Hex in High Heels

Linda Wisdom

SOURCEBOOKS
AN IMPRINT OF S
NAPERVIL

D1040596

Published by Sourcebooks Casablanca, an imprint of Sourcebooks, Inc.
P.O. Box 4410, Naperville, Illinois 60567–4410
(630) 961–3900
FAX: (630) 961–2168
www.sourcebooks.com

Printed and bound in the United States of America
QW 10 9 8 7 6 5 4 3 2 1

To all my fans who have embraced my hexy witches with such wonderful enthusiasm. You are what keeps me going. Thank you from my heart.

Chapter 1

"YOU TURNED THEM INTO TEENAGERS?" JAKE HARRISON howled, which sounded eerily like his Were–Border Collie self, even though this morning he was deliciously human. He was lounging in a red vinyl and chrome chair by the 1950s diner table on display in the back of the vintage shop, long legs stretched out comfortably. Dressed in his usual faded jeans and flannel shirt, Jake's shaggy black hair was in need of a trim and his black eyes were bright with laughter. One hand rested idly on the Select-O-Matic jukebox on the table, while the other held a paper cup filled with coffee. The rich scent of cinnamon mocha filled the air.

"They were lucky that's all I did to them. And let me tell you, there's nothing scarier than trophy wives suddenly reverting to pimply face, original nose, stringy hair teens. Not one of them was a cute kid, either. All of their so-called natural beauty came from a surgeon's knife, hairdresser's skill, and make-up." Blair Fitzpatrick stood a short distance away, studying with satisfaction the primary colors adorning the walls of her shop, Blast from the Past. She specialized in selling vintage items and liked to make her shop bright and welcoming to tempt customers inside. But what really revved her engines was the way Jake was looking at her, with a dark gaze that held more than a hint of hunger. Yep, Jake was the one who really stirred her hormonal cauldron.

"Some people just don't understand that my gifts are meant for the greater good." She sat down across from him and sipped the caramel latte Jake had brought her that morning.

He grinned at her. "Oh yeah, anyone can see that revenge spells are for the greater good."

"You craft the right spell, and husbands and boyfriends think twice about cheating on their women. A woman who's illegally run up a man's credit card suddenly finds the bill in her name, or worse." She absently touched her curly, dark auburn hair to make sure her '40s updo was still in place. Each week Blair took the time to decorate the shop in a different theme. This week was the 1940s and she was dressed accordingly. "Two small examples."

"It's a good reminder never to piss you off."

Blair rested her chin on her hand and studied his silky black hair and lean, rough-hewn features. In human form, Jake was one hot-looking guy; and even in dog form, any woman would want to adopt him. But she knew she could look into his dark eyes all day and never see all that was within. Jake had kept his Were nature secret for a long time and even now, despite her witchy senses, she couldn't detect a hint of *Canis lupus familiaris.* That didn't stop her from gazing at his mouth and imagining it on hers, or his hands running over her body or... wowza! Was it hot in here or was she having a hot flash? "I have to say, you'd come out pretty good even as a toad or a warthog."

"Blair!" A young woman's voice echoed through the archway separating Blair's shop from fellow witch Stasi's lingerie boutique, Isn't It Romantic. "It's Horace again."

"'It's only for three days,' she says," Blair grumbled, rising to her feet. "'Trev's taking me away for a romantic long weekend. Ashley will watch the shop, so no worries there,' she assures me. If Stasi wanted no worries, she should have taken Horace with her. But I suppose her wizard boyfriend wouldn't be too keen on that. Not that I blame him." She walked through the archway into the neighboring shop. A moment later a multi-colored spike of light flashed between the shops, and Horace the gargoyle's yelp of pain was heard. Blair returned, rubbing her hands in a gesture of a job well done.

"Stasi only tells me no!" the gargoyle yelled after her.

"Yeah, well, I'm in charge now."

Jake glanced at Felix, the Kit-Kat clock on the wall, and stood up, pulling on his fleece-lined denim jacket. "You're going?" she protested.

"Agnes asked me to replace some boards in their front fence and I promised to do it today."

"And you decided to do it while she's at her hair appointment," she guessed.

He nodded. "Floyd, I can handle," he said, naming the town's mayor. "But Agnes seems to feel she should be out there supervising, when she doesn't know a thing about carpentry. Plus that heavy stuff she calls perfume makes me sneeze. With luck, I'll be done before she gets back. I'll see you later." With a wave of his hand he was gone.

Blair resisted to the urge to let her own inner teen-ager peek out the window and watch him walk down the street.

While she and Jake had become closer since the dramatic events of last Samhain, they still weren't as close as she'd hoped. She knew the man was interested. He stopped by just to chat a couple of times a week and often brought her favorite latte and muffins with him. Who could resist a man who brought her something that, in her mind, was better than roses?

Every so often Jake still showed up as his Were–Border Collie alter ego, and while Blair complained about the shedding—things could be worse.

She stared at the colorful flyer announcing the upcoming annual Winter Carnival, sponsored by a nearby resort. The town of Moonstone Lake was gearing up for attracting the tourists. Maybe the carnival preparations would provide the opportunity she'd been waiting for to pull Jake closer.

Jake glanced at the note Agnes Pierce had left him with her ideas for a new fence and tossed it into his toolbox. He'd rather be back at Blast from the Past, laughing and talking to Blair. Instead he was out in twenty-degree weather, freezing his ass off. Still, it was a job and he liked keeping busy.

He looked up as a buzzing sound blasted from his cell phone and he snatched it from the top of his toolbox.

"Come on, Agnes, give me a chance to get started," he grumbled, flipping open the phone. "Jake here."

"For someone who's kept out of touch for so many years, you sound very healthy."

A black haze covered Jake's eyes as he stared off into the trees.

"How did you get this number?" he spoke slowly and evenly, reining in the fury that threatened to bubble to the top. The last thing he wanted was to show how this call affected him.

"You're a smart puppy. I'm sure you can figure that out for yourself." The woman's voice held a cold bite. "We need to talk."

"Really. I thought we were doing that now, *Mom*. But I'm pretty busy at present, so let's get together later. *Much later*."

"It would be in your best interest to speak to me now." The icy edge to her tone could have frozen his ear.

"And it would be in your best interest to lose my number."

"This isn't over," he could hear her say as he clicked off the phone.

Jake's grip tightened until the cell phone snapped in his hand.

"Damn that bitch," he muttered angrily, feeling power begin to course through his veins. His steps turned into long strides as he headed for the cover of the trees. Within moments, fur covered his body and a sleek black and white Border Collie raced across the snow-covered ground.

The winter air made Jake's nose tingle as he leaped over fallen logs. He skidded on a patch of ice, but quickly regained his balance and was off and running again. A deer, sensing the dog's anger, took off in the opposite direction.

Rage. Don't need it. Hate her. Leave me alone.

His stride lengthened as he ran up a hill, halting for a moment at the top to catch his breath. A rustling sound not far off caught his attention and he lowered his head to the ground, creeping along the snowdrifts as the scent of enemy tickled his senses.

Jake rounded a stand of trees and came face to face with a coyote. The coyote's grayish-brown head snapped upward, a low growl emerging from behind his bared teeth as he tried to establish dominance against the dog staring him down. The Border Collie rumbled deep in his chest as his mouth widened in a doggy grin at the idea of an old-fashioned critter rumble.

Bring it on, dude. This is my territory, so I guess I'm just going to have to kick your furry ass.

Without any further warning, the coyote leaped. Not to be outdone, Jake bunched his muscles and met his adversary in mid-air with a snarl. The battle had begun.

The coyote wasted no time twisting his head to clamp his jaws on Jake's neck. Jake yelped and managed to get loose before too much damage was done. He knew his foe wasn't Were and didn't have his strength, but he wasn't about to make it easy on the animal.

Jake danced around, yipping canine insults, jumping forward to nip the coyote's haunches, then leaping back. Each time the coyote got in a bite or a scratch, Jake returned the favor with some damage of his own.

His blood sang with the glory of battle, every sense heightened as he threw himself into the fray. If he wasn't mistaken, the coyote was enjoying this just as much. Jake had no doubt that they'd leave the impromptu battleground bloody and satisfied.

Oh yeah, I really needed this.

Jake felt more than a few aches and pains, but he was grinning; he hadn't felt this good in a long time. He wasn't in the mood to return to the Pierces' to pick up his toolbox; Floyd would see it and stick it in his shed. He'd call the older man that night and explain that something had come up. His features darkened briefly at the memory of just what that something was.

He tipped his head up, sniffing the air, and then did what he did best—he followed his nose to the lake.

Blair had changed out of her vintage dress into clothing more appropriate for the cold weather and stood near the water's edge.

"Aren't you afraid the lake monster will show up and eat you?" Jake teased, walking toward her.

She turned her head and flashed him a bright smile. "Hey you." Her smile dimmed. "What happened?"

"As in what?"

She quickly conjured up a mirror and showed him a face marred with scratches and what looked like a nasty bite on his neck.

"Fixing Floyd's fence proved to be more dangerous than I thought."

She shook her head at his glib answer. "Try again, pooch. Agnes stopped by the shop and asked if I'd seen you. She said your toolbox was left there and what looked like pieces of your cell phone." She reached up and lightly traced one of the scratches. "I have a salve that would speed up the healing process."

He shook his head. "I'm fine."

"I thought shifting healed a Were."

"Not so much if you're *Canis lupus familiaris*. We tend to have a slower healing rate. Besides, these cuts are a badge of honor, courtesy of a coyote that won't be coming around here again any time soon." He stood next to her. "See any signs of life out there? Beany and Cecil show up on the *Leakin' Lena?*"

Blair smiled and shook her head. "Cecil was a sea serpent. Besides, the lake monster is only an urban legend."

"I don't know, stranger things have happened in this town." He grinned as he nudged her shoulder with his arm.

"Says the guy who once turned into a dog to save my life." She laughingly bumped him back. She tipped her head to the side and reached up, pulling a tuft of grayish-brown fur away from his throat. "Hm, from a new playmate?"

"I doubt he'd see it that way." He deliberately kept his gaze on the lake. "You know, I had no choice that night. You hadn't paid me for those new shelves yet."

"Goof!" But Blair was smiling as she turned back to the lake and its serene pale blue surface that echoed the moonstone gem for which it was named. "If there was a lake monster, surely one of us would have sensed it by now. In all the years Stasi and I have lived here, we've never even seen a sign of a living creature in the water."

"Maybe he or she is shy." His fingers itched to brush the stray strands of hair away from her face.

"Isn't it enough that the town has witches and a Were Border Collie? We have any other creatures around here, and we'll end up as an offshoot of *Ripley's Believe it or Not,* or a late night documentary on the Sci Fi Channel."

"So what brings you out here when the temp is dropping like crazy?"

"Sometimes I like to come out and just look at the water. When it's calm and beautiful like this I can't believe it was ever any other way," she murmured, tucking her hands into her pockets. She cast him a quick glance, her bright, blue-green eyes loaded with humor. "I can't believe any self-respecting lake monster would have allowed its home to be damaged by magick. And speaking of magick." She poked her finger against his chest. "Why didn't you ever mention you were Were? And don't say you didn't have any chances, because there were plenty of times you could have said, 'Oh, by the way, I'm a dog. Honest.'"

Jake shrugged his shoulders. "I had more fun showing up as the dog, even though you weren't always that welcoming."

Her jaw dropped. "You tracked muddy paw prints all over my new comforter!"

"And you gave me a bath." His grin widened at the memory. He reached out and took her hand. "Come on, little witch, you're beginning to look like a Popsicle. I'll walk you back to your place. I might even let you play nurse."

"Fine, change the subject. It won't stop me from continuing to ask," she said as they walked down the path toward the building where she and Stasi had their shops and home.

"Okay, I'll tell you—once you admit you and Stasi used to use binoculars to spy on me."

She cast him an innocent look that battled with the amusement dancing in her blue-green eyes. "We never did anything like that."

His chuckle floated in the frosty air. "One, I have Were super sight. Two, the sun tends to reflect on the lenses." He laughed as she muttered under her breath.

Chapter 2

"ASHLEY'S PICKING ON ME," HORACE GRUMBLED, making his way into Blair's shop. It took some huffing and puffing on his part, but he finally got his leathery wings going enough to allow him to fly up and land on one of the counters. The eight-inch, gray-stone gargoyle had an elongated snout that resembled a monkey's, long arms, and short legs, along with pointy horns and leathery-looking wings. His long tail curved up behind him as he skated across the glass counter.

"He told a customer her thong showed all her cellulite," Ashley, the young woman who helped out in Stasi's shop, called through the archway.

"You know very well you're not supposed to speak to the customers. You do it again, and you'll be wearing a muzzle." Blair adjusted the display of World War II pinup photos. "Stasi warned you about doing stuff like that."

"I don't care. A thong wasn't a good look for her, and someone needed to tell her the truth." He used his claw the way humans use a toothpick, examined whatever he dug out from between his fangs, then tossed it to the floor.

Blair shot him a warning look and zapped it quickly away.

"Don't think you can hang out here," she warned him. She set her iPod in its dock and switched on 1940s-era

Big Band music to play softly in the background as she rearranged her collection of World War II memorabilia, including ration books with tokens and a gas mask, courtesy of fellow-witch Maggie from when she lived in London during the war.

In keeping with her theme, Blair was dressed in a black rayon, satin-backed crepe dress with a sweetheart neckline and cap sleeves. The gores of the skirt were spliced with a floral print of tiny red rosebuds; it was impossible for her to walk without swishing her hips. She glanced down and adjusted her seamed stockings. Black leather open-toe pumps completed the look. Her gold ankle bracelet, sporting a tiny golden broom with a blue topaz on the handle, winked as she walked.

"When's Stasi coming back?" Horace asked, flopping back on the glass and waving his arms and legs as if he was making a snow angel.

"Sometime tomorrow." Blair paused at the front window, adjusting a few items in the display, then standing there and looking out.

"I wish she'd taken me with her." Horace heaved a deep, dramatic sigh.

"Oh yeah, every witch wants to take a gargoyle along with her on a romantic getaway." She craned her neck to look down the street.

"He's across the street at the hardware store."

"He who?" she said, blushing.

"Jake, that's who," Horace hooted. "That's who you were looking for, isn't it?"

"No." She stopped herself from touching her nose. She had this deep fear that a lie would cause her nose to grow.

She still wondered why Jake had gotten into a battle with a coyote the previous day. She'd posed a lot of questions as she'd treated his cuts and scratches, but he remained mum on all of them.

She vaguely noticed the sound of the small bells tinkling over Stasi's door as a potential customer walked inside.

"Interesting that a lingerie shop would smell like a forest," a woman's voice murmured. One of the quirks of Stasi's shop was that each woman who entered encountered her favorite smell.

Interesting that a woman would instinctively choose forest over, say, vanilla or lavender, unless she's in to pine air freshener. Oh well, to each her own, Blair thought to herself, returning to her post at the window. She watched a figure racing up the street and resisted the urge to duck out of sight even though it was apparent he was heading straight for her. "Yikes!"

"Get rid of it!" The twenty-something man shouted as he ran into the shop and grabbed her arms. "*Please!*"

"Let go of me, Kyle."

He jerked away and backed off. "Please, Blair. I swear I'll never do it again. I'll be so faithful to Abby, I'll be a saint."

Blair watched the man's face turn a stunning shade of royal blue and couldn't help but smile. "Wrong answer, Kyle. All you have to do is go one month without lying to or about Abby, and so far you haven't been able to do either."

"That other girl meant nothing." He walked in jerky circles, his arms waving up and down at his sides.

"You're quickly moving up to cobalt." She narrowed her eyes on him. "Do you love Abby, Kyle?"

"Yes." His face lightened to cerulean.

"See, you just told the truth! Keep it up. Don't cheat on her, and show her just how much you love her," she advised. "Do you think it was easy for Abby to ask for this revenge spell? She cried the whole time she was here. You got caught and then you tried to lie your way out of it. Dumb, Kyle, really dumb. You broke her heart and she came to me for vengeance. And now you're paying the price." She could have felt sorry for him; except she knew as long as he lied to the woman he claimed to love he was doomed to go around with a blue face. But her voice softened. "Be honest with yourself, Kyle. Do you really love Abby?"

The young man looked about as miserable as any guy with blue skin could look. "I love her so much it hurts."

She nodded at his admission. "Then show her. Don't tell her you're working when you're really out drinking with friends. Don't make up excuses for forgetting her birthday. Start thinking about her and her feelings, because if you don't, you will lose her. There are a lot of guys out there who'd love to have her as a girlfriend."

He looked off into the distance. "Okay, I'm going to prove it to her." His smile was a bit off-putting, since even his teeth were a pale shade of blue. "I was really pissed at you when this first happened, but now I see that you wanted me to do the right thing. I'm not going to lose Abby and she won't have to see me with blue skin." He ducked his head and left the shop.

"How interesting."

Blair turned around to face a tall woman standing in the open archway to Stasi's boutique.

Not human and wearing a glamour to hide her true nature.

Blair wasn't an excellent shopkeeper for nothing. Her smile was welcoming, even if she was on guard against the mysterious woman. She noted that the visitor wore a classic Chanel suit—very overdressed for the casual mountain town. She wondered if she was visiting one of the nearby resorts.

"I hope you don't mind. The young lady mentioned you are a witch who crafts vengeance spells."

Blair cast a quick glance to one side and noticed that Horace was posed like a statue. The expression on his face told her he hadn't missed the stranger's glamour spell either.

"Yes, I do, for those who deserve justice."

The woman stepped forward and moved around the shop, glancing at the 1940s vintage items. She paused to study a bronze silk evening gown draped on a mannequin.

"I have a son who has hurt me deeply," she said, leaning over to closely examine the beading along the deep neckline. "While I don't believe in revenge, I do believe in justice."

Blair stood still, her smile fixed, but she was wary. Something wasn't right. "What has he done to hurt you?"

She straightened up and viewed Blair with dark eyes. "He refuses to help our family. Not financially, but emotionally. To be a part of what we have."

"Would there be a reason why he's acting this way?"

The woman reached into her bag and pulled out a checkbook. "Only that he chooses to hurt us all. How much to force him to realize the error of his ways and return to the fold? And I would prefer that his skin not turn colors." Her lips narrowed with disapproval.

Blair wasn't sure what the woman's son had done or why, but she suspected he had done it for good reason. "I would need to meet your son first."

"Why?"

"Because I can pick up better vibes that way and see what spell works best," she lied.

"That's impossible." Her words dropped like ice cubes.

"Then I'm afraid I can't help you."

"All I need is a spell." She opened her checkbook and drew out a Mont Blanc pen. "If you give me that, I can do the rest."

Now Blair was really getting ticked off. "That's not how I work." Her voice also had noticeably cooled.

The woman's head snapped up, surprised at the strong negative response.

"Then no wonder you have to work so hard, selling these old toys," she murmured, dropping the checkbook and pen back into her bag and abruptly walking out of the store.

"What is she?" Blair wished she had the senses to see past a glamour spell, but she had never had that gift.

"Not good," Horace said, stretching his arms over his head. "And she knew I wasn't real. You should have seen the look she gave me. You wouldn't have sold me to her, would you?"

"You were safe." Blair watched the woman ease her way into the back seat of a black Lincoln Town Car that smoothly pulled away from the parking space. "But there was something familiar about her."

Now that he considered himself safe, Horace ambled over to the other end of the glass display case and settled down to pore over a colorful catalog. "Cool dollhouses."

"And expensive."

"Think whoever makes them could make a pad for me?" His claw traced the lines of a three-story Regency-styled home. "Something with a lot of red, maybe a disco ball and big mirrors over the bed and on the walls." He wiggled his hips.

"Okay, that is just nasty." Blair stuck out her tongue. "Thank goodness there's no way you could afford it." She returned to her post, gazing idly out the window.

"I need to start asking for a salary. I do my share of work here, too," Horace said absently, flipping through the rest of the catalog.

"Like that'll happen."

"At the rate you're moving it'll happen before you manage to seduce Jake into bed."

"I prefer the subtle approach," she said primly.

"You? Prim? Yeah, pull the other leg." He swiveled his head around. "Please. *Ow!*" He brought the singed tip of his tail around and licked the injured appendage. "Bitchy much?"

Blair knew she should apologize, but Horace ought to know she was a little sensitive where Jake was concerned.

"We'll have a full moon next week," Horace commented in a thinly veiled attempt to change the subject. "Anyone coming up for it?"

"We know Jazz will be coming for sure." And she knew Jazz's reason for coming. Namely to drop off those damn bunny slippers of hers since she claimed it was Blair's turn to look after them while Jazz and Nick took a vacation. As far as Blair was concerned, they had plenty of other witch friends who would do a much better job of dealing with Fluff and Puff, the bunny slippers from hell. Jazz could dump them with Thea, who'd take them shopping for designer bunny-ware, or even Maggie, who'd dress them in camo and take them on one of her bounty hunting runs. They'd love either of those options, and Blair would be bunny slipper free. Why did she get all the creature-sitting duties?

"Thea said she would come up, but I'll believe it when I see it—she's working on her next book. Maggie plans on coming if she's not on a job. She hasn't been up here in months," Blair remarked. Her witch friend Maggie enjoyed working security details with a motley crew of creatures as her backup. She had moves Lara Croft would envy.

Blair sighed. It had been at least two hundred years since all thirteen of the witches who'd been banished from the Witches' Academy in 1313 had been together at one gathering, but they individually managed to hook up with each other from time to time.

"The good thing is, the lake's back to normal, we're back to normal, and the town is even sort of back to normal. Whoa mama!" Horace's head swiveled almost 180 degrees as he noticed a shapely brunette walk by. "Tell me she's stopping in the boutique."

"She's kissy face with a football player type," Blair was happy to say as she settled in a red vinyl chair.

"Aw, those guys always turn to fat." He slowly flew over to the diner table and plopped down next to Blair.

Horace stretched out on the table as if he was sunning himself, even though it was a balmy thirty-two degrees outside. "Maybe if you dressed sexier, the dog would sniff around you more," he mused, raising one claw upward and examining the long, curved nails.

While he was a proud card-carrying coward, Horace had the equipment to fight back if he was backed into a corner. "C'mon Blair, show off the girls." He eyed her sweetheart neckline with a critical eye. "Shorten the skirt." He tried again to check under her skirt but smoke curling up from the tip of his tail quickly stopped him. "More uplift here, nip in there, maybe some fuck-me stilettos. You got a smokin' bod, girl. Show it off more."

"Wonderful, I'm reduced to getting compliments from a creature."

"What if we place a personal ad for you again?" Felix, Blair's Kit-Kat clock, chimed in.

"With you writing the ad, no thank you. Last time a snake shape-shifter contacted me!" She shuddered.

"You should have let me write the ad," Horace said. "You would have had much better luck."

"I didn't even want Felix writing an ad," Blair pointed out.

"Hey, gorgeous. Having a good day?" Blair turned to see a familiar male figure standing in the doorway.

Her lips opened in a big smile as she looked at the handsome Were who made her heart skip more than a few beats. She was pleased to see that his scratches and cuts were much better and even the bite mark on his neck had healed faster than it would have on a human.

"I am now. You look much better." *And yummy. And kissable. And jumpable.*

"I'm feeling more like myself, thanks to you. A good night's sleep can help the healing process, too."

"And what about poor Wile E?" she asked, standing up and moving over to one of the glass cases.

Jake grinned. "He's probably off somewhere licking his wounds and wishing he hadn't met me."

"Oooh, puppy with attitude," she drawled with a provocative smile as she leaned her hip against one of the glass display cases.

Jake's cocoa brown eyes flared with a speck of heat, but he didn't move any closer. Then he smiled as the bouncy sounds of the Andrews Sisters' *Boogie Woogie Bugle Boy* floated through the air.

"Hey, hexy woman, you look ready to dance at the USO Canteen."

She gave a hip-swinging movement. "I feel it, too." She held out her arms. "C'mon on, handsome, give it a try."

Blair's smile widened as Jake moved forward and swung her around in jive moves that soon had her laughing and breathless. He may have been tall and muscular, but he was light on his feet and never came close to the display cases or the shelves. Luckily, the shop was large enough they could dance with total abandon to the 1940s hit. She was still laughing when the song stopped and so did they, in total sync.

She looked up, losing herself in his warm gaze and starting to move that extra inch that would put her right against his chest.

The heat in Jake's gaze cooled as he dropped a kiss on top of her head and moved away. Blair immediately missed his warmth and was tempted to step back into his personal space. As if he guessed her intent, he moved across the length of the store until he stood near one of the display cases.

Rats, bats, and frog tails!

"I wondered if you'd like to go down to Grady's tonight and get some dinner?" Jake asked idly, seeming to be interested in a collection of metal soldiers in blue and gray uniforms.

Yes! "Why, Jake Harrison, are you finally asking me out on a date?" she asked coyly.

His smile melted her insides until they were all warm and gooey. "Maybe I am, or maybe it's one of those 'we both have to eat, so why not eat together?' And since it's the twenty-first century, I'm even willing to let you pick up the check."

She gave him a look that pretty much said *not with this witch, pal!*

"I'll come by when you close up." He tapped the glass case with his fingertips and sauntered out.

Blair took the opportunity to return to the door and look out. There was something about watching a tall, sexy guy in snug jeans walk away. Especially when he had a world-class ass like Jake's.

"It's about time that Were got smart," Horace said. "Although you still could have sped up the process with some sexier clothes. Or no clothes." He quickly cupped his claws over his tail before she could zap it again.

"Really?" Blair asked, her mind still on Jake's exit.

"Oh yeah, at this rate the two of you will be getting it on hot and heavy. You'll get regular sex and not be so cranky," Horace said.

"There is no way I'll discuss sex around you." She really needed to get Horace off the sex issue. Her hormones had been playing havoc with her lately and she didn't want to talk about it.

Blair returned to the window and watched several men outside hanging glittery white and blue banners across the streetlights announcing the upcoming Winter Carnival. It should be big this year, with the backing of nearby Snow Farms Resort. The resort had recently been taken over by a new owner and, not one to miss an opportunity, Floyd Pierce had immediately offered him the opportunity to help sponsor the carnival. Moonstone Lake's mayor was a blowhard, but he knew how to bring business into the tiny mountain town, and with Agnes as the power behind him, the deal was easily sealed.

"What to wear. What to wear," Blair murmured, mentally surveying her closet. Grady's place was more a tavern than a restaurant and the witches considered his barbecue to die for, but that didn't mean Blair was going to stint on date wear.

Jake returned to the workshop behind his cabin in hopes a few hours of hard work would center him before he picked up Blair for their dinner date.

"Why did I ask her out?" he muttered, pushing the buttons that disarmed the alarm and unlocking the door. With a small fortune invested in woodworking tools, he didn't take any chances—not to mention his inventory, one of his closely kept secrets. "We're completely different species. We have completely different needs." Yesterday's round with the coyote had proven that. Jake had looked even worse than when Blair saw him by the time he and the coyote had limped away from each other, in unspoken agreement that the battle was a draw. But it had been a good fight, and the two combatants parted with respect. Would Blair understand that?

He clicked on a space heater then turned on his CD player, cranking up Coldplay's "Viva la Vida" with no concerns, since his nearest neighbor lived far enough away to give him the privacy he desired. He could work late into the night without worrying that the sound of his power tools would disturb anyone's sleep. Never mind that his own sleep had been disturbed more than once lately by thoughts of a saucy little witch with a quick tongue and a sexy smile.

From the first time Jake had set eyes on Blair, he'd felt a stirring down deep that refused to go away. A part of him yelled that he'd found his mate. Only trouble was, she wasn't a species his Pack would accept. She didn't turn furry—even if she did have the ability to snap and snarl without the benefit of fangs. Although why it mattered to him, he didn't know. He'd left his Pack years ago because they couldn't accept that he was a throwback to a different branch of the *canidae* family. Jake had a hard time knowing just where he fit in, so instead of pursuing Blair full out, he had kept to his Were–Border Collie self. It had been easier to snuggle up to her when he was cute and cuddly, and safer to hop on her bed and settle at her feet while she shouted and waved her arms, trying to remove his furry self.

He grinned at those memories. Especially the knowledge that Blair liked to sleep in the nude. That was a picture he wasn't about to forget any time soon. Something else ran through his mind. In the few years he'd known Blair, he also knew that no one else had shared her bed. He felt a familiar heaviness in his groin that happened pretty much any time he thought about her.

No, Blair was a big hands off for him. He might have left his Pack—by his choice, not theirs—but he still knew that Weres and witches didn't mix.

They say that "witches and wizards don't mix" either, but Stasi and Trev found a way. And let's not forget the "witches and vampires don't mix" that Jazz and Nick ignored.

"Yeah, well, they didn't have to answer to my Pack, which has its own way of dealing with anyone who doesn't conform to their rules—even if a particular Were no longer considers himself a member," he muttered, switching on the coffeemaker then heading for his power saw.

An intricately designed dollhouse resembling a British country estate sat on a nearby worktable awaiting his final touches and the custom-made furniture and tiny rugs and curtains supplied by a fellow craftsman. Plans for his next project lay on a drafting table. But it wasn't easy to keep his mind on work right now.

And once again the question of why he had asked Blair out for dinner raised its furry head.

Hell, he might be Were, but he was also a healthy male and no matter what, Blair was the only one who caught his eye. He picked up his saw and put Blair out of his mind—for now.

"You can be one hot little witch when you want to be, Blair," Felix said, his tail picking up speed as Blair walked back into the shop, having made a quick trip upstairs to change her clothes for her evening out. "*Très chic.*"

"I try." She paused long enough to admire her reflection in a mirror. Since Grady's dress code was pretty casual, she'd opted for a dark teal, hip-skimming cowl-neck sweater over a pair of black jeans. Her gold ankle bracelet with the broom charm was draped outside her high-heeled boot. She had released her 40s updo and allowed the curls to fall free around her face.

"You are one witch loaded for bear... or should I say Were?" Felix chuckled.

"Give us all the details when you get back," Horace demanded from his sprawled position on the counter. "And don't leave anything out."

"I'm amazed you don't want pictures, too," Blair retorted, emptying her cash register and stowing the bills and change in the enchanted moneybag that boded ill for anyone who dared steal it.

The gargoyle perked up. "Yeah! You've got a camera phone. I wanna know if what they say about Weres is true. You can find a way to take pictures. Or just make his pants disappear."

"*Horace!*" A flick of Blair's fingers had the gargoyle tumbling head over heels off the counter and across the floor.

"For Fates sake, doesn't anyone have a sense of humor around here?" He slowly got to his feet and rubbed his butt as he limped away. "I have one simple request and I get zapped for it."

"What'd he do now?" Jake asked, stepping inside the shop and stopping short when he looked at Blair. The hand passing over his black hair betrayed his nervousness. "You look great," he finally said. "I feel low-class next to you."

"No way," she assured him, liking his casual look of flannel shirt and jeans. Jake took her faux-fur hooded jacket out of her hands and helped her put it on.

She locked up the shop and moved down the sidewalk next to Jake. With the streetlights made to look like old-fashioned gas lamps, the light was soft and didn't war against the stars shining in the clear sky. Blair breathed deeply, then wished she hadn't when the icy air hit her lungs.

"I guess there are some things you witches can't handle," Jake gently teased, taking her hand.

She was glad she hadn't worn her gloves as she felt the warmth of his calloused fingertips.

"There are a few."

Jake pulled her to a stop. "Are you sure eating at Grady's is fine with you? I mean, we could go up to one of the resorts for dinner, if you'd rather."

She shook her head. "Give me a beer and Grady's infamous barbecue and I'm a happy witch."

"No eye of newt or bat wings?"

"Oh puleeze, that's so thirteenth century," she pooh-poohed. "Not that I was around then."

As they walked, they passed a few of the locals, who smiled and greeted them. A few knowing glances were directed their way.

Since Grady's BBQ Pit and Tavern was also located at the edge of town, it wasn't a far walk. The old one-story wooden building looked like a shack but was sturdier than most modern buildings.

Grady, a tall, bald-headed man in his seventies, was busy in the kitchen when they walked into the crowded tavern. Blair noticed an empty corner booth and nabbed it while Jake went to the bar to place their orders. He returned with two glasses and a pitcher of beer.

As he sipped his beer, Jake looked around the room. There wasn't one person there he didn't know personally. But suddenly he had a flash of memory of what had happened in the town the previous October.

"Do you ever think about Samhain?" he asked softly, although there wasn't much chance of anyone eavesdropping with the jukebox turned up high.

Blair had started to take off her coat, but the chill that invaded her bones at his words made her decide to keep it on for a little while longer.

"Not if I can help it," she murmured, nodding her thanks as he poured beer into a glass and handed it to her. "There's something about an angry mob and insane forest Fae trying to burn you at the stake that doesn't invite Kodak moments."

"You could have had those memories erased along with everyone else," he reminded her.

Eurydice, their former headmistress and head of the Witches' Council, had told Blair and her friends that their memories could be altered like the townspeople's memories, but they had chosen to remember. In case they ever had to fight the battle again, Jazz, Nick, Stasi, Trevor, Blair, and Jake had agreed it was necessary. The six magickal beings never spoke of that night, when a renegade band of forest Fae led by "Reed Palmer," disguised as a human, had almost succeeded in poisoning the lake and destroying them all. But it didn't mean that their recollections had faded over the past few months.

Blair still experienced that dark hint of fear any time she went out to the lake. While she enjoyed going out there for relaxation, there was also a bit of concern that the lake would retain some of the taint.

"It was tempting, but Stasi was right. It's better to remember the past in order to be prepared for the future." She sipped the cold yeasty drink that Grady brewed in his basement.

Jake's dark brown eyes turned almost black. "You almost died that night. If I hadn't…"

"But you did. You turned all furry and saved the day when you killed Reed," she said quickly with a big grin. "Not to mention totally surprising the hell out of me when you shifted. And to think I was feeling sorry for a poor homeless dog!"

"I was getting pretty sick of Pupperoni," he told her, grinning back. "Try Beggin' Strips next time, okay?"

"Deal." Blair laughed as she slipped off her coat and let it slide down behind her.

"Here you are, kids," Grady announced, setting down two platters along with a bowl of thick, rich barbecue sauce. "Tri-tip dinners for two with all the trimmings and extra sauce."

Blair immediately picked up one of the seasoned fries, dipped it in sauce, and brought it to her lips. She closed her eyes as the flavors exploded in her mouth. A soft moan escaped her.

"Damn, woman! You trying to get me shut down for illicit behavior?" Grady scolded with a smile. "You know how old Sheriff Carson is about goings-on in public places," he said.

"Old Sheriff Carson is five years younger than you," she reminded him.

"Old fuddy duddy with that tin badge sure doesn't

act it. He should have retired years ago." He scanned the table, saw that they had all they needed, including extra napkins, and left them to their feast.

"You know what? Let's talk about anything *but* last Samhain. Since you showed up furry at your little play date yesterday, it's obvious you don't need the full moon to shift."

Jake shook his head. "You need the full moon when you're young, but after you reach maturity, you can shift at will. Some prefer sticking to a ritualistic full moon ceremony, but I like the idea of running free whenever I choose. Plus, the dark of the moon makes for good hunting."

"That makes sense. So tell me, Jake, why does a Were move away from his pack when it's a known fact that Weres stick together no matter what?" The minute she saw his face, she realized that it wasn't a question he would readily answer.

"I prefer being on my own and this town gives me what I need," was all he said. "Plenty of land to roam."

"Lots of rabbits and squirrels for you to hunt." She shook her head. "I'm still trying to get my head around the idea you're a Were." She kept her voice low; his species wasn't "out" like the witches were. "Although I'm more used to Were wolves and panthers and such."

"Mine is a story that's hard to tell. I don't talk about it much." He noticed Blair's expression, as if she expected him to tell all anyway. "Like I just said, I don't talk about it."

"Oh. I thought you meant you hadn't talked about it before, but you would now." She used the side of her fork to cut through the tender meat and brought the spicy goodness to her lips. They tingled.

"It's not like you and Stasi talk very much about your pasts."

"We're pretty much an open secret here, at least among the townsfolk who've lived here for more than a few years. And since we conjure up a few spells to keep the town safe from developers, people don't mind as long as we stay sort of low-key."

"Then what was with this deal about banishment that the head witch talked about?" Jake asked.

Blair refused to allow the mention of Eurydice to ruin her appetite. Not when all this fantastic tri-tip sat in front of her. No to-go bags tonight. If she took any home, Horace would gobble it up in no time and what he missed, Stasi's magickal dog Bogie would grab. "I guess, like you said, some stories are hard to tell," she replied.

"*Touché.*" He saluted her with his fork. "You seem to do pretty well."

"We have. We've all made our way in the world in our own unique ways, and we're all happy with our lives. None of us have done deliberate harm to anyone." She nodded when Jake indicated the pitcher then her near-empty glass. He topped it off, then his own. "We've come a long way over the centuries."

Jake held his glass near hers and they bumped glasses for a toast. He flashed an appreciative smile as he watched her eat. "It's nice to see someone not pick at their food or approach it as if it's the enemy. Female Weres are hearty eaters, too."

"I guess I'd qualify on that count."

"Blair's as good a customer as you are, Jake." Grady stopped by the table. He glanced down at Blair's half empty plate. "I guess everything's fine."

Jake looked at Blair's open and clearly happy face. "Perfect, Grady. Just perfect." He noticed she didn't blush or look away. Instead she looked him square in the eye and there was a hint of mischief in her bright blue-green gaze. Mischief he wouldn't mind pursuing to see just what would happen.

Oh man, this witch was trouble with a capital T.

Chapter 3

THE EVENING DIDN'T END WITH DINNER; THEY remained at the table and shared a second pitcher of beer while they enjoyed the music and dancing. The tavern's occupant's age ranged from early twenties up to a few couples in their seventies and eighties, so Blair and Jake sat back and watched the show.

Blair almost choked on her beer when Mrs. Benedict and her longtime beau, Mr. Chalmers, got up and cut a rug to the sound of Steppenwolf screaming from the jukebox.

"Who knew she could shake her booty like that?" Blair remarked, chuckling.

"You think they'll ever get married, or just keep on with their affair?" Jake asked.

This time Blair did choke on her beer. Jake quickly got up and slapped her on the back so hard she almost fell out of the booth.

"I'm fine!" she choked, holding up her hand.

Jake immediately dropped down next to her. "Your face is purple."

"At least it's a color I can wear," she wheezed, struggling to regain her breath. "Mrs. Benedict and Mr. Chalmers are…?" she wig-wagged her hand.

He nodded. "Oh, come on, you had to know they were more than just platonic friends. I found out a year ago when I went over there early to chop wood for Mrs. Benedict and saw Mr. Chalmers slipping out the back door, looking pretty pleased with himself. I waited about ten minutes, then went over to knock on Mrs. Benedict's door." He leaned over to confide, "She was wearing a robe and her cheeks were pretty flushed, and not because the oven was on."

Blair took another gulp of her beer. "No more, please. I really don't want to consider them in that position. In *any* position. How will I look her in the eye when she brings over some of her cookies or sourdough biscuits? I so can't think of her having a sex life!" She buried her face in her hands.

Jake grinned. "Just be glad you weren't the one who showed up that morning. At least I didn't get there ten minutes earlier. As it was, I never chopped wood so fast in my life. She was inside humming *Papa Loves Mambo*."

Blair looked up when the door opened, then ducked down behind Jake's broad shoulders.

"Floyd and Agnes just came in," she hissed. "She'll want to talk me into helping with the carnival."

He looked over his shoulder. "Too late, she saw you."

"Blair, there you are!" the mayor's wife trilled, tottering over on her high heels with her portly husband behind her.

"Agnes," Blair greeted the woman.

"What wonderful luck to find you here." Agnes plopped down across from them in the booth. She wiggled her fingers to direct Floyd to sit next to her. "Grady, could we have two root beers, please?" she called out.

"Floyd can pick them up here," Grady yelled back.

Floyd sighed and lumbered to his feet.

"The new owner of Snow Farms Resort had us up for dinner and to discuss the carnival," Agnes related with a light in her eyes. "What a lovely man. So gracious, and friendly, too. He feels, as we do, that the carnival can be so much more than it's been in the past. He's going to see if he can persuade some professional skaters to come up here to give us an exhibition. Now we just have to hope the lake freezes over in time, and with our cold weather, we should be lucky that it does. The poor man has so much on his shoulders, what with the previous owner being arrested for renting out private penthouse suites to use for Lord knows what. There was even talk that teenage girls were involved." Her lips pursed tightly. "Not only that, but he had been overseeing the carnival account and that money is now gone. Our funds are somewhat low," Agnes confided. "Thank goodness Snow Farms Resort is willing to help out. I'm sure we can bring the carnival to life, even after all these upsets."

Blair managed a smile. *"We" as in anyone Agnes could coerce or blackmail into doing most of the work while she supervises and takes all the credit.* She mentally smacked herself upside the head; while Agnes did manage to take all the credit, she also was an excellent organizer and got everyone going in the right direction—a job that no one else really wanted.

"You and Stasi will help us, won't you?" Agnes asked. "We thought if the weather stays cold enough the lake will freeze, and we could even use it for ice skating. Look at all the snow we've been getting, and the carnival is just around the corner."

Blair swallowed her horror and mentally counted the days. Jazz would be up next week for their centering ceremony and the carnival was only a few weeks after that.

"We had hoped—" Agnes frowned at her husband as he swallowed half his drink. "That doesn't look like root beer." She snatched the glass out of his hand and sniffed, recoiling with horror. "That's bourbon!"

Floyd took it back. "No, a very fine Irish whiskey." He downed the rest before she could steal it back again.

Agnes leaned over. "Floyd, you are a role model for this town," she said in an undertone. "They can't see you drinking alcohol in public. Do you want people thinking you're a drunkard?"

"Nope, can't be that lucky. Just ask Blair," he groused, craning his neck to stare longingly at the bar.

"Ask me what?" She felt that sense of horror again.

Agnes leaned across the table until Blair had no choice but to inhale the heavy gardenia and jasmine scent of White Shoulders that wafted off the woman. "While the resort will do what it can, we have to do our part, too. I thought you and Stasi could help us with some…"

"Some…?" Blair prompted when she didn't go on.

Agnes mouthed the word *magick.* "We thought you could do something… perhaps with decorations… and perhaps convince the printer to print our flyers for free," she whispered. "You know what I mean. One of those spells."

Blair could sense Jake's suppressed mirth as his thigh pressed warmly against hers. She rested her arms on the table and leaned across toward Agnes, making sure to breathe shallowly. She dared not breathe through her mouth or she'd taste the damn perfume, too, and no way she wanted to ruin the tasty memory of her dinner.

"What you're asking for isn't allowed, Agnes," she whispered back. "We have very strict rules we have to follow." When she again sensed Jake's swallowed chuckle, she *casually* ground her heel into his toes. His work boots wouldn't allow much damage, but he got the message.

Agnes's overly plucked eyebrows rose. "You have rules?"

Blair nodded. "We have to answer to someone, and we must be careful how we use our *magick,*" she mouthed the last word.

"And they wouldn't allow you to help us out? It's for a worthy cause," Agnes persisted. "What if I speak to whoever is in charge? Perhaps they'd make an exception."

"I'm sorry, but they wouldn't see proceeds used for renovating the town center as a worthy cause. Don't worry, I'm sure Stasi and I can come up with other ways to help." Oh yeah, Stasi was so going to hate her for this, but there was only so much quick thinking she could do in one evening and she'd pretty much reached her limit. Plus, Stasi had gone off on a romantic getaway, leaving Horace with her. Yep, this seemed only fair.

Agnes frowned in thought as she sat back, then suddenly brightened. "I know what you could do to help us add some wonderful ambiance to the carnival. Being... what you are... I would think you'd know"— she paused as if looking for just the right word—"well... small people."

Blair sifted through Agnes's attempt at political correctness. "Small as in...?"

"Elves."

Blair was beginning to be aware of a headache pounding its way out of her forehead. She picked up her beer glass. "Why do you want to know if I know any elves?"

Agnes brightened. "Think how festive it would be
with booths out by the lake and the ice-skating. And
the resort has offered to host a lovely formal dance as
a finale."

"Gee, that all makes sense why she'd want elves,"
Jake said quietly enough for Blair's ears only.

"I personally don't know any elves, but I'll see what
I can do," Blair said, immediately tossing that idea out
the window. Elves were too much trouble, and that was
the last thing she wanted.

"Wonderful." Agnes turned and pushed Floyd so
hard he almost fell out of the booth. Or it could have
been the three Irish whiskies he had sneaked while she
was talking to Blair. "You two go on and enjoy your
evening. And thank you, dear. Oh Floyd, there's Ted.
I need to speak to him, too, and see if he'll provide the
lumber for the booths." She turned back to Jake, who
cringed under her thousand-watt smile. "I know you'll
help build them, Jake."

"I'm looking forward to it," he muttered, in a tone
that hinted the exact opposite, but then few were able
to hold out against Agnes. Like Blair, Jake chose his
battles wisely.

"I'll be right there." Floyd wasted no time in heading
for the bar after casting them a look of apology for his
hell-on-wheels wife.

"Maybe she should run for mayor at the next elec-
tion," Jake chuckled.

"No, she'd hate all the official paperwork that Floyd
thrives on. Agnes loves being the power behind the
mayoral throne. Plus, if one of her crazy schemes goes
wrong, she can proclaim it was the mayor's idea and she

told him he needed to try something else. But if it works out, naturally it was all her doing."

He grinned and shook his head. He slid out of the booth and stood up, wrapping his hand around Blair's wrist and pulling her to her feet. "Come on, hexy lady, dance with me." He led her to the small dance floor on the other end of the tavern. Jake kept hold of her hand while he paused long enough to peruse the jukebox's offerings. Considering Grady's varied clientele, his music was just as eclectic, from big band to country western to rock and roll, and even some heavy metal. Jake inserted quarters and punched the buttons. A moment later, "Save a Horse, Ride a Cowboy" flowed out of the speakers.

"Let's show them how it's done," he said, swinging her into his arms.

Blair laughed, enjoying this fun side of Jake. She was used to the somber-faced handyman who wielded a hammer and saw with great skill, with wry humor that seemed to show up more in his canine form; now she was seeing a more playful side, and she liked it a lot. She kept up with him step by step and after the song finished and another started, they stayed out on the dance floor. By the time they'd finished a fourth dance, Blair was ready to sit down to catch her breath.

"You could have warned me what a great dancer you are." She finished her beer and when Grady stopped by to see if they wanted refills, she asked for a Diet Coke. "I didn't expect a major cardio workout."

"I'll be honest, I haven't danced too much the past few years. After our dance in the shop, I should have known you could boogie like a professional dancer,"

Jake admitted, requesting a Coke for himself. "You also do a great jive."

"Thanks, you're not so bad yourself. I never knew a carpenter could be so light on his feet."

"Uh, no offense, but could you word that another way? I don't want any of the guys here to think I'm looking to change teams."

Blair thanked Grady for her drink, then pressed the icy glass against her cheek. "I don't think that's something you have to worry about," she said huskily.

Jake's dark eyes heated with pure lust as he stared at the glass pressed moistly against her ivory skin. Keeping his gaze on her, he emptied his glass in record time. Blair took her time, even pausing to lick droplets of Diet Coke off her lips.

"You are one dangerous witch," he growled—a real growl, as only he could.

Blair almost cheered at the thought that she was throwing him off balance. Not that she was expecting to be carried off to his cabin tonight. Although, she wouldn't protest if he did decide to play the part of the Alpha male to her witchy female and steal her away for some hot and heavy sex. There was something about the *Me Tarzan, You Jane* scenario that revved her engines. And at that moment Jake was seriously revving her engines.

Plus, she was afraid if she was too forward (heaven forbid she jump his bones on the first date!), that he'd run for the hills—literally—and she'd never see him again. She'd really hate to throw out a *bring 'em back alive* spell if she didn't have to. Although the longer she stared back at him, the more tempting the thought became.

She glanced up at the old-fashioned clock that hung on the wall near the dartboard. "I should go. I'm going to have a busy day tomorrow, rearranging the shop."

Jake nodded and slid out of the booth, stopping to snag his jacket from the other side and then helping Blair on with hers.

They stepped outside and Blair giggled when her breath showed in white puffs in the icy night air.

"Oh yeah?" Jake pursed his lips, and his breath puffed out in perfect circles.

Blair flicked her fingers at him. "Amateur." She closed her eyes and slowly exhaled, her breath turning into an old-fashioned witch riding her broom with a cat perched on the end. It dissipated in a cloud of silver sparkles.

"No way I can compete with that, and I'm not even going to try." Jake took her arm in his, tucking it against his side as they walked up the sidewalk. He grimaced at the icy air assaulting their faces. "I guess I should have picked you up in my truck. Are you sure you can walk safely in those boots?"

She shook her head. "There's no ice. Besides, I know you're here to catch me if I start to fall." She shot him a flirtatious smile. "I like to walk when nights are this pretty, even if it's so cold."

"One question I've always wanted to ask."

"Ask and I might answer," she replied.

"Why are you and Stasi are always willing to let them hold the carnival at the lake every winter? I mean, you own that property, and you and the other witches go out there each full moon, so why not find a way to keep it to yourselves?" Jake asked.

"We believe the lake is here for everyone, and it is a lovely spot. All we want is to keep the lake and surrounding area safe from developers. People love having the carnival booths around the lake, even if visitors have to park in town and hike there—it doesn't seem to deter them," Blair replied, enjoying the sounds of their boots on the wooden planks that made up the sidewalks of Moonstone Lake. She loved this town. She glanced in the drug store that had been owned and operated by Kenneth Fogerty for the past fifty-three years. Lights showed in the back and she could see rusty-colored tufts of hair on the pharmacist's head as he worked in the back of the pharmacy. She wondered if the elderly man would ever retire. She doubted it. One morning they'd find his eternally sleeping form seated in the ancient chair behind the counter.

"A sense of family," she said abruptly.

"Hm?" Jake looked down at her. "Come again?"

"We're a family. In your terms, a Pack. All of us who've lived here in Moonstone Lake for years." She threw out her free arm in a graceful arc. "How many winters have we been snowed in because of heavy snow-storms? How many summers have we worried about fires, and even rode out a few? No matter what, we've always worked together to help each other. We all stuck together even when this was a small mining camp. Yes, there were bar fights and killings over claims, but those of us who wanted a secure and law-abiding town fought for it and we won. So many stayed on and in the process left something tangible for their descendants."

"Maybe you should be mayor."

"No way. I like what I'm doing. Finding pieces of the past and giving them new homes."

Pretty soon they stood at the back stairs that led up to Blair and Stasi's apartment. Their living space encompassed the entire second floor of the building, with their shops downstairs. Faint barks could be heard from above.

"Maybe Bogie thinks his buddy is out here," Blair said softly.

"You really love yanking my chain about that, don't you?" Jake grimaced as he realized there was definitely a pun in there. Luckily, Blair was kind enough not to jump on the opportunity to tease him.

"Thank you for dinner and the dances." She stood on the second-to-last step, putting herself at eye level with Jake. "I enjoyed myself."

"I did, too." He reached up and brushed away a strand of hair the breeze had caught and left at her lips. As he did, his fingertips rested momentarily against the moist skin and he paused, looking into her eyes that shone with brilliant blue-green light.

"You have the most beautiful eyes." His words were so soft she had to strain to hear them. "Cute nose. Kissable..." He then chose to take action instead of talking about it.

Finally! Blair tasted sharp yeast and barbecue spices as Jake's mouth moved over hers. He threaded his fingers through hers, keeping their entwined hands at their sides. She wanted to complain about the lack of full contact, but she found it arousing because Jake had a way of making her forget everything but the feel of his lips, his taste, and the warmth of his fingers. She closed her eyes and allowed her senses to fan out and enjoy it all. The warm, woodsy scent of his skin teased her nostrils, and the warmth of his mouth chased away the night chill. Her tongue danced with his, curling around and inviting him inside. When they finally parted, they were breathing harder than they had after dancing.

"I should have known," Jake rasped.

"What?" She felt pretty dazed herself.

"That you'd kiss like a dream come true." And just like that, he seemed to fade into the darkness.

Blair stared into the space where Jake had been. "Ooookay." She turned around and slowly climbed the stairs. Pleasantly warm air wafted across her face as she entered the kitchen. She leaned down to pat Bogie on the head before the dog drifted in the air toward the family room, where his favorite blanket awaited him. The sound of the TV told Blair she wasn't alone. "How was your date?" Stasi called from the family room.

"You're back? I thought you'd be gone another day or so." Blair nuked water for tea in the microwave, then dropped an orange spice teabag into the mug.

"Trev got a call about an important case he's been dealing with for the past two hundred years, so we came back here tonight."

"We'd rather hear about your date," Trev called out. "Horace said you were smokin' hot tonight."

Blair walked into the family room and found Stasi and Trev lolling on the couch. Anastasia Romanov, smartest witch in the class of 1313, sported yellow fleece pajama pants and a yellow thermal shirt dotted with pink beach umbrellas, her golden-brown hair fanning out as she snuggled back against Trev's broad chest. Trevor Barnes, hotshot wizard lawyer, was equally dressed for comfort in flannel pajama pants and a navy T-shirt as he lay stretched out with Stasi lying between his legs, his arms draped loosely around her waist. Blair glanced at the TV.

"I'm impressed. You got him to watch a chick flick!"

"We flipped a coin," Trev explained.

"And you lost?"

He nodded.

"What was your choice?"

"*The Matrix,* but he would have settled for *Terminator.* Turns out my buttoned-down attorney boyfriend loves those shoot 'em up films." Stasi reached into the bowl of popcorn that rested on her tummy.

Blair settled in the oversized comfy chair she liked to call her own and pulled off her boots. She stretched her legs in front of her and wiggled her toes. Just like magick, her gold ankle bracelet with its broom charm returned to her ankle.

"I gather from the goofy smile on your face that you had a nice evening." Stasi tossed a piece of popcorn into the air and slightly behind her. Trev leaned forward to catch it in his mouth.

"Wow, nice trick. Are you guys available for birthday parties?" Blair picked up her mug and sipped her tea. Not that she needed warming up. Jake had jacked up her internal thermostat nicely, but drinking the tea gave her something to do.

"Weddings, funerals, you name it." Trev reached around Stasi and stole a few more kernels.

"Come on, give. Horace already told us you two went to Grady's, so just tell us the juicy parts. How does Jake rate as a kisser?" Stasi asked.

Trev almost choked on a piece of popcorn. "Get to the point, love."

Blair sputtered into her tea. "Stasi! Who even said he kissed me?"

"I only have to look at your face to know he kissed you. I just want details."

"Wait a minute, is this what you two did when Stasi and I first went out?" Trevor asked.

"'Course not." Horace ambled into the room and hopped up onto the coffee table. "I wanted facts, I wanted pictures, and I got bupkus. How am I supposed to keep my scrapbook up-to-date if you guys don't give me something to put in it?"

"Yes!" Stasi squealed, almost upsetting her bowl of popcorn. "C'mon, Blair!"

"We had dinner, we danced for awhile… and Agnes asked if we'd do some witchy stuff to help with the carnival." She helped herself to a handful of popcorn.

"Witchy stuff as in…?"

Blair waved a hand. "As in using a few spells to obtain good deals from the printer and stuff, since most of the carnival funds were embezzled. I already told her it's against the rules. Just like last year, she wants to hold the carnival along the lake. There would be booths, and the new owner of Snow Farms told her he'd try to get some professional skaters up here for a skating exhibition. And he's hosting a formal dance up at the resort. But," she held up her hand for emphasis, "here's the biggie. She's hoping we can bring in some elves."

"Elves?"

Blair nodded.

Stasi mimed a gagging action. "Why?"

"Beats me. She seems to think they'll add a festive atmosphere to the carnival."

"I could see elves running around the town for Yule, but not for a winter carnival. Although I've heard that most of the time they're more of a headache than they are good background." Trev stretched his arms over his head and yawned, then carefully dislodged Stasi so he could climb off the couch. "Sorry ladies, but this guy's beat. I'm for bed." The scorching look he shot at Stasi from his deep blue eyes communicated that he hoped she felt the same. She offered him a soft look of apology.

"I'll be there in a minute," she assured him.

He dropped a kiss on the top of Stasi's head and moved toward her bedroom.

"He's a keeper," Blair told her once the wizard was out of earshot.

Stasi smiled. "I know. I think Jake is, too."

Blair's snort was unladylike. "If he comes to his senses. Although I have to say, he is a fantastic kisser."

Stasi threw up her arms in a victory gesture. "And?"

"And he kissed me and sent me upstairs."

Stasi's glee left as quickly as it had appeared. "No invitation for coffee at his place?"

"Nope."

"No asking to come up here for coffee?"

Blair slowly shook her head from side to side. "Good thing he didn't, since I didn't know you were back."

"Did he say he'd see you soon?"

"Stasi, this town has a population of 148. I see everyone who lives here at least twice a week, and sometimes more."

"So what are you going to do?" Stasi saw the determination in her friend's eyes and knew the Were didn't have a chance—once Blair had her teeth in a problem, she didn't let go.

She sat back with her fingertips pressed together. "I won't make it easy, but I'm going to make sure he finds out just how much fun this witch is." The two witches grinned conspiratorially. "And if I volunteer to work on setting up the carnival, I should be able to spend more time with him. Plus find a way to explain to Agnes that elves aren't a good idea."

"I wouldn't worry. After all, how could Agnes find any elves without our help?"

Blair thought about it for a moment. "You're right. It's not as if there's an elf employment agency out there."

"So what else has been going on?"

Blair brought Stasi up to speed, telling her about Jake showing up scratched and cut after his scrap with a coyote and the strange woman coming into the shop wanting a revenge spell that Blair refused to craft.

She finished her tea and rose to her feet. "Go show your sexy wizard you're not ignoring him. I'll take care of the lights." Stasi scooted out of the room grinning in anticipation. With a snap of Blair's fingers, the lights and TV switched off.

It wasn't until she was settled under the covers and ready to drop off to sleep that a vague memory teased Blair's brain.

Wait a minute—there is *an elf employment agency.*

Chapter 4

"FOUR MORE DAYS 'TIL THE FULL MOON." BLAIR STARED out over the lake's gentle blue surface, reflecting the late-afternoon sun. She rubbed her nose with her gloved hand, but the warmth only remained a short time before the icy air chilled it again. Stasi stomped her feet against the snow-dotted ground and tucked her hands under her armpits. "Jazz is right, winter is never fun out here. If it gets any colder, we'll need to find a way to hang portable heaters under our robes, because even long underwear won't make a difference."

"You'd think our magick could handle that, but since it doesn't work I'd say Eurydice has something to do with it." Blair tugged her leopard-print fleece hat further down on her head, ignoring the fact she'd be stuck with nasty hat hair later in the day. It was Saturday, but since she didn't have a date, who cared? "It would be nice if she'd hand out a list of dos and don'ts, since she's so insistent we walk the straight and narrow."

"The list seems pretty basic. Don't irritate vampires, Weres, wizards, trolls, gnomes, elves, goblins, Fae, Druids, Mother Nature, or Cupid." Stasi wrinkled her nose. "Is there anyone left?"

"You forgot the most important one when it comes to our personal well-being: don't piss off the Witches' Council." Blair started to take a deep breath, but the icy cold air reminded her it wasn't a good idea. She settled for cupping her face in her hands and breathing in and out a couple of times to warm herself.

"I try not to mention them out loud." They walked side-by-side back toward their home.

"True, big ears and all that."

Stasi glanced at the friend who was closer to her than blood. "Thinking about Jake again?"

Blair nodded.

"Did the kiss help you decide anything?"

"Definitely, but I'm trying to be subtle." Blair was convinced the wheels and gears in her brain could easily be heard.

"Your definition of subtle, or mine?"

"Sort of a cross between the two." She dug her hands in her pockets and found a couple of Hershey's Kisses. She handed one over to Stasi, unwrapped the foil on hers, and popped it into her mouth. Blair firmly believed that her thought processes improved when she had chocolate in her system. "I've said it before: there's no doubt about Jake. He's interested, but for some reason he's holding back, and I need to find out why."

"It's the Were thing. They all think they're superior to us," Stasi replied thoughtfully, nibbling on her chocolate Kiss. "I don't understand why the other magickal beings don't like witches. We're all so wonderful. What's not to like?"

"Nasty hexes over the centuries, a few—or a hundred—wars. That type of thing." Blair searched her pockets again for more chocolate but came up dry. She made a mental note to stop by Lancaster's Old-Fashioned Chocolates and Candies without delay. She considered their hand-dipped milk chocolate graham crackers health food. And she thought she'd add a few coconut haystacks, along with Hetty Lancaster's sinfully rich truffles, to her purchases. Her mouth was already watering at the thought.

"But that wasn't us," Stasi pointed out, then reconsidered. "Well, some of the wars had to do with witches, but not us *personally*. We all get along. Well, to a point," she had to concede. "And it's not the way it was centuries ago."

"Thank the Fates," Blair muttered, her mind still on the array of handmade chocolates at Lancaster's.

Stasi stopped and spun around to face her friend. "You're thinking about chocolate, aren't you?" she accused.

Blair stepped around her and continued on. Witch on a mission—and with chocolate as the goal, there was no stopping her.

"You are!" Stasi stayed on her heels.

"You're having regular sex with a guy who's obviously giving you Grade-A orgasms." She ignored Stasi's hot blush. "I don't have that pleasure. And while Flipper," she said, referring to her trusty dolphin vibrator, "can take the edge off, it's still not the same as the real thing."

Stasi narrowed her golden-brown eyes at her friend. "Then stop being subtle and do something! When has a stubborn man ever stopped you before?"

"It would have been a lot easier if he was human instead of Were. Although love spells can be trouble, too. But I don't want to get him with magick! It has to be his idea."

They reached the back stairs leading up to their apartment.

Stasi shook her head. "Go get your chocolate. I'll start the laundry." She climbed the stairs. "But I want some champagne truffles!"

"Done." Blair's mouth was watering more by the second as she thought of the rich chocolate she'd find in the small shop.

She'd barely stepped foot inside the bright teal and hot pink décor of Lancaster's Old-Fashioned Chocolates and Candies when the seductive scent of chocolate flooded her olfactory senses. She breathed in deeply. *Ah, Nirvana!*

"I see someone's in chocolate withdrawal." Hetty Lancaster, a fortyish petite brunette with dancing blue eyes, stood at a marble counter pouring rich chocolate fudge to cool before slicing it into bricks.

"I had two chocolate Kisses in my pocket, but Stasi was with me, so I had to share. All it did was prime the pump." Blair leaned over the glass counter, careful not to drool on the pristine surface. "What's that?" She pointed to colorful bricks of fudge.

"Something new. It's marbled orange fudge, like the orange and vanilla ice cream bars." Hetty inclined her head toward a plate on the counter. "Try some."

Blair picked up a piece and popped it into her mouth. "Oh, this is good." She stole another. "Okay, I need some of this, too. Along with milk chocolate with and without nuts, the mint chocolate, peanut butter and chocolate, rocky road, and some milk chocolate-coconut haystacks. Oh, and six—no, make that eight—milk chocolate dipped graham crackers. And a dozen champagne truffles." She surveyed the displays, seeing even more she wanted—but eating herself into a chocolate coma wasn't a good idea. She also knew she'd have to hide it from Bogie and Horace, who were as much chocoholics as she and Stasi were.

"How I love customers like you." Hetty efficiently boxed up the requested items. "And how I hate that you can eat this much and not gain an ounce."

Blair knew she had her magickal metabolism to thank for that, but it wasn't something she advertised too widely. Although she knew she'd make a fortune if there was a way to bottle it.

"You have turtles today." She gazed longingly at the round candy made from caramel and nuts topped with chocolate.

Hetty tossed a couple into a box. "By the way, you might want to hide somewhere. Agnes is on the prowl for volunteers. She was in here a few minutes ago."

Blair shook her head. "Too late. She ambushed me at Grady's the other night, and I already said Stasi and I would help out, but she's not going to get us to do more than I offered. Do you notice it's usually the same people doing all the work for every town function? Why can't she find other victims?"

"Because she knows who will work and who won't. Plus, she wants to impress Snow Farm's new owner."

"There are days I wish someone would run for mayor against Floyd, because then we wouldn't have to deal with Agnes and all her town promotion schemes," Blair grumbled. It wasn't that she didn't like Floyd and Agnes, and she was very much aware of what the couple had done to revitalize the town. But she sometimes wished they would find other minions to help with their plans.

"No one wants the job," Hetty said, placing Blair's purchases in three teal-colored bags with the shop name printed in hot pink script. "You can't blame them. Most of us have our own businesses to run, and Floyd's retired and happy to handle all the little things that come up with the town."

"Headaches, you mean." Blair handed over her Visa card.

"Exactly."

Blair tried not to wince at the amount printed on the charge slip, but she knew that Hetty's candy was well worth the cost. When her husband divorced her four years ago and moved down the mountain, Hetty had taken over running the shop, making her chocolates, and raising her fifteen-year-old son, all with equal efficiency. Blair noticed that Hetty's gaze kept veering toward the front window.

"Looking for anyone in particular?"

Hetty picked up the plate of samples on the counter and moved over to the back table to replenish it.

"Vic should have been back with Jason by now," she murmured. "It seems he brings Jason back later every time he has him." She twisted her fingers, showing the fear and tension she'd been trying to hide.

Blair was aware that Hetty's ex-husband had an abusive personality that he had taken out on his wife, who had kept the violence quiet for her son's sake, so nothing was ever done. Blair had even once less than subtly offered to work a severe punishment spell on Vic—any penalty from the Witches' Council be damned—but Hetty begged her to leave him alone, fearing the man would retaliate, since he knew what

Blair's major gift was. Blair had accepted the woman's decision, but she didn't like it and swore that if Vic ever got out of hand, she'd zap him but good.

"And you don't dare complain to your lawyer about this?"

"I got the shop and physical custody of Jason in exchange for not bringing up... things. Vic enjoys reminding me he can take me back to court any time he chooses, and he knows I can't afford to keep on doing that." Her eyes started to light up when a black Dodge Charger rolled to a stop in front of the shop, but the light dimmed when it was apparent that the tension level inside the vehicle was high. "Please no," she whispered.

Blair watched Jason jump out of the car as Vic streaked out of the driver's side and reached the boy in just a few steps, grabbing his wrist so hard Blair imagined she heard the bones grind. Judging from Jason's wince of pain, she feared she wasn't that far off.

"Stay here," she ordered Hetty, who had started to move forward. "I promise everything will be all right." Blair was out the door in a flash.

"Listen, you fuckin' snot, you start treating me with the respect I deserve or you won't be living with your bitch of a mother anymore, do you hear me?" Vic's fingers tightened further on Jason's wrist until the boy looked as if he would cry.

"Vic." Blair's tone held about as much warmth as she'd bestow on a cockroach. Actually, she considered cockroaches many levels above Vic.

He looked up. At first glance, Vic was handsome, with his ex-football player body and the bad boy charisma he exuded—until his darker side came out in full force, usually with harsh words and fists. Blair doubted he ever kept a girlfriend for long once they got to know the real him.

The creep had once cornered Blair and it had taken a pretty nasty jolt to his genitals for him to get the message she wanted nothing to do with him, but he hadn't forgotten, or forgiven, her rejection. She saw that now in his sinister gaze.

"Back off, witch. This is family business," he snarled.

"I'd call it child abuse." Her eyes lit on the dark purple, finger-shaped bruises on Jason's wrist.

"If you interfere, she'll never see him again."

Blair's temper could turn white-hot, but when she was beyond furious she tended to turn cold and right now the temperature in Antarctica was balmy compared to her.

"I don't think so, Vic. Don't look at Hetty and don't you dare blame her," she snapped. "Right now, this is between you and me. This has to do with you being such a bully and what you've done to her and your own kid over the years, and your insane ability to get away with it. Guess what? Ain't gonna happen anymore." She took another step forward, feeling her power flow out through her fingertips. She made sure Vic saw and felt it, too. "Jason, honey, go on inside to your mother now." She kept her eyes trained on Vic.

The boy looked a combination of scared and relieved, but followed her direction and hurried into the shop and into his mother's arms.

"Here's the deal," Blair said conversationally. "You are going to treat Jason like the wonderful kid he is and you will treat Hetty with the respect she deserves. If you want to terrorize someone, go find a fetish club, where a nasty old Dom in a leather bodysuit and stiletto boots can stomp the shit out of you, but you *will* leave them alone. You got me?"

He crossed his arms in front of his chest and leaned against the car. "And if I don't?"

"Then you will hurt as you've never hurt before. Bad boy. Mad boy. I won't be coy. No more hurt, no more pain. You… will… stop or you feel all you inflict. Make it so."

Vic swatted at the dark blue sparks that rained over him. "What the fuck?"

"I made it easy for you," Blair told him. "Any time you try to hurt Hetty or Jason by word or deed, you will find you can go no further. Your body will refuse to go any further. The same goes for any woman you try to abuse. Women, and children, are to be cherished and respected, not terrorized. And there's no way you can take this spell out on anyone."

He straightened up and started for her.

She held up a hand. "Don't even think about it, Vic." Her low voice throbbing with power got his attention more than her words. "You've always mocked Stasi and me as a Halloween joke. You have no idea what we're capable of, and trust me, you really don't want to know."

"Is there a problem?"

Blair spared a quick glance to her left and saw Jake standing nearby. While his loose-limbed stance appeared casual, she could see the tension in his shoulders and the sharpness in his gaze.

Oooh, my knight in shining fur.

"I don't think so. What about you, Vic?"

The man appeared to grind his teeth. "Tell Hetty to make sure the little fucker's ready on time from now on." He reached inside the car and pulled out a duffle bag, tossing it to the sidewalk. He walked around the car and pulled open the door.

"Just don't forget what I said, Vic. The consequences wouldn't be pretty," she reminded him.

As he revved the engine and roared off, his extended middle finger appeared over the top of his car.

"Charming." Jake walked over to her.

"That's Vic." Blair looked back at the shop's window and saw Hetty standing there, one arm draped over Jason's shoulder. "Just a second." She walked to the door and opened it up. "He won't hurt you again, Jason," she told him. "And he'll actually behave."

"Blair, I…" Hetty looked worried.

She shook her head. "It's nothing major, just a little something that will remind him of his manners. There's no way he can beat someone up just because he feels the need. And there's no way he can fight it or have the spell erased. The only one strong enough to eliminate the spell is Jazz, and you know she'd only strengthen it if he were crazy enough to go to her. I've wanted to restrain him for some time, and now it's been done."

"But he's really strong," Jason pointed out. "You know he'll try." He glanced down at his wrist, which was purpling more by the second.

"If he does, he'll find he can't move. Can't raise his hand, can't even try anything through his lawyer, because who's going to believe that a witch hexed him that way? People like the idea of hexes, but most still refuse to believe it can be done." She offered them a smile before she ducked out again.

"I see you did a bit of shopping." Jake eyed the bags. "Are there rumors of an impending chocolate shortage in the world that I haven't read about?"

"Most of it's for Stasi." She decided not to divulge one of her vices. She was looking at a prime male specimen who had her mentally drooling even more than she actually did when walking into Hetty's shop. Even though it was a cold day, Jake wore only a flannel shirt over a faded red T-shirt. She figured his Were metabolism kept him warm except on super cold days. "What are you up to?"

He glanced across the street where his dark silver Suburban waited. Several large boxes were in the bed of the truck. "I'm heading down the mountain to drop off some things and pick up some supplies."

She summoned a bright smile while a tiny voice inside chimed *Take me along! Take me along!* like an energetic puppy. Any minute she'd be sitting up and begging with her tail wagging merrily away.

Instead she took a step backward. "Well, have a good day, and thanks for being there in case Vic got out of hand. Although I guess he'd be a poor substitute for a coyote." She grinned.

Jake smiled back and nodded, then strolled across the street to his truck.

"I really must work on my conversational skills," she muttered, heading home with the intention of diving wholeheartedly into her chocolate stash.

❖ ❖ ❖

The witch is making me crazy. Jake downshifted as he reached a treacherous turn on the winding road. *My life is making me crazy.*

For a moment back there, he'd been tempted to ask Blair to go along with him. His errands wouldn't take all that long and he'd suggest they have some dinner, maybe even catch a movie. This time they could have a date that wasn't under the ultra-watchful eyes of the whole damn town. He wanted to go out with her again, have the chance to kiss her good night again. Fill himself with the unique, sassy taste that was all Blair. Then thoughts of kissing her started to wander into forbidden territory.

While she knew of his Were nature, did she honestly know what being Were meant? What the darker side of his personality could entail?

When he swung the truck around another curve, a faint tinkle of chimes sounded in the air. He glanced briefly at the gold chain that swung from the rearview mirror, a chain he had once worn around his neck as a symbol of his status as the second-in-command's whelp. Suspended from the links were small charms etched with ancient symbols. It was the only thing he had taken with him other than his clothing when he left the Pack, and reminder enough of why he hadn't asked Blair to go with him. It had been a gift from his father when he had reached puberty, and Jake couldn't bring himself to throw it away.

"If she finds out the truth about what I left behind with the Pack, there'll be Hades to pay. I'll be lucky to end up with even a small patch of fur left on my ass."

"It's like Indian summer today," Stasi commented as she and Blair took advantage of an unseasonable warm front to bask on their rooftop patio under the winter sun. Stasi was celebrating the warm day with summery capris and a sleeveless top, while Blair wore denim cutoffs, a dark yellow T-shirt, and tooled brown leather ankle boots with a three-inch heel. A straw cowgirl hat was tipped forward over her eyes. She looked ready for a night down at the nearest country-western honky tonk instead of an afternoon of vegging out.

Blair pushed back her hat and surveyed her bare legs with a soft sigh. "If I'd known we'd have a great day like this, I would have gone for a spray tan. Magick tans still are hit and miss for me."

"You're not the only one. The last time I tried it, I ended up looking so blotchy you would have thought I had some sort of horrible skin disease, and then it wouldn't go away for two weeks." Stasi smothered a yawn.

Blair curled her lip as she observed her friend's sleepy manner. "Do *not* mutter you had a long night, or I will have to hurt you.

Stasi's satisfied smile told it all. "Fine, I won't." She stretched her arms over her head and yawned again, then yelped when Blair zapped her bare leg. Bogie floated his way into her lap and snuggled in as she swung back and forth in the wood slat porch swing. "Jealous much?"

"I'm taking the Fifth." Blair spotted a tall figure in the distance and frowned. She dug the binoculars out of the nearby storage box and brought them up to her eyes — taking careful note of the angle of the sunlight. Her frown turned to a smile as she remembered Jake's teasing.

"Jake?"

"Jake—in his shirt-sleeves, now there's a happy thing. He's chopping wood for Mrs. Benedict and it looks like Mr. Chalmers is supervising. Although it seems the couple have some additional ways of stoking up a fire." She quickly explained Jake's revelation about Mrs. Benedict and Mr. Chalmers' love life.

Stasi broke out into a broad smile. "I'm so glad! They're really meant for each other. I think it's wonderful that they're still able to express their love."

"Then Mr. Chalmers should be out there showing off his muscles and chopping that wood."

Blair settled back to enjoy the sight of the smooth play of muscles as Jake swung the axe, turning the wood into neat kindling while the elderly man stood nearby. She knew she could easily eavesdrop on their conversation, but chose not to. It was simple enough to see that Mr. Chalmers was talking about what he could accomplish "back in the day." She didn't miss that he held a biscuit gleaming with butter in one hand. The elderly widow was known for her sourdough biscuits, and there was no doubt she had been baking that morning. According to Mrs. Benedict, her starter originated from an ancestor's sourdough starter back in the 1800s. Blair's mouth watered for one of those warm-from-the-oven biscuits.

She straightened up when Jake finished stacking the kindling against the side of Mrs. Benedict's cabin and shook Mr. Chalmers' hand. He paused at the back door, obviously to say something to Mrs. Benedict, and then left carrying a cloth-covered plate in one hand.

"I'm off." Blair hopped to her feet.

Stasi opened one eye and nuzzled her dog. "The witch is on the prowl."

"You got it." She stopped in the apartment long enough to apply a dab of coral lip gloss and a spritz of cologne as well as to pull a fleece jacket out of her closet and tie the sleeves around her waist in case the air started to grow chilly.

"Just act casual," she reminded herself as she headed for the rear path that would take her past Jake's two-story, A-frame cabin.

When she reached the outskirts of his property, Jake was coming out of his cabin, talking on his cell phone. Judging by his dark expression, he wasn't happy with whatever the person on the other end of the line was telling him.

"Yes, I know that," he growled, as he crossed his backyard. "And I'm out of it. I have been for years. The best thing you can do for both of us is to not contact me again." His mouth worked as if he was coming up with some prime cussing. "I've said my piece. For once respect it!" As he turned toward the rear building that housed his workshop, he saw Blair standing nearby. "I've got to go." He slapped his phone shut and stuck it back on his belt. "This isn't a good time, Blair."

She sensed that his irritation and the weariness that lined his features had nothing to do with his chores at Mrs. Benedict's. And while his greeting wasn't a "hi, good to see you, sit down a spell," she made no move to leave.

"I was just talking a walk."

"When you take a walk, you go out by the lake."

She was pleased that he remembered. "A witch has been known to change her mind now and then."

"Not you. You never change your mind about anything." He stopped by the workshop but didn't reach for the lock.

"I did with the dog," she said softly. "I even let him sleep on the end of my bed."

Jake combed his fingers through his hair, allowing the shaggy strands to settle back in their haphazard way. He leaned against the building with his arms crossed in front of his chest. Still not a welcoming move, but he wasn't ignoring her, either.

Blair didn't miss that his dark eyes scanned her length of bare leg. She was glad she hadn't changed into jeans, even if by now the sudden drop in temperature meant that her legs were starting to turn an unattractive shade of navy. She untied her jacket and shrugged it on, zipping it up. There was no use for the rest of her to turn blue.

"And I don't even like dogs all that much," she continued.

A brief uplift of his lips showed he wasn't entirely impervious to her words. "You must have a soft spot, then."

"Only for the moon-challenged, although I guess I'd have to say that's not truly you, is it?"

"Like I said, family background." The minute he said that he looked as if he'd regretted saying even those two words.

Blair wasn't one to ignore any opening. "You never talk about your Pack. Are they Border Collies too? Yorkies?" she prompted when he didn't reply. "Pugs? Did you try to herd them and they didn't like it?"

A short bark of laughter escaped Jake's lips and he looked down, shaking his head. "It's not like that, Blair."

"Then what is it like? What's so wrong with telling me? Is it some big secret, that if you told me you'd have to kill me?" She winced a little. "Hm, scratch that. We won't look at it that way, 'kay? It's just that I want to know."

Jake's head shot up. Anger darkened his eyes. This time the anger was well and truly directed at her. "Why do you have to be such a nosy witch? What is so important about me that you have to know every facet of my life? Can't you understand that I might like to keep some things private?" He straightened up and walked back to the house, entering the rear door and closing it with a final click.

Blair shifted from one foot to the other. "So I guess that's a no on discussing your family tree?" she called out, not expecting a reply and not receiving one. "Some people were just brought up not to share," she muttered, heading back to her house. "See if I talk to you at the town meeting tonight, then."

Jake stood at the kitchen window and watched Blair walk away, the toes of her boots scuffing any rocks in her path. Tiny spots of magick sparkled over her head, which he took to mean she was thinking way too hard and her temper was simmering. A part of him hoped she'd look back, while another part of him hoped she wouldn't. He knew his words hadn't made her happy, but he needed to say whatever it took to get her to leave before the fury that was eating like acid deep down inside him bubbled up and out. Before he pulled her into his arms so he could reacquaint himself with her spicy taste and the slender curves of her body. Before he could give in to the side of him that wanted even more from her than he knew he could give her.

"Trust me, Blair, the last thing you want to know is anything about my family tree," he murmured, turning away.

Luckily phone calls from the family were few and far between. They always made him uneasy and this one was the worst of all, because his mother had called him again insisting she needed to speak to him. He'd already broken one cell phone because of his temper, and he refused to do it again.

As far as he was concerned, it was same old, same old. *He must return to the Pack.* Why, when he'd been doing just fine on his own, thank you very much. *Didn't he understand he needed the Pack as much as they needed him?* Why did he need a group that had always made a point of telling him they *didn't* need him? *The Pack believed in all for one, one for all. That included him.* Not the way he saw it.

"Fuck that," he muttered, spearing his fingers through hair that hadn't seen a comb since he showered and dressed that morning. He started to wonder if that coyote was in the area and ready for another go-around.

Once upon a time the Pack, and his own family, hadn't cared what happened to a whelp that was considered nothing more than a stain on the Pack. Punishment was often and brutal to the youngling who didn't understand why he wasn't like the others. He was a throwback to an affair several generations back; a reminder no one cared to have around because he was considered a weak link.

As he grew older, Jake saw no reason to stay and left before he was tossed out of the Pack. While Pack Weres normally preferred to stick together, he quickly discovered he could do just fine on his own. After all, a Border Collie didn't exactly go big game hunting. While Pack members gloried in working together to bring down a deer, he was content with catching the occasional rabbit or squirrel and just roaming the woods.

And once he visited Moonstone Lake a few years ago, bought his cabin, and built his workshop, he knew he'd truly come home. He had done odd jobs around the town, worked on projects in the workshop that brought in the majority of his income, and wasted no time in noticing a sassy, red-haired witch. But then, who wouldn't notice Blair, with her flair for the eccentric and warm manner that included hugs for all? Not just her love of the eclectic, but the sheer color she seemed to bring into everything she did. For someone who'd been brought up in a world of black and white, he had first found her amusing; amusement quickly turned into fascination, and that later turned into something else, as he started to see the world as she did, in brilliant color.

Blair's warm, loving touch was a part of her sharing nature and held a sincerity he'd never encountered before.

Avoided as being different, cut off from the warmth of his Pack's social interactions, most of Jake's experience with touch had involved either discipline or sex, as he grew up and had the occasional hook-up. Blair had complained long and hard about the dog, but there'd been many a night he'd woken in the middle of the bed with her hugging him like a stuffed animal. He was always happy just to go back to sleep.

Here he wasn't treated like a worthless Pack whelp. Here he wasn't treated like the bottom of the heap.

Here he was treated fairly and kindly. And that's all he wanted.

His nostrils flared, catching one last hint of Blair's perfume.

Well, maybe not all.

Chapter 5

"TIME IS SHORT, BUT THAT'S NEVER STOPPED US before," Agnes enthused from the front of the town hall. "And I know you all will help make this the best winter carnival yet."

"My feet are freezing," Blair said under her breath.

"Floyd's already talking about bringing up a bond issue to cover the cost of putting a new furnace in here," Stasi whispered. "Ted over at the hardware store said it's cheaper just to invest in electric socks and wear more layers."

"Not if the socks short out every time you wear them." Blair shifted in her chair, which felt like concrete under her butt, then glanced over at Jake sitting a few rows away. He hadn't looked her way once, but she knew deep down that he was aware of her because she could feel it. *Why is he frowning?* She started to lean forward in her chair when he did, then she caught herself and leaned back. She had no doubt something was bothering him and even more certain that his mood had nothing to do with her.

"You're drooling again," Stasi said under her breath.

"No, I'm not." *No way I'll drool over that grouch. I should go out and find me a nice big Werepanther who can kick his canine ass.* She scanned the room, trying to see what was upsetting Jake, because apparently there was something in the room he wasn't happy about. But looking around didn't send up any red flags for her.

"And now let me introduce the new owner of Snow Farms Resort, Roan Thorpe," Agnes's voice cut into Blair's thoughts and brought a scowling Jake upright in his chair.

Blair looked up at the stage at the tall man striding to the podium. His midnight-black hair seemed to hold a silver sheen under the lights.

"Ho boy," she muttered.

"Hubba hubba," Stasi added with a broad smile.

"You're taken," Blair reminded her *sotto voce.*

"Yes, I am and very well done, if I do say so myself, but that doesn't stop me from looking."

It only took another glance in Jake's direction to see his anger level rising even if he was holding it under control admirably. She should have guessed right away.

"This guy's a Were! And if I'm not mistaken, Jake not only knows him, but I'd bet my favorite spell book that they have some history," she whispered for Stasi's ears only.

Stasi's head swung around so fast she almost suffered whiplash. "*What?*" Her squeak came out louder than expected. She turned to the front of the room and took a longer look. "Oh boy, you're right— that's one powerful Were up there, and I don't think he's a Werepoodle, either."

Blair nodded. "Not even close. Look at Jake—I'd swear steam is coming out of his ears." She scrunched down in her chair a bit as if trying to avoid what she expected could be some Were fallout. "This isn't good."

"We've already had not good. We need all good now." Stasi offered up an apologetic smile when the woman seated in front of her turned around and frowned at her while mouthing *please be quiet!*

Blair turned her attention from the man standing at the podium and concentrated on Jake, who was looking grimmer by the second. She was positive that Jake and the new owner of Snow Farms Resort were familiar with each other, because every so often the man would look directly at Jake and each time he did, Jake scowled back. It didn't take long for the answers to start clicking in. Roan Thorpe must be part of Jake's former Pack. Her stomach knotted up so much she wondered if she'd be able to eat anything ever again. She turned her attention back to the speaker before she did something stupid— such as stand up and demand to know what the Were had done to Jake. After all, she had no right to do such a thing.

But she was sure going to find out what was going on.

Witch on a mission.

The minute the meeting was over, Blair jumped out of her chair and headed for the coffee urn, where Agnes was steering their guest. She knew she wouldn't get any answers out of Jake, but that didn't mean she might not find out something from Roan.

She had to admit the Were was in the hot category, with his carved features and dark hair, but she could also easily sense his untamed side. This was no happy-go-lucky dog of any kind. She was positive Roan Thorpe was the kind of wolf Little Red Riding Hood would have wanted to avoid at all cost, because he'd snap her up without a second thought. Luckily, Blair wasn't wearing her red hooded cape and her grandmother had been gone for many centuries.

"And here's our dear Blair and Stasi," Agnes chirped, as she handed a cup of coffee to Roan.

"They're always so generous with their time when we have our town activities."

"Blair Fitzpatrick," Blair said, holding out her hand. The minute Roan's large hand engulfed hers, she felt the Were magick wrap around her skin. She made sure to respond with a little power surge of her own and inwardly smiled as he straightened up and shot her a considering look.

"Stasi Romanov." Stasi did the same with a more polite smile than Blair had been able to muster.

Agnes beamed at the threesome and left them when someone called her name.

"So you're the town witches," Roan murmured.

Blair's smiled remained fixed. *So, it's going to be like that, is it?*

"We don't see ourselves that way."

His dark eyes surveyed her in a way that would have had her hackles rising if she'd had any. Oh wait a minute, that was more his thing.

"So in your own way, you've pretty much ruled the mountain all these years, haven't you?" His voice may have been soft, but they easily heard each word.

"More like protected the land," Stasi retorted. The lawsuit against her last autumn had resulted in more than Stasi's finding the love of her life in Trevor Barnes, wizard attorney: gentle Stasi's snark level had risen and she wasn't above using it when necessary.

"Just as my kind do."

"Except we don't go all hairy every full moon and chase rabbits and squirrels," Blair offered with a broad smile.

Roan's dark narrowed gaze warned her he didn't like her flippancy. As if she cared.

"It's a well known fact you witches love to court trouble. Never tease a tiger, Witch Fitzpatrick. You'll get eaten."

"Then aren't I lucky you're not a Weretiger?" She smiled, an innocent expression on her face. "You know the limerick about the lady from Liger?"

While his smile might have appeared warm to a casual observer, the fury simmering in his eyes told the witches a different story before he moved away.

"I take back the hubba hubba." Stasi nibbled on a Snickerdoodle.

"Ditto." Blair refilled her coffee cup and surveyed the array of baked goods, finally settling on a brownie. She needed chocolate... bad.

"Don't toy with Roan." Blair almost dropped her brownie when Jake seemed to materialize before her.

"Then you do know him." She was positive she spoke the truth, but she still wanted some verification.

Jake's mouth tightened to a thin line. "You might say that—since he's the Pack leader's heir apparent."

"He's what?!"

"Close your mouth, Blair, before you attract flies," Stasi suggested softly. "And as for Roan, let me say he's not a very nice Were, even if he is apparently our new neighbor."

"If Roan's here, that means the Pack isn't far behind." Blair's mind whirled madly. "Most of this mountain is protected. We made sure of that years ago."

Jake shook his head. "That won't stop him, or the Alpha." He looked up and faced the Were across the room, who returned his gaze. Jake drew so close to Blair, she could feel his heat.

"Uh, Jake, you're giving out mega vibes that pretty soon everyone here will sense," Blair whispered, as he bumped up against her. "Are you trying to herd me?"

"If I thought it would do any good, I would," he snarled.

"What the hell is wrong with you?" Her glare could easily have blasted a hole through him.

Jake's jaw flexed. He took a deep breath and looked off in the distance. "Roan Thorpe is also my brother." He turned away and headed for the door.

It took Blair a moment to recover as she picked her jaw up off the floor. "Stasi, tell me he did not say that Roan is his brother."

"I can't, because that's exactly what he said."

"Roan's wolf, so how can Jake's Were half be dog? There is no way he can drop a bombshell like that and just leave," Blair fumed.

"But he did drop that bombshell. So what's next on the agenda, oh wise one?" Stasi chose a brownie.

Blair stared after Jake, then swung her gaze across the room to Roan where he stood talking to Agnes.

"Pull out your No More Ms. Nice Witch persona, babe. I don't know what's going on, but judging by the 'I am Alpha male and you shall do my bidding' vibe, we could end up with a fight on our hands."

"I love these custom dollhouses," Blair commented, leafing through a toy catalog that had arrived in the Wednesday afternoon mail. "I just wish they weren't so expensive. Look at this one. It's a French chateau with antique furniture that looks so authentic you'd swear they were Louis XV. And a haunted house that's priceless. The bedposts look like a stack of skulls! I could easily have sold that last October."

"I love the one that looks like a Southern plantation house. Just looking at it makes me feel like Scarlett O'Hara," Stasi said.

Blair looked up when a familiar classic aqua and white T-Bird whizzed past her window and made a turn around the building.

"Jazz is here," she said, heading for the door and flipping the sign from Open to Closed.

"You look great!" Blair hugged Jazz after she climbed out of the car. Irma, the ghost who inhabited Jazz's T-Bird, and her ghostly dog Sirius floated through the door on the passenger side. Blair looked around apprehensively. "Where are the fuzzy ankle biters?"

Jazz grimaced as she stamped her feet up and down. "You so wouldn't believe what they did. I thought you were having a warm spell up here?"

"We were until two days ago." Stasi stepped in and hugged her, too. "And now everyone's hoping for snow for the winter carnival."

Jazz shivered at the mention of snow. "I thought you've had more than your share of that nasty white stuff already."

Blair watched Jazz pull a bright yellow leather tote bag out of the back seat. "Packing light, aren't you?"

"There's no packing light for Jazz," Irma commented, resting her ghostly hand on Sirius's head. "While all she gives me are a few catalogs from which to choose my clothes." Irma had been stuck in the same 1950s outfit in which she had committed suicide until Jazz had finally found a way for her to update her wardrobe.

"Your wardrobe changes are easier than mine—if I used your method my charge cards wouldn't be maxed out all the time, but where's the fun in that?" Jazz pointed out. She hefted the magickal tote bag. "You'd be amazed what I have in this bag—it'll hold as much as I want to put into it. It was a birthday gift from Thea—and a lot safer than Croc and Delilah. Magickal crocodile stilettos are all very well, but they totally fixated on my housemate. It got so Krebs was afraid to go to bed without having me check out the room first. They managed to sneak through all the wards I put around his space. Not to mention they were always getting into my makeup."

"How are they doing living with Mindy?" Stasi asked, aware that Jazz had passed the sexy shoes on to the blond elf who used to work for Dweezil, the owner of All Creatures Car Service, where Jazz worked as a driver. Mindy now ran her own limo service in San Diego.

"She loves them, and vice versa, because she caters to their makeup and perfume addictions. She even bought them the whole new MAC makeup line, so they'd stay out of hers. I wish I'd thought of that. Still, they're much happier with her, even if I hear they're still pining for Krebs."

The three witches and two ghosts walked (and floated) upstairs. Bogie barked a hello at Sirius and the two dogs headed for the family room.

"This will warm you up." Blair poured cinnamon spice mocha coffee into a dark orange mug with *Witchy Woman* in script across it and handed it to Jazz. "So what's got you in a snit? And don't say you're not in one." She indicated the sparks flying around Jazz's head.

Jazz sat at the table, sipped the hot brew, and released a blissful sigh. "Fluff and Puff have found another way to make my life miserable."

"I didn't think they could get any worse." Stasi sat down across from her.

Jazz turned away and leaned over, tugging off her Ugg boots. Sounds of coughing and choking sounded from her ankles.

Blair and Stasi looked down.

"What the—?" Blair's jaw practically dropped to the floor.

"How did they do that?" Stasi whispered.

Jazz grimly looked at the outside of her right ankle, where Fluff and Puff now resided as a tattoo. The bunny slippers continued to cough and choke, spewing out bits of the boot's shearling lining.

"You better not have ruined the lining," she warned them. "And no complaints. You did this to yourselves, so you have to pay the price."

Puff raised his head and snarled at her while Fluff continued hacking as if he was ready to cough up a hairball, which he did a second later. The three witches groaned in unison.

"I told them they were staying here with you and they told me they weren't." Jazz crossed her legs with her right leg on top, the foot swaying to a beat only she could hear. "I woke up this morning to a strange feeling on my leg and found them literally attached to me. At least they didn't choose the ankle with my ankle bracelet. I hate to think what they would have tried. One of them probably would have swallowed the broom charm."

Blair couldn't hold back her grin. "Oh, this is good. Very good." Her grin soon turned into laughter that wouldn't stop. Stasi joined in the mirth, but Jazz didn't look the least amused.

"This isn't funny!" Jazz argued. "My ankle itches all the time now."

"You should have heard her this morning. The language was very unladylike," Irma confided, leaning over to inhale the coffee in Blair's mug. Her look was so wistful that Blair almost offered her a cup, but she didn't want coffee all over the kitchen floor. Ghosts couldn't hold food, of course—it went right through them. "Even the carriage house shook, the way she stomped around the house ranting and raving. But those little critters weren't going to move from her ankle no matter what spells she tried, and she tried a lot of them. They made sure to stay put."

Blair regretted she was drinking her coffee at the time because she almost spewed it everywhere.

"Wait a minute." She held her hand up, palm out as she fought her hysterical laughter. "Are you saying they *cursed* themselves onto your ankle?"

Stasi was already cradling her face in her hands while her shoulders shook with mirth. "I love it! The curse eliminator is cursed!" Her voice was muffled by her hands.

"I am not!" Jazz insisted, in a voice a few octaves too high.

"Sure you are!" Blair howled, practically bouncing out of her chair. "This is priceless, Jazz!"

"For someone whose success rate as a curse elimi-nator was almost 100%, she's sure losing ground. After all, she couldn't get me out of the car for over fifty years," Irma chimed in.

Jazz ground her teeth so hard it was amazing they weren't stubs.

"Okay, not funny."

"Are you kidding? I haven't laughed this hard in ages." Blair held her stomach and hooted. Stasi kept her face buried in her arms on the table, her shoulders shaking.

Jazz's foot jiggled faster as her agitation level rose. Fluff and Puff screamed out their protest as her movements increased, but they didn't try to escape her ankle, nor did she stop her action.

"Oh wait!" Blair jumped out of her chair and ran into the family room. She returned with her cell phone and started snapping off pictures. "We so need proof of this."

"What are you doing?" Jazz leaped out of her chair and tried to grab Blair and the phone, but Blair hopped out of her reach, busily punching numbers.

"*Yes!*" She held up her phone in victory.

"I think this would make a great holiday card," Stasi said, not even wilting under Jazz's glare. "Who all did you send it to?"

Blair's grin broadened until it threatened to split her face. "Everyone." She looked down when her phone twinkled "All Star." "Maggie loves it."

"You *witch!*" The plates and glassware trembled under Jazz's fury as she advanced on Blair.

Blair remained just out of her reach, looking down again when she heard "When You Wish Upon A Star" and reading another text message. "Lili is using it as her screensaver."

Fluff and Puff's laughter added to the chaos.

"Just remember who does the revenge spells here, Jazz," Blair thought it judicious to mention. "You didn't like that humongous zit you got when your lost your power last year, did you?" She wasn't making a threat, just letting her friend recall that she also had a lot in her witchy arsenal.

Jazz stopped and stared downward. "This is all your fault and once you're off my ankle you will pay like you've never paid before."

Then she glared pointedly at Blair's cell phone, but nothing happened.

"I wasn't even bringing it in here without a protection spell," Blair explained, tucking the phone in her pocket. "You have to admit you would have done the same if it had been me."

"I'm off to lie down. You all wear me out." Irma winked out to the guest room.

"You know what, why don't we all calm down?" Stasi took the role of peacemaker, which was her usual post when things got too heated. "Let's have a leisurely dinner and catch up. Any new gossip?" she asked, opening the freezer and pulling out a container of beef stew while Blair got up and rummaged for the ingredients for dumplings.

"I talked to Thea the other day. She said she'd be up here this month," Jazz reported.

"Fantastic! We haven't seen her for ages," Blair commented.

Stasi dumped the frozen stew into a large, copper-bottom pot and turned on the heat. Well familiar with the kitchen, Jazz went exploring and found some sugar cookies. She cooed with delight as she bit into a chewy cookie, breaking off a small piece for Bogie, who'd shown up for his share, and ignoring Fluff and Puff's pleas. "As long as you're on my ankle, you're not getting a thing," she warned the slippers. "Did Mrs. Benedict make these?"

Blair nodded. "She dropped them off the other day. Her grandchildren were coming up and she baked I don't know how many dozen cookies."

Jazz used her forefinger to sweep the multi-colored sugar sprinkles off her lip and into her mouth, looking pensive. "Seriously, Fluff and Puff are driving me crazy. We've barely gotten over the damage they did to Cupid's front lawn, even if he deserved it." She ignored the cheers and raspberries coming from her ankle. "He was hopping mad and that was not a pretty sight."

"I loved that they sought revenge on my behalf." Stasi flashed them a warm smile.

"Good, then you can get Trev to handle the lawsuit Cupid's threatening to file against them—and me, since I'm supposed to be in charge of them. Yeah, like that'll happen." Jazz started to take another cookie, but Stasi took it out of her hand, reminding her dinner would be ready soon. "I saw the banners up for the Winter Carnival. What is Agnes up to now and what does she want you to do?" She did her part by pulling out plates and silverware and setting the table.

"As much as possible," Blair said. "And by the way, Roan Thorpe, the new owner of Snow Farms—who just happens to be a Were and part of Jake's Pack—is involved, too. Not to mention it seems he's Jake's brother."

Jazz looked up sharply. "What? When did all of this happen? And I gather it's not a good thing."

"Very much not a good thing. Roan Thorpe has this 'me Were, you witch' attitude," Stasi said. "Then there's Jake with his 'I wish he was on the other side of the universe' attitude. No Brady Bunch vibes there."

"We don't like him," Blair said, stating the obvious. "And if things get worse I may be coming up with some innovative revenge spells against Roan. He and Jake could be the main attraction on *Jerry Springer,* because I can't see them on *Oprah* or *Dr. Phil* willing to talk their feelings out."

"It's always the quiet ones that hand us the surprises. Plus you have to wonder if trouble doesn't sometimes follow us." Jazz finished setting the table and set out glasses filled with Diet Coke. "So Stasi, where's your sexy wizard?"

"Working on a case. He was up last weekend anyway, and he knows at the full moon I like to be with my sister witches. This time is just for us."

A soft pinging sound was heard from the family room, along with *You have wallmail.*

"I'll go." Jazz left the kitchen then called back. "Thea's at the B&B and will be here in time to go out to the lake tonight. And there's another from Maggie. She'll arrive in a half hour or so."

"Tell them we'll hold dinner for them," Stasi called back, returning to the freezer for another container of beef stew while Blair doubled the ingredients for the dumplings.

Suddenly feeling a strong urge to look out the window, Blair wandered over to the sink and looked out. Jake had installed motion detector lights along the side of the stairs last November, so she could easily see the familiar black and white dog sitting near Jazz's car.

For one long moment their eyes met, then the dog stood up and loped off.

You're a fool, Jake Harrison, and I intend to prove it to you.

She pasted a smile on her lips that wouldn't have fooled anyone and returned to making dinner.

The five women wore pale blue robes and matching moonstone pendants and rings. The silken fabric lifted and fluttered in the night breeze as they walked along the lake's edge until they reached a flat-topped boulder that jutted out over the water. They walked with sure-footed grace along the length of the large stone's surface until they stood on the tip of the rock, presenting an ethereal picture as the full moon cast silver rays over them.

"May our sanctuary provide us with continued protection and strength," Stasi intoned, taking multi-colored dust out of the gold mesh bag she held in her hand and sprinkling it over the water.

"May our sanctuary give us sustenance and nurture us." Blair followed with a pinch of silvery dust.

"During this full moon we ask that our sanctuary always be there for us in our time of need." Jazz opened her bag with its dust spilling forth the color of creamy pearls.

Thea stepped forward next. "May our sanctuary offer us the strength we need during harsh times." She pulled out her red silk bag, watching the red dust glimmer before it dusted the water's surface.

Maggie, taller than the others, was last. "And may our sanctuary always give us peace." Magickal dust the deep shade of sapphires floated in the air before settling on the lake.

As the last dust touched the water, the color of the lake turned the rare translucent color of a moonstone, echoed in the gemstone pendant each woman wore. At that moment, all five women's moonstone pendants and rings glowed bright. When a star shot across the velvety night sky, they looked at each other and burst into joyous laughter.

"And thank you for making sure the lake monster didn't rise up and eat us!" Jazz shouted across the shimmering water as she spun in a tight circle.

"Will you ever grow up?" Thea shook her head as she dropped her hood. "You say that every time I'm up here."

"Growing up wouldn't be any fun." Maggie dropped her hood also, shaking out her shoulder-length blonde hair.

"No, she'd rather encourage the lake monster to rise up and seek out a late night snack," Blair said.

"Raise your hand if you vote we should push Jazz out front if a lake monster does show up." Stasi raised her hand and the other three did the same, while Jazz shook her head.

"And you call me the immature one," she grumbled.

Five heads lifted when a faint howl rippled through the air, followed by several more.

"I thought there weren't any wolves around here," Thea said quietly.

"There aren't." Blair spun around to face the direction from which the howls had come. She, Jazz, and Maggie took several steps then stopped, their heads cocked to the side. A moment later, they heard the chilling howls again.

"There are now," Maggie said, flexing her fingers as if readying for a battle.

"And we know it's not Jake," Stasi said. She exchanged a telling look with Blair and Jazz, because they all knew exactly why there were wolves out there now. The Pack was gathering. She rubbed her arms. "Let's get back to the apartment and into warmer clothing."

As they turned to retrace their path along the lake's edge, Blair looked over her shoulder at the lake. A faint undulation appeared in the center, the watery rings moving in ever-increasing circles toward the water's edge.

"Maybe it's true after all," she commented. "Maybe there *is* a lake monster."

Thea followed her gaze. "I haven't been up here as much as some of you, but I've never seen a sign of anything like that. It's got to be a local legend to keep kids from rowing out there late at night." She suddenly seemed lost in a world of her own that the others took to mean she was thinking of a new book idea.

"That doesn't mean there isn't something living in the lake," Jazz said, pausing to look out over the lake, quiet now except for a few lingering ripples on the serene surface.

"I think it's a good thing—helps to prevent someone from coming out here during the full moon in hopes of catching us dancing naked around a bonfire," Blair joked.

"Oh right, someone would be dumb enough to come out on a night like this when they could be sitting in front of a roaring fire?" Jazz shivered under her thin robe. "I love you all, but doing this during the winter really sucks. Even thermal underwear isn't helping."

"I've already turned into a witchcicle," Thea complained with a hint of a whine as she rearranged the flyaway strands in her glossy black cap of hair. "Can we go back now?"

As the five women took the path leading back to Blair and Stasi's building, they didn't notice the faint outline of a scale-covered head popping out of the water and gazing in their direction.

"This is nice," Blair said, looking around the crowded family room. She was ensconced in her favorite over-sized easy chair with a pillow behind her back while Stasi curled up in a big brick-red chair. Jazz and Thea sprawled on the couch while Maggie flopped on the loveseat on the other side of the coffee table. Each witch held a glass mug of Irish coffee. "We haven't had a group this large in ages."

"I wish I knew why Lili hasn't made it up here in awhile," Stasi commented. "Has anyone talked to her on the phone lately? It seems the only way I can contact her is by wallmail."

"Same here," Jazz replied and the others agreed. She glanced at Maggie. "Maybe we should hire you to track her down."

"Lili's fine." Maggie took a sip of her whiskey-laced coffee, then set the mug down and reached behind her back to twist her blonde hair into a braid. "If she wasn't, I'd sense it. I always know when one of you is in trouble."

"Then your so-called senses must have been on vacation last year when Moonstone Lake was pretty much going nuts," Jazz muttered in her cup as she inhaled the whiskey and coffee.

"You three seemed to handle it pretty well." Maggie punched her pillow into a more comfortable shape. "Otherwise, I would have been up here."

"We barely handled it," Stasi told her.

"Welcome to my world. So what exactly is going on with the resort up the road? You said Jake's *brother* owns it now?" Maggie asked.

Blair nodded. "We met him and didn't like him. He's got an agenda. We're just not sure what it is."

"And Jake doesn't like him and vice versa," Stasi added.

"How did a Border Collie Were end up in a wolf pack?" Thea asked. "That normally doesn't happen."

Blair and Stasi shook their heads.

"Maybe Mom got too frisky one night; but Jake won't say a word about it and believe me, I've tried to find out," Blair replied. "With Roan up here I have an idea we'll find out pretty soon."

Stasi set her cup to one side as the microwave oven dinged. "Popcorn's ready." She disappeared into the kitchen and returned with a large bowl of buttered popcorn that she set down on the coffee table. She set a smaller bowl on the floor and Bogie immediately dug in. Fluff and Puff looked hungrily from their spot on Jazz's ankle, but they knew enough to stay put.

"Go ahead," Jazz urged them with a smile that bordered on evil. Puff snarled and nibbled on her ankle instead. "Ow! Hey!"

"How's your latest book going, Thea?" Stasi asked.

"Fine." Thea's dark eyes darted around. "Is that a new painting?"

"No," Blair replied, searching her friend's face. "Is something wrong?"

"Nothing that I can't handle." Thea now showed great interest in her French tipped nails. "It's been a busy time for me. It was pure luck I could make it up here for this. I'll have to leave first thing in the morning, so I can catch a flight to New York. I'm meeting with my agent and my editor."

"Is it time for a new contract?" Blair asked.

"Lots of things going on." She offered up a tight-lipped smile.

The other four shared a silent conversation that agreed they weren't going to get anything out of Thea.

Blair looked around at the friends who'd been with her for so many centuries. She felt as if she should snap a photo to keep close at hand, because these moments were few and far between.

Their lives had changed over the years, luckily, more for the good than the bad. But now their lives were changing at such a swift rate that she wondered if they were all equipped to handle what could be racing their way.

Still, if they could deal with what had happened over the last seven hundred years, she figured they could handle anything.

Chapter 6

WHILE BLAIR AND STASI LOVED HAVING COMPANY, they also enjoyed saying good-bye and knowing their space would be all theirs again. Blair stood outside, bidding farewell to their friends.

Thea left first, then Maggie, after assuring them she and her crew would be there in a flash if they needed help. Jazz hoisted her magickal tote bag into the back of her T-Bird.

"If Irma's not here in three minutes, I'm leaving without her," she announced, looking down at Fluff and Puff, who gave her their best *we're going with you so forget any witchy mischief* expressions. "I should have worn my Uggs this morning. Wearing them all day would have changed your nasty little minds, even if you have nibbled off most of the shearling lining."

"Look who I met!" Irma floated out of the trees accompanied by a ghost wearing an old-fashioned coat, tapestry waistcoat, and long trousers that even in ghostly form looked the worse for wear. His graying beard was neatly trimmed and tufts of hair sprouted from under his top hat.

"Professor Peggins?" Blair squeaked, staring at the self-proclaimed man of medicine she and Stasi had worked for when they all first arrived in the town. The Professor had later died after imbibing too much of his own potent medicine.

He sketched a courtly bow. "At your service, m'dear. I must say you look well, although wearing such form-fitting trousers isn't very ladylike." He eyed her dark brown relaxed leggings and cream-colored basket weave sweater with a critical eye.

"You haven't been here since you left this realm."

"Ah, but I have." He held up a finger for emphasis. "I've just make sure to stay out of your and Anastasia's way for fear you'd find a way to send me back to that ghastly realm. I rather enjoy lounging at Grady's saloon. While I can no longer drink spirits, I can at least inhale them. Also, those ghastly Fae creatures were here last year and while many of us were not entirely aware of what they were, we did know enough to stay away from them. I wasn't entirely sure of their origin, but there was no doubt they meant trouble."

Blair briefly closed her eyes. Now she remembered why she and Stasi had suffered so many headaches years ago when they had to listen to Phinneas go on and on and on and... on.

"Which is why Phinneas is coming with me," Irma's announcement sent Blair's eyes flying wide open. Irma was beaming at Phinneas as if she'd just discovered the highlight of her semi-dead existence.

"Terrific, everyone's got a boyfriend but me," Blair groused under her breath before explaining, "Irma, he can't go with you. He can't leave the area."

"If I can go where I want, so can he." Irma looped her arm through Phinneas's, and he patted her hand.

"You were a cursed ghost; he's not, he's tied to a realm," Jazz explained, ushering Sirius into the back of the T-Bird where he settled in. "Different rules."

Irma glared at Jazz as if the red-haired witch had just told her she couldn't have what she wanted most. Which at the moment was the transparent man standing beside her. "I'm not leaving Phinneas."

Blair counted to ten—four times, but it didn't help.

"It doesn't work that way, Irma. Whether Phinneas likes it or not, he has to return to his realm, and that's set here." She turned to the male spirit. "In fact, why are you still here, when you should have gone back on October 31st?"

"It is not that difficult to remain behind if one wishes." He puffed up with peacock pride. "Others have succeeded and so have I."

"Fine, Irma stays with you and Fluff and Puff can suffer along with me on Nick's idea of a getaway. He booked us for a midnight river rafting excursion," Jazz explained. "I asked for a vacation in a luxury hotel, but now that there's this vampire travel agency offering up all sorts of adventure trips for the nightwalkers, he wants to do this. Fates know why."

Fluff and Puff's alarm sounded loud and strong.

"Don't forget their little bunny slipper life vests," Blair teased.

Except Fluff and Puff had other ideas. Jazz fell backwards against the car as sparks erupted from her ankle. Before Blair could jump away, the sparks swarmed around her ankle—and now Fluff and Puff were firmly attached to her.

"No!" she cried, stomping around, but they weren't about to budge.

Jazz looked down at Fluff and Puff, then up at Irma.

"Perfect! I'll see you in a month. Have fun!" She wasted no time hopping into the car and speeding around the corner of the building, with Sirius barking a good-bye but making no move to return to Irma.

"You traitor! You come back here!" Blair sent out a wave of power, but clearly the car was protected and there was no way she could bring it back. "Coward!"

"I hope she has Jonathon look in on Sirius while she's gone," Irma said, referring to Jazz's mortal housemate, also known as Krebs. "He likes listening to music during the day."

Blair glared at the two ghosts standing arm in arm, then stared at her new bunny slipper tattoo with a look fit to hex.

"None of this is good."

"Let's go upstairs." Irma steered Phinneas to the stairway. "You must tell me more about that wonderful tonic you concocted. It must have been a true miracle drug. I've always suffered from aching joints. This sounds like something that would have worked wonderfully for me."

"She always forgets she can't have aching joints now, and she would have been under the table with one sip of that tonic. I can't do this," Blair mumbled, resisting the urge to kick something. Mainly herself.

"Not a good day, huh?" Jake, choosing this unfortunate moment to appear, walked over and glanced down at her ankle, where Fluff and Puff were looking all too proud of themselves.

She turned to face him. Someone else she wasn't too happy with. Blair enjoyed being in the know. Jake had managed to hide his Were nature from her for months when she usually picked up on these things, and he still hadn't told her how he did it. She had no idea how long he'd known that Roan had purchased the resort, and this was only a small percentage of why she was ticked off with him.

"Fluff and Puff didn't want to go midnight river rafting with Jazz and Nick," she replied. "Irma has met a man—Professor Phinneas Peggins, who Stasi and I worked for over 100 years ago and would have been perfectly content never to see again—and then there's you, who's turned into my biggest problem of all." Showers of sparks erupted all around her. A witch with a temper was a dangerous thing, and Blair was well on her way to being dangerous. "An arrogant Were's in town, and you are acting like a real dickhead." She spat out her words with enough power to push Jake so hard he rocked on his heels. He held up his hands, palms out, then growled as the power burned and stung his skin. Blair glared at him, unwilling to apologize. She didn't like harming anyone, but at the moment she was more than willing to throw a little pain Jake's way.

"What the fuck is your problem?" Jake's snarl was more canine than human and his eyes darkened with anger.

"You." She pointed at him, but kept her magick contained. "Why have you kept so many secrets? How did you manage to mask your Were nature from me? And what, for Fates sake, is going on in your Pack?"

He winced at the high pitch in her voice. "That's the operative word, Blair. Secrets. As in something no one else needs to know." *Something* you *don't need to know* rang loud and clear between them.

Anger and hurt was a bitter pill for Blair to swallow. Logically, she knew she had no right to demand answers from Jake. Flirting aside, they'd only had one real date, so it wasn't as if they were an actual couple. But she knew the attraction was there, even if Jake seemed to have a reason for backing away from her. She wanted him to let down his guard. Except the wall he'd erected between them was high and strong.

Blair was a very determined and a very talented witch, but she knew if she were going to take down his wall and find out just what could be between them, she'd need all her power at her fingertips.

"Then tell me just one thing, Jake. Why is Roan here? Why would he choose this mountain? Do you think there's more to his purchasing the resort than just wanting to get into the hotel business?"

Jake's look was intense, but he replied calmly enough. "I don't think Roan would do anything the Alpha didn't sanction. With Roan now living up here, you will see more Weres hunting in the woods. If you think he's up to something, ask him yourself. You don't usually seem to need to consult with anyone else."

"But you have an idea why he's here, don't you?" she pressed. "When I met him at the town meeting he had that *witches are beneath me* attitude. Silly wolf."

A ghost of a grin touched Jake's lips. "As in, he should know better?"

"As in, I won't accept that attitude," she admitted. "It doesn't make any of us happy that we're pretty much magickal outcasts, but then many have rued the day they underestimated us. You might want to remind your precious brother of that the next time you see him."

"I don't—" He bit down on his words before he gave away more.

But Blair was like a terrier with her favorite toy. "Don't what, Jake? You don't intend to see Roan? No running in the woods with the crew and howling at the moon? Isn't he going to be kind of hard to avoid, since he'll only be eight miles up the mountain? Plus, I thought all good little doggies had to be with the Pack. Gee, there's another mystery: Packs are always together, it's practically a hard and fast Were law. So tell me the truth. Why aren't you with your Pack?"

Jake growled under his breath as he walked over and pulled her into his arms so fast she literally fell against him. But his kiss was far from angry. He nibbled on her lips until they parted for him, then his tongue took the admittance she granted him. He tasted wild and free, of the forest he roamed during the night and the freedom he gloried in. He tasted so good she wanted more and she took it.

Blair lifted her hands to cup his face, feeling the rough skin against her palms, and blindly ran her fingers over the sharp-planed features, then up to tunnel through thick hair that felt like black living silk curling around her fingers.

"Come upstairs," she murmured, moving her lips enough to whisper in his ear as she nibbled on the lobe. "Come with me, Jake." His labored breathing and the stillness in his form told her he was seriously considering her suggestion. Taking courage in that, she reached down and palmed his fly, feeling the hardness that strained the zipper even as one of his large hands slid under her sweater and cupped her breast. Her heart skipped a beat as she felt the coolness of his skin touch her. She arched up against him and ground her hips against his, but before it could go further, Jake jerked back. Only pure luck kept her on her feet and allowed her to rein in her seriously runaway control. "If our roles were reversed, there would be a name for you." Her voice was harsh with the emotions running wild through her.

Jake didn't look any calmer. "You think it's easy for me?" he ground out. "I want you, Blair. I want you so bad that my blood practically boils, but it can't be. You know it and I know it. My nature... isn't a good balance for yours."

"Then stop kissing me! Stop looking at me the way you do!" She blinked back tears she refused to shed. "Stop being so damn..." She threw up her hands and turned away. Except her temper wasn't about to cool down that fast. She spun on her heel and launched a jolt of power at him so that he landed on his ass, his legs sprawled out. A fire bolt followed, landing all too close to the vee of his thighs. Jake swore and scrambled backwards.

"Damn it, Blair! What are you trying to do?" he yelled.

"Be grateful I didn't aim a little closer." She turned back to the stairs and ran upstairs, slamming the door behind her.

Jake started forward as if to follow, then stopped. His fists flexed at his side and he looked ready to pull a tree up by its roots with his bare hands. Instead, he strode away, radiating fury.

"Damn his furry hide!" was heard above a loud whirring sound.

Stasi slowed her steps and peered uncertainly into the family room. She stared at her housemate wielding the vacuum with one hand and a dust cloth with the other. Vases and figurines shifted to allow her to dust under them, then shifted back to their spots. The furniture did the same. An unfazed Irma and Phinneas sat in the chairs conversing in low voices.

"What are you—?" She then became aware of the newcomer to the group. "Professor Peggins?"

"Hello, dear." The professor smiled warmly at her. "How nice to see you after all these years. I understand you have a beau now. Good for you! You used to be such a shy thing, I thought you'd never find a man. But, as I always say—"

"And nice to see you too." Stasi quickly crossed the room and waved a hand, stopping the vacuum cleaner, and grabbed the dust cloth out of Blair's hand. "What's going on?" she whispered. Suddenly she realized something else was new. She glanced down to see Fluff and Puff coughing from the faint cloud of dust the vacuum had brought up. "Are you kidding me?"

Blair took a deep breath, then another. "What's going on? Let's see, where shall I start? Fine. Irma somehow met up with Phinneas. She wanted to take him with her, and when she was told it wasn't possible, she voted to stay here. Phinneas apparently has taken to hanging out at Grady's so he can at least inhale the alcohol fumes, since he's beyond drinking now. Fluff and Puff heard that Jazz was going midnight river rafting with Nick, so they jumped ankles. Oh, and Jake is arrogant, and stubborn, and if I could, I'd zap him into his furry self 24/7." She snatched the cloth back and sent it sailing to a high shelf, where it busily did its job while books obligingly moved out of the way.

"So he kissed you senseless again, then did something stupid." Stasi had no trouble interpreting this outburst.

All the air seemed to be let out of Blair and she dropped into a chair. When she looked up, her blue-green eyes shimmered with the tears she'd been holding back by sheer force of will.

"Is there something seriously wrong with me? I mean, I know I have my moments, but am I so bad, that a man will kiss me, then tell me it was wrong?"

"No!" Stasi perched on the chair arm and hugged her tightly. "You're the best friend a witch could have."

"I just don't understand it." Blair absently reached down to scratch her ankle. "Ow!" she yelped, jerking back her hand, then snarled at Puff. "You bit me, you little shit!" Puff growled back.

Stasi soothed Blair's wound with a healing spell. "Behave yourselves," she chided the slippers-turned-tattoo. She turned back to her friend, clearly choosing her words carefully. "I know the attraction between the two of you is there," she said slowly. "But maybe that's not enough. What if now it has something to do with Roan moving up here? Maybe Jake has a good reason for keeping you at arm's length." She paused. "When he's not kissing you senseless, that is."

"I think he only did it to shut me up. I was asking him if he knew why Roan came up here and bought the resort." Blair pulled her pillow out from behind her back and hugged it against her middle. "And why he's no longer with his Pack."

"So he kissed you. The male sex was designed to make us nuts."

"Trev doesn't make you nuts."

"He irritated me plenty when I first met him, especially when I had to look at those red hearts all the time after Cupid cursed us with them to show we were soul mates. Thank the Fates Cupid finally took the hearts away, or I'd be more than just irritated with them." Stasi looked around. "Wow, you did a great job cleaning around here. Temper tantrums seem to have their positive side."

"It was that or look up the worst oozing rash spell I could conjure up," Blair said testily. "I'm beginning to reconsider my choice."

"So let's backtrack here. Fluff and Puff jumped to your ankle because they didn't want to go river rafting with Jazz and Nick. Irma now has a boyfriend and is staying here, and you had a fight with Jake. Then Jake kissed you, which made you even more angry with him, which turned you into mega-cleaning witch. Is that everything or have I missed something?"

"Isn't that enough?" Blair tossed her pillow to the floor and stood up. She started to rub one ankle against the other until she remembered Fluff and Puff wouldn't appreciate it and knew how to retaliate.

"The Fae haven't returned, have they?" Phinneas spoke up. "Could that be upsetting your young man?"

"They're well and truly gone," Blair assured him.

"Good. Nasty creatures, them. They wanted us gone, you know. They knew once we were all banished, the townspeople would feel our loss. As time went on, with no sense of connection to the past, their descendants would gradually desert the town. I don't think you realize how much the living still feel the presence of the dearly departed and how much solace they draw from that. Without it, the need to relocate can be strong. In their quest to have the land to themselves, those Fae tried to make sure all of that would happen."

"The Fae never admitted that," Blair said, surprised by his revelation.

"One of the ladies of my realm overheard them talking. It seemed the bakery they had made their headquarters used to be a mercantile in her lifetime. She liked returning there to relive old memories. Lovely girl. Of course, she's nothing like you, dear." He smiled and patted Irma's hand. She literally glowed under his attention.

"I may be sick," Blair muttered. She got up and headed for the kitchen, where she pulled two cans of Diet Coke out of the refrigerator.

"Eurydice needs to know this about what the Fae had planned," Stasi said, following her. She took the second can and pulled a couple of glasses out of the cabinet. "For all we know, they could try it elsewhere."

"I'll leave that less-than-pleasant task to you. She likes you better." Blair would never admit it, but the head of the Witches' Council and headmistress of the Witches' Academy scared the ever-living crap out of her. Conversely, the head witch generally looked upon Stasi with favor. Stasi had been her star pupil—before their whole class got expelled into the mortal realm, of course.

"I'll contact her later tonight, then." Stasi sipped her drink. "As for the Were, are you thinking what I'm thinking?"

"I don't know, Brain, do wolves really pretend to be sheep?" Blair quipped, falling back on their habit of quoting from the animated series *Pinky and the Brain*.

"Goof. From what Roan said that night at the meeting, he's discovered we own a lot of the land around here."

"Meaning he has good lawyers who will dig for that info. It's not like we hide the fact." She paused. "Well, okay, in a sense we do, since Ebenezer Sneed handles all that," she amended. Mr. Sneed was the wizard financial manager who oversaw their portfolio. "And he's very protective of his clients, so he wouldn't willingly reveal any details."

"The resort's main land holdings are devoted to the ski runs, and no matter what, I can't see them leveling the runs. Would they really want to move up here to a tourist area, even if it is remote? Packs need plenty of land for their hunts…"

"He seems to think he can make us an offer we can't refuse," Blair said wryly.

"True."

Blair nodded. "So why hasn't he approached us directly?"

"Maybe he's waiting for the right time. He couldn't exactly start discussing business that night. Plus, he'll be around a lot because of the carnival. He'll look for our weak points, then he'll move in for the kill." Stasi winced as she realized the significance of the last word. "Sorry about that."

"We don't really have any weak points." Blair mentally leafed through her favorite revenge spell book. She always liked to be prepared.

Stasi was equally deep in thought. "Maybe he has a mate. If so, she might stop in the shop and turn out to be talkative."

Blair jumped up and went over to the phone, quickly punching in numbers. She smiled. "Agnes, hi, it's

Blair. When do you think the committee will want to get together and look over the lake to figure out where to place the booths? Well, what about noon tomorrow? And you'll call Roan? Terrific!" She paused, her smile slipping a bit. "You did what? When did you call them? Uh, Agnes, it's never a good idea for a human to deal with the preternatural community unless they know what they're doing. No, of course, I don't doubt your people skills, but we're not exactly talking people here. Who did you call?" She looked at Stasi with a panicked expression while keeping her voice calm. "All right. We'll see you tomorrow." She hung up and stared at Stasi in mute horror.

"Fine, a meeting at noon tomorrow, but what was the rest of that about?" Stasi asked.

"Agnes contacted Mickey Boggs to hire elves for the carnival."

"Not him!"

Blair nodded.

"We have to stop her. He's the worst you can deal with."

"She already signed a contract, and his contracts are always ironclad, even for mortals."

Stasi closed her eyes. "Oh no! If he can't find elves for her, he could send anything up here."

"Well, if nothing else, what Agnes did has gotten my mind off Jake." Blair was lying and Stasi knew it, but it still made her feel better.

Blair spent the evening on the Internet researching Jake's Pack, and what she read didn't make her feel any better.

"This is a large Pack," she told Stasi after viewing the information on the website accessible to the supernatural community only. "That's probably why they're looking for new territory. I wonder how they'd feel about relocating to the Rockies or Sierra Nevada?"

"Who's that?" Stasi was standing behind her and reached over her shoulder to point at a formal photograph of a striking silver-haired woman who looked to be in her sixties and the gray-haired man next to her. They could feel immense power emanating from the screen.

Blair felt her jaw drop. "It says her name is Vera and she's the Pack Alpha female. She's the woman who came in asking for a revenge spell against her son!" There was something about the woman's eyes that niggled at the back of her mind. "And that's Baxter, the Alpha. I do not get these family relationships."

"She looks like a true bitch." Stasi giggled at her pun.

"She could be more than that," Blair said thoughtfully. "Too bad we weren't able to purchase the resort property years ago."

"But we own enough property that if Roan thinks he can expand their hunting grounds, he'll soon find out it won't be possible," Stasi reminded her.

"No kidding." Blair shut down the computer and closed the top.

"Perhaps Phinneas and I could go up to the resort and see what's happening," Irma suggested, materializing in their midst with her arm looped through the Professor's. Her cheeks were bright pink and Blair really didn't want to speculate on why.

"I explained to dear Irma that it would be very easy to pop up there," the former charlatan medicine man explained. "I've actually done it a few times. Why, have I ever told you the story about the time when I—"

"Go for it," Blair told them and a second later they winked out of sight. "Maybe we can keep them busy and out of our hair."

"I'd rather hope they'll discover something," Stasi said.

Blair cocked her head to one side as a faint sound came from outside. She went to the kitchen door and opened it, stepping out onto the landing.

The Border Collie sat at the bottom of the stairs with ears cocked up.

"What? After acting like such an idiot, you think I'll invite you up?" Blair exclaimed.

The dog yipped once and lifted a paw in entreaty.

"Please, pathetic is so not your look." She crossed her arms in front of her chest. She wasn't about to make it easy for him.

He bobbed the paw up and down and cocked his head to one side.

"I'm mad at you!" Blair declared fiercely, trying desperately not to smile.

"If anyone overhears you they'll wonder why you're talking to the dog as if he understands you," Stasi murmured from behind her. "Come on up, puppy."

He looked toward Blair, obviously waiting for her to issue the invitation.

"Great, you're willing to come in when you're a dog," she muttered. "Just don't expect me to brush you."

As he loped up the stairs, he flashed her a doggy grin and moved into the kitchen.

"And stay off my bed!" She followed him in.

"Did you ever stop to think maybe we can find a way to get him to talk about Roan and Vera?" Stasi whispered. A canine growl from the kitchen gave her her answer. "Or not."

"Damn dog slept on the bed anyway," Blair muttered as she and Stasi held on to their travel mugs of coffee while they took the path to the lake. "It took a whole lint roller to get the fur off the bedspread. I know he's just getting back at me for zapping him."

"It seems he deals with you better when he's a dog than when he's in human form," Stasi commented. "Do you think there's therapy for that? Hmm, would you see a psychologist for humans or for pets?"

"Ha ha, so funny. Not." As they approached the lake, they could see the small group of people walking around part of the lake's perimeter.

Blair sensed Roan's power the minute she and Stasi entered the clearing. And she was in no doubt the Were was using it to his advantage to charm Agnes and her tittering friends who flocked around him.

"It's like leading lambs to the slaughter," she muttered, lifting her mug for a sip of coffee and purposely turning away. She didn't need to look to know the moment Roan approached her because his power rolled in front of him like a strong wave.

"Good morning, Blair, Stasi." His smile was too wide and white for Blair's taste. She didn't miss that he was casually dressed today, even if his jeans bore a designer label. His charcoal wool sweater flattered his broad shoulders and she was positive that dirt wouldn't

dare mar the polished surface of his black leather boots.
Ordinarily, seeing a man like that would have had her
drooling big time, but nowadays she realized that a guy
who got down and dirty was more her style.

*And there's Mr. loves-to-relax-by-picking-a-fight-
with-a-coyote now.*

Her gaze drifted right beyond Roan to Jake, who had
joined Agnes's group.

Jake looked her way, then briefly glanced at Roan.
His eyes darkened and seemed to bore right through
him. For a second he raised his head, his nostrils flexed
as he scented the air. He reluctantly turned his attention
back to Agnes when she laid her hand on his arm.

"What's going on between you and Jake?" Roan's
words were more a demand than a question.

None of your damn business. "Why don't you ask
Jake?" *He can tell you he's slept in my bed more than once
and one day chewed my favorite slippers.* She smothered
her smile at the muffled dangerous rumbling sounds from
Fluff and Puff inside her high-heeled boots. It appeared
they weren't any fonder of the Were than she was.

The Were didn't look pleased, but he didn't pursue
the subject, either. He looked down at the ground.

"You might want to tell your little fuzzy friends that
they'd make a tasty snack."

Blair almost fell on her ass when her right leg started to
lift upward with intent to do damage to the Were. It took all
of her willpower to keep it planted firmly on the ground.

"They don't respond well to threats."

"Who said it was a threat?" Abruptly, he changed the
subject. "Whoever handles your financial affairs is very
skillful at hiding your ownership of the surrounding

land," he commented, turning to gaze at the lake and the trees beyond. "Is there any reason why?"

"Probably because we like to keep our private business just that… private," Blair replied. "And if you found out even a little, it means you have people performing illegal activities. I don't like people digging into my life."

His smile wasn't the least bit pleasant. "There's nothing wrong with asking if particular parcels of land are for sale. Even if your people say the land isn't for sale at any price."

Now Blair's suspicions were running high. "That's right."

Roan turned back to her and speared her with his dark eyes. A wave of something feral washed over her as his eyes flashed a hint of yellow. "There are those who would pay handsomely for land like this."

"If they have that kind of money, they can find their land elsewhere." Blair momentarily bared her teeth. She might not have fangs, but she could push back, too, and she was more than willing. Stasi walked up behind her and offered up enough serenity that Blair could keep her power under control, although she noticed that Stasi's hold was tenuous.

Roan's power started to press at her, and she instinctively drove back hard enough that he almost lost his balance. She wanted to smile when she saw the banked fury in his eyes. Good. Let the wolf know the witch wouldn't bow to his will. Her blue-green eyes glowed with determination and she was prepared to stare him down, even as she reminded herself that could be a fatal mistake with a predator.

"Stop it, both of you." Jake's command barely broke through their silent battle. When they ignored him, he stepped between them and broke the energy that crackled in the air. Roan's glare sliced through Jake and his growl demanded Jake give in to his power. But Jake held his ground, returning his gaze with equal darkness.

Roan's lips tipped briefly upward. "Well, well, well, the whelp has developed some balls."

"This isn't your territory, Roan," Jake said softly but with equal menace. "You are on Blair and Stasi's turf, and you will treat it as such."

"Not for long, whelp. Don't mess with me. Things have changed since you ran off. We're not all in agreement where you're concerned." Roan turned and returned to Agnes and her group.

Blair exhaled a deep breath that she didn't even know she'd been holding.

"I *really* don't like him," she muttered.

"What part of *don't mess with a powerful Were* don't you understand?" Jake looked ready to take a bite out of her himself. "I'm sure they taught that at the Witches' Academy, or did you miss that class? Don't you *realize* how dangerous your actions were? He has enough power in one paw to snap you like a twig!"

"I'd like to see him try." Blair sounded more confident than she felt. The first thing she had done was take stock of Roan's power, but she also knew she could conjure up a hell of a mange spell once she got back to her workroom. Her mind was already busily sorting through what ingredients she would need to make Roan's condition as miserable as possible. She always believed in conjuring her revenge spells for maximum effect.

Jake stuck his face in hers. "Didn't you hear me? Don't even think what you were mentally spelling," he ground out.

"I was not!"

"You were so. Magick was sparking all over you."

Blair looked at Stasi, who nodded. "You were starting to turn into a magickal fireworks display."

"I wasn't thinking of a harmful spell, just one that would turn him all ugly and miserable. And he'd have to be shaved and use a nasty smelling medicinal shampoo."

"And he'd report you to the Witches' Council so fast you wouldn't know what hit you." Jake kept his voice low, even though they all knew Roan could easily hear them. "I may be out of the Pack, but I am still aware of what goes on there. Roan is one of the most powerful Weres on this continent, which is why he's heir to the Alpha. He could tear you apart with a single thought."

"No one pushes us around," Stasi told him with the same ferocity. "And if anyone knows that, you do."

"Yes, I know what you're capable of, and I'm sure Roan is, too. He has the resources to find out anything he wants, and right now he's focusing on you. And Roan is aware of everything I do." Jake's dark eyes flared with a fire that instantly warmed her, then just as quickly cooled. "Don't toy with him, Blair. You'll only get hurt."

She met his eyes, refusing to look away. "I'm already hurt." Her words were nothing more than a breath in the air.

"Blair! Stasi! Girls, would you come over here, please?" Agnes called out.

Blair was the one to break eye contact as she and Stasi stepped away.

"And here we thought Jazz and Maggie were the only ones to deal with big bads on a regular basis," Stasi said.

Blair tipped her chin upward when Roan glanced at her and smiled. *No gauntlet, no firing shot, but war has been declared, and buster, you are so furry toast.*

"You look very nice today, Agnes." Stasi smiled at the mayor's wife, who was arrayed in a teal wool pantsuit.

The woman lit up. "Thank you, Stasi. I do love those new foundation garments you showed me a few weeks ago," she said in a lower voice. "I know you girls must be careful with your gifts, but is there a way you might be able to make the ground out by the lake more even? Or perhaps move the rocks out of the way and then put them back afterwards? Do you think that would be allowed?"

"I think we could do that, Agnes," Stasi replied. "We'll manage it one way or another."

"Good." Agnes pulled a clipboard out of her huge black leather tote bag and made a few notations. "Also, our elves are arriving early. Roan has graciously offered them rooms at the resort."

Damn! She'd forgotten all about that! "I'm just curious, Agnes. How did you learn about Mickey Boggs's agency?" Blair asked.

"Roan suggested him. He said Mr. Boggs would be able to provide all the elves we needed."

Blair and Stasi exchanged a speaking glance.

"Did he mention how he knew of them?" Stasi questioned.

"Oh, he said he's used the man to provide holiday help at his hotels. He owns five other hotels," she confided. "We're very lucky he purchased Snow Farms. We could have ended up with someone who isn't as helpful… or charming." She winked.

Blair mentally visualized herself gagging. "Very true. Oh! Marva's calling you." She quickly gave Marva a mental push who appeared startled as Agnes's name erupted from her fuchsia painted lips.

"Coming!" Agnes trilled, tottering quickly toward her friend.

"Let's see, Jake's big bad Were brother shows up and buys the resort just miles from where Jake's settled, even though they apparently hate each other's guts. We know that same Were has been running around in the forest, and not alone, because we heard him and his furry minions at the last full moon," Blair mused. "Mr. Fur and Fangs thinks he can scare us into selling him our land. And a royal bitch of a Were is also skulking around town, trying to buy nasty spells. Yep, it's just another day in the witchy neighborhood."

Chapter 7

"WHAT ARE YOU DOING?"

Blair ignored Stasi's question as she curled up on their rooftop swing with a heavy fleece blanket wrapped around her. The twinkle lights that rimmed the walls were off, leaving them in darkness except for the waning moon overhead.

"Focusing." She was staring out through the trees toward a beam of light that flashed a sharp yellow a short distance away.

Stasi, with Bogie floating beside her, settled on the other side of the swing and pulled up the end of the blanket, draping it over herself and her dog. "You're not doing a Call, because I don't sense one."

"Probably wouldn't do me any good if I did do one. He's so stubborn, he'd find a way to ignore it." Blair shifted restlessly and combed her fingers through her auburn curls that the evening breeze had ruffled. "Jake is canine *domesticus* but his Pack is pure wolf. Interesting mix."

"All wolves are arrogant," Stasi agreed. "But Roan does it with a capital A. So listen: I asked Trev if he'd look further into Roan and his Pack for us. He has resources we don't have access to unless we went to The Library, but The Librarian still hasn't forgiven me for telling him he sucked."

Blair grinned. "I wish I'd been there for that, or at least seen a video of The Librarian's face when you said it."

"It wasn't one of my brighter moments. Trev said he's heard of Roan, and Roan's stepfather, who's the Pack Alpha. So Vera is Roan's mom, but we don't know what her game is, or what happened to Jake and Roan's dad. Trev says they've never crossed paths and Weres tend to have lawyers within their Packs to handle their legal affairs. They like to preserve their anonymity. Still, they have yet to deal with Trev's people," Stasi said with a great amount of pride. "He's also making sure there's no way Roan can try to trick us out of the land. He said he'll talk to Mr. Sneed tomorrow."

Blair thought of the elderly wizard who'd handled their business for the last 130 years and knew he wouldn't mind Trev's involvement. Ebenezer Sneed had talked of retiring soon, and she and Stasi had discussed having Trev's firm handle their business dealings when that happened. It might be a good time to start making that transition.

"I get the feeling that Roan doesn't intend to cheat us out of the land, even if he doesn't mind using intimidation to get it. He probably wants a fair and square deal so he can proclaim he did the two little witches a favor by taking all that nasty ole land off their hands." She continued watching the ray of light, then stood up, dislodging the blanket. Stasi quickly grabbed it up, watching with a knowing eye as Blair purposefully pulled on her high-heeled boots.

"Are you going where I think you're going?" she called after Blair, who'd already headed for the stairs.

"You betcha. I'm going for some answers, and he's giving them to me whether he wants to or not."

"Okay, I'll just sit here and watch the fireworks."

Blair stopped and looked over her shoulder. "Don't wait up."

Stasi grinned. "I hadn't planned to."

"Light come to me and guide my way. Make it so," Blair whispered, holding up her cupped palm. A second later a tiny ball of light appeared in her palm, sending out a golden glow that lit up the path before her. "So much nicer than a flashlight." She took off down the narrow path between the trees that was behind the main part of town and led to a few of the smaller roads where many of the residents lived. When Blair reached Jake's A-frame cabin, she was surprised to see the light she'd viewed from her place hadn't come from there, but from the building behind the house that she knew was his workshop. Sounds of Keith Urban rolled outward, along with a deeper voice that she was astonished to realize was Jake's.

"What do you know? The dog can sing." She tried knocking on the door, but soon realized there was no way, even with his Were hearing, that he could hear her over the loud music. Or was he ignoring her? "Knock, knock, knock, let it rock. Make it so." She made a fist and tapped on the door, almost getting blown off her feet as the pounding sound echoed around her so loudly it was like a small thunderstorm. "Whoa." She windmilled her arms to keep her balance, then quickly jumped back when the door was thrust open.

Jake's dark expression couldn't have been more forbidding. "What the hell are you doing here?"

"And hello to you, too." She tried walking past him, but he stepped to one side, effectively barring her entrance. For one moment a cold ball of uncertainty

plopped in her stomach. "Oh… uh, if you're not alone…"
*She was going to go home and drown herself in the tub.
She was going to go home and find a spell that would
turn a Border Collie into a warthog. She was going to
go home and sulk for the next hundred years.*

Jake's tension seemed to leave his body. "I'm alone."
He stepped outside and closed the door behind him,
setting the lock.

Blair craned her neck, but he'd closed the door so
quickly, she couldn't catch a glimpse of the interior.
"Don't tell me. You've got mega doggy quarters set up
in there. Equipment for doggy agility tests, a big bed,
abundance of toys."

He looked as if he wasn't sure whether to bark or laugh,
so he blended the two together. "Why are you here?"

"I was out taking a stroll and thought I'd stop in and
say hi." Her smile didn't thaw his cold demeanor. "Hi."

"Try again."

"I want to see what's behind the curtain." She sighed
when he looked confused. "You know, don't go behind
the curtain… *The Wizard of Oz.* Didn't you ever read or
watch the classics? We all like Margaret Hamilton's The
Wicked Witch of the West portrayal much better than
Billie Burke's version of the good witch Glinda with
all that tulle and the crown and wand. Wayyyy over the
top. Although none of us wanted the green skin." She
stopped as if she'd run out of breath.

"I was more a *Playboy* and *Dog Fancy* man myself."
Jake stared down at the golden glow still in her palm. She
shrugged and released the light. Like a firefly, it drifted
off into the dark night until it winked out of sight.

"Invite me in for coffee?"

"Isn't that something a guy would say?"

"It's the new millennium. Women can do the asking now."

"It probably didn't stop you during the last millennium, either." He headed for the back door and Blair stayed on his heels, determined to shatter the door to splinters if he dared close it on her again. But this time, he pushed it open and gestured for her to enter first as he reached inside to flick a switch.

Blair walked into the kitchen and dining area and took a quick look around. The last time she'd been in his house, she'd only seen the living room—and for a short time, at that—before he'd taken her home.

"I'm impressed." She idly ran her fingertips across the counter but couldn't find a smudge of dirt or grease. She wouldn't have been surprised to find even the top of the refrigerator dust free—and she couldn't say the same for own fridge. "There's days even our kitchen isn't this clean."

"What did you expect? Dirty dishes piled in the sink, pans covered with congealed grease?" He sounded amused. "I may like a good roll in the dirt, but that doesn't mean I like to live in it. I even change the sheets once a week."

"Were they changed recently?"

If she hoped to trip him up, she was sadly mistaken. Jake lounged against the sink and crossed his arms in front of his chest. He watched Blair circle the cooking island and investigate the breakfast nook with built-in table and benches against the windows for a great morning meal view. The idea of Blair sitting there with a cup of coffee in the morning was tempting.

"Did you want to check the cabinets, or maybe bounce a quarter off the sheets?" he asked, eying the moonstone pendant set in gold resting between her breasts. He wondered if it was a trick of the light that the stone glowed from within as if it had a life of its own. For all he knew, it could have. While he'd observed Blair a lot since he'd first arrived in town and discovered the sexy witch, he still knew only a fraction of who she really was.

On that last Samhain night, he'd seen a witch with great courage who faced down an angry mob intent on destroying her and her friends. He still remembered the ferocity that etched her features and lit a fire in her eyes as she echoed the spell Stasi had begun. A spell that shattered the illusion spell surrounding the forest Fae who were bent on killing them.

He hadn't thought twice that night when Reed Palmer, disguised as a human, ran toward the three witches with a blazing torch in his hand. Jake had shifted without hesitation. The dog saw danger to one he cared for and there was only one thing to do. He destroyed a creature who deserved to die.

He knew if he hadn't acted quickly that night, Blair wouldn't be standing in front of him right now, looking like a bright ray of sunshine. Her dark auburn hair glinted copper and gold and curled around her face with a life of its own. He knew from experience how silky it was to the touch. But he still didn't know if her whole body felt just as silky. For once she hadn't responded to his retort, but stood watching him with a look he wasn't sure he could read. She called to him like a Siren luring a mariner to his doom.

Still, some dooms were a very good thing, if a hexy seductress was involved.

"Why me?" he asked, the words sounding strangled in his throat.

"I don't know," she said honestly. "I admit in the beginning, it was this lust at first sight thing, because we all enjoyed watching you work with your shirt off." She winced. Definitely too much information when she was trying to make him think she *wasn't* some crazed stalker. "It's just something I feel inside that warms me up when I see you." She shifted from one foot to the other, waking up Fluff and Puff, who grumbled in unison. The usually self-assured witch suddenly looked unsure. "I thought…" she waved her hand in the air and for once no magick sparkled around her, only uncertainty. "I'm sorry."

"For what?"

"For thinking the feeling was mutual. Because you kissed me—more than once, I might add. And when we went out to dinner that night, I thought there was something there, but I guess I was mistaken. I promise I won't bother you again." She started to brush past him, but he grasped her shoulders and turned her to face him.

"You're not mistaken, Blair, but you have to understand something. My life is complicated." *If she only knew!*

"And mine's not?" she laughed. "Jake, even to many of my own kind, I'm considered an outcast. Thirteen of us stood together and refused to name the witch who cast an illegal spell. We all were expelled from the Witches' Academy and banished to the outside world for one hundred years—as long as we stayed out of trouble. That was in 1313, and we're all still out here!

The Witches' Council keeps adding time to our banishment because we don't adhere to their antiquated rules. For all I know, just saying that could add a few—or fifty—years on to mine. Sometimes I think they have some crazy agenda for us, but they don't bother giving us any hints. Stasi and I have changed our identities so many times, it's amazing we haven't suffered from personality disorders."

"And you'd know it if you were?"

She punched his arm in retaliation for his wry comment, but the blow was half-hearted.

"I'm just saying, you don't hold the patent on complicated lives. It's how you handle it that counts."

Jake was silent for so long, Blair thought he was either going to usher her out of the house or be his stubborn self and refuse to answer.

"I'm a throwback in my Pack," he said finally. "A dog, Border Collie at that, and not a wolf like the others."

"But you're a very handsome Border Collie."

He waved off her attempt at humor and directed her to the spacious living room. "If I'm going to say anything more, I'm going to need some Dutch courage." He pulled open the refrigerator door and brought out a bottle of beer. He held a second one up in silent question. "Or if you'd rather, I've got some Chardonnay."

"The beer is fine, thanks." She wandered around the family room and realized she was stepping into strictly guy territory. She smiled at the big screen TV, complete with a sound system that looked as if it belonged on the Starship Enterprise, a navy couch that showed more than a little wear, and dark burgundy easy chairs meant for lounging while watching the big game. "Wow. Do you need a PhD to operate all this?" She perused his DVD collection and was surprised to see some of her favorites there. She smiled as she fingered the plastic case marked *Young Frankenstein.*

"No, a Master's degree works just fine." Jake gestured for her to take a chair, but she chose the couch, pulling off her boots and curling up in a corner before reaching out for the bottle he held out to her. He settled on the coffee table in front of her, holding his beer bottle by his fingertips, dangling between his thighs.

"So your Pack are wolves, but you were born *Canis lupus familiaris* instead of *Canis lupus,*" she mused after taking a sip of her beer. "Any chance you were adopted?"

Jake chuckled. "Unfortunately, not a chance—in human form, I'm the spitting image of my father, while Roan is identical to my dad in wolf form." Blair didn't miss the way his grip on the bottle tightened.

"But they let you live, even though you're not wolf." She rolled that over in her mind. "I don't know a lot about Weres, but I do know they don't like to keep anyone they consider unworthy. That they're pretty rough on them and are known to toss them out of the Pack at best, kill them at worst."

"I walked away from the Pack because there was nothing there for me. I haven't looked back since. I've made a new life and am happy with it."

"Is that why your last name is different than your brother's?" she asked, her gaze holding his steadily.

He was silent for a moment, meeting her eyes with a proud look that turned her inside out. "When I left the Pack, I walked away with only the clothes on my back and left the family name behind. Thanks to finding

someone who could create valid looking ID, I left Jake
Thorpe with the Pack and turned into Jake Harrison."
He tipped the bottle upward and allowed the cold, yeasty
brew to flow down his throat. When he straightened up,
he noticed her pendant emitting a soft glow. "Why is
that happening? I don't recall seeing it do that before."

Blair looked down and frowned. "I don't know.
Maybe it's picking up magick I'm not sensing. Just be
grateful we don't have red hearts dancing around. Let
me tell you, those red hearts dancing around Stasi and
Trev's heads for weeks was enough to make me scream."
She stroked the moonstone, rubbing her fingertips over
the milky blue surface with the lightest of touches. The
stone appeared to shine even more.

Jake stared at her hand, feeling a reaction as if she
was touching him instead. Stroking him with the same
feather light touch she gave the stone. He couldn't
remember ever being this hard just from watching a
woman. But then, Blair wasn't just any woman.

"Change of subject noted, answered, and now ignored.
So why weren't you thrown out of the Pack or killed
immediately?" She noticed he didn't wince at the latter
words. She hadn't expected him to. Even if she didn't
know a lot about Pack behavior, she did know that they
didn't tolerate differences well, and Jake's canine nature
would be abhorrent to his kind.

Jake sighed. "You're not going to give up, are you?"

She grinned. "I'm Irish to the bone. Is that enough of
an answer?"

"Okay," he replied after taking another swallow.
"Okay. My old man was second-in-command to the
Pack's Alpha and Vera was his mate. After I was born

and my Border Collie nature was apparent, my mother
was accused of having an affair. My old man beat her so
badly it should have killed her. Considering the accusa-
tion of infidelity, she was lucky she wasn't killed. Her
situation was precarious until Roan was born. By that
time the healer, who'd been with the Pack for decades,
had done some digging and learned an ancestor on my
old man's side had an affair centuries ago that produced
a pup instead of a cub. That created a recessive gene
that had been resting in the family DNA on the paternal
side for the last few hundred years or so. For obvious
reasons, it was a little known fact. They probably hoped
it wouldn't show up again. They couldn't find anything
in my mother's DNA, so they don't know what triggered
it. That recessive gene was passed down to my old man's
eldest son. Me."

"And I gather your mother wasn't too happy
about this."

Jake's lips twisted in a parody of a smile. "No, but she
used the information to reclaim her status. She broadcast
to all that she should have known better than to mate
with someone so inferior. She also said she should have
fought with the alpha's mate for that position instead."

Blair grimaced. "Hmm, gives one the warm
fuzzies… not."

"All of you witches stuck together over the years.
A Pack sticks together, too, but only when they're all
alike. Anything different is treated like shit. When
you're bottom of the Pack, you learn just what rough
play means, and you either learn to fight back, or you
end up a punching bag. Just because you're the second-
in-command's son doesn't mean you don't have to

fight for everything. Even more so when you don't fit the Pack expectations. And with Roan being perfect in every way, my imperfections were pointed out as often as possible."

"No wonder you left," she said, aching for his pain. "Why would you want to stay with ones who were that cruel? Did the healer think your young would be born Border Collies?"

Jake shook his head. "It's been many generations since that happened, so she thought it would only happen again if my mate had the same recessive gene. It was something no one really tracked all those centuries ago. When I was young, my mother liked to tell me that no female worth her salt would want to mate with me. The healer felt the young would have the wolf blood; but there was still no guarantee. My old man… died around then, and even to his last day he didn't want to look at me…"

Blair was positive there was more to it, but she'd give Jake time before she'd get the rest of the story out of him. "And your mother?"

He dropped his head to look at the rug. "She was all into power and becoming Alpha." He heard the shifting of material, then saw a pair of bare, coral glossed toes standing in front of him. The jasmine and vanilla scent of her skin washed over him as she tipped his chin upward with her fingertips. He scooted backwards when she sat down straddling his thighs and draped her arms over his shoulders. "It was always more important than family."

"One more question." Blair grinned at his pained expression. "I promise this is the last one."

"Last one."

"How did you hide your Were nature from Stasi and me? We can always pick up on Weres, but we never did with you. You must have used an illusion spell." She wasn't going to tell him that she guessed that was what his mother had done when she came into Blast from the Past.

He reached inside his shirt and pulled out a leather cord holding a small bronze medallion. Blair didn't have to touch it to sense the incredible power in the metal. She could sense the masking spell, and she knew the protection spell also embedded in the metal would singe her fingers.

"I didn't want any problems any time I ventured into another Pack's territory, since they'd have the right to jump me if I was there without permission. Once I left my Pack, I was a loner. A rogue. Luckily, I was able to find a witch to enspell this for me," he explained. "It works on every creature but members of my own Pack. She said there was no way I could hide myself from them, since the Pack has blood ties. There were times I wanted to tell you the truth about me, Blair. Maybe that's why I showed up at your place so often in dog form. I hoped you'd figure it out yourself—since you're such a smart hexster," he teased.

She wrinkled her nose. "I guess I'm not as smart as I thought I was, because I never connected the two. Whoever crafted this did a good job."

Jake pulled off the medallion, setting it on the coffee table. The moment it left his body, Blair felt his Were magick reach out to her in a wave that left her a little giddy.

"Now it's definitely all you." She smiled warmly and leaned over to kiss his forehead with the lightest of touches. Her smile suddenly shifted to something with a different meaning.

Jake blindly set his beer bottle on the floor and cupped her head with his hands, pulling her back against him.

He already knew Blair's kiss was like the witch herself: saucy, open, and hot. He quickly discovered that this time she had amped it up. Her exotic scent wrapped itself around him with a seductive intent he could taste. He tunneled his hands under her sweater and found silk that couldn't compare with what it covered.

"Front clasp," she murmured against his lips before she resumed nibbling on them. "If you rip it, you'll be buying me a new one and trust me, Stasi won't give you a discount."

Jake would have laughed, but what Blair was doing was re-circuiting his brain waves to south of the border. Her hips rocked against his, the vee of her hips rubbing against the fly of his jeans in such a way he was harder than ever and his head felt ready to explode.

"You're killing me here," he breathed.

"Do you want me to stop?" she whispered in his ear as she bit the lobe just hard enough to cause pain that radiated through his body and settled in his cock.

He rocked his hips back at hers. "No way."

He could feel her smile against his cheek. "Good. Beep beep. Beep beep. Take us where Jake sleeps. Make it so!"

"Holy shit!" Jake's words were swept away as he felt a roaring in his ears and a sense of disorientation, then found himself sprawled in the middle of his bed with Blair on top of him. And if he wasn't mistaken, his T-shirt and flannel shirt were magickally missing, along with her sweater. Her bra was the same cinnamon color as her sweater and warmed her skin tone.

She smiled and shrugged. "I thought I'd save us a little time."

"You're still wearing too many clothes." He reached for the front clasp and released it. He drew in a deep breath when the material parted to reveal the creamy pink-tipped globes that his mouth wanted to worship. So he proceeded to do just that.

Blair closed her eyes and whispered words he couldn't understand, but the meaning became pretty clear once his jeans went the way of his shirt and so did hers, along with her bra and a sexy pair of thong panties the same color as her bra.

He managed to sit up while keeping his mouth on her breast and edged his way backwards on the bed. He rested against the headboard with his arms wrapped around her. Blair's fingers tightened against his scalp as he returned to figuring out just what she tasted like. He rolled the pink nipple with his tongue, feeling it harden and peak, then he turned his attention to the other nipple, while he felt her fingertips dig through his hair.

But it wasn't enough. Not when there was more luscious skin to investigate and taste. Along with what he knew would be heaven itself.

"No backing down now, puppy dog," she whispered with a teasing nip along his jaw line.

With a quick twist of his body he had them both lying on the bedspread, Blair underneath him now. "Trust me, calling me a puppy dog isn't a good idea right now," he suggested, moving his attention further south. The ginger-colored curls invited him to delve beneath, but first he rested his palm against her, feeling the heat against his skin and inhaling the rich scent of her musk. A soft growl escaped his lips before he slid down further and rested his lips against her pelvic area before he gave one long lick. She shuddered beneath him.

"If you dare stop now, I swear I will make you sorrier than you can imagine." Blair's voice came out strangled as she moved against his mouth.

"Not a chance." He mentally filed her scent in his memory; he knew nothing could ever make him forget it. He gently pushed a finger inside, feeling her inner muscles grip him tightly, and pulled it back out, bringing it to his mouth for that first taste. All it did was make him hungry for more, which he made a mental memo to check out again… later.

Her inner lips were plump and dark pink from his kisses, inviting him to investigate further, but another part of his body was demanding its share of attention, too. As if his cock called out Blair's name, she reached down and stroked the tip that gleamed with a drop of liquid. He hissed at her touch as she rubbed her thumb over the sensitive skin.

"You do that, hexy, and I won't last long," he warned her.

She smiled at the nickname. "We wouldn't want that happening, would we?" A purring sound started deep in her throat.

With good reason Jake had never liked cats, but the feline purr coming from Blair was something altogether different and aroused him even more. He suddenly reared up and plunged deep inside her. He lifted her thighs, wrapping them around his waist as he buried himself to the hilt. He cupped his palm over the tattoo, ignoring Fluff and Puff's protests and the tiny bites stinging his skin. This was a moment he didn't intend to share with anyone. Blair threw back her head, letting out a cry that was as glorious as music while she met him at every thrust.

She was hot, wet, and oh-so-sweet, a perfect fit for him, with inner muscles that gripped him like a silken glove that refused to let him go. With each plunge, he felt his control start to splinter like shattering glass.

Blair suddenly laughed, throwing her hands out and sending showers of magick all around them, lighting up the room with multi-colored sparkles and with her joy. At the same time, Jake felt something hot and incredible surround him as she joined him in a release that seemed never ending.

"That was fantastic." Blair emitted a soft sigh as she curled up next to Jake, with one silken thigh thrown carelessly over his.

He knew he was grinning because his face hurt, but he couldn't stop. He barely had the strength to brush her hair away from his nose before he sneezed.

Blair lifted her head slightly, then her body, as she moved over him. "Say something!"

"Give me a chance," he begged. "I think I blacked out at some point."

Her blue-green eyes twinkled with lust. "Really?" She drew out the word. "Let's see if we can repeat the performance, then." She trailed her lips down his chest.

Jake discovered that with Blair's attention centered on him he could indeed go for an encore.

By morning it was Blair who couldn't move. She felt so boneless she was amazed she didn't just flow right off the bed. She was warm and cozy under the covers. No wonder, with Jake's body curved around hers giving off so much heat it was like having her very own personal electric blanket. She murmured an inarticulate protest when Jake slid from the bed. He dropped a kiss on her lips and whispered he was going to take a shower and not to worry about coffee, it came on automatically.

A moment later she heard the sound of running water and just after that the rich aroma of coffee came wafting upstairs.

"Nirvana." She smiled and burrowed into the pillow that smelled like a combination of Jake and herself. "Should I surprise Jake in the shower, or sleep a little longer?" She yawned deeply. "I choose door number two."

Except sleep wasn't meant to be. The doorbell began to chime insistently, as if either the button was stuck or an unwanted visitor had their finger on it.

"Give it up!" Blair groaned, pulling the pillow out from under her head and plopping it over her face, but it wasn't enough to muffle the unrelenting sound. She tossed the pillow across the room and sat up. "Okay, that's it. Ding dong bell, not so merrily. This I say verily. Silence! Make it so." She smiled as the chimes abruptly stopped. And groused when the visitor began knocking on the door. "Okay, that does it. It can only be Stasi, and she's going to know right away I am not happy about this."

She muttered a few choice curses as she climbed out of bed, wrapped the sheet around her like a toga, and made her way downstairs, careful not to trip on the trailing fabric.

"Honestly, Stasi, did I ever bother you and Trev? Couldn't you…" her reprimand trailed off as she found herself facing a woman who wasn't Stasi and wasn't a witch. Her silver hair was pulled back in a French twist and if Blair wasn't mistaken the woman's suit was from St. Johns' new collection. She didn't look the least bit cold, but that didn't surprise Blair either. She already had a good idea that the woman's blood was as cold as her furry heart.

"I was given to understand that Jake Harrison lived here." The woman's voice was as cold and distant as her features. Not by a flicker of the eye did she indicate she'd met Blair before. Her aristocratic nostrils flared as she inhaled the scent of sex and Jake on Blair's skin, making her aware just what had been going on—more than once—to Blair's satisfaction. Her lips curled up in a sneer when she noticed Fluff and Puff on Blair's ankle. They looked up at the female Were and snapped and snarled at her, but remained safely attached.

"Yes, this is his house. And you are?" Blair now knew exactly who Vera was, but she figured two could play the clueless card. The Were mother had been polite to Blair the day she came to her shop requesting a revenge spell against her son. That attitude was completely gone this morning. She half turned at the sound of Jake coming down the stairs. He was shirtless, one hand holding a towel as he dried his hair.

He stopped short at the sight of the visitor.

"What are you doing here, Vera?"

"I had no idea you had… company." Her dark eyes turned to ice chips. "A *witch* at that." She made the term sound like something she'd scrape off the bottom of her Chanel pumps.

Blair knew she should have kept her mouth shut. But the bitch—and here she could truthfully use the term— had started it and Blair firmly believed in having the last word. No insult left unanswered. She stood tall and with as much dignity as she could muster, even if her sheet was slipping dangerously to the south, she turned to Jake.

"And I repeat what I asked you last night: are you absolutely *sure* there's no chance you were adopted?"

Jake had to give Blair credit. Vera had been known to reduce lesser wolves to tears, or worse, but Blair just flat out looked her in the eye and gave as good as she got. Not by a twitch did he betray his amusement; he knew his mother too well. She would see it as weakness and use it to her advantage, in the process doing her best to decimate Blair. Although right now his money was on the witch.

Then his attention fixed on the intricate pendant she wore on a gold chain and the implication he knew it carried.

"Congratulations, Vera, I see you got what you always wanted." He continued walking down the stairs until he stood behind Blair. He could smell his scent on her skin, sense the tension in her body that she didn't show, and just knew she was itching to say something that would only make the situation worse than it already was, because that was Blair's nature. He glanced down and saw her fingertips tapping against her sheet-clad thigh. He immediately reached down and threaded his fingers through hers before she started tracing runes that might cause something that couldn't be reversed.

"May I come in?" Vera asked, completely ignoring Blair as she looked at Jake. "And get rid of the witch. She has no business hearing Pack business."

"Okay, witch is standing right here and her hearing is absolutely perfect." Blair's hair started to lift into the air as her temper started to rise. "And *the witch* is *not* going to do anything just because you demand it. You should have realized that the other day." A slight widening of the woman's eyes told her the comment hit its mark.

Jake looked from one to the other. "What about the other day?" he asked sharply.

Blair didn't say anything and neither did Vera.

He growled under his breath and turned back to his dam.

"I assume you're staying at the resort?" Jake waited for Vera's nod. "I'll see you there. Don't come here again." He then closed the door in her face.

"And they accuse me of being rude." Blair tossed a corner of the sheet over her shoulder.

He knew she could see how he felt in his face and in his stance. "What the fuck happened between you and Vera?"

"Nothing." At least she wasn't lying. While she could see Jake and his mother had issues, she wasn't about to tell him that Vera had wanted a revenge spell to use on him. She thought about conjuring up something special to keep on hand to use against Vera, just in case. "You know what? I'm going upstairs to get dressed, then I'm heading out." Despite the bulky length of sheet, she gracefully ascended the stairs. "I suggest you shave and put on something nice for your meeting with Mommy Dearest."

Jake figured Blair used magick to dress, because she was downstairs in seconds.

"Last night was beautiful, Jake," she said quietly, before she opened the door. "Don't let her demean it." She stood up on her tiptoes and brushed a kiss across his lips before she slipped out.

Jake thought of the plans he'd made when he woke up that morning. He was going to make breakfast for Blair and himself, then tempt her back upstairs for a repeat of last night, because he was learning he couldn't keep his hands off her and he was already hungry for another taste. But it wasn't to be.

And just what had gone on between Blair and Vera?

At the same time, did he really want to know?

So instead of a blissful morning rolling around on his bed with Blair, he was entering the wolf den he'd hoped never to see again.

"I told her my life was complicated."

Chapter 8

"Wow, TALK ABOUT GOING FROM A TOTAL HIGH TO A TOTAL downer," Stasi said. Getting her boutique ready for the week ahead, she opened the armoire doors and hung up delicate camisoles in winter colors of ice blue, silver, and white. Once they were displayed to her satisfaction, she scattered vanilla and lavender scented sachets across the bottom, giving the armoire a delicate and delicious scent. "This Vera sounds downright nasty. I'm scared to death of meeting Trev's mother, although he says she's wonderful. She sure doesn't sound as intimidating or nasty as Jake's mother. I didn't believe what Trev told me, because he's perfectly capable of lying so I wouldn't stress out over meeting her. But I do believe what Mae told me. She said his parents had one of the most civilized divorces in history, and that all Trev's mother wants is for him to be happy." She smiled with fondness at the thought of Trev's assistant, who enjoyed instilling fear into the young legal associates she felt obligated to train; but she had already shown she had a warm spot for Stasi.

"Well, I don't think Jake ever went to his mom for comfort after he had a nightmare. That bitch of a Were is more the type to cause one." Blair flicked the top of Horace's head with her fingertip when he twisted around in a vain attempt to look up her sweater as she sat on the counter. The disgruntled gargoyle grumbled his way back to the opposite corner of the counter. "New sachets?"

"None of these have even a hint of a spell in them," Stasi said, picking up a blue silk rose sachet and waving it back and forth to release the calming scent of lavender and vanilla. "Bespelled sachets are a thing of the past for me now, even if I do have a capable attorney on retainer."

Blair hopped off the counter and wandered around, picking up a book here and there. "*50 Ways to Hex Your Lover,*" she chuckled. "Isn't that the title of the spell book Jazz was late returning to The Library?"

"Yes, but this is fiction. I still wasn't going to put the book out until after she left. It's still a sore point with her. It's a cute book, though." Stasi carefully wrapped a narrow white and silver garland around a basket handle. She glanced down at Blair's ankles. The blue topaz in her broom charm winked in the light while Fluff and Puff grinned at her from their spot on her other ankle. "Jazz is well and truly gone on what's probably the river rafting trip from Hades, guys. There's no reason for you to continue to torment Blair. She can't send you back."

"Wanna bet?" Blair mumbled.

Fluff rattled away while Puff just yawned.

"Wouldn't you know they'd think being a tattoo is more fun? Although they weren't happy when we covered them up last night. There are just some things they don't need to see." She looked down at the sound of the protests. "Hey, I don't care what goes on with Jazz, and I sincerely doubt you're allowed to do any peeking when she's alone with Nick. Right now you're with me and as long as you insist on staying with me, you'll follow my rules. If you don't like it I'll find a way to zap you two right back to Jazz and that raft."

Fluff and Puff erupted in protests.

"Oooh, tough witch," Stasi teased. "As if Jazz would allow herself to be found right now. So, on a scale of one to ten, where does Jake rate?"

Blair's grin split her face.

Stasi broke out laughing. "Okay, off the charts. I get it. At least his dog self already knows you snore."

"Do not!"

"Do so!"

"You do, Blair," Horace added. "But they're cute girly snores. Not train whistles, or anything."

"If Blair would hang me in her bedroom once in awhile, I could offer up my opinion, too," Felix called out from Blair's shop.

"And that's why I don't." Blair frowned in response to a rumbling sound in the street as a flash of color went by the shop window. She walked to the front of the store and looked out. "Wow, there's an RV that's seen a lot of country and looks it. Yeesh! It looks like someone barfed all over it."

Stasi followed her to the window and looked out. She grimaced at the vivid greenish-yellow vehicle parked in front, effectively taking up several parking spaces. "Uh, Blair? Why doesn't this look good? And I don't just mean the RV, either."

Blair experienced the same really bad feeling. She wasted no time running for the door. "Oh no! Because it's not, and it's all Agnes's fault!"

High-pitched chattering voices could be heard as the RV's door opened and a stream of men, none of them over three feet tall, poured out of the vehicle.

Blair hissed a curse when she saw the sign *Elves 4 Your Party* painted on the RV's door.

"Agnes will have a stroke," she muttered, practically running to the RV. "Hold up!" She held up her hands to stop them. "What are you doing here? You're supposed to go up to Snow Farms Resort, where you'll be staying while you work at the carnival."

"Hey, toots." A bearded elf smoking a large cigar that smelled like something out of a dung heap ambled up and winked at her. He wore a wrinkled T-shirt carrying unidentifiable stains, one of them moving, and dirty jeans that hung at his hips and revealed eye-bleeding red boxers. She tried not to stare at something that seemed to be crawling along the point of one of his ears. "No one told us witches lived around here. Good to see ya." He glanced down at her ankle where Fluff and Puff gnashed their teeth. "Wicked cool tat. Who inked it for ya?"

"*Hey!*" Stasi clapped her hands on her rear and spun around to glare at another elf who was grinning broadly. "You pinch me again, you little pervert, and you'll find yourself stuffed face first down a reindeer's butt!" Sparks flew out of the finger she pointed at her attacker.

"Oooh, I like 'em when they talk dirty." He pursed his lips at her in a parody of a kiss that had Blair and Stasi gagging. "Hey, baby, whatcha doin' tonight? I got me a private bunk."

Blair pointed at the one she took to be the leader. "You do not move one inch."

"I want you to remember this moment the next time you call me gross," Horace grumbled from just inside the shop door. He waved his claws to keep the cigar smoke away.

Blair pulled her cell phone out of her pants pocket and quickly punched in Agnes's number. "Agnes, you need to get over here right away," she ordered without bothering with a polite greeting and hanging up without saying good-bye. This was no time for proper etiquette. She sensed the situation wasn't going to improve once the mayor's wife got a look at the creatures that passed for the cute and smiling elves she thought she'd hired for the carnival.

"So, babe, whaddya do for fun around here?" Another elf with a fuzzy beard belched loudly as he lifted his beer can. He drank deeply then crushed the aluminum container against his forehead and dropped it on the sidewalk.

Blair closed off her nostrils to keep out the alcoholic fumes. She flicked her fingers at the flattened can and it immediately flew back up, smacked the elf in the face, and dropped into his hand.

"Okay, okay, I get the idea," he mumbled, tossing the can over his shoulder to land on the RV steps.

Blair narrowed her eyes at him. "One of my favorite computer games is Elf Bowling. Now I know why."

She was never so thankful the town wasn't all that big, because it wasn't long before Agnes's navy Lincoln Continental rolled down the street and parked behind the RV. She climbed out of her car and tottered over on high heels.

"What is going on?" she asked, staring at the bus and its inhabitants in horror. She took several steps back as a couple of them advanced toward her. "And what are… they?" She clutched her handbag to her chest.

"*They* are the elves you hired through Mickey Boggs," Blair informed her, wrinkling her nose against the beauty shop vapors that rolled off Agnes's obviously recently permed hair. Great, first the beer fumes, now hair salon chemicals.

Agnes reached inside her tote bag and pulled out a pair of glasses, perching them on her nose. One look showed her that nothing had changed as one elf leered at her while another idly scratched his butt.

"These aren't elves," she proclaimed, waving her hand in front of her face as if to stave off the stench of beer and body odor. "I don't know what they are, but they're certainly not the cute Santa-type elves Mr. Boggs assured me we'd receive." She started to take a deep breath and immediately realized it wasn't a good idea. She pinched her nostrils shut. "They'll just have to go back and I will demand an immediate refund of my deposit. This is unacceptable."

"Who's the broad?" the head elf asked Blair, crooking his thumb at Agnes.

"The broad is Mrs. Pierce, the mayor's wife, and the one who contracted with Mickey for your services," Blair explained, keeping a safe distance from the drunken elves who were still climbing out of the RV and making a wide circle around her. Considering most of them were only in sleeveless undershirts or, Fates preserve her, no shirt at all, she was amazed they weren't freezing in the cold winter air. Of course that was unlikely, given the high alcohol content that had to be coursing through their veins. "Except you guys are not what Mickey said he was sending her. Tell me something, have any of you ever worked for Santa?" She sincerely doubted it, but she wanted to give it a shot. "Do you understand what that kind of elf gig involves?"

"That piker?" He snorted. "No elf in his right mind wants to work for him. Trust me, he's not as jolly and ho-ho-ho as everyone thinks he is. And he pays shit for all that he wants us to do up there. Do you know he won't even put central heat in the workshop? The Elves' Union said we didn't have a proper grievance against him, so we gave him and the Union the finger and struck out on our own. Mickey took us on and he gets us pretty decent gigs." He peered at Agnes, who rapidly backed up, then he turned back to Blair. "I'll stay with you, sweetcakes. I hope you got a big bed. I like lots of room." He grinned, sidling up to her.

"Do not even think it." Blair let him see just enough of the power radiating from her to warn him not to try anything. Stasi went a step further and zapped the one who'd goosed her. "Besides, you're supposed to stay up at Snow Farms." The idea of the grungy elves staying at the exclusive resort was enough to bring a smile to Blair's face. Since Roan Thorpe had persuaded Agnes to have elves at the carnival, he could just deal with them.

He continued to stare at Blair's breasts until she zapped him between the eyes. "Okay, I get it. Don't ogle the boobs," he sighed. He gestured toward Agnes as he idly dug his finger in his ear. He pulled out the digit, inspected something wiggling on the end of his fingertip, and scrubbed it off on his grungy pants. Agnes almost fainted. "So she's the one in charge and not the dude up at Snow Farms?"

"She's the one paying the bill."

"Oh no, I am not! I will not pay for these… these…" For once words failed the woman as she fanned her face with her handbag.

"Alberic," he told her. "The name's Alberic."

"And I'm Elrohir." An elf with green-stained teeth that matched the wispy hair sticking out on his head in all directions grinned up at Agnes. His eyes, a brilliant amber, glowed as he studied Agnes the way a PMSing woman looked at a hot fudge sundae. "You know what they say about good things coming in small packages, baby? That's me."

"This is so wrong," Agnes wailed as Stasi took charge and guided the nearly hysterical woman into her shop.

"You," Blair pointed at Alberic, "come with me. The rest of you go back inside your RV and *stay there*." She speared Alberic with a look that said it all. "And don't you dare touch a thing." She waited until he moved to enter Stasi's shop ahead of her. No way she'd have him walking behind her!

Alberic groaned his disappointment as he sauntered inside.

"Blair, is there a problem?" Cliff, who owned Sam's Dry Cleaners, called from across the street. He eyed the RV and its residents with a wary eye.

"All taken care of, Cliff. Thanks!" Blair called back with a confidence she didn't feel. She flashed him a smile and walked inside the shop, where she heard Stasi's soothing tones, Agnes's shrill ones, and Alberic arguing with Horace. "Absolutely not!" Agnes was railing at Alberic. "We cannot allow *things* like you around small children who could be corrupted just by looking at you! Mr. Boggs will just have to give the deposit back, and we will not pay him another penny. This is fraud! You are not the cute elves I ordered!"

Blair sighed as she saw the arrogant stance Agnes took when she felt she was in the right. A posture that meant nothing would move her.

"Lady, I don't give a diddlysquat what you say. Mickey negotiated our contract and that means we get paid, along with having our food provided for us and a place to park our RV. We haven't had a gig in some time, so there's no way you're going to back out of this one. You should be grateful you don't have to house us, too." He gestured toward the street where the RV was now rocking with the hip-hop sounds of Trick Trick in gloriously explicit stereo sound.

"I am sure they have all the food you will require at the resort along with a large parking area to hold that *thing* out there." Agnes did her best to stare him down.

"Yeah, well, that's why we're down here. I drove up to that hotel first. Thorpe took one look at us and said there was no way we he'd allow us to *sully,*"—he made quotation marks with his fingers—"his precious resort. He said it was better if we stayed down here, since the carnival was held down here around some lake. When I started to point out the terms of the contract, he said we had two minutes to leave before he set the dogs on us." He shot Blair a telling look.

"I didn't know they had guard dogs up there," Agnes wheezed.

She breathed through her nose and swung around, grasping Blair with one hand and Stasi with the other, pulling them into Stasi's stockroom.

"Do something," she ordered under her breath, turning toward Stasi. "Your boyfriend is a famous attorney. Can't he help? He said he was a wizard, so wouldn't he know what to do with elves and a contract I refuse to honor?"

"Stasi and I talked to Trev the minute you told us you hired them through Mickey," Blair told her. "He said there's no way to get out of a contract drafted by Mickey Boggs. His paperwork is as ironclad as a contract can be."

"But those creatures out there aren't elves!" the woman wailed.

"But they are," Blair said gently, feeling sorry for her. After all, she was a human and had no idea what trouble can be brewed if you worked with the wrong members of the preternatural community. "True, they aren't the storybook elves you hoped for and I'm sure you even asked Mickey for that kind of elf. But the creatures out there *are* actual elves. You contracted with Mickey for elves, and that's exactly what you got."

Agnes sighed. "There must be something we can do. We can't have them running around town. What if we appeal to Mr. Boggs?" She turned to Blair with a clear "*by* we *I mean* you *appealing to Mickey Boggs*" look. "Surely he would understand the worries we have about this… wouldn't he?"

"Mickey understands money and that's all he understands," Blair told her. "What if we ask Grady if they could park on that empty lot behind his restaurant?" she suggested. "It's plenty big enough for the RV and far enough off the road that they'd be out of public view."

"I don't want them here at all!" Agnes groaned. "You saw those little men. They're disgusting!"

"We'll tell them they have to bathe, wear appropriate clothing, and behave," Blair assured her, fighting down an irrational fear that her idea might not work out, because their luck wasn't going that way lately.

"You gonna be back there much longer?" Alberic called out. "I gotta take a dump."

Agnes's eyelids fluttered and she started to tip to the side.

"Breathe, Agnes, just breathe," Stasi ordered, looking around and finding a paper bag, which she fitted over Agnes's nose and mouth.

"Floyd won't be re-elected after this," she moaned into the bag. "Roan *couldn't* have known Mickey Boggs would send up such horrible creatures."

Blair walked out to the shop and immediately zapped Alberic, who had started to finger a pair of lace thong panties.

"They're for my girlfriend!" he protested. "I'll pay for 'em."

Stasi sighed, walking in behind Blair. "Just take them, but nothing else."

Blair wasted no time in calling Grady, who was willing to allow the RV to park there even after she tried to explain the elves wouldn't be what he'd expect. He was used to Agnes's schemes sometimes going haywire, and he seemed to understand the need to get the elves out of sight fast. She quickly ushered Alberic outside and toward the RV, giving the head elf quick directions to Grady's BBQ Pit. She just knew the elderly man wouldn't be happy once he saw what she couldn't adequately describe, but she couldn't think of any other place where there was enough room to park the RV and keep it out of public view. "Do *not* go near the restaurant until we come down there, and do us all a favor—think about all of you taking baths and putting on clean clothes."

She waited on the sidewalk, watching the smoking vehicle lumber its way down the street and turn up the road toward Grady's.

"I was hoping for all these cute little elves in a wonderland setting," Agnes sighed. "Little red and green outfits, with the hats and bells and curled toe slippers."

"It's not Christmas, Agnes. It's a February winter wonderland. We would have been better off with penguins," Blair said then quickly added, "Toy ones, not real."

"We're going to need someone to keep them in line," Stasi brought up.

"I know the perfect candidate for herding a bunch of unruly elves; too bad he's probably visiting his mom at the moment," Blair said, wishing she was a fly on the wall for that meeting, but shape-shifting wasn't one of her skills. Plus, with her luck, Vera would be carrying a can of Raid and wouldn't be afraid to use it.

Agnes fingered her handbag and seemed to have recovered her composure. "Stasi, dear, do you have any more of those French corsets you showed me a few weeks ago?" she whispered. "Perhaps red or purple? Floyd so enjoyed what I purchased, that I thought I'd pick up a few more."

"I'm outta here." Horace hopped off the counter and disappeared into Blair's shop.

Blair did likewise.

Jake left his truck in the care of a parking valet whose jacket bore the name Snow Farms Resort embroidered in dark green on the front pocket. The young man refused the money Jake held out.

"We're not allowed to accept tips from Pack members, Mr. Harrison."

Jake's grin showed a lot of teeth as he tucked the bills into the man's pocket. "Good thing I'm not family, then." He headed up the steps to the lobby and crossed the marble floor toward the front desk.

A clerk spied him and immediately picked up a phone and spoke quietly into it.

"Your mother is in the Crystal Room having her tea, Mr. Harrison," she told him before he could say a word. "She would like you to join her there."

"I guess it's too early for a drink," he muttered, thinking a couple of shots of JD would go down very well right about now, but he'd settle for a strong infusion of caffeine.

He followed the clerk's directions to a large lounge that offered a few tables and a bar along one end. He ignored his mother seated at a table by the window and paused long enough at the bar to request a cup of coffee before heading her way.

"Vera." He accorded her the barest of nods, hating himself for waiting until she gestured for him to be seated. He told himself it was only good manners and not his bowing to the Alpha female.

She gazed at his worn jeans, work boots, and navy T-shirt topped with an open navy and green plaid flannel shirt.

"I would have thought you would dress appropriately for this visit," she murmured, picking up the china teapot and starting to pour the contents into a second delicate cup.

"I'm dressed appropriately for my work. And no tea for me, thanks." He glanced up with gratitude when a waitress left the coffee in front of him. He wished he'd asked the bartender to add a shot of Jack Daniels to it after all. "So when did you move up the food chain to become Baxter's mate? And what happened to Suzanne?" He mentioned the Alpha female he'd known as the Alpha's mate.

Vera fingered the oval pendant she wore; it featured a gold wolf's head with dark emeralds for eyes. He knew the Pack leader wore a larger version but with black diamonds for the eyes. The pendants were passed down over the years to each successive Alpha and his mate. Jake knew for a fact that the pendants were also drenched in blood from battles instigated so that the winner would have the honor of wearing them.

He'd never been so grateful he had been born a dog instead of a wolf and had never been considered worthy of fighting for even a lower position, much less Alpha. That was another reason why he was able to exist so easily away from the members of his Pack. He'd never been part of their social structure, so he didn't need them the way they needed each other. He truly was a stray dog.

Vera squeezed a hint of lemon into her tea and added one lump of sugar, stirring her tea with a silver spoon.

"Suzanne stepped down as Alpha in 1943," she replied. *Barely four years after he'd left the Pack.* That was one nice thing about being a Were. They aged a lot slower than humans, so Jake looked to be in his mid-thirties, rather than his actual ninety-seven years.

"Stepped down, or was forced out?" He knew his mother well. She'd coveted the Alpha female's pendant of authority for as long as he had lived among the Pack. And while Suzanne had been the warm and fuzzy part of Pack life, Vera could easily have taken her on and won. No one had fought Suzanne for the honor because they all knew she was the heart and soul of the Pack and looked after them the way a nurturing mother would. No one could have continued her work with the same fervor she showed. Vera was the exact opposite. She'd pushed his father to fight for Alpha rank and he died in a fight that had lasted as long as snapping your fingers. Jake had left the next day and never looked back. His mother hadn't bothered finding him all these years. So why was she bothering to talk to him now?

"Stepped down." Her dark eyes were cold as ice. "She's been in seclusion since then."

Jake felt a lump in his stomach at her words. He knew there had to be a lot more to the story than an Alpha female giving up her pendant and position, not to mention her mate of many years, without a fight, but he also knew that his mother was more than capable of fighting dirty, while Suzanne would have given up her position if she thought it was for the good of the Pack. "What's going on, Vera? Why is the Pack moving in up here? And don't say they're not. That's the only reason Roan would be here—and the parking valet talked about Pack." Acid dripped in his gut as he watched his mother's features soften at the sound of her younger son's name. His brother was apparently heir apparent for the position of Pack leader as long as he was willing to fight dirty enough to keep it. Knowing Vera, Roan had been raised with that intent and his eye was on the prize.

Jake picked up his cup and drank down the hot brew while Vera appeared to consider her answer. Before he could blink, his cup had been refilled. Roan clearly believed in hiring an efficient staff.

"Over the years the Pack has almost doubled in size. Baxter feels it's time for it to split before hostility grows too high. That means we need a new territory for the second Pack. The resort's sale came at an opportune time and we took advantage of it. Naturally, Roan will lead the new Pack."

"Talk about timing. What a perfect chance to give Roan the responsibility he craves and get him out of your fur all at the same time." Jake tipped his chair back and barked a short laugh. "Of course. And with Roan up here as Pack leader for the new Pack, you wouldn't have to worry about his mate fighting for your position. Was this your idea or Baxter's?"

Vera picked up her teacup, pinky delicately extended, and sipped her tea. "It was a Pack decision. Besides, what is the problem with a Pack living up here? It's not as if there isn't plenty of open land for hunting."

Jake sat forward, the front legs of his chair thumping on the floor. "Plenty of open land as far as you're concerned might not be other people's idea of plenty of open land. What you really want is for Blair and Stasi to sell you *their* land, since they own a good portion of the area." He shook his head. "Ain't going to happen. They want to keep the land untouched and they know the best way for that to happen is to keep it all their own. They've protected it for over 100 years. No way they'll change their minds just because you want them to."

Her lips stretched in an icy smile. "People often change their minds if offered the right incentive."

Jake rested his arms on the table. "Get this clear, Vera. We're not talking about novices fresh out of the Witches' Academy. They've been in this world longer than you and I combined have been on this earth and they have power you can't even imagine. I've seen them at work. You haven't. The land belongs to Blair and Stasi and there's no way they'll give it up just because your precious Pack thinks they should have it. And speaking of Blair, what was going on between you two this morning? Why do I get the idea you'd met each other before?"

"I have no idea what you mean."

"Of course you don't." Past experience told him if his mother didn't want him to know something, he wouldn't be able to pry it out of her. He knew the same would happen with Blair.

Her face was a perfectly smooth-featured mask showing absolutely no emotion. Thanks to her blood-lines, she had never needed Botox injections or a few nips and tucks to look as icily elegant as she did then. "You have no idea what is involved here."

He stood up, pushing the chair back with more force than necessary. The legs made a scraping sound on the polished wood floor. "I have a pretty good idea, and it's apparent your showing up this morning had nothing to do with seeing how your son was doing. Do us both a favor, *Mom,* and don't bother me again." He walked off.

"There's more, Jake!" she said after his departing figure, but he ignored her.

Jake's steps faltered as he crossed the lobby and saw Roan standing near the front desk. The younger Were pushed away from the counter and walked toward him.

Roan's dark red sweater was cashmere and his designer jeans fit him like a glove. Jake knew he should have felt like a poor relation in flannel and frayed denim, but he had moved beyond any sense of inadequacy years ago. He felt no sense of family with the woman who'd borne him and the man he had once called brother. Even though they'd shared the same den years ago, Roan was a stranger to him, and vice versa.

"So you saw Mother," Roan spoke first, watching him with the same dark eyes Jake had.

"Oh yeah, great conversation, caught up on old times, you name it. Just one of those Hallmark moments." Jake started to walk away, but Roan moved to block him. "Look, Roan, what promised to be an incredible morning for me turned into a shitty day because Vera decided to make an uninvited morning visit. Right now, all I want is to head home."

Roan's dark eyes examined him. "What did she tell you?"

"That you're going to find a way to cheat Blair and Stasi out of their land because you want it all for yourself. Do yourself a favor. Don't even think about it." A gentle snarl vibrated deep in Jake's throat. He might be a dog, but he was a dog who'd killed more than squirrels and rabbits.

Roan showed his status by not stepping back, but smiled and cocked an eyebrow. "So that's how it is. You're fucking the red-haired witch. I thought I smelled her on you. What we need is for the good of the Pack, Jake. Just because you've been away from the Pack for so many years doesn't mean you still can't have feelings for what goes on. And what about Jennifer? Why didn't you ever contact her after you left?"

Jake froze. "That bond was broken when I left the Pack, Roan. And it was between Jennifer and me. It had nothing to do with anyone else."

"That's what you think. Think about it, Jake. She could easily be your way back into the Pack," Roan said in a silken voice, one that implied so many possibilities for Jake if he returned to the furry fold.

So why did Jake read something more ominous into it?

"Why am I so important all of a sudden?" Jake demanded. "I'm not like you, Roan. And no matter what any of you think, I don't give a damn that I'm no longer with the Pack. I'm happy with the life I've made for myself, and I don't need any of you." He stepped around Roan and this time, the younger Were didn't try to stop him.

Jake wasn't surprised to see his truck idling in front of the resort when he stepped out. He settled behind the wheel and started up the engine, turning on his CD player and listening to Nirvana. His visit to his mother had turned out as badly as he expected, but it was nothing that a little rock 'n' roll wouldn't cure.

"Thank the Fates I'll be back to normal once I get back to Moonstone Lake." He shifted gears and did a passable imitation of getting the hell out of Dodge.

During the ten minute drive he mentally smacked himself upside the head for letting Blair get away that morning. He decided he'd head straight for her place. After last night, he doubted there would be much trouble talking her into a little *them* time.

He guessed he'd also have to admit that Blair was right. They were good together. She knew about his animal nature, she'd seen him kill, and she understood that wasn't everything that made up Jake Harrison. He also suspected that if he was stupid and tried to back off now, Blair would go after him with a ferocity that would make his mother look like a mewling puppy.

Memories of just how he had given in to the saucy witch's charms, and how often, brought a ball of heat to his gut. He pressed down a bit harder on the accelerator and the large engine roared.

But whatever ideas Jake had come up with involving Blair and whipped cream screeched to a halt when he reached the town's outskirts and heard what sounded like a battle.

"Why do I have the feeling I'll find Blair in the middle of whatever's going on?" he muttered, speeding up to reach Grady's BBQ Pit a few seconds faster.

It was a good thing Jake didn't try to anticipate what he'd find, because the scene that spread out before him was way beyond anything he could have imagined.

An RV the size of a train, and the color of barf, took up most of the open lot above Grady's place. And if he wasn't mistaken, there was an army of elves that had to have come from the Underworld swarming all over the place, most of them bare ass naked, while Agnes was standing nearby screeching like a banshee, with her partner in crime Marva standing next to her as pale as a ghost. And yep, there was Blair, smack dab in the middle of the insanity.

Jake pushed open his door and climbed out of his truck.

Blair was retreating to the sidelines, her gray wool peacoat flaring open to reveal a cobalt sweater and dark wash jeans that hugged her curves. It wasn't easy for Jake to keep his mind on the problems at hand when the witch had that spark of ire in her eyes. She glanced over her shoulder at his approach. She looked as if she wanted to grab him, and not in a good way. He hadn't realized he'd left the truck's engine running until it abruptly died. Blair at work.

"Do not even *think* of leaving here," she called between clenched teeth.

"I wasn't planning on it," he told her, ready and waiting to see the show or dive into the fray if need be. He was nothing if not adaptable. He continued walking toward her. "What the hell is going on here? Why haven't you gone off all hexster on them?" he asked.

"Probably because with the mood I'm in, I'd end up blowing up the whole area. While you were swapping memories with your mom, Agnes's elves showed up," she said, sweeping her arm in a graceful arc toward the scene before them. "If I wasn't trying to avoid adding another 50 years to my banishment, every one of the little buggers would be toast by now. In the short amount of time they've been here, their RV has increased the smog level by a good thousand percent, they've flashed every woman who's had the bad luck to cross their path, drunk a couple of cases of beer, and almost given Agnes a heart attack. And it seems Roan told them that they couldn't park that nauseous hunk of metal up at Snow Farms, but that there was no reason why they couldn't stay down here. Then there's what's gone on in the last five minutes, when one of them flipped up Marva's skirt to reveal a very scary pair of granny undies, and now Grady's threatening everyone with his twelve-gauge shotgun."

Resisting a strong urge to laugh, Jake followed her gaze and saw the elderly man standing at the back door with the large weapon clutched in his trembling hands. Jake pinched the top of his nose and closed his eyes, while the sounds went on around him. He dearly hoped the shotgun wasn't loaded, but knowing Grady, it was not only loaded, but his ammunition wasn't buckshot or rock salt.

"Blair, that horrid little man must be stopped!" Agnes shrieked. "He's urinating against a tree!"

Blair's ire seemed to include the world around them. Jake looked past her and saw a few other elves choosing various trees and bushes for the same purpose. Hell, even when he was in dog form, he only watered plants out of humans' sight.

Jake strode purposefully past Blair and approached the RV. "*Enough!*" His roar rivaled any Alpha Were and broadcast enough power to stop the elves; although he wished a few had finished pissing before they turned around or fell back on their bare asses.

He paused long enough to make sure Agnes wasn't going to faint, then he quickly steered the woman and Marva toward a nearby picnic table and sat them down with Stasi there to pat their hands and offer comfort. Then he turned to confront the elves.

Blair quickened her pace until she almost plowed into Jake's back. He could feel her power increasing until it was getting hard for him to breathe.

"Okay, you can back it off a bit and dial down on the magick," he advised under his breath and relaxed when she did. "These guys *can't* be elves." His Were sense of smell was pretty offended by what was in front of him and considering that as his dog self he had tangled with more than his share of skunks, that said a lot.

One grungy looking elf, with a smelly cigar poking out of a corner of his bearded mouth, ambled over to him. "Who're you to talk, Rover?" He grinned, displaying discolored teeth. "Easy to tell what part of the dog park you're from, and it ain't no leader of the Pack."

Jake's growl moved up his throat, but to give the grimy elf credit, he didn't back down.

"This is Alberic. You might call him the boss of this group." Blair didn't sound too happy about it, either. "Agnes hired elves through Mickey Boggs and this is what she got. And sad to say, they are real elves."

Jake swallowed a curse. "Agnes didn't listen to you when you told her it might not be a good idea?"

"She thought she was getting a great deal on some cute elves to run around the carnival as local color, so to speak, and also man some of the booths. Instead, she got *them*. I was thinking maybe you could, you know, kind of herd them."

Without looking behind him, he snaked his hand back to grasp the back of Blair's neck and brought her forward. She cast him an apologetic look and mimed zipping her mouth shut.

"Let's get something clear, shall we?" He spoke to the elves in a low voice that fairly vibrated with power. "The nice people around here don't know what I am, and I intend to keep it that way. So if word gets out I will know who opened their mouth and then I will head over here to have a *chat* with them. Got me?"

Alberic apparently was now wary enough to realize that teasing Jake any further might not be in his best interests. "Look, we're here to do a job and that's it. We were told to come up and play the part of cute smiling elves and when the time comes, we will. But give us a break. We drove straight here from a fair in Texas. We're just blowing off some steam, okay?"

"Blowing off steam is one thing. Disrespect to the people who live here is another," Jake said.

"You weren't due here until next week. Why are you here now?" Blair asked.

"We were told there was no problem if we showed up early. That no one would care if we hung out." He idly scratched his chest. He leaned over and confided, "Although that old broad over there isn't too happy about it."

"Mrs. Pierce is still a lot younger than you and as such she will be treated with deference." Jake easily guessed the elf's age to be a couple of centuries. "Not to mention that she's basically your boss up here. And if you can't behave, this witch and myself will make your lives very miserable." His eyes flared gold with power.

Blair took this as her cue to speak up and lay down the law. "So there's going to be rules, such as no pissing against trees or bushes, keeping all your trash picked up, no getting drunk, no walking around naked. And you will all be polite to everyone."

"Anything else?"

Blair glared at his cigar. "I'm sure Agnes has a plan for how you're to dress and behave for the carnival. And considering you're in the woods, it's a given there's no smoking up here. "

Alberic sighed. "Mickey said this was an easy gig. He was going to give it to another group, but then he changed his mind."

Blair had a pretty good idea why Mickey had chosen these guys instead, and she spelled it R…o…a…n. "Yeah, well, he told Agnes he was sending up cute elves and look what we got," she countered. "Maybe I should also explain that Grady is really good with that shotgun and he's been known to shoot first and ask questions afterwards." She stalked off to tell Grady he could stand down.

"Sassy kid," Alberic said, casting an admiring glance at Blair's backside. He turned back to Jake. "You banging her?" The look on Jake's face forced him back a few steps. "Hey, I can ask, can't I?"

"No, you can't," Jake advised with a show of teeth. "You can start following those rules by persuading your buddies to get dressed and clean up all the trash around the RV."

"The contract states our food is taken care of," Alberic said.

"You are kidding, right?"

"It's in the contract."

"Fine, we'll get that straightened out. Just do your part and behave, okay?"

Jake left Alberic and walked over to Blair, Stasi, Agnes, and Marva. "They'll still need to be fed."

"I guess I could fix up a few pans of lasagna," Agnes said slowly.

"Lasagna?" One of the elves perked up at the word and practically climbed up her leg like a dog ready to hump her calf. She uneasily shifted her legs to one side. "With real ricotta cheese and fresh mozzarella?"

"And garlic bread?" another asked. "I like lots of oregano on mine."

"None of that eggplant shit, but lasagna with real meat in it?"

"Uh, yes." Agnes started to warm to one of her favorite topics: cooking. "I also make my own sauce from scratch, with lots of garlic." She frowned. "I guess garlic wouldn't bother you, since you're not vampires."

"Agnes makes wonderful lasagna," Marva chimed in.

Pretty soon the elves had surrounded Agnes with hopeful expressions at the idea of real home cooking. Stasi mouthed that she was heading back to the apartment and left.

Jake gently pulled on Blair's arm. "Let's get out of here while we can." He drew her back to his truck. He looked at his vehicle. "It'll start up now, won't it?"

"Oh." She muttered under her breath and waved her hands over the hood. The engine started up immediately. "I just wanted some backup if they got rowdy... wait a minute!" She shrieked when he picked her up, planted her on the passenger seat, and quickly buckled her in.

"Things are settled and Agnes is planning their dinner menu," he told her, running around the hood and climbing in.

"Where are we going?"

"Back to my place. Any objection?"

"Is your mother there?"

"She was still having tea in Snow Farms' Crystal Room when I left. And if she shows up at my place again, you have my permission to zap her back to... wherever you want her to go."

"Hm, very tempting. Her being up there isn't far enough away for you, is it?" She stretched her arms over her head.

"The other side of the world wouldn't be far enough away," Jake said grimly.

Blair glanced down at her watch. "Tell you what, let's go over to my place. Stasi put a roast in the crock pot early this morning and it should be ready soon."

Jake considered a moment, hunger winning out over lust. He wasn't much of a cook. "My mouth's watering already."

She smiled at him. "As long as you stay your nonfurry self. It's nicer to sit across from you at the table than to have to put a bowl down on the floor."

He put the SUV in gear. "Sounds good to me. It's been a long day."

Blair shuddered. "You're telling me." She half turned in the seat and leaned against the window. "I'm never opening the door in the morning again. So how did your meeting with your mother go?"

"Let's just say it was a meeting I don't care to repeat."

"I don't care what you say. You *had* to have been adopted."

Chapter 9

BLAIR WAS RELIEVED THAT THE ELF SITUATION HAD calmed down without any bloodshed or violence — namely, violence on her part, because she had been ready to turn everyone into toads, and that was exactly the kind of thing that kept getting her banishment extended. Jake had shown up just in time. She had never needed the big he-man figure to ride in on a white horse — or silver truck, as the case may be — but she was glad that he had arrived to back her up. And now that one situation had been taken care of, she was ready to move on to another. The one that had to do with Jake and the family that seemed to want him back. The hard part was getting Jake to talk about it. Once they reached Blair and Stasi's apartment, she and Stasi urged him to sit while they made the final preparations for the meal.

"So, Roan is your brother, and your mother is also up here now?" Stasi asked, peeling potatoes while Blair dug out the vegetable steamer. Bogie floated around their ankles in a never-ending figure eight.

"That's it." Jake accepted the cup of coffee Blair set in front of him. "I'm sure Blair told you that she met her."

"I said very little." Blair knew she was caught in a lie, but when all was said and done, Vera was Jake's mother and she was trying very hard not to refer to the female Were in some pretty unladylike terms. "So what happened up there, other than the two of you sharing a pot of tea?"

He looked at her steadily and she returned his look, not the least deterred by his glare. "I had coffee."

"I never did think you were the tea type. So what happened?"

"You're not going to let go of this, are you?"

"Nope," she said with a smile.

"It's one of her more annoying qualities," Stasi informed him. "If you'd like, I could make up a list for you, for future reference. Anyway, you certainly won't win this time, because I'd love to know all about it, too."

Jake groaned. "I used to have this nice quiet life."

"Yeah, well, consider it over," Blair said cheerfully. "So tell all. Why did your mother come up here? I personally couldn't see her out on the slopes or even sitting in front of the fireplace with a hot toddy. And don't say it's so she can visit her baby boy, because after this morning's conversation, I know better."

"Fine, I'll tell you everything after dinner," Jake said. "You'll just have to hold on to your curiosity until after you've fed me."

The two witches exchanged a silent conversation.

"Okay," Blair agreed, although she looked as if she couldn't wait that long.

"Deal," Stasi said, setting a pan filled with potatoes on the stove, then pulling cans of beef gravy out of the cabinet. She glanced at the large crock-pot and its contents. "We could end up with a lot of leftover roast."

"Oh, no!" Blair immediately knew what she was thinking and was determined to nip that thought in the bud. "They're Agnes's problem, not ours. She should have listened to us and not blindly gone ahead and dealt with Mickey. If she had, we wouldn't have all those elves running around."

"I've never heard of Mickey Boggs. Who is he, besides someone who sent the elves from Hades to our formerly quiet town?" Jake said, smiling his thanks as Blair refilled his coffee cup.

"He's a troll that runs a temporary employment service for elves, dwarves, sprites, pixies, and whatever else needs a job. He figures if you qualify as a supernatural creature, you qualify to work for his agency," Blair explained. "There's a lot of seasonal work for elves between Christmas, spring festivals, summer carnivals, and even the fall season, and he manages to keep them busy, even though the ones he sends out are pretty much scraping the bottom of the barrel. He'll hire the ones that nobody else would touch."

"How can he stay in business if he's sending out creatures like the ones he sent up here?"

"He's very skilled with the terms of his contract," Stasi said. "All Agnes asked for was elves. Since cute-type elves will go to a more reputable agency, he sends what he has. And since technically he sent elves up here, he's not in breach of his contract. Plus, there are always new suckers looking for a deal; he doesn't have to rely on repeat customers."

"Is there any chance he had no idea they were so disgusting?" Jake sipped the hot brew.

"No chance at all. Mickey knows exactly what he's doing." Blair kept an eye on the cooking potatoes while mixing up corn bread and sticking a pan in the oven. She knew with Jake's Were metabolism, he'd be one hungry puppy and there really wouldn't be as much roast leftover as Stasi thought there would be. Her lips twisted in a brief smile.

"What's so funny?" Jake narrowed his gaze at her.

"You wouldn't find it as amusing as I do."

"Meaning it has to do with me." His nostrils flared when Stasi lifted the crock-pot lid and checked the contents. The rich scent of cooking meat filled the air.

"Everyone needs a hobby."

Jake settled back and watched the easy way Stasi and Blair worked in the kitchen, managing never to get in each other's way as they quickly worked to finish dinner preparations and get the food on the table. Conversation was relaxed and filled with laughter. The teasing soon went three ways, with the two witches making him a part of it. He'd known Blair and Stasi for as long as he had lived in Moonstone Lake, and worked for both of them off and on. He'd sensed their power right away, but was polite enough to wait until they let him in on their secret. But now he saw them as the fascinating women they were. He saw that Blair's sense of humor had some interesting quirks, and that Stasi wasn't the sweet pushover so many thought she was. He also knew just how tough these witches were and what they could do when their backs were against a wall. He had to admit he was happy to have them on his side.

Blair had kicked off her boots and Fluff and Puff's happy chatter joined the group as she padded barefoot around the kitchen.

"They still haven't left your ankle?" Jake asked.

"I think they're enjoying their spot too much, even if they complain when I wear boots." Blair glanced down at Fluff and Puff, who threw her air kisses.

"But they're slippers," Jake pointed out, and was immediately assaulted by Fluff's and Puff's loud and energetic protests. "Sorry guys." He was quick to apologize, especially since they looked as if they were considering bolting from Blair's ankle and attaching themselves to his. He growled at them, but they didn't seem the least bit intimidated.

"Maybe we could send them up to visit Vera." Blair's smile widened at the idea. Ear-piercing chatter from the floor level let her know it wasn't a good idea. "No offense, but they don't like your mother either."

"We promised to leave that subject alone until after dinner," Stasi reminded her, as she carefully pulled the roast out of the crock-pot and set it on a serving platter while Blair used a bit of magick to mash the potatoes while she rescued the corn bread from the oven and quickly whipped up honey butter.

"Here, make yourself useful." Blair handed flatware and plates to Jake. He was quick to set the table, since the more he smelled the food the hungrier he grew. Horace waddled in, having conveniently waited until dinner was ready, and they sat down.

Two bites into his meal, Jake was sighing with bliss. He only cooked for himself enough to keep from starving and avoid eating at Grady's or Ginny's Sit 'N Eat every day. He realized he could get used to this sense of togetherness real fast. Especially if that included seeing Blair sitting across from him at every meal.

He was surprised to see a hint of pink come into her cheeks as he looked across the table at her. And if he wasn't mistaken, there was a hint of something else more elemental in her eyes that had him momentarily forgetting his food.

"Behave, you two." Stasi smiled as she cut her meat.

"As if you do when Trev is here." Blair turned back to her own food. "I swear it's amazing the kitchen doesn't go up in flames."

"But nothing good ever happens out here," Horace groused from his side of the table, where he was ensconced in a special gargoyle highchair. He dug into his food with such gusto that the others tended to ignore his less than perfect table manners or the food dropping to the floor that Bogie quickly snapped up. "I always know when something's going on because they wrap me up in a deaf and mute spell."

"Poor baby," Blair said with a lack of sympathy. "It sucks to be you."

"So where did you live before you came to Moonstone Lake?" Blair asked, dipping into the honey butter for her corn bread.

"I lived in Oregon for awhile. Then I moved to a small town in the upper part of Washington and later on I found a nice place north of San Francisco. I moved around so people wouldn't notice I don't age that fast. I'd get new ID, sometimes a new name."

"How old are you?" Blair asked curiously, casting out her senses but unable to discover what she wanted to know.

He grinned at her question. "I'll tell you mine if you tell me yours."

"Never ask a witch her true age," she said primly, then looked down when Fluff and Puff started to speak up. "If you say one more word, I'll start wearing socks 24/7, and I'm talking nasty, itchy wool socks."

The bunny slippers knew when to be quiet.

"Weres don't age as quickly as humans. I was around for the World Wars. Both of them."

Stasi considered him for a minute. "Under 100?"

He nodded. "Just barely." He cast Blair a heated look. "I never did it with an older woman before. I've got to admit it was pretty hot." He grinned, enjoying her obvious discomfiture.

Blair's cheeks flushed dark pink again and Stasi looked away to hide her grin.

"I'm always a cradle snatcher." Blair wasn't happy with herself for allowing him to get under her skin. Well, at least that way. The further they got into their meal, the higher her impatience level rose. She was itching to know what had happened at the resort and she knew she wouldn't get a word out of Jake until after dinner. And watching him nibble on his food, she'd swear he was deliberately dawdling.

"Great roast, Stasi," he said, taking a third helping of the meat and mashed potatoes.

Blair narrowed her gaze. Yep, he was definitely taking his time. Damn him!

"Any dessert?" he asked with a hopeful look.

"Later." Blair picked up the plates while Stasi gathered up the serving dishes. "You're safe from KP duty tonight, so be the big he-doggy and relax in the family room while we take care of this. Then we can sit down and *chat*." She issued him a look that warned him that his time for putting it off was growing shorter by the second.

Jake was no fool. He took his coffee and escaped to the family room with Bogie and Horace right behind him. He settled into one of the oversized chairs and stretched his legs out in front of him. A sense of contentment washed over him and he felt ready to doze off with the soft chatter between Blair and Stasi as background. His extra sharp hearing allowed for eavesdropping, but the idea of a short nap was more tempting.

"So what's Blair like in the sack?" Horace asked, jerking Jake out of his light doze. "*Hey!*" He slapped his smoking horns with his claws and spun around to glare at Blair, who stood in the doorway.

"Warning one, Horace," she told the gargoyle, pointing her forefinger upward and blowing on it as if it were a smoking gun. "Do you really want to try for two?"

"No." He catapulted himself onto the loveseat and plopped down on a pillow with his arms crossed in front of him. If it was possible for gargoyles to sulk, Horace was turning it into a fine art. "There are days she's really evil," he grumbled as Blair turned back to the kitchen.

The clatter of dishes was short-lived and Jake could hear the dishwasher humming away as Blair and Stasi walked in. Blair carried a bottle of Baileys liqueur while Stasi had two coffee mugs hanging on her fingers and a coffee carafe in her other hand.

"Thank you, ladies, for a great meal," Jake smiled.

"You're very welcome. And now dinner's over. Time to talk." Blair poured Baileys into his mug while Stasi freshened his coffee.

He took a sip, allowing the mixture of caffeine and alcohol to warm his veins. First he told Stasi what he'd told Blair the night before, then continued into his meeting with his mother.

"Vera's now the Alpha female. Since she's into power, I'm sure it didn't take her long to seduce Baxter and then fight his Alpha female for the position.

Suzanne was only Alpha for as long as she was because Baxter thought highly of her and she truly cared about the Pack. Vera said Suzanne stepped down in 1943," he ignored their looks of surprise when he mentioned the year, "but I know it really means that Vera deliberately called her out even though she knew Suzanne wasn't a true fighter. Vera wouldn't want to intimidate Suzanne into just handing over the pendant. She'd want to show dominance, demonstrate that she was the better Were for Alpha female. From what I remember of Suzanne, she would give up her position rather than fight over it. She always kept the Pack's well-being foremost in her mind. She might have thought they'd be better off with a more dominant female Alpha." His face twisted in a grimace. "Baxter's Pack is one of the largest in the country and he's always ruled it with an iron paw. Everyone knew that Suzanne was his soft spot. She was more a mother figure than a ruling Alpha, and Vera always hated her for having the position that she felt she deserved." He looked down at his hands twisting in aimless patterns as they hung between his spread thighs.

"What would happen to this Suzanne once she wasn't Alpha?" Blair asked. "I thought it was a standard practice for Alpha females to be very strong physically and mentally. You're making it sound as if she wasn't."

"She was very strong in other ways. She looked after anyone who needed help and was there to advise any youngling who didn't feel comfortable going to their parents." It was obvious that the female Were held a soft spot in Jake's heart and Blair wondered if he was one of the Weres Suzanne had advised. "Even when I was still with the Pack, she was urging Baxter to consider splitting it before it grew much larger. There were always battles to move up the chain of command, although no one dared challenge Baxter. He fought hard and dirty. But none of the females had challenged Suzanne. She made sure there was day care for the whelps, even counseling services were made available. Packs stuck together, but ours was stronger because of her, not because of Baxter."

"And with Vera?" she asked.

He shook his head. "Knowing her, she ignored all that Suzanne worked for—or found someone to run it for her. Vera has always been interested in Vera." He paused for a second. "And I'd say she's up here to help Roan acquire your land. A real power trip for her, with her mate leading one Pack and her son the other."

"Tell them good luck on that," Blair scoffed.

"How much land around here do you own?" Jake asked.

"A lot," Horace piped up as he busied himself cleaning his claws. He didn't wither under Stasi's warning glance, instead opting to mimic zipping his mouth shut.

Blair and Stasi looked at each other.

"The resort's land was a parcel we weren't able to purchase and this sale went through so quietly we didn't know about it in time," Blair said finally. "We've spent quite a few years acquiring land whenever we could. It was our way of protecting the area. What we hadn't yet bought, we cast a 'not interested' spell on until we could. Which obviously doesn't work on Weres," she said ruefully.

"Has your agent mentioned anyone contacting him or her about buying your land?" Jake asked.

"Ebenezer called a couple of weeks ago to say that a developer had shown some interest, but he gave them the same spiel he gives anyone else who calls, 'the owners aren't interested in selling.' They wouldn't find it easy to look for a legal loophole in getting the land because they'd only end up buried in paperwork. Ebenezer loves nothing more than mountains of paperwork."

Jake shook his head. "The Pack will do whatever it takes to get what they want, and it won't necessarily be a legal loophole. They haven't been stopped before and they don't expect to be this time."

"Remember last October when we were almost burned at the stake? After that, there's nothing a Pack of Weres could do that would scare us."

"I don't know about that. They can be truly nasty creatures. Present company excluded, Jake." Irma popped into view, seating herself on one of the easy chairs with Phinneas perched on the arm.

Blair's and Stasi's screams were shrill enough to make Jake clap his hands over his ears.

"The least you could do is give a warning and not just appear like that!" Blair gasped, holding her hand over her heart.

"Sensitive ears, here," Jake muttered, still feeling a ringing sensation bouncing around inside his head.

Unfazed, Irma looked from one to the other. "Do you want to hear what Phinneas and I found out up at that fancy hotel, or not?"

"They popped up to the resort to do a little eavesdropping," Blair explained to Jake. "They promised to be careful so no one would notice them. Please tell me you stayed out of their way."

"That's not easy to do since they saw us, but I had a lovely cover story all ready just in case. I spoke to one desk clerk who was just lovely. I told her I'd been there on my honeymoon and liked to revisit the place. She's very sweet but not very bright, because she believed me," Irma chattered away. "I admit I did peek in on some of the rooms and suites and even nosed around the spa." She turned to Stasi. "No wonder you and Trevor enjoy going up there so much. Too bad it's only open to Weres now."

"No wonder Trev couldn't get a reservation," Stasi commented. "I'm going to really miss their famous chocolate soufflé."

"It's a far cry from that small mining camp that used to be up there," Phinneas said, pushing his ancient spectacles up on his long nose. "Why I remember—"

"Not now, please, Phinneas," Blair interrupted. "Just tell us what you learned."

Irma rummaged through her black clutch handbag. "We did our best to eavesdrop, but we weren't able to find out anything from anyone working there. Thank goodness they assumed we were just there reliving our past and left us alone. All of their conversations had to do with their work and they felt they weren't being paid enough. But the resort owner, Roan something, and his mother were talking in his office about his plans to turn the resort into a Pack colony and now all they needed was the surrounding land, which they're confident of getting. It all sounded like some kind of cult to me." She sniffed and turned to Jake. "Do Weres have cults?"

"Not exactly."

"I'll call Ebenezer in the morning and warn him he might get another call," Blair said. "Anything else?"

"Many of the Weres working there are lovely people, for wolves, but the ones in charge have nasty dispositions and like to show their teeth. I wouldn't want to spend much time around them. After awhile, Phinneas and I were told to leave. They actually told us that we weren't wanted there. Very rude." Irma smothered a yawn. "I wish I could tell you more, but we can always go back up there and make sure to stay out of their way. I'd like to see more of the spa. Good night, children." She smiled and winked out of sight with Phinneas close behind.

"They're staying here together?" Jake asked.

"Yes, and none of us want to think what they might be doing," Blair said.

Stasi glanced at the clock. "I'm off to message Trev." She left the room with Bogie and Horace trailing behind her.

Jake waited until she was out of the room before he turned to Blair. "Her way of leaving us alone?"

"More like her and Trev having phone sex," she replied. "He was supposed to come up last weekend, but he's in the midst of a big case that's giving him fits. And I'm sure when he finds out why he couldn't get a reservation up at the resort, he'll want to make their lives miserable. Stasi will tell him not to worry, even though we'll both miss the spa and their chocolate soufflé," she said with a sigh.

"How do you two get involved in so much drama?" Jake asked, moving over to the chair Blair was curled up in. He picked her up easily then sat down with her in his lap.

"We're just lucky, I guess." She looped her arms around his neck. "Still, you have to admit we are fun."

"Crazy fun." He kept his arms loosely around her waist. "It's going to get nasty, Blair."

"Nothing we can't handle."

He smiled and shook his head. "Have you ever gone up against Weres before?"

"No, but that won't stop us. We're very tough." Her eyes lit up.

"I said that Baxter's only soft spot was Suzanne, but I'm sure he has feelings for Vera, and I think it's safe to assume she's not bothering to keep him calm the way Suzanne did," he said quietly. "He's always been a vicious son of a bitch who'd kill you as soon as look at you. He and Vera are a perfect match."

"Then why did an Alpha like him mate with Suzanne, when she sounds more like a pussycat than a wolf?"

He was quiet for a long time before he answered. "This goes back years before I was born, and it's a story that's rarely mentioned. Suzanne was very beautiful. What I heard was that Suzanne was in love with my father and vice versa, but Baxter also wanted her and what he wanted, he got. He made sure that Suzanne had no choice but to mate with him."

"Don't tell me. And Vera was in love with Baxter?"

He shook his head. "I'd say Vera was only ever in love with Vera. She settled for my old man, who was second-in-command. Vera…" he was hesitant to even say the words.

But Blair wasn't. "Was willing to take second best and bide her time until she could get what she wanted." Her blue-green eyes glittered with fury. "Honestly, Jake, this kind of story belongs on a soap opera."

"Vera knew how to push my father's buttons. She'd hint that he could be Alpha if he'd gather enough of the

Pack on his side; let them know he'd be a better Alpha if only they would side with him. Instead, he was killed, because all she cared about was being top bitch."

"No wonder you left." Blair lightly brushed his hair away from his forehead, allowing the silky strands to slide between her fingers. She left them there, gently combing through his hair in a comforting gesture.

"It was as good a reason as any. I just wanted out." A sigh escaped his lips at her soft touch.

"I'm still amazed that you managed so well all these years without your Pack. Without that connection that so many Weres require."

"There were times when it wasn't easy; at first I was so angry I welcomed getting into fights with strange Weres. But that wore thin, and I did my best to fly under the radar if I had to venture into other Pack territories," he admitted. "Once I got the charm that hid my nature from other supernaturals, I felt a lot safer. But despite the fact that growing up I never really felt a part of the Pack, there were times I wanted to die from sheer loneliness. There have been Weres banished from their Packs who do die because they can't handle being on their own."

His remembered emotional pain was echoed in her eyes, which glittered with tears.

"But you survived and that says a lot. You're a stronger Were than all of them put together," she said, continuing to soothe him with her touch.

He smiled. "If life was the way it should have been, Baxter would have mated with Vera and my father would have been with Suzanne, but Baxter and Vera fucked up two lives that suffered for their selfishness."

He closed his eyes, savoring her tender contact and the sweet scent of her skin.

"Did Suzanne and Baxter have children?" she asked softly.

He shook his head, but not enough that the action would dislodge her touch. "Suzanne had been badly injured when she was young and required surgery."

"But don't Alphas look for a fertile female to carry on their own bloodline?"

"Yes, but lust overrode Baxter's need for his own heir. If he was desperate for one of his blood, he would have found a way to do it, but he's never acknowledged anyone as his blood. Roan's a lot like him, and probably why Baxter named him his heir. That, and I'm sure Vera insisted on it."

"You guys would be a family therapist's dream." Blair idly combed the sides of his hair back with her fingers. She liked that he kept the black locks slightly shaggy; it suited his laidback style. "You took after your father, didn't you? It's obvious that Vera and Roan are type-A personalities and you're not. Although no way I'd call you submissive."

"My dad was happy with his position as second. He knew he wasn't cut out to be a leader." Jake's features tightened. "But that didn't stop Vera from pushing him into a fight that sent him to his death. And once Vera challenged Suzanne, she had exactly what she wanted. But I was already gone; I had no idea."

She used her hands to smooth over his beard-rough features, soothing the bitterness that lay over him.

"What do you think you could have done?" She kept her voice soft.

"Tried to talk my old man out of fighting for Alpha. Reminded him that listening to Vera only brought him pain."

"Would you have been able to succeed?"

Jake thought about it for a moment. "No, but I would have felt better if I'd at least have tried. Didn't you ever wish over the years you'd done something differently?"

"Many times, but I also knew there were some things I couldn't change. Fate is one of them." She pressed a butterfly light kiss against his brow. "Sometimes we can change the direction of our lives, but sometimes we're destined to follow the path we were given. You followed your path and look where you ended up." She brushed another kiss across his forehead and down his cheek to a corner of his mouth.

"With you?" He smiled, having no difficulty knowing what he should say.

"With me," she confirmed, turning her attention to the other corner of his mouth with a bit of a nibble along with the whispered kiss. "And what a good boy you've been, too."

"I admit I never expected to have a hexster in my life."

"Well, maybe I can't turn furry once a month, but I do have a few surprises you might like better, because trust me, the last thing you want anywhere near you is a witch suffering from PMS." She smiled against his cheek.

"Come on, baby, show me your stuff," he growled… literally.

He shifted her in his lap until she moved enough to straddle him. She knelt on the chair, with her knees on either side of his thighs and her hands resting lightly on his shoulders while her bottom was snuggled against his lap. Jake placed his hands on either side of her waist... and waited. He cocked an eyebrow in silent inquiry.

Blair smiled and leaned forward as she purred, "Come on fur boy, let's conjure up some sexy magick." She snapped her fingers. The lights immediately blinked off, but the thick darkness was staved off as the candles scattered around the room immediately flared to life.

Chapter 10

BLAIR SLID HER MOUTH OVER JAKE'S, TASTING HIS coffee and Baileys, knowing he tasted the same from her. But she also savored the dark flavor that was intrinsically his. She ran her tongue across his lower lip, which obligingly opened.

"Um, this is nice." She drew his lip between her teeth and gently pulled back.

Jake gripped her hips and kept her centered on the part of him that needed her most. Only too happy to help out, she rocked back and forth over an erection that was threatening to rip his jean's metal zipper to shreds.

"Very nice," she continued, now focusing her attention on his ear.

Jake found it hard to breathe as Blair nipped on his earlobe then ran the tip of her tongue against the ultra-sensitive spot just behind his ear.

"It would be real easy to rip those jeans right off you," he said hoarsely, then groaned as she giggled softly in his ear. He settled for sliding his hands under her sweater and finding the lace edging on her silk camisole. "What color?"

"Mocha with cocoa lace." He shuddered as she breathed the words in his ear.

He groaned again. "Panties?"

"Thong, same color." She continued leaving butterfly kisses along his jawline. She knew there was nothing better than an old-fashioned make-out session.

Jake closed his eyes and searched for air, but his starved lungs couldn't seem to find any.

"You're killing me here." He hissed a curse when her nimble fingers danced over his zipper and pressed lightly against the bulge.

"I don't know, you feel awfully alive to me."

"Miss Fitzgerald, are you trying to seduce me?" Jake asked.

Blair giggled at the famous line from *The Graduate*. "All I need are black sheer stockings, which I have tucked away in my dresser. And ribbon garters." When Jake leaned forward, she returned his kiss with equal hunger, holding nothing back.

"Black stilettos?"

She nodded. "But of course, and a black lace teddy would be a nice touch, too."

"I was right, you're trying to kill me with mental pictures." Jake slid his hands up under her camisole to find warm silky skin. His Were nose caught the scents of jasmine, sandalwood, and vanilla; he'd never smell them again without thinking of her. His pillows held the same fragrance, and he already knew he'd sleep well with the aroma surrounding him.

Blair released his shirt buttons and dotted kisses across his chest, the crisp dark hairs tickling her nose.

"Good thing this is a big chair," Jake's voice was raw with desire.

"And that we're flexible." She tugged at his zipper and palmed his cock as it sprang free. "No boxers or briefs. What a wild guy you are."

Jake didn't see himself as wild. Not when the woman seducing him was weaving a spell that ensnared him as closely as any trap. But this was a trap he'd willingly be caught in. He grasped her head, bringing her face to his, their tongues tangling as they kissed deeply, and by then neither cared if they had to breathe. He pushed her jeans down and tried to wiggle out of his—her sweater was hiked up to her neck and his flannel shirt hung open while her hands danced under his T-shirt.

Oh yeah, it wouldn't be long before he'd revisit that nirvana that was Blair.

But even knowing wasn't the same as feeling. She rose up on her knees and slowly lowered herself onto his aching cock, enveloping him in wet heat. Once she was all the way down, she stopped. He felt the tiny pulses of her inner muscles as she tightened them around him. He sucked in a breath, wondering just how much sensual torture she was going to give him before she put him out of his misery. The tiny logical part of his brain whispered the hope Stasi wouldn't walk in at the wrong moment.

"We're entirely alone," she whispered in a silken voice that promised pure pleasure, as she answered his unspoken question. "Stasi won't disturb us—you might say I hung a witchy necktie on the doorknob."

He smiled. "There's no door, much less a doorknob."

"I'm very innovative." She rocked slightly, increasing the pressure.

Jake's breath hitched at the sensation as electricity shot all through his body. He gripped her hips, planning to direct what was happening, but he quickly learned that his hexy lady had plans of her own.

She straightened up slightly, changing the angle yet again. Each time she moved, Jake felt ready to shoot out of the chair. He arched up, feeling her even more deeply. He watched her eyes shine in the candlelight and inhaled the scent of her arousal, which was more potent than any perfume.

He pulled her toward him, pushing up her camisole and unhooking her bra. Her breasts gleamed in the soft light as he cupped his palm to the rounded skin. This time she was the one to hiss in reaction as he rolled her nipple between his fingers before leaning forward to take it into his mouth. He felt her cheek nestle against his hair while she wrapped her arms around his head.

It wasn't until then that he realized just how much Blair's touch meant to him. For one who wasn't used to experiencing much physical contact, it was like rain in a parched dessert. Suddenly, Jake wanted this woman to hold him forever.

When he used his teeth on her nipple, he felt her move faster against him and he rocked up against her. The need increased to a pleasure-pain that was ready to explode, and his arms tightened around her as her movements quickened.

"You can't scream this time," she murmured in his ear, her breath raspy with the knowledge of what was to come.

"Men don't scream," he whispered, nuzzling her ear. "You were the one doing the screaming last time." He reached down and found the tiny hooded bundle of nerves. As he rolled it between his fingers, Blair started to keen softly and as the chain reaction hit them both, he covered her mouth with his. But while Blair's scream was kept quiet, her magick went flying around them and the room lit up with golden sparkles.

Jake was wrong. It wasn't nirvana he experienced, but something so intense and addictive that the minute they collapsed in each other's arms he couldn't wait to experience it again. He held Blair in his arms, her face nestled against the crook of his shoulder as they slowly recovered.

"Not looking. Not seeing a thing." Horace walked through the room with his claws over his eyes. "Just going to the kitchen for a drink of water. I'll be gone before you realize I was even here."

"*Augh!*" Blair screamed as Jake jerked upward, almost dumping her off his lap. He managed to grab hold of her before she landed on the carpet.

"Get out of here, Horace!" Her voice threatened dire consequences as the gargoyle appeared to be peeking through his claws. "You don't even drink water, and you don't need to walk through this room to get to the kitchen!"

"Yeah, well, if I were you, I'd tell Stasi I want my money back on that push up bra. It does nothing for you." He scurried into the kitchen before she could retaliate and made sure to leave the kitchen via the other doorway that led down the hall to the bedrooms.

Jake breathed in sharply through his nostrils. "At least he didn't come in a few minutes earlier. Or did he?"

"That's one thing I'll find out in the morning, and he'll be one sorry gargoyle if he did."

Jake had never felt closer to Blair, but the mood had been broken, and this probably wasn't the time to see if Blair truly could accept his animal nature the way she claimed she could.

"I'd better go." He stood up, setting Blair on her feet. "Ted dropped off the lumber for the booths and I want to get an early start setting them up tomorrow. Are you coming out to help paint?"

"Stasi and I will be there," she promised.

She didn't try to argue, just followed him to the back door, where he grabbed his jacket off the coat rack and stepped outside. He turned back and brushed the back of his fingers down her cheek.

"You're making me crazy, you know that, don't you?"

Her blue-green eyes glinted with humor. "Welcome to the club."

Jake was going to leave her with only a light kiss on the lips, but the minute his mouth covered hers he knew it wasn't to be. Their kiss threatened to start the fireworks all over again until Blair moved back a step.

"Good night, hexy," he murmured, gently pushing her back into the kitchen and closing the door.

"Hexy?"

Blair turned to face her best friend, who stood just inside the kitchen. "Seems he likes calling me a hexster."

Stasi grinned. "Oh, that's very cute. I went ahead and wallmailed Ebenezer and left him a message that the order still stands on the land up here not being for sale, no matter what price anyone offers."

"If they're smart they won't try to bully him. He loves nothing more than going toe-to-toe with the Were community." Blair switched off the lights and they headed down the hallway together, parting at their bedroom doors. Blair went inside to her private sanctuary.

With the chill in the air, Blair opted for a pair of lilac fleece pajama pants and matching sweatshirt top. She noticed the glow in her eyes as she brushed her teeth and washed her face.

"Too bad he's not still here to keep this glow going." She headed for her bed and shivered at the feel of the cold sheets.

"Can I sleep in here?" Horace called out, opening the door a crack and peeking in. "Stasi's talking to Trev again and even a silence spell isn't working tonight."

"I thought you adored phone sex," she teased, nodding that he could enter.

"Yeah, but only when it's me doing it." He walked in and hopped up to sit on the end of the bed. He groomed his horns and sat down as close to cross-legged as a stone gargoyle could. "And I didn't see a thing, I swear." He held up his claws in his own version of the Boy Scout salute. "So can we watch TV? There's a Nicole Kidman marathon on cable. *Practical Magic* just came on." The Australian actress was a favorite of his, and they'd smuggled him into the theater more than once so he could see her on the big screen. He'd been so excited that he not only behaved during those trips, but he hadn't hogged all the popcorn, either.

"Sure, go ahead." She piled up her pillows behind her, ready to watch with him.

If nothing else, watching the cinematic witches and their erratic love lives would take her mind off Jake.

Or not.

It hadn't taken Jake long to realize that leaving Blair was a big mistake for him. Sleep was non-existent; he finally fled to his workshop, where he could lose himself at his drafting table laying out plans for his new project. Even then, memories of her laughter and her taste and touch haunted him.

"Hey poochie!" Blair's shout brought his head up off the drafting table where he'd finally fallen asleep not long before dawn. "Come on out, I brought breakfast."

He almost fell off the stool as he straightened up and wiped the sleep from his eyes. It wasn't the first time he'd fallen asleep at the drafting table, so the aches and pains in his body from the unnatural position were nothing new. He dry-scrubbed his face with his hands but knew he'd need plenty of coffee and a hot shower to finish the job.

Jake left the workshop and locked the door behind him, turning to Blair, who stood near his kitchen door. He laughed at the sight before him. Blair wore a red wool hooded jacket and carried a large basket with a towel draped over it. He inhaled the mouth-watering fragrance of eggs, bacon, and pancakes coming from the basket. Her mouth was slicked with a warm red shade that he ached to kiss off her lips.

"Hey, Red Riding Hood, are you off to see Grandma?" he asked, walking toward her.

"Nope, just looking for a sexy wolfie, and while you may look canine, you do have your *lupus* side." She grinned. "Hurry up. The food's getting cold and so am I."

Jake pushed open the back door and ushered her into the cabin. Thanks to the timer on the coffee pot, the hot brew was waiting.

"I'll be down in a minute." He loped upstairs while Blair unpacked the contents of the basket onto the table.

Jake took the fastest shower in history to wash the cobwebs out of his head and returned downstairs, pulling on a clean T-shirt. By the time he reached the kitchen, a breakfast feast lay before him.

"I'm impressed." He sat down, unsure where to start first. He helped himself to eggs scrambled with bits of green and red bell pepper and hints of onion, along with smoked bacon, and golden fluffy pancakes. There was a pitcher of maple syrup between their two plates, and two glasses held orange juice, which he knew wasn't in his fridge. He hadn't stocked up lately, so all anyone would find in there were some containers with what looked like science experiments inside and a few bottles of beer. He forked up some of the eggs and savored the taste.

"I heated up everything in the microwave," Blair explained, digging into her own plate. "I tried calling you to invite you over for breakfast, but when I couldn't reach you on the phone I figured you were locked in your workshop. I know you won't answer your cell when you're in there, so I thought I'd bring breakfast to you."

"Ginny will wonder where I am." He grinned. "While I do some cooking, I tend to eat breakfast at Sit 'N Eat." Ginny's family had been running Moonstone Lake's popular café since the 1800s.

"She'll survive without your business." She poured syrup on her pancakes and cut them into bite-size pieces. "So, what were you working on in your secret lair?"

"Finishing up a custom piece." What would it be like to see Blair sitting across the table from him every morning? She'd taken off her red coat to reveal a faded sage-green sweatshirt over a striped shirt with a frayed collar that she wouldn't have to worry about while working at the lake today. He slid along the breakfast nook's bench seat and reached for her hand. "You make me smile."

Blair's face lit up as if he'd given her a truckload of diamonds.

"I'm just happy I don't have to put your breakfast in a bowl," she teased. "So are you going to tell me about your new project? I know you've built some furniture and you do a lot of carpentry in the area, but what else goes on out in your secret lair?"

"I build custom pieces," he admitted, now working on the pancakes that he had covered with butter and syrup.

"Custom as in furniture?"

He exhaled a deep breath. This was something he had always kept to himself, but maybe it was time to reveal a little. "Actually, more like dollhouses."

"Dollhouses?"

He nodded. "I build custom dollhouses, and I try to put a twist in each one. I've built English country homes, French chateaus, a Swiss chalet, a Southern mansion, recreations of a family home — but I might put in a secret room, a dungeon, or family portraits that look a bit off. I have a source that creates the furniture and the small figures for the houses, but I do the designing. You might see an elegant Regency-style chaise with skulls for legs or a four-poster bed that's twined with snakes. A collectibles seller in LA sells them through their catalogs and on line."

"Wait a minute! Are you JH Creations?" in her excitement Blair almost bounced off the bench. "You built the house that looked like a cross between a movie star mansion and the Addams Family house? I wanted that one so bad, but your prices are way too high for my budget."

"They're worth it. Besides, you wouldn't want that dollhouse. You'd want something that was definitely you." He thought of the drawing on his drafting board. One he didn't want her to see because that dollhouse was very much Blair.

"I could see one for Stasi as a Barbie's Dream House with a peaked black hat for a chimney. What about me?"

"Modern, elegant, with a touch of Edward Gorey for spice."

"I could live with that; it would mean no pastels. They do absolutely nothing for me."

Jake glanced up at the clock. "While I'd love nothing better than to relax here, I guess we'd better head out to the lake. I dread to think how much trouble the elves will cause if they're out there, and knowing Agnes, she'll put them to work, too."

Blair slid out of the bench and began gathering up the dishes. She rinsed them off in the sink and left them on the counter. "We haven't received any frantic phone calls from Agnes, so that's a good thing."

Jake chuckled. "Or she's locked herself in a closet and refuses to come out."

"Won't happen. Floyd doesn't have the *cojones* to take on those elves and Marva's such a wuss she won't go within ten feet of them without Agnes pushing her." She pulled on her coat and retrieved her gloves from her pocket while Jake got his jacket.

"I put the boards on a sled last night, since my truck can't get back there." He walked around the back of the shed and pulled out a sled piled high with boards and the tools he'd need to put up the booths.

"No harness?"

He shot her a glare that she returned with her most innocent gaze. "Sorry, I couldn't resist."

"Just remember it can go both ways. You start with more dog jokes, and I'll be loading you down with brooms and cauldrons," he warned her, starting off for the lake.

Blair walked past the sled until she was walking side by side with him. "We're more Oreck than brooms, and no way I'd ever try flying on one. That's so twelfth century. Plus I'd suggest you forget mentioning the ugly black dresses and striped stockings. So not us." She looked back at the sled piled high with boards. "How many booths are you putting up?"

"Agnes wanted about fifteen. Some of the high school kids are coming out to help paint them. With all the cold, dry weather they'll dry just fine."

"Oh sure, if they remember to get up at a decent hour. We are talking teenagers, you know. So you've got me this morning and Stasi will show up this afternoon. She'll watch both shops then I'll take over. Felix and Horace offered to watch the shops, but not a good idea. Horace would probably give away Stasi's stock as long as he got a peek at any part of female anatomy."

"You witches sure have your share of oddball sidekicks."

"You have no idea."

When they reached the lake, Blair took a deep breath, relishing the scent of pine mixed with the cold air.

They found a casually dressed Agnes and Floyd along with ten elves who, while they were attired in grubby clothes, at least looked cleaner than they'd been the day before. And when Alberic turned toward her, he didn't look at her breasts first.

"Hey toots!" He grinned and waved the unlit cigar that had been clamped in his mouth. "Don't worry, I'm only chewing on it. We're here to help." He gestured for his friends to help Jake unload the wood from the sled. "We're good at this stuff. You know those cartoons about the elves coming in during the night to help the baker or the shoemaker? Some of us have really done that kind of shit."

"Good." She was still surprised to see them bathed and shaved, and even their pointed ears didn't have any creepy crawlies on the tips. "You... uh... you look really good."

He leaned toward her. "You know that Agnes dame ain't so bad. She makes a fuckin' good lasagna, too. After dinner she sat down with us and gave us the scoop."

"The scoop?" Blair was afraid to speculate.

Alberic nodded. "She was really upfront, even telling us what she paid Mickey. That troll bastard Mickey lied to us about what Aggie's paying him, and that means he should be paying us a whole fuckload more than he is. She was pretty pissed about that and said we should be getting what we're worth. She wants us to stand up to Mickey and demand the money he cheated us out of. She also said we can't look like bums, that we wouldn't be taken seriously as long as we didn't clean up our act. She wants us to call that Stasi chick's boyfriend and see if we can retain him to sue Mickey. She feels we have a good case. I gotta say she's pretty savvy for a human."

"That's something I'd like to see." Blair had never been so happy that Trev was meant for Stasi, because she had a feeling it was Stasi the elves would now latch on to. She tapped into her inner witch to see if there was any guilt or sympathy for her friend. Nope, not a bit. Stasi could take care of herself.

"Blair, dear, you're here!" Agnes tittered, as she approached her. "I'm sorry, the rhyming was unintentional." She pressed her hand against her throat as she leaned in closer. "Could that mean something I should worry about?"

Blair shook her head. "You're safe. We don't always rhyme our spells." She looked to one side of the lake, where a crew of men had been busy smoothing out the ground and boards were now unloaded from the sled and laid out for each booth space. "I'm amazed with the improvement you've made with Alberic and his crew. And overnight, no less. I don't think I could have done as good a job as you have."

Agnes's smile brightened under her praise. "I admit I love to cook and making several batches of lasagna wasn't all that difficult. Actually, I made ten batches. I wasn't certain I wanted to sit down with them for dinner when they invited me, but they turned out to be very polite, with halfway decent table manners—at least, better than I expected. Although some have no idea what napkins are used for, but I quickly corrected them on that," she said graciously. "And the stories they told about their travels was heartbreaking. That horrible Boggs creature sends them all over the country for such little pay and without providing for any type of medical insurance or any benefits at all! No wonder they live like animals. No one's ever truly cared for them before. Those that are married said their wives don't want them to come back."

Blair got a sick feeling in the pit of her stomach. "Agnes, you sound like you want to..." she gulped, "adopt them."

"Oh, no!" she trilled. "But they do need to settle down and feel their own self worth. They can't do that if Boggs keeps exploiting them."

"Then call Dr. Phil. Agnes, these aren't cute puppies or kittens or even a baby left on the doorstep," she reminded her. "They're supernatural creatures. Elves can be helpful, but then they can turn around and be as mischievous as Chaos."

"I truly feel these elves are the helpful kind. They were receptive when I suggested they clean up their RV, and we talked about repainting it so it would look more respectable."

"Brownies love to clean. Elves prefer taking things apart—or building something." Blair winced when she heard boards hit the ground with a clatter and one of the elves shout "Sorry!" "Especially any elf Mickey sends."

Agnes firmed her lips and shook her head. "I think you're wrong, Blair. They were meant to come here, so they could find a new purpose in life." She smiled and patted Blair's hand. "Don't worry, dear. Everything will be fine. You'll see. I know last Halloween's festivities didn't go well, what with so many of us being ill and all, and our Christmas even seemed to lack something because none of us were still feeling up to snuff. But I know our winter carnival will make up for it all. Especially with Roan helping out."

"I'm sure he'll make all the difference."

Blair's sarcasm was lost on the woman, who turned at the sound of her name. "Mrs. Benedict promised to bring out hot drinks and snacks later this morning. Off to do my thing." With a wave of her fingers, she was gone.

"So, Blair, are you going to stand there and look gorgeous, or are you going to do some actual work?" Jake called out.

"Coming." She decided that hammering a few nails might not be such a bad idea for therapy after all.

Two hours later, Blair decided that form of therapy wasn't right for her.

"No offense, but it wasn't my fault!" she told the elf, Jericho, who was bouncing around, sucking his injured thumb.

"You almost broke it!" he wailed around his reddened digit, stuck in his mouth. "Hit the nail, not the thumb!"

"Go back to painting," Jake suggested, walking up and taking the hammer out of Blair's hand and replacing it with a paintbrush. "It's less painful to anyone else."

She stared at the bright blue paint that stained her jeans. "I painted myself more than I painted the boards. That's why you put me back to hammering."

"It's safer than you breaking everyone's fingers." He dropped a kiss on top of her head and gave her a gentle push.

"You didn't tell me this was fast drying paint." She had chosen her oldest jeans so she wouldn't worry if she ruined them. It appeared she'd made the right decision. She sighed and returned to the group of townspeople and elves brandishing paintbrushes on the booths already put up by Jake in record time.

They all took a break when Mrs. Benedict and Mr. Chalmers showed up with thermoses of coffee and hot cocoa and plates loaded down with cookies and brownies.

"You all know how to put on a good feed," Alberic took a seat on the log Blair had appropriated. He sat back, his short legs swinging back and forth as he gripped a cup of coffee in one hand and several cookies in the other. Cookie crumbs decorated the front of his sweatshirt. "This helping out is nice. 'Course, if we were back at the RV we'd be downing beer and grog. Aggie doesn't like us doing that. Most clients would rather we stay out of the way and just come out when it's time for us to do our gig."

"Did you ever stop to think it might have something to do with the way you looked and acted? If you were anything like you were when you first showed up here, I'm surprised the other clients didn't run you out of town."

"Oh, we've been run out of town." He waved his cookies in the air. "More than once, even. They claim we're bad for the children, but we've never harmed one child." He grew pensive. "We wouldn't do that. Children are precious to us."

"Do you have children?" Blair asked, feeling a surge of sympathy for the small creature.

"Hades no! Whiny rug rats with snotty noses, always needing their nappies changed. Not to mention a nagging wife. Just ask Barris over there. He's got fifteen. Children, not wives. That's why he's on the road so much," he confided. "Nice guy, but dumb as a stump. Never stopped to think that every time he visited his wife when we were in his hometown he'd have a new little one months down the line. It took us three days to fully explain it to him. And he still didn't really get it." He shook his head in wonderment.

There was no way Blair was going to pursue that subject. The last thing she wanted to know was the sexual practices of elves.

"But that doesn't mean I don't like the little rug rats. Just means I don't want any of my own." He finished his last cookie and eyed the butterscotch brownie in Blair's hand. "Are you going to eat that?"

She obliged by handing it over.

"Aggie is a strange old bird, but not too bad," he went on. "She and some of the other ladies are making us new costumes for the carnival. She took one look at what we've got and said washing them would only make them fall apart. Plus, she doesn't want us wearing green or red. She thought we'd look good in blues and whites to go with the carnival's color scheme." He looked across the way and watched Agnes direct several men in placing the booth just the right way. "She's a bossy thing too. Amazing her husband stays with her, but I think she's good for him."

"She is?" Blair wondered what the elf saw that she never had.

"Sure. Floyd's not too assertive. He needs her to push him along. And she needs someone to push. You see? The perfect pair."

Blair studied the couple and could see what Alberic meant. Agnes was speaking to Floyd, flailing her arms around, with the man nodding and doing her bidding. Her gaze shifted to the left where Jake was setting up boards. She watched the play of his muscles with feminine enthusiasm and enjoyed the sight of his tight ass under the snug denim as his legs flexed when he picked up boards. She silently vowed to have a better look first chance she got. When he straightened up he looked her way and grinned. But it was the lambent heat in his eyes she felt the most.

"Good thing you two hit the sheets. If you hadn't worked off some of that sexual tension, you'd end up setting fire to the whole forest," Alberic commented. "Hey!" He massaged the back of his head that Blair had just thumped. "He didn't say a word. I figured it out."

"And you were doing so well, too." She finished the last of her coffee and took the empty cup over to the trash bag.

"Ms. Fitzgerald."

Blair tamped down her inner bitch as she turned around to greet the owner of a melting chocolate voice she was sure had seduced many a woman into bed. Even if she wasn't lusting after Jake, she wouldn't even want to shake paws with this guy.

"Mr. Thorpe." She was determined to be polite even if it killed her. Or him.

"Please, call me Roan." He flashed her a toothy smile. "And if I can call you Blair?"

"Feel free. It's protected." She knew many creatures protected their names, with a name that was for public use and one for close friends and family only. She was only too happy to let people know her name wouldn't give an enemy any advantage. She ran her eyes over Roan's pressed designer jeans that held a perfect crease and a dark brown cashmere pullover. He showed no signs of feeling the chilly air, but then she didn't expect him to unless he was trying to fit in around humans. "Come here to help out?" What she wouldn't give to have a paintbrush in her hand right now. Or even that evil hammer that hit everything but the nails.

"I just came out to look things over." He surveyed the lake and the surrounding land.

Blair tensed when his gaze paused at the rock that hung over one part of the lake, where she and the others stood once a month. She shouldn't be worried; the rock held no magick of its own and they always made sure all traces of their presence were erased when they left. Although the lake held special value for the witches, not too many preternatural creatures would be interested, but you couldn't be too careful.

"I'm surprised you didn't fix this up as a tourist stop. Bring in some sand for a beach to use during the warm weather. You could clear out some of the trees and even build a small restaurant and rest area. Of course, you'd need a road to accommodate vehicles coming back here. I don't think you'd want an RV park back here because you'd have to clear out too much land. And that's never good. Still, it's valuable land going to waste."

She bristled at his words. "Land never goes to waste, *Mr. Thorpe*. It gives back when it's well cared for. You, of all creatures, should know that. Weres need the forest for hunting, a place where you can run free. Some of us witches prefer to keep the land intact."

He swung back to her. "I'm glad to see that you understand our need for plenty of space for our hunts."

She knew exactly what he meant and she mentally tossed his words into a trashcan. But her stress level inched up a bit when she saw Roan's attention wander toward Jake. She could tell that the Border Collie Were appeared to be ignoring them as he worked with a couple of men and elves, but she also sensed that he was aware of every movement Roan made and heard every word his brother spoke. She wanted to assure Jake she could take care of herself, but she liked the idea of readily available back up.

"You chose the wrong mountain to settle on, Roan," she said softly, "There's no additional land left for your Pack, unless you can persuade the government to give up what they own, and I doubt that will happen. I hope your Pack likes to ski and snowboard, because the resort is well known for the slopes there."

This time his smile showed more teeth and a strong hint of wolf. "Too bad you're a witch, Blair. You'd make an excellent Were."

"Now that's just being mean."

Blair felt the change in the atmosphere the same time Jake did. Roan's look of satisfaction as he looked toward one of the paths that displayed a new arrival didn't give her any warm fuzzies, either.

The woman who walked toward them looked as well put together as Roan himself and was so beautiful Blair was certain all the men's jaws had dropped. For once the elves didn't utter any chauvinistic comments that would earn them a smack upside the head, probably because they were as much in awe as all the other males around. She had never been so aware of her grungy appearance, tousled hair, and the paint under her nails. She quickly jammed her hands in her jeans pockets to hide the smudges of paint on her fingers.

But then she noticed the expression on Jake's face. He looked as if he'd just been struck with a two-by-four.

Now Blair didn't just feel a tad overwhelmed, she felt sick to her stomach. Jake knew her.

"Jen, over here," Roan called out.

The woman's steps seemed to flow with animal grace as she moved toward them in her stiletto boots that weren't made for the rough ground but didn't seem to deter her steps a bit. Black hair with the sheen of a raven's wing was swept back in loose curls that highlighted lavender eyes even Elizabeth Taylor would envy and full lips glossed in red.

Blair didn't feel any better when the woman veered toward Jake instead of Roan.

"Jake!" The woman's face warmed in a smile as she walked quickly his way and threw her arms around him.

Luckily for Blair's state of mind, Jake didn't look as happy to see her; stunned seemed more like it.

"Another Pack member?" Blair wondered how the beautiful Were would feel if her nasty little paws fell off—literally.

Roan's all-seeing eyes took in her expression and appeared to be pleased with what he saw. "A little more than that—Jennifer was chosen to be Jake's mate when they were pups. She comes from a bloodline as superior as our own and has no recessive genes. Our healer thought mating Jake and Jennifer would ensure he have quality cubs."

For a second she thought seriously about throwing up on his highly polished boots. Or setting them on fire. "Yeah, you wouldn't want puppies instead of cubs, would you?"

"Exactly."

Blair always prided herself on having the last word, but this was one time when nothing came to mind— except maybe to shriek at that sexy Were to get her French manicured paws off Blair's boyfriend or be prepared to lose a limb.

Chapter 11

"THERE'S STEAM COMING OUT OF YOUR EARS." LUCKILY, Stasi had shown up ready to do her share of work and was quickly filled in on the morning's events, including Roan and the mysterious Jennifer's arrival that still had Blair seeing red. After Roan delivered the verbal blow to Blair, he sauntered over to where Jennifer still hung on to Jake's arm. Even if Jake looked as if he would prefer to be anywhere else, Roan looked too smug for Blair's peace of mind.

"Jealousy doesn't become you," Stasi murmured, nudging her friend. "While you look good in green, you don't look good with green skin."

Blair unconsciously touched her face. She was tempted to conjure up a mirror, but she really didn't want to know if her jealousy had done that to her.

"So what's with her?" Stasi looked over to where Jake and the female Were were talking. She was smiling and looking hopeful as she gazed up at Jake, while he just looked pained.

"It seems he has a fiancée." Blair ground her teeth.

"A *fiancée?*" Stasi's voice raised an octave. "That bastard." She glared at Jake with enough force that he started shifting from one foot to the other.

"It's one of those bonds chosen at birth."

Stasi shook her head. "I thought mate bonds didn't happen until Weres reached maturity."

"They probably don't, but this is more like selective breeding on their part." Blair focused on relaxing her jaw. "Something about her bloodlines, not having any recessive genes, and hopefully insuring no puppies in the litters."

Stasi took the paintbrush out of her hand, while Blair actually fought to retrieve the brush that seemed to be aiming itself at the female Were. "Go home, change your clothes, and take over the shops," Stasi said softly. "I'll keep an eye on things here. Believe me, if anything happens I will take care of her… uh, it."

Blair heaved a big sigh. "You're so good to me."

"Oh, girls!" Agnes was heading their way.

Blair muttered a soft curse but forced herself to smile. "I'm heading back to the shops. Stasi's taking over for me, Agnes."

"I thought we'd do a potluck dinner tonight at the town hall to thank everyone for their help today," she said.

Blair's first words were intended to be *no thank you,* but Stasi cut her off at the pass.

"What a wonderful idea! We'll bring a main dish. And for now, Blair needs to get back and play shopkeeper." She gave Blair a less than gentle shove that rocked her back on her feet.

"More like going through my super duper book of revenge spells," she muttered, walking off without another look in Jake's direction. She doubted his *fiancée* would be helping with setting up booths. She didn't look as if she did anything more physical than maybe bring down a rabbit when she turned furry and even then she'd be careful not to break a claw. "Mange. Mange is good. Six months' case of fleas." She walked back toward her home. "Rashes. Oozing sores." Her mood lightened as her ideas turned more creative and downright gross. She was even smiling by the time she reached the building with a shower and a change of clothes in mind.

But her smile didn't last long, because one question sounded loud and clear in her mind.

Jake had finally opened up about himself and his Pack. Yet he had managed to *forget* to mention he also had a fiancée, who, judging by her reaction to Jake out by the lake, didn't seem to have any trouble with his having been away from the Pack for so long.

Or was this some kind of plan to bring him back? And if so, why?

Jake watched Blair leave and judging by the red and black sparks flying around her head, she wasn't in a good mood. Since her skills ran to revenge spells, he feared she was planning something pretty nasty and he could end up the unlucky victim.

"We need to talk, Jake," Jennifer said, keeping her hand on his arm. "It's been so long."

He didn't view her touch as anything more than the Were's need for physical contact. They couldn't go a day without hugging or stroking each other. Well, except for his mother. She didn't like having her fur mussed. He was amazed she'd bothered with sex to have him and his brother. He'd never looked up the moon phase when he and his brother would have been conceived. A Were's sexual hunger grew ravenous during the full moon. Even Jake's urges were stronger then, although he insisted on controlling it. Jake refused to be out of control. He'd accepted that he was different, and he was happy with the life he'd created.

And now here was Jennifer, acting as if their bond was still to be finalized. "Jake, aren't you going to introduce us?"

The lesser of the two evils and if I can get her on my side, I'll live to see the next full moon.

"Stasi Romanov, this is Jennifer Santiago, a member of Roan's Pack," he said before turning to Jennifer. "Stasi owns Isn't It Romantic, the lingerie boutique and bookstore in town."

"Lingerie and books?" Jennifer's laughter was musical to go with her perfect features. "What a curious combination."

"Romance novels," Stasi explained. "Most of my lingerie stock comes from Europe, and I like to match the books to the lingerie. Many of the tourists staying at the resort patronize the shop. Hopefully, that will continue."

"I'll have to stop by and take a look." She smiled at Jake. "A woman never has enough sexy lingerie."

Stasi smiled sweetly. "Do that. I'll take anyone's money." She turned to Jake. "Do you want to show me what you need done?" She held up her paintbrush. Jake automatically stepped back as if he feared the brush would land on his chest, but then he remembered he wasn't facing Blair.

"Sure. Excuse us, Jen." Jake gratefully took his chance for escape and led Stasi over to booths that still needed painting.

"It was nice meeting you," Jennifer called after her.

"You, too." Although Stasi might not have sounded particularly sincere, she still had the polite bit going on.

Jake deliberately chose one of the end booths.

"How mad is she?" He squatted down and pulled out a screwdriver to open a can of paint.

"Think Mt. Vesuvius and Mt. St. Helens combined, and that's only the starting point." She waited a beat. "You hurt her, Jake. You never said one word about having a fiancée. It wasn't good for Blair to find out this way."

His shoulders stiffened. "Jen's not my fiancée. She's the Pack's attempt to strengthen the bloodline. Since my parents came from strong lines, they want to increase it with Jen's family line. They came up with this plan when we were young and it was not my decision."

"If that's what they want, why didn't they match her up with Roan?" She glanced up and noticed that Roan had reached Jennifer before one of the elves had. A low snarl of warning from Roan kept the little guys at bay.

"I don't know, since that would make a hell of a lot more sense." He kept his voice low. "When I left the Pack—"

"Don't tell me, tell Blair," she interrupted him. "Unless I'm badly mistaken, she's the one who matters. If you're smart, you'll find a way to tell her before the potluck; I'm sure Jen will be there along with Roan and a few others."

"Do you think she'll bother to listen before she lets loose one of her infamous revenge spells?"

"That could be tricky. You'll need to be fast and find a way to make her listen to you, but I think you won't have to worry about her taking more than a few strips off your hide." She thought for a moment. "Well, maybe she will. But if you're lucky she might kiss it all better after she finishes. You're the Were. Show her that side."

LINDA WISDOM

"I told her my life was complicated, but she didn't believe me."

"And I'm sure she told you yours is no biggie compared to ours. Okay, I know what to do. Go off and do what you need to do. I'll take care of this."

Jake straightened up and smiled. He pressed a light kiss against her forehead. "Thanks, Stasi."

"Don't thank me. I have to live with her, you know."

Jake moved off, aware not only that Stasi's attention was on him but that Roan and Jennifer also watched his movements. He felt his temper heat up, all of it directed at Roan, since he knew who was the instigator. He felt his muscles tense and begin to bunch up with the anticipation of getting into a pissing contest with Roan. Sensing Jake's fury, Roan flashed a smile that declared loud and clear that he was confident who the winner would be in that battle.

That's what you think, Jake thought to himself. *Things have changed over the years, and you're not the only one who can fight dirty.*

"And you'll be nice tonight." Stasi and Blair chose to drive down to the town hall since they had a large pot of chili and pans of corn bread in the back of the SUV.

"Yes, Mother," Blair drawled with teenage sarcasm for what had to be the millionth time.

"I watched Agnes out there this afternoon and I swear she was in her element. Oh, I don't just mean directing everyone. She's always loved doing that, and we've all let her because none of us wants the job, but I swear she was practically mothering those elves, and they ate it up."

"She was that way this morning, too. If she adopts them, the town will never be the same. Although I have to admit I'm impressed with her getting them to shower and wear clean clothes along with pretty much keeping their grubby little paws to themselves."

"And none of them tried to pinch my butt or even look at my breasts." Stasi parked in the small parking lot behind the town hall that was already filled with cars and trucks, including a snazzy BMW that they knew didn't belong to anyone in town and a few other vehicles they didn't recognize.

Once out of the Explorer, Blair opened up the back and reached for the large pot.

"Blair." Stasi stopped her before she picked it up. "Please remember what I said about Jake. He has no feelings for that Jennifer at all."

"Judging by what she purchased in your shop, she has feelings for someone." Blair recalled standing there and watching Jennifer pick out a couple thousand dollars worth of lingerie. Only Horace's swift intervention had kept her from "tweaking" one of the scented sachets Jennifer also bought.

"Easy to tell that Grady chose the music," Blair commented as Lynyrd Skynyrd belted out "Sweet Home Alabama" from the hall's aged stereo system.

"Personally, I would have chosen 'Animal I Have Become' and see if any howling would come up."

The hall was already half filled when they stepped inside and headed for the long tables set up for the food offerings. Along the way they smiled and greeted friends and Blair determinedly didn't look for Jake. Not that she had to. She already knew he wasn't there.

She would have sensed him the minute he entered the hall.

But Roan was there, along with Vera, Jennifer, and several other Weres.

Blair kept her smile firmly fixed on her face as Roan introduced her and Stasi to Vera, who once again didn't let on she'd already met Blair. Blair was only too happy to keep up the pretense while hearing faint sneers from Fluff and Puff. For a moment she was tempted to let them out, but knew it wouldn't be fair to anyone else in the large hall. The men and women that accompanied Roan were introduced only as colleagues.

She thought all was well until Mrs. Benedict cornered her while everyone was lining up to get their food.

"Is there something different about those resort people?" she asked Blair in a soft voice.

"As in what, Mrs. Benedict?" Blair leaned down a bit, since the elderly woman was five feet nothing and almost as round as she was tall.

The woman appeared to choose her words. "As in, they're like you, but not like you." This time she whispered, although she had herded Blair into a corner so they couldn't be overheard. Blair hoped there was enough background noise that none of the Weres could easily eavesdrop. "I couldn't say this to many, but I know you would understand. Ever since last fall I've sometimes sensed people aren't, well, normal. Sometimes I even feel there's something odd about Jake. Not odd as you two are, but different. And I sense the same with those resort people. And it doesn't feel right."

The last thing Blair wanted was the elderly woman

worried. "Maybe there's just something you don't like about them."

"Well, that Roan Thorpe thinks he's hot stuff, as you girls would say, but I don't see it. Also, have you heard wolves howling some nights lately? It surprised me, because there haven't been wolves up here for years. I mentioned it to Floyd and he almost clapped his hand over my mouth." She appeared more angry than upset by that. "He said we mustn't worry Mr. Thorpe about such things. He wants the man to think it's a paradise up here. Although I can't imagine Mr. Thorpe buying the resort without having done a lot of research on it first."

"That sounds like Floyd," Blair said dryly, positive she was one of the few who saw humor in the thought of Floyd protecting Roan from the possibility of wolves in the district. "I wouldn't worry too much about it, Mrs. Benedict. Ten to one someone's dog got out and was having a high old time in the woods. Remember last month when the Morrises' husky was out and about? And he howled every time Floyd tested the town's warning siren?"

"That's true. Carrie Anderson got the children a dog. Some type of retriever that she lets run wild, and he digs everywhere. I shooed him out of my garden just this morning. While there isn't anything there right now, I don't want him returning in the spring. Maybe that's what I heard, since I know the Morrises are keeping their dog inside." She sniffed, catching sight of Mr. Chalmers, who had been filling plates for the two of them. "Oh dear, he knows he can't eat that. The doctor told him he has to watch his salt intake." She patted

Blair's hand. "Thank you for listening to an old lady's worries without laughing at me." She bustled off.

And that was when the hairs on the back of Blair's neck stood on end and she felt electricity zinging through her veins.

Jake had just entered the hall.

Damn it! Why did Blair have to make it difficult for him?

She had dragged Stasi to a crowded table with no room for him. She had even conversed with every damn person, and Were, in the room except for him. By the time dessert rolled around and Agnes stood up at the front thanking those who had worked out by the lake today, he was ready for a confrontation and the little witch was going to listen... or else.

He waited until she left the table to use the ladies' room and he was there in a flash. When she exited, he grasped her wrist and dragged her out through the back door.

"What are you doing?" She pulled back, but there was no way he was letting her go, even if he had to throw her over his shoulder.

"We are going to talk," he said grimly, hauling her over to his truck, pushing her up into the interior, then activating the lock while he loped around to the other side. He knew she could easily have disengaged the lock and considered it lucky that she didn't. Not that her closed expression looked all that promising.

"Why didn't you tell me, Jake?" she asked quietly, too quietly. "It's not as if you didn't have any chances. Even if it were not something most people would bring

up in casual conversation, you could have found a way
to say, 'Oh, by the way, I'm engaged.' You could have
said it any of the times you were over for dinner. Or
when you revealed your Were self to us last fall. Or
maybe the night you took me to Grady's." The lights in
the parking lot were dim, but the inside of the truck was
as bright as day thanks to Blair's anger. "Or gee, one of
those times we had sex?"

Her voice cut him to ribbons and he knew he
deserved it.

"There was no reason to mention something that was
no longer an issue."

"No longer an issue? So the woman who's considered *no longer an issue* just came up here for the spa
or skiing? And she sure hung on to you a lot today. I
thought you told me everything important that night."

"I did tell you everything that was important. Jen
wasn't part of that. She never has been. I had no idea
that she was going to show up here or that Roan would
claim she was still my fiancée, when it's not true. He
obviously said it to get a rise out of you, and it looks like
he succeeded," he said, twisting sideways to rest one
arm on the steering wheel and the other along the top of
the seat. Blair had scooted as far back as she could until
she almost climbed up the door. Her arms were crossed
across her chest as she stared at him. It didn't take an
expert in body language to tell she still wasn't happy
with his explanation.

But now he realized there was no more anger in her
eyes. There was hurt. And he knew he was the one who
had put it there.

"The families spoke of a bonding match when the

time came; it was one of those unspoken agreements that when Jen and I reached maturity we would become mates. But I knew I didn't feel anything toward Jen other than the affection I'd feel for a sister, although her interest in me was stronger than that. I couldn't understand that since I wasn't exactly prime match material. Personally, I don't think she loved me as much as the idea of loving someone who was an outcast. Being enthralled by a bad boy. Because I wanted to do the right thing, Jen was the first to know when I decided to leave the Pack," he said slowly. "She even offered to leave with me, but even if I had loved her, I wouldn't have allowed it. She's the type that needs the Pack. I don't."

Blair relaxed, but only a bit. "If she's up here, that means they want you back in the Pack. Why?"

He shook his head. "I don't know and I don't care, because I have no desire to return. I can't believe Roan would want me back, even if I'm no threat to his position. Vera sure wouldn't and I wouldn't be surprised if she doesn't have her own agenda in all this. The only woman who has my attention is the one sitting across from me." He raised his hand to her cheek. She lifted her hand to cover his with her own.

"I have a temper."

He grinned. "I know."

"I was going to give you an oozing rash."

"I was afraid of that."

"She's very beautiful."

He gazed deeply into her eyes. "She's not you."

"Oh, puppy, you just said the right words." Blair threw herself against him. He was lucky the door was secure or they would have tumbled to the ground.

Jake grasped her face and brought her to him, kissing her deeply and with the hunger of a man who needed a Blair fix. He nudged her lips apart and swept his tongue, relishing her taste, inhaling the jasmine and vanilla fragrance that wafted from her warm skin with the sharper tang that announced her arousal. Her moan, traveling up from deep in her throat, assured him there was no vengeance on her mind, just old-fashioned desire. She inclined her head enough to nip his throat before she returned to his mouth, while she tunneled her hands under his shirt to circle his nipples and pinch them hard enough he felt it all the way down to his cock, which was trying to stand at attention even if his jeans were in the way. While he devoured her mouth, he blindly fumbled with his fly, almost tearing off the metal buttons as he tore it open. She shifted around to push down his jeans while he worked on her jeans. The scarlet ribbons tied in a delicate bow on her hips were a surprise, but he wasted no time loosening them and pushing her scanty panties down.

"I've only ever truly wanted you," he growled, gripping her hips and pulling her down on him.

She hissed with delight and threw her head back as she wiggled until she was firmly seated on his hips. She made short work of pulling off her sweater and camisole and each rocking of her hips sent shock waves through his body.

Jake already knew that sex with Blair was incredible, but what was going on now was even hotter and wilder. He ignored the steering wheel jammed in his side and the gearshift that could seriously ruin the moment if they weren't careful. He ignored the thought that someone could walk out into the parking lot at any time, although their body heat had steamed up the windows so that he assumed no one would be able to see in.

"No one can see in or even sense what we're doing," Blair breathed in his ear, nipping his lobe with her tiny sharp teeth.

His laughter rumbled up his chest. "A bit of your hexy doing again?"

"Of course." She ran her nails down his chest, scoring lightly around his nipples. "I want to be mad at you." She kissed him again, tasting him, offering her flavor in return as she moved her hips in a rhythm that brought shock waves through both of their bodies.

"I want to fuck you until the world knows you're mine."

She pressed down hard with her hips as she leaned toward him. "No reason to do that when I'm already yours. But I won't stop you from doing it again. At least we won't have to worry about Horace showing up." The rocking of her hips increased in tempo until she felt the fire build hot and fast within her. Jake's hold on her body kept the intensity strong and before she knew it, they both exploded. If he hadn't been holding on to her, she would have slid off him and the seat.

Blair collapsed on top of Jake, struggling to catch her breath.

"At least we didn't shatter any windows," she said.

Jake wanted to remain there, with Blair wrapped in his arms, but he knew even with her masking spell they couldn't stay there forever. As if she knew it too, she slowly straightened up and pulled up her jeans without bothering to fix her panties and pulled down her sweater while Jake rearranged his clothing. A moment later he helped her out of the truck and she looked as neat and tidy as she had when she had first arrived at the hall. He wanted to drag her back into the truck and recreate every second spent there.

When she started back for the building, Jake pulled on her hand. "There are those in there who will know what we did out here."

She knew exactly who he meant. Once they went back inside, the Weres with their supernatural sense of smell would have no doubt that she and Jake had engaged in wild screaming sex out here.

Her face glowed from a combination of sex and devilish behavior. "Exactly."

"How did they leave the hall without anyone noticing?" Blair grumbled as she and Stasi went through their kitchen with Jake following them.

"Who cares?" Stasi directed Jake to set the pot and corn bread pan in the sink. As usual, they hadn't brought back a speck of food. "It's not nice to gloat, Blair. Especially about having sex in the parking lot." She patted Jake on the shoulder. "No, she didn't tell me. Her self-satisfied smile said it all, and I'm pretty sure all the elves knew, too."

"Maybe next time we should just put up a sign to announce it to everyone," he drawled.

"Nah, more fun to let them guess." Blair grinned.

"I'm off to bed." Stasi wiggled her fingers at them and headed down the hallway with Bogie floating after her. "Good night, you two."

"Now, where were we?" Blair walked into Jake's

arms for his kiss. But it was sadly short-lived. The lamp in the room suddenly flashed red.

"Someone's breached our wards." Blair moved toward the back door, but Jake pulled on her arm to stop her.

"Stay in your room, Stasi," he called out. "I'll take care of this," he told Blair firmly.

Jake's nostrils flared as a familiar scent reached him while Blair whispered the words to stop the flashing lights.

"You know who it is, don't you?" She followed him to the back door, which he pulled open with more force than necessary and stepped out onto the landing. "Jake?"

Blair stood on her tiptoes behind him and looked over his shoulder. "You have got to be kidding me. It's not even a full moon and they're out there?" Anger mixed with magick sent painful heated prickles through Jake's body.

When she started to step around him, he pushed her back, keeping one restraining hand on her hip to keep her in place even as she practically bounced up and down on her toes.

About fifteen wolves sat in a half circle in the yard below. The largest wolf was all black, while the others were varied shades of gray, silver, and white. One female wolf peered up at them with large, dark lavender eyes. The black wolf stood up and stepped forward. While he didn't make a sound, his entire body seemed to throb with menace.

"Do not even think about it." Blair shoved by Jake, succeeding this time because she pushed magick through her hands so he couldn't stop her. It was sheer willpower that kept him on his feet. She moved to the railing and curled her fingers over the wood as she leaned over to look the Alpha wolf squarely in the eye. A deliberate action—it wasn't done to a Were unless you were willing to fight, and Blair preferred to think of herself as more of a lover type. But she wanted to make sure the Were got the message loud and clear. "You are in *my* territory now, wolf, and you are here uninvited, I might add. You have insulted me by coming to my door. So do us both a favor and leave."

"Very subtle, Blair," Jake muttered.

"I'd rather shoot witchflame at them, so don't talk subtle to me. I mean it, Roan. Return to the resort. Return to your territory."

The Alpha looked up at her and bared his teeth as his fur bristled with anger.

Jake's hackles rose in response, a growl sounding from deep within his chest. This time he was able to move forward and keep Blair slightly behind him.

"I fight my own battles, Jake," she whispered. "This is my home."

"We're in this together."

Blair flashed a smile that was just as feral as the wolves.' "The odds are in our favor."

Blair didn't need a translator to know that Roan was trying to intimidate her. To show her that he could come to her home any time he chose. Bringing other wolves with him was nothing more than more terrorization. She was so glad they didn't know that it wouldn't work with her.

She didn't have to raise her voice, but she did so deliberately. "You think you can move in here and take over, but it won't happen if I have anything to say about it." She drew on her power, feeling it wrap around her and flash through her veins, crackling from her hair that flew around her face even with no breeze in the air, and dancing over her skin. "I'll make you a deal. You stay on your property and we'll stay on ours, and never the twain shall meet."

The Alpha wolf stared at them for several long moments before slowly turning away and walking off. One by one, the wolves followed him.

Blair watched them leave, feeling the tension still tight in her muscles and also in Jake's.

"He doesn't give up—and if I'm not mistaken, you pissed him off," Jake said quietly.

Blair finally released the breath she'd been holding. "I know, although you seemed to give as good you got, too." She returned to the warmth of the kitchen, Jake following her, and closing the door after himself.

"What is going on?" Stasi burst into the kitchen, a frazzled Bogie and Horace on her heels.

"We had unwanted visitors." Blair started rummaging through the cabinets. "Don't we have some brownies somewhere?"

"That bad, huh?" Stasi glanced at Jake. "She goes chocolate crazy during times of stress. What happened out there?"

"Members of Jake's former Pack showed up looking all big and mean. Yeah, like that would worry me." Not finding any brownies, Blair settled for pulling out a box of brownie mix along with a bowl and mixing spoon. She soon had the brownie batter mixed up and poured into a pan, and waited impatiently for the oven to preheat.

"And you were mad at me for 'ruining the moment.'" Horace used his claws to make quotation marks.

Jake couldn't stay still. He needed to get out there,

shift, and run. While he was at it, he'd make sure the wolves had returned to the resort.

"I'd better get going," he said, reaching for his jacket that hung on the rack by the door.

Blair shot him a sharp glance. "Are you sure it's safe?"

"Of course," he lied. The last thing he wanted was for her to follow him.

Blair started to raise a hand with color warming her fingertips, but Jake shook his head. "I don't need a protection spell, Blair. I'll be fine," he assured her. He walked over, kissed her warmly, and slipped out the door.

"So sweet." Stasi dug through the refrigerator for a bottle of wine and then pulled out two glasses.

"Could have gone way beyond sweet until Roan and his motley crew showed up and ruined everything," Blair grumbled.

She resumed searching the cabinets. "Do we need frosting? Of course we do," she answered her own question as she found the powdered sugar, cocoa, and vanilla. She turned to find Stasi seated at the table, two glasses of wine in front of her. Stasi was leaning forward, gazing at her, her chin resting in her cupped hand. "What?"

"I'm just looking."

"Looking for what?"

"Red hearts dancing over your head."

Stasi's teasing comment hit Blair like a ton of bricks aimed right at the chest. Her mouth gaped open like a fish then suddenly snapped shut as she realized she couldn't breathe. She bent over, her hands on her knees, as she struggled to fill her suddenly non-working lungs. The idea of seeing red hearts over Jake's head slammed through her mind, and she just knew that Stasi would see it as perfect payback for all the teasing Blair handed out when the hearts were part of Stasi and Trev. She resisted the temptation to conjure up a mirror to make sure her head was heart-free. She had very strong feelings for Jake, but had they gone that far?

Stasi leapt up and searched through the drawers for a paper bag, which she clapped over Blair's mouth and nose. "Breathe slowly," she ordered, keeping the bag secure.

Blair blinked rapidly, watching the multi-colored spots dance before her eyes.

"Not funny!" she wheezed.

"Who was being funny? All anyone has to do is look at your face to know the truth. Same with Jake, even if he's more reluctant to admit it. You two just didn't end up with the mamboing hearts." Stasi's smile broadened. "It's so nice to see someone in the same predicament."

"Except you weren't interested in Trev at the beginning."

"I was, but I didn't want to admit it because of the lawsuit." She suddenly giggled. "Oh, this is going to be fun."

"Oh sure, except this time we're up against a bunch of nasty Weres, including the champion bitch of all time." Blair shoved the pan into the oven and set the timer. "Doesn't matter. They won't win."

"We are witches, hear us roar," Stasi proclaimed.

"Damn straight."

Jake winced when he saw the noxious mess Roan and his Pack had left in Blair and Stasi's yard. He should have known they'd return after he and Blair had gone back inside, so they could leave their opinion of Blair's speech.

"She's going to be royally pissed about this," he muttered, heading into the woods, where he shifted to collie form. After he made sure Roan and the others had left the area and weren't going to cause Blair any further trouble tonight, he'd return for his truck and head home. He set off at a leisurely trot, easily picking up the trail. It was obvious that Roan hadn't seen any reason to mask their trail, because he wouldn't have expected anyone to follow them and probably didn't care if they did. Jake didn't intend to catch up with the Pack, but he did want to know where they were headed. He hoped if he stayed downwind they wouldn't realize he was on their tails.

He wouldn't admit it to Blair, but seeing the group of wolves, watching them turn to leave together, Jake had been reminded of how it had felt growing up an outsider in his own Pack. More keenly than he had for a long time, he felt the longing for the connection of running and hunting with them. A longing he'd have to find a way to disconnect again; he would never be a part of the Pack. And no matter what Jen had told him about their match still being on, he had no intention of going forward with it. No reason to mate with one female when another had his heart.

Jake enjoyed traveling through the forest at night. Too bad this journey wasn't for fun.

Tonight he kept his eyes forward and his senses on high alert. He lowered his body, his hackles up, when a familiar scent reached his nose. He bared his teeth and released a growl from deep inside his chest as a wolf-shaped shadow appeared before him.

You want a fight? Buddy, you've got one. Jake bared his teeth, ready to do battle. But the shadow came no closer and before Jake could make a move, a faint pinging sound echoed in the air and something sharp struck him in the shoulder. He yelped and twisted his body into the air, falling to the ground and lying on his side. As his eyes slid closed he saw the blue-feathered dart sticking in his fur.

This isn't good.

Chapter 12

BLAIR HAD GONE TO BED IN A CHOCOLATE COMA, shedding her clothes along the way and crawling under the covers with her pillow snugly over her head. She figured if she was lucky, she could sleep until it was time to open the shop.

"Get up, Blair!" Stasi pulled on her shoulder so hard Blair snarled that she was going to dislocate her arm if she wasn't careful. But Stasi was past caring.

"Leave me alone!" Her voice was muffled under the pillow.

"Trust me, you want to be up." Without a hint of regret, Stasi threw the covers back and tossed the pillow to one side so that a naked Blair was exposed to the morning's cold air. Stasi dropped some clothing on her back and deposited a cup of coffee on the night table. "Get dressed and come outside with me."

"This better be good." Blair shivered in the chilly air as she gathered up the clothes and started to put them on, punctuating her movements with sips from her coffee mug. She suddenly stopped as she realized her friend wasn't smiling. "It's not something good."

Stasi shook her head. "Ebenezer called this morning. It seems Roan Thorpe called him first thing this morning and offered a lot of money for the land. He was kind enough to pass on our 'no thanks,' but Roan said we might want to reconsider our answer. Ebenezer told him not to hold his breath, bless his cranky wizard's heart. Then Roan told him if we rejected his offer, we would truly regret it this time." Blair barely had her jeans zipped up and sweatshirt pulled over her head before Stasi was dragging her out of her room and out the back door.

The putrid smell was the first thing Blair noticed when they got outside. She tried to control her gagging reflex and it wasn't easy when she saw Horace prowling among the brown piles that could be only one thing. It didn't help when Fluff coughed up something nasty and Puff followed suit.

"Wow! This is high quality shit!" Horace shouted up to them, poking at one pile with his claws.

"At least he means literal shit and not drugs," Stasi commented with a sigh, staring at the mess. She pinched her nostrils shut with her fingers. "Ugh! It's even worse when you breathe through your mouth. What did they eat?"

"Those assholes!" Blair exploded. "They did this on purpose!"

"Can we keep some of it?" Horace looked up and asked with longing. "You know, I bet this would be good for gardening, too."

"I don't even want to know what else he wants it for. You better take a disinfecting bath before you even step one foot inside," Stasi told him. "Make it a steam bath."

"Wait a minute," Blair said slowly. "He loves it, so there's no reason why he can't help us do something useful with it. Horace, will you pile it all in some bags for me?"

The gargoyle brightened up. "Sure!"

"Use the small shovel in the gardening shed," she advised. "There's also some burlap bags in there you can use."

"What are you going to do?" Stasi noticed the crafty expression on Blair's face.

Blair smiled and held up her hand, a small hint of witchflame glowing in her palm. "I'm just planning on returning something to its owners." She paused and looked down when Fluff and Puff started chattering away and pointed with their ears. "What do you mean—?" She turned in a tight circle then stopped at the sight of the familiar dark silver Suburban parked nearby. "Jake."

"Jake what? Oh, no." Stasi saw what Blair did.

"Look what I found." Horace had abandoned the wolf poo to head a short distance into the woods and returned with a clump of black fur in his claws. "It's Jake's fur and there's some drops of blood on it."

Blair didn't hesitate to run back up the stairs and snatch up the phone, quickly punching in numbers. Stasi followed. "I got his voice mail." She tried another number. "I know he doesn't answer his phone if he's working, but I don't think that's why he's not answering. Something's wrong." She suddenly got a sick feeling in the pit of her stomach. "He didn't leave all that long after they did. What if—?"

"They wouldn't dare hurt Jake," Stasi assured her.

"Maybe not physically, but who says they didn't find a way to make him suffer." She lightly pressed her fingers against her stomach that was roiling with acid. "I need to go to his cabin."

"I'll go with you." Stasi grabbed two jackets and handed one to Blair.

They took the path that would get them there the fastest and found Jake's cabin and shed locked up tight. Blair pounded on the workshop door but there was no answer. She refused to believe that Jake was in there and ignoring her. They returned to the cabin's back door.

"What locks up tight can unlock with light," Blair whispered, pushing power into the doorknob. Once they heard the lock disengage, she twisted the knob and nudged the door open.

"It feels empty," Stasi whispered, as they stepped into the kitchen.

"Too empty." Blair headed for the stairs. "I'm going to find something personal of his to use for a location spell."

Once upstairs, she paused to look around the loft bedroom. The bed was still unmade from the day before and through the bathroom door she could see a towel hanging over the shower door. There was no sign that Jake had been there in the last twelve hours.

"This is incredible," Stasi breathed, craning her head to look upward.

Blair looked up. A skylight covered most of the roof, and windows surrounded the loft bedroom. It gave the feeling of being outside and she was sure it appealed to Jake's Were nature. She looked around on the nightstands and chest of drawers to find the right item for her spell and was drawn to an agate that twinkled with light. When she picked it up, she felt a bond to Jake, which told her he handled it a lot, so she hoped it would be enough to help her find him.

"I don't want to waste any time." She sat down on the floor and folded her legs under her.

Stasi sat across from her. "If Emma was here she could use her crystal," she said.

"What she does is much stronger than what I'll do, but I have a feeling I shouldn't wait too long. And this should work." Blair felt a weight in her chest, squeezing the breath out of her lungs. "He's in trouble. I can feel it."

She cradled the agate in her palms. "Stone so bright. Stone so light. Lead us to the missing one. Give me the sight. Make it so," she uttered to seal the spell. She set the agate on the floor between them.

Stasi repeated the words after her, lending her own power to strengthen it.

For a moment, the stone remained unresponsive, then a swirling mist appeared on one side, slowly dissolving into a tiny scene.

"What is that?" Blair squinted in hopes of better seeing the scene displayed among the mist.

"It looks like—" Stasi shook her head as if she refused to believe what she saw. "Bars."

Blair's heart almost stopped when she saw the familiar black and white furry mass lying on a concrete floor with the shadow of bars striping the figure. "Stone of light. Stone of sight. Show us more," she ordered.

While the picture was still fuzzy, they saw enough.

Blair's Irish temper was as legendary as Jazz's and right now she could blow as easily as Mount Vesuvius.

"That wolf bastard. I'll kill him for this." She set the stone down gently then jumped up and paced the room. "I have to get down there."

"I'm going with you."

Blair shook her head but Stasi remained adamant. "You're too upset to drive, Blair. Besides, you have no idea what you might find when you get there. Backup is a good idea and you know it."

Blair and Stasi raced from the cabin with Blair pausing only long enough to relock Jake's door. Her mind reeled with all sorts of revenge. Most of her ideas would be illegal among the magick community, but she was willing to put up with thousands of years of banishment if it meant she could avenge what she feared had been done to Jake. And if she was too late, Roan and his Pack would discover just how pissed she could be.

"I went back out there and did some snooping around. I found this," Horace announced, walking out of the trees holding up a blue feathered projectile.

"A tranquilizer dart." Blair felt her mood darken even more. "You got all of those bags of wolf poo ready?" She watched Stasi run up the stairs and return with both of their purses.

He nodded. "Are you thinking what I think you're thinking?"

"You have a problem with that?" she asked even though she already knew what his answer would be. Horace never disappointed her when it came to mischief.

"I thrive in chaos." His dark eyes brightened at the idea of creating havoc.

Blair quickly conjured up paper and pen and wrote something out, handing it to Horace. "Say the first paragraph to get you to where you need to go. The second paragraph will set things off, then read the last paragraph to get you back home. Make sure to do it as fast as you can so they can't catch you."

"And do it right." He grinned, waving the paper in the air. "Thanks for letting me be part of the fun."

Stasi ran for her Explorer and Blair climbed into the passenger seat.

"How could they do that?" Blair exploded as Stasi started up the engine.

"Ultimate cruelty." She aimed the SUV toward the main road.

Blair was positive her stomach was boiling over with acid by the time Stasi reached the bottom of the mountain. It was made worse when they had to stop for directions twice.

By the time they pulled into the parking lot and Blair jumped out of the vehicle, she was ready to throttle anyone in her way. She knew that was an excellent reason for Stasi to be with her. She'd need her friend's calming influence to get through this without turning anyone into warthogs or worse.

The minute they entered the animal shelter they heard the varied howls, yips, and meows from the inhabitants.

"Can I help you?" A volunteer from behind a waist-high counter asked with a bright smile.

"Yes, I was told my Border Collie was brought in here." Blair mustered a smile she didn't feel.

The volunteer's smile dimmed. "A male Border Collie was brought in last night."

"That's got to be my Jake," she said brightly. "I didn't realize he got loose and I'm sure I'll have to pay something to retrieve him. I'm really sorry this happened."

"Um, ma'am, I'm afraid it's not that easy. The police brought him in here because he mauled a child," she said slowly. "He's been labeled dangerous and is in quarantine for now. Naturally, he can't be released."

"*Dangerous?*" Blair's voice indicated just who the dangerous one was. "My dog has never bitten anyone. In fact, from what I've been able to learn, a vindictive son of a bitch lied to get my dog out of the way. So there was no mauling, and I want my dog *now*."

"Blair, if they succeed with this farce of Roan's, the shelter will have to destroy him," Stasi muttered under her breath.

"I'm not leaving without my dog." Blair refused to back down.

"I'll get the supervisor." The volunteer practically ran to the back room.

"We have to get him out of here." Blair's mind whirled with possibilities, but for now her pressing need was to see Jake and make sure he was all right. "And damn the consequences."

By the time the shelter's supervisor arrived, Blair was loaded for bear, but she forced herself to relax and offer a friendly smile overlaid with concern. She was determined not to give the supervisor any reason to call the police because a dog owner went ballistic. Keeping her magick under wraps wasn't easy, since her temper was feeding it.

She waited while the supervisor explained Blair couldn't just take her dog home even if she had the proper paperwork—paperwork that Blair magickally produced when asked for proof she was the owner, including the dog's vaccination papers and a clean bill of health from a local veterinarian.

"Then I want to see him," she insisted. "I want to make sure he's all right."

"He's been sleeping a lot, and I doubt he'd know you were here," the supervisor went on. *And I know why.* Blair silently vowed extra retaliation for the tranquilizer dart.

Luckily, Stasi quickly intervened and with a magickal soft nudge she and Blair were escorted to a rear room.

Blair's heart sank when she looked at the red tag attached to the kennel bars, labeling the dog as dangerous. A sluggish Jake was sprawled on a blanket in one corner of the concrete floor. His chest rose in shallow breaths. For a moment Blair feared she was too late. She tamped down the darkness inside her that threatened to erupt.

"Jake?" She crouched down, her fingers wrapped around the bars.

"I wouldn't get too close," the supervisor warned, but one fulminating look from Blair had her backing off.

"Jake? Look at me. It's Blair."

The dog had trouble lifting his head and whimpered, but his tail slowly thumped against the floor a few times.

"Don't worry, we're going to get you out of here," she whispered low enough for only him to hear.

He whined softly in response, but his eyes were still hazy.

Blair looked over her shoulder and caught Stasi's attention.

I need five minutes, she mouthed.

Stasi gave a brief nod. "Play statues, if you please." She touched each woman on the arm and they immediately froze. "Do it fast," she told Blair.

Blair quickly released the lock and pulled open the gate, kneeling on the cold concrete floor.

"Okay, baby, we need to do something you might not like, but it's the only way I can get you out of here without any trouble." She frowned at the odd-looking metal banded collar around his neck. She knew that Jake never wore a collar when he was in dog form. It was easy to guess it was an unwanted gift. A quick scan told her the collar held enough magick to keep him in canine form. "We'll deal with that later," she said grimly. "But first things first." She placed her palms gently along the dog's side. "Dog so mighty. Dog go small. Come be six inches tall." Jake's body shivered as pink and gold sparks traveled from Blair's hands and covered him. The sparks cleared away to reveal what appeared to be a toy dog that she immediately picked up and gently tucked inside her bag. She took a deep breath and concentrated. "Old dog gone. New dog here. Sit and stay until we are clear. Make it so." She waited until the vision of a Border Collie materialized on the floor before she left the kennel, quickly locking the gate. "Okay."

Stasi released the two women and chuckled as if one of them had said something funny.

"I can't bear to see him like this," Blair said, squeezing out a few tears. "You said he mauled someone and I refuse to believe he'd do that. I'm going to the police and finding out exactly what happened. This is ridiculous." She brushed past the women and headed for the exit.

"She raised the dog from a puppy," Stasi explained as they all left with a tearful Blair leading the way.

"We need to get out of here pretty fast," Blair said as they drove away from the shelter.

"How long do you think the illusion spell will last?"

"Ten minutes. As long as there's no disturbance back there, it could last even longer." She carefully took the small dog out of her bag and settled him in her palms. He lay inert, appearing to barely breathe.

Stasi took one look and pressed harder on the accelerator. "I did something for that 'just in case' factor. They saw a sedan and not an SUV, and they think you were a brunette and I was Asian."

"Wow, you thought of everything. I am really impressed."

"Just don't tell Trev. He winces any time I bend the law—human or magickal—a bit." She didn't hesitate in increasing their speed. "I magick myself out of one speeding ticket and you'd think I'd robbed a bank."

"They put a collar on him," Blair whispered, her fingers hovering over the dog.

"A collar? He's never worn one."

"He's wearing one now, and it's bespelled to keep him in dog form." She felt her temper rise again. "I'll have to get it off. If only he would have let me use that protection spell for him last night! Of course, they'd find a way to get back at us. And what better way than to tranq him, throw him in a shelter, and make sure he's on their most ready to kill list?"

"We've got him now," Stasi assured her. "And we'll soon have him free."

Blair glanced at her friend, grateful that Stasi would do anything she could to help her and Jake. Her friend who once wouldn't break one teeny tiny magickal rule was now helping Blair break more than a few laws, and looked as if she was having a blast doing it.

As the Explorer sped up the mountain, Blair thought of Horace's errand.

"I wonder how Horace did with the poop bonfires?"

she mused, keeping Jake warm within the folds of her jacket. Stasi cranked up the heat and Blair directed the vents toward him.

"What do you think? This is probably the most fun he's had in ages."

For the first time in the past ninety minutes, Blair smiled.

"I hope he took pictures."

"It was awesome!" Horace bounced up and down in his excitement as he met Blair and Stasi at the kitchen door. "Let me tell you, wolf shit smells really bad when it's set on fire. I put bags outside of every door, so they got it everywhere. That Roan dude was royally pissed, too. And I left a bag at the end of one of the ski runs and someone ran right into it!" he chortled. "Talk about brown skid marks," he snickered.

"He enjoyed his task way too much," Irma told them, drifting into the kitchen with Phinneas behind her. "Where did you get the toy dog? Oh no! Is that Jake?"

Blair didn't answer as she swiftly walked down the hallway to her bedroom, where she laid the tiny dog on her bed.

Horace skidded to a stop and hopped onto the end of the bed while Irma and Phinneas crowded around. "Whoa! What did Jake do to have you turn him into a toy?"

"It was the only way I could get him out of an animal shelter that would have destroyed him." Blair's heart tightened with worry as she heard the soft whimpers coming from the dog. She knelt by the bed and gently ran her fingers over his fur. When one finger got too close to the collar, she felt a shock that not only zapped her but Jake. "Damn it! It won't allow me to get too close, much less remove it. Shocks like that could end up killing him."

"Let me see what I can find on enchanted apparel and accessories." Stasi ran out of the room.

"Doggie so tiny. Doggie so small. Doggie grow tall. Make it so!" She lightly pressed her fingers against Jake's back legs and watched while her power shimmered over him and he lengthened to his usual size. His *woof!* wasn't as strong as usual but he licked her hand. As he tried to scramble up, he fell back, panting.

"It's the collar," she told him. "It's keeping you in canine form and it's protected. We need to find a way to get it off. Still, you're out of that shelter. Good thing, because if they decided you weren't dangerous, you would have been neutered and put up for adoption." The dog's soft growl told her his opinion of that. She smiled. "You're safe now. Ten to one you're still feeling the effects of the tranquilizer dart they shot you with. Horace found one out in the woods." Her smile disappeared and anger started building up again. "Thank the Fates my location spell worked." She stroked his head and looked into his dark eyes, still glazed from whatever he'd been shot with. "I'll get you feeling better. I promise," she whispered, dropping a kiss on his head.

She heard the phone ring and ignored it. A moment later the ringing stopped, so she knew either Stasi had picked up or the voice mail had kicked in.

"I bet you're hungry, too." She smiled at the sound of a tiny whine. "That we can take care of. Let me get you something." She climbed off the bed, careful not to jostle him. "Gee, Jake, it seems every time you're in my bed you're in dog form." She dropped another kiss on his head and left the room.

"Man, they did a number on you." Horace could be heard chattering away as she left. "I bet you'd love what Blair had me do this morning. We're talking bags of burning wolf shit all over the place up there. They were running around putting out the fires and gagging at the smell. Most fun I've had in centuries."

"Great, now he'll want to help us all the time," Blair muttered, heading to the kitchen for coffee for herself and to figure out what she could give Jake.

"We have a voice mail from a royally ticked off Roan," Stasi announced from her spot at the kitchen table, where piles of spell books were scattered across the surface. "He seems to think we had something to do with the stinkfest up at the resort. I vote we call him back never."

Blair looked at the coffeepot-shaped clock that perked on the wall. "The shops!" she groaned.

"I called Ashley and Jordan and asked if they could work today," Stasi said. "They jumped at the chance to earn some extra money, so I opened the shops for them and warned Felix to behave. Horace can stay up here."

"He's back there telling Jake all about his big adventure." Blair poured herself a cup of coffee then rummaged in the pantry. "Jake really needs to eat something. Do we have any cans of dog food left?"

"No, but I think there's still some roast beef he could have." Stasi put one book aside and picked up another. "So far no luck in finding anything on enchanted dog collars, although I did find a great spell to look ten pounds thinner."

"The trouble is, it's someone else's spell. We really need to know what they did."

"That would mean confronting Roan."

"I know." Blair sipped her coffee and sat down at the table, pulling one of the books toward her. "Too bad these never have a table of contents." She studied the elegant calligraphy that detailed a spell to change a gown's design and color. "I want to see if there are other options first."

"We could go to The Library."

"Where The Librarian would give us riddles instead of answers. No thanks. We'll figure this out for ourselves."

They both looked up when the phone rang again. Stasi checked the Caller ID. "It's Trev. Hi." Her voice lowered to a purr then turned sharp. "What? They can't do that, can they? Fine, did that son of a bitch tell you what he did? Because there's no way we can allow him to get away with something so nasty."

"What?" Blair was positive this had something to do with Jake, but Stasi just waved her hand at her to remain quiet.

"Their actions have to have broken some magickal law," she argued. "And in a sense, they involved humans by dumping Jake at an animal shelter!" Her expression tightened. "You know what? I'm not talking to you anymore." She clicked the phone off. "It isn't any fun when you can't slam the receiver down."

"What did he say?"

Stasi returned to her chair and sat down, then brought a book toward her. Her golden-brown eyes glinted with fury. "It seems Roan called Trev, stating that we vandalized the resort and if Trev can't 'control his witch bitch,'" she hooked her fingers in quotes, "then Roan would take further steps."

"And wouldn't Eurydice love to hear that?" Blair leaned back in her chair and closed her eyes. "So Trev's coming up here to yell at us?"

"Probably." Stasi linked her fingers together and stretched them out in front of her.

"You don't seem too worried about that."

"Once he sees what's been going on up here, he'll understand why we did it." Stasi glanced at the clock. "He'll probably make it up here later this morning, which is actually a good thing, because he might be able to think of something we haven't. For all we know, a wizard spelled the collar, not a witch. Your call, Blair, but I think we should wait for Trev to get here before we consider going up to the resort. If nothing else, we'd have an attorney with us to bail us out of jail."

Blair looked toward the hallway.

"Go back and be with Jake." Stasi gave her a gentle push out of the chair. "We both know I do better with the books than you do."

Blair didn't hesitate to get out of there as soon as she had pulled some of the roast beef out of the refrigerator. Stasi was right. She enjoyed diving into books, while Blair preferred winging it.

"I even managed to stick one of the bags in the spa area." Horace was still talking. "You should have seen all those female Weres running out of there and not even bothering to wear towels. 'Course they don't care about being naked, do they? I really wish I had taken a camera with me. Or even video. I could have put it up on YouTube. But I guess Stasi and Blair would have taken it away from me."

"You're right, we would have." Blair pointed toward her dresser. "Take my iTouch into Stasi's room and knock yourself out."

"I'm out of here." And he was.

Blair sat carefully on the side of the bed. She smiled down at the look in Jake's eyes that seemed to send her a *thank-you.*

"Why do I feel that's for me sending Horace out of here?" she chuckled, setting the meat near his muzzle. He nosed the roast beef and wolfed it down in no time. "He rarely gets a new audience for his stories, and he's seeing this morning as a true accomplishment." She ran her fingers down his side. She winced when the dog whined and tried to move away from her. She gentled her touch and carefully probed again. She was positive if he had been in human form she would have seen bruises. "The collar must also be keeping you from healing." She chalked it up as another reason for her to go after Roan and his Pack. At the rate her temper was growing, she doubted even Trev with all his wizard power would be able to keep her off Roan. She wasn't reckless enough to think she could win a physical battle, but she could sure do some damage. She mentally catalogued what silver she had in her jewelry armoire. She cupped her moonstone pendant in her palm, watching the stone glow a soft blue and turn warm against her skin.

"Too bad Jazz is off with Nick. She'd love this kind of confrontation," she told Jake, pleased to see he had eaten all the meat. "Same with Maggie. She's fought rogue Weres before and won the battle." She couldn't resist fondling his ears. "But I need to do this myself. I won't let them get away with this. They can't think they can come in here and do what they want."

Garbled sounds from her ankle reminded her that she and Jake still weren't alone. "Sorry guys. You've been pretty quiet lately." She pulled off her boots and socks. Fluff and Puff uttered a grateful thank you and started babbling away.

Jake uttered a soft woof and panted. His back legs scissored.

"Don't tell me. You've got to pee. And I guess you can't exactly use the bathroom, can you?" She held out her hands as he tried to scramble to his feet. "Okay, let me help you. No trying to jump off and onto the bed until you are feeling better. Maybe I could shrink you again and put you in the tub."

Jake barked to let her know that wasn't an option.

"Okay, let's get downstairs, then."

With Blair on one side and Stasi on the other, they helped the dog limp downstairs where he issued them a "don't follow me" look as he slowly made his way to the trees. After a few minutes he limped back to them and they helped him up the stairs.

Blair finally curled up on the bed with Jake lying with his head in her lap, pulling her quilt, with its splashes of vivid cobalt, emerald green, and hot pink, over them for warmth. She put on the TV for him while she read. She was grateful that Ashley and Jordan were reliable and she didn't have to worry about her shop. Worrying about Jake was about all she could handle for now.

"What the hell were you thinking, Stasi?" Trev's roar was heard a second after the door opened. "Do you realize how many mortal laws you two broke?"

"What we were thinking was that we were saving someone important. Take a look and you'll see exactly why we did it."

A moment later they stood in the doorway and Trev, face still flushed with anger, looked down at the dog, who tried feebly to get to his feet then sank back into Blair's arms.

"They tranqued Jake last night, somehow manufactured a story that he was dangerous, and found a way to dump him at a shelter that wasted no time in putting him on a list to be destroyed," Blair said from her spot on the bed. It took all her willpower not to burst into tears at the thought of what could have happened. Jake lifted his head momentarily then returned it to its place on her lap. "That they left their shit all over our yard is the least of our worries, but I figured it didn't hurt that Horace was willing to return it to the owners, so to speak. I used a location spell to find Jake, and then Stasi and I broke him out of the shelter. Whatever was in that tranq dart is still in his system, and I'd say they gave him one nasty beating before they left him at the shelter. He's also wearing a collar that prevents him from shifting back to human form and from healing while he's a collie."

"I looked in our spell books and can't find anything to help us," Stasi added. "Can you come up with something?"

Trev pulled off his coat and walked toward them, holding out his hands. He skimmed them lightly over Jake and stepped back.

"The collar is providing a blanket spell. It's preventing any reversal magick to be used to help him." He frowned in thought. "Are you sure Thorpe did this?"

"Great, the lawyer using the 'innocent until proven guilty' defense. What do you need, Trev? Paw prints? Yes, they did it!" Blair insisted, along with Jake's soft whine. "They were in the yard just last night. I know it was them who left the piles of wolf shit out there, they were the ones who hurt Jake, and they were the ones who tried to have him destroyed without them doing it directly. To give them clean paws, so to speak."

Jake pawed at her, but it didn't stop her temper from sparking around her.

Trev breathed heavily through his nose. "If that's the case—" He held up his hand before the two witches started in on him. "Hey, I'm a lawyer! Let me do this my way. *If* they are behind this, then the case needs to be brought before the Alpha, who will determine punishment." He winced as both Blair and Stasi shouted him down. "I'm trying to keep you two out of trouble! You already vandalized the resort. If they report you to the Witches' Council, you'll be in a lot of trouble."

"Actually, that was me who left the burning bags of shit up there." A smug Horace sauntered in with Blair's iTouch in one claw. "And I did a really good job of it, too."

Trev looked pained. "And who told you to do it?"

"What? I can't think it up myself?" Horace drew himself up, looking as offended as a gargoyle could. "I have a brain, ya know."

Trev closed his eyes and pinched the top of his nose with his fingertips.

"Mae said I should have read my horoscope today."

Chapter 13

"SO WHAT DO YOU THINK WE SHOULD DO?" BLAIR asked, gently stroking Jake's muzzle but keeping a safe distance from the collar to avoid inflicting further pain.

"Other than going up to the resort and turning Roan into a pile of slugs?" Stasi added.

"Too clichéd. I'd rather go for something more gross." Blair continued to stroke Jake's silky fur.

"Fine, let me make a call." Trev pulled his cell phone out of his jacket pocket and left the room.

"When did you stop being the voice of reason?" Blair asked her best friend. "Usually you're the one trying to talk me out of getting into trouble."

"When I realized creating trouble was more fun." Stasi went to the door in hopes of eavesdropping. "He's talking to Roan," she whispered. "He's using his lawyer voice and sounding not too happy. I'm not sure if the 'not happy' has to do with us or with them."

"Probably us," Blair sighed. As soon as Trev returned, she spoke before he could say a word. "I'm sorry for dragging you into this, Trev. This is my problem, not Stasi's and not yours. Right now, Jake is my priority. He has no Pack to protect him, so I hereby vote myself a part of his Pack. He'll never be alone again."

"And me," Stasi chimed in.

Trev looked at Jake. "You are one lucky dog to have Pack members like these two." He heaved a deep sigh. "Actually, make it we three. We'll get this settled without any backlash." He took Stasi's hand and tugged on it. "Come on. We need to talk."

"I'm part of this Pack too, aren't I?" Horace asked. "I did my part to revenge what was done to Jake."

Blair wasn't sure whether to laugh or cry, so she settled for a bit of both. She leaned over and buried her face in Jake's ruff, wincing when the collar zapped her and backing off before it could hurt him again. "You're probably thinking you were better off without us," she whispered. He pawed at her hand reassuringly.

For the rest of the day Blair left Stasi and Trev alone as they sat in the family room and conversed in whispers. She watched Jake sleeping, hoping his slumber would allow the drug to run its course and he'd be more like himself. Visualizing Roan as something covered with warts or pustules occupied her as she did laundry and stopped in the shop once to check on things. Assured everything was fine, she left Jordan to his work and returned to finish up the household chores.

Too bad a domestic routine couldn't take her mind off Jake.

But then, her mind hadn't been off the subject of Jake for some time now.

This totally sucked.

Jake never minded shifting to dog shape and exploring the woods at night or sometimes even during the day, but to be trapped in this form without a way of shifting back was pure hell.

He had been under the effects of the tranquilizer dart when the blows rained down on him. It wasn't the wolves that attacked him, although they hadn't minded taking a couple of chunks out of him, but those in human form who had their own form of punishment. Boots kicked him, fists struck him, and wooden sticks beat him. Silver burned the pads of his feet. They were still tender and luckily, Blair hadn't seen the burns yet, or he knew she'd be after Roan in a witchy second with no holds barred.

The spelled collar felt like a noose around his neck. He imagined it gradually tightening with each breath he took. For all he knew, it actually was meant to do that. He didn't completely recall the collar being fastened around his neck, but then the last twenty-four hours had been pretty much a blur for him. All that mattered was that Blair had found him and used her hexy wiles to rescue him.

What if the collar can't be removed?

"You're going to behave when we go up there tomorrow, right?" Trev was asking Blair, including Stasi in his request as they all gathered in the family room after Trev carried the still weak dog out to one of the large oversized chairs.

"Of course we are." Stasi wrinkled her nose at him.

"Witch's honor." Blair held up her hand.

Jake wished he could chuckle, because from his vantage point he could see that Blair had her other hand behind her back and her fingers were crossed.

"If she's anything like Jazz, she doesn't mean it," Irma said from her perch on the loveseat with Phinneas seated beside her.

"They hurt Jake," Blair pointed out. "If we can't find out what to do, he could end up as a dog forever! Sorry sweetie." She patted Jake's head then turned back to Trev. "Roan did this on purpose. He realized he can't scare us, so he's using Jake as a pawn to force Stasi and me into selling our land to him."

"Can you prove that?"

"Stop acting like a lawyer, Trev!" she snapped. "We should send the elves back up there, but as their grungy selves, not the cleaned-up elves they are now."

"The carnival's almost here," Stasi said. "We can't have this battle going on then. We have to settle it now or at least avert any disasters."

Trev closed his eyes and rubbed his forehead. "I used to have this calm life. And now Mae is laughing herself silly." He stood up and grabbed Stasi's hand. "Come on, witch o' mine. You're going to have to make this up to me big time."

Jake whined his own form of apology and looked up at Blair.

She smiled and leaned down to ruffle his ears. "Hey, I'm going to fix this," she assured him. "And you know I never break a promise." She groaned as the phone rang, but got out of her chair and snagged the cordless phone lying nearby.

Jake rested his head on his paws, cocking an ear to listen in. He could hear Ginny's voice as easily as if she was in the room. And she was asking for Blair's help.

"No, it's fine. Come on over," she told the tearful woman.

She looked down at Jake. "Since I can't go after Roan tonight, I'll settle for second best." She glanced at Irma and Phinneas, who had their heads together, whispering

Fates-know-what between them. She was afraid to ask. "Ginny can't see you two; you can stay here, but please, no trying to interfere."

"Ginny's that sweet girl who owns the café, isn't she?" Irma asked. "If someone's hurt her, you'll fix it. You always do." She beamed at Blair as if she was a beloved granddaughter.

"I'll fix it, all right." She headed to the kitchen.

Jake slowly got climbed down off the chair and followed her.

Barely five minutes had passed before there was a knock on the door and Blair got up to answer it.

Jake looked up at a Ginny he'd never seen before.

Gone was the lovely Asian woman's usual smile and sunny nature he saw every time he went into the Sit 'N Eat. Tonight, her face was splotchy from tears and her eyes were swollen and black from smudged mascara. She walked into Blair's arms for a hug.

"Hey puppy." Ginny stroked Jake's head as he nudged her, offering comfort in his own way. "When did you get a dog?"

"He's visiting," Blair explained. She steered Ginny to the table and sat her down before moving to the stove to fix tea.

"I can't believe he did this to me," Ginny sniffed, pulling out a crumpled tissue, blowing her nose and wiping her eyes. "Why?" she asked, the age old question every woman asks when a man does her wrong. Blair sent a box of tissues over to the table to sit by Ginny's elbow.

With a spurt of magick, Blair had the tea ready faster than a microwave and brought two cups to the table along with a plate of peanut butter cookies. Jake stretched out under the table. He had always been curious about Blair's side business of creating revenge spells, and he had an idea he'd learn a lot tonight.

"Drink your tea, then tell me exactly what happened," Blair urged her, knowing the calming herbs she had slipped in would help her friend.

Ginny sipped the tea. "You know Dave and I have been dating for the past year."

Blair nodded, silently urging her to continue.

"He was even talking about moving up here, since all his business is conducted online." One tear escaped and trailed down her cheek while her nose dripped.

"I never had any reason to think he wasn't what he portrayed himself to be," she whispered, continuing to sip her tea. "I even met some of his friends. We went away a few times for really nice, long weekends at these gorgeous resort hotels."

"Which your mother still doesn't know about, right?"

"She still thinks I'm a virgin, and it's safer to have her thinking that. He even hinted at marriage." Her cheeks bloomed a bright pink.

Blair could easily see and feel her friend's pain, but she knew the worst was yet to come. And she already knew she'd do all she could to help her friend to feel better and see that justice was served. "So what happened?"

Ginny stared at the tabletop as if she couldn't bear to look at Blair.

"Dave and I talked about my ideas for expanding the café when Lyle's lease runs out next year." She mentioned the shop that was next door to her café. "Lyle doesn't plan on renewing it, because he wants to retire and see the country in his RV. Dave's always been very lucky with his investments, and he suggested I set up a portfolio."

"Oh Ginny." Blair knew exactly where this was going, but she knew Ginny had to be the one to say the words.

"It was a sure thing. I would double my investment and have more than enough to expand the café. Except now Dave is gone. Both his phone and email are no good and when I went to his house, I was told it was a rental and he moved out owing six months rent." Ginny buried her face in her hands, sobbing so hard her shoulders shook. "And all my money is gone."

"How much?" When Blair heard the amount she almost fell off her chair. She mentally amped up what she'd need for the spell. "Did you go to the police?"

Ginny nodded. "I used to watch those shows where women said they were too embarrassed to go to the police because they felt stupid at being scammed. I always thought they were crazy to get taken in, and now I'm one of those stupid women!"

"No, you're not. It's all Dave's fault and you remember that. What did the police say?"

"I filed a report and it turns out that he ran the same scam with three other women. The detective I spoke with said if Dave is found I can sue him for my money, which I bet he's now spending on another woman before he cons her out of her money." Ginny sighed. "That's why I called you."

Blair studied her hopeful expression. "You want vengeance."

Ginny nodded. "And not just for me, but for the other women, too. At least I have the café. I didn't take out an extra mortgage or borrow money I couldn't afford to pay back. One of the women did that and she's losing her house. I just can't tell my mother what happened or I'd never hear the end of it."

"How are you going to explain not having any savings?"

"Hope she doesn't ask?" Ginny's sniff held a hint of laughter.

Blair tapped her fingers against the table as she thought for several moments. Ginny remained quiet, only getting up to fix herself another cup of tea and this time taking a cookie along with sneaking one under the table to Jake.

"I can't get your money back," Blair said finally. "That's beyond my capabilities, but I can make sure that no one will be scammed by him again. And maybe even make it easier for him to be caught. And I'll make a charm for you to keep in the café to help increase business, even if it's only that everyone will decide they want dessert or an appetizer at dinner. But I really think you need to tell your mother. Mrs. Chao will probably lecture you for the next ten years, but she'll also be grateful that you and Dave didn't get married, and you can remind her of your narrow escape."

"She'll probably just remind me it would have been nice if he'd given me children first. So you can help me?" She reached inside her jacket pocket and pulled out a bag. "Luckily, I kept something of his when I tossed everything else out." She handed Blair a key fob with a key still attached. "The key is for the house I thought he owned."

"I'll work on it tonight. Stasi and I have to be somewhere in the morning, but I'll come by tomorrow afternoon."

"Make him suffer." Now that Ginny had shared her tale of woe, she was ready for bloody retribution.

"Make all his teeth fall out, or make his face break out in massive acne—or how about he develops crabs? And I don't mean those little ones either, but real ones!"

"Okay Ginny, now that you're starting to bounce back, let's not bounce back too hard." Blair followed her to the door. "I'll see you tomorrow afternoon."

Ginny hugged her tightly. "You are the best. Thank you."

"No thanks are necessary. I'm just glad I can help."

Once Ginny was gone, Blair crossed the kitchen to a bare wall. She pressed her fingers against the surface and whispered words under her breath. A moment later, a click revealed a cabinet door that she slid open.

"Can't have the magickal goodies getting mixed up with the flour and sugar." She looked through the contents of the shelves, pulling out several bottles, and a small stone bowl and pestle. She moved everything off the kitchen table and laid out a cloth before setting out her materials.

Jake moved out from under the table and took up a spot near the pantry.

"And I liked Dave, too," Blair told Jake. "I can't believe that something negative about him didn't tickle Stasi's or my senses. I didn't sense any magick, so he's just a regular conman who needs to be brought down a few pegs." She returned to the hidden cabinet and pulled out a spell book. The leather cover was cracked and worn, many of the pages yellowed and curling. No wonder it was in such battered condition—Blair had started writing her spells in the book when she attended the Witches' Academy in the early fourteenth century. "The key fob will be perfect for directing the spell toward him. Let's see what will provide the best effects." She carefully leafed through her book.

By the time Blair finished with her tasks, Jake had been dozing for some time. She cleaned up the kitchen, then went to her bedroom for some much needed sleep.

She had just started to fall off to sleep when her door opened wider and a furry body leaped onto the bed, curling up at the foot of the bed with nose to tail.

"I really hate Roan," she said sleepily, digging her toes against Jake's back.

"They'll want a proper act of contrition on your part," Trev instructed during the drive to Snow Farms Resort. "You'll have to take all the blame for Horace's actions. Especially since you directed him to go up there."

"They beat Jake and put an enchanted collar on him so he couldn't return to human form and *they* want *us* to play nice?" Blair's lip curled. She sat in the back seat of Trev's new Cayenne. "They're lucky that all I told Horace to do was surround them with bags of flaming wolf poo. He could have been let loose to try some of his own ideas, which can rival Fluff and Puff's." Muffled sounds from her ankle argued that they could have done a lot more damage than anyone could imagine. Blair was wearing all black, including her favorite black patent leather boots with three-inch spike heels, which she felt enhanced her witchy image — and right now, she needed all the help she could get.

"How did you all manage to survive all these centuries?" he asked.

"Very nicely, thank you very much," Stasi said. "We don't like bullies, Trev, so don't even think of trying that tactic with us. Roan is a bully, and I'm not too happy with what he's done, all in his idiotic quest to acquire our land."

Trev turned the Cayenne over to a parking valet, who looked at them as if they were something he'd wipe off his shoe. One fulminating look from Trev's glittering cobalt blue eyes ensured he wouldn't abuse the vehicle.

Trev entered the building with Stasi on one side and Blair on the other.

"Trevor Barnes to see Roan Thorpe," he told the desk clerk, who picked up the phone and murmured into it.

"Mr. Thorpe's assistant will be out momentarily." Her eyes were cold as she gazed at the two witches.

"Guess no more spa treatments or chocolate soufflés up here," Blair muttered.

"I wouldn't even want to think what they'd slip into the soufflé," Stasi whispered back.

Blair was surprised to see Jennifer Santiago walk out. As before, her Were grace was apparent in her walk and she knew the Were's lightweight wool suit cost more than half her own wardrobe.

"Being Roan Thorpe's assistant must pay well." She returned Trev's warning glare. "It's just an observation."

Jennifer's smile turned wary when she saw Blair.

"Right this way." She directed them down the hallway to a conference room where she offered coffee, which they all declined. "Mr. Thorpe will be with you in a moment."

"Making us wait to show who's in charge?" Blair asked Trev. "Stasi and I took business classes when we started our shops," she said in answer to his skeptical look. "She aced the classes. I passed."

"Sorry to keep you waiting." Roan breezed in. He frowned when he noticed the bare table. "Didn't Jen offer you coffee?" He glanced at his assistant, who cringed under his regard.

"Yes, she did, but we're fine," Trev said.

Blair stood looking at the Were, at the arrogance stamped on his features, and felt her temper rising like lava in a dangerous volcano. "Give me the spell to release Jake's collar."

Roan ignored her demand and kept his gaze trained on Trev. "It took my staff most of the day to clear out the mess your witch's minion left."

"I am not anyone's witch but my own! And all I did was return what you left behind on our property." Blair released just enough power to float in the air between them. "Right now I am a pissed-off witch who resents that you intruded into our territory without permission."

"So I was allowed to be at the lake that I understand you two own, but not visit you at your home?" he drawled.

"You weren't invited, and the way you showed up revealed grade-A arrogance. Your Pack has grown and you need land. Fine. Montana and Wyoming have a lot, and I bet you could even find a ski resort for a nice cover up there, too, or even build your own wolfie compound. Just not here."

"We're not Fae, Blair. We aren't being deceptive, as they were last year. From the beginning we have been upfront with you about purchasing more land. And I'd like to add we have no wish to move out of the state. Now, as to the damage done yesterday…" He snapped his fingers and Jen immediately placed a sheet of paper in his hand. "I have the costs of cleanup here."

"Damage? Did you not hear me? You left it in our yard. I just returned it. And it was nothing compared to what you did to Jake. I want that spell." Her power moved up a notch until the air was close and difficult to breathe.

He speared her with a steely glare but she didn't back down an inch. "Pack members play rough."

"Pack members don't throw an enthralled collar on each other. That's cruel—I can't even say inhuman, since you aren't human. Why did you do it?"

Roan turned to Trev. "Did you know she was this much out of control?"

"I'd say she has a valid question, Thorpe," Trev said easily. "I did some research late last night, and I found a very old law that had to do with collaring a rogue Pack member if they were considered dangerous to the Pack. Except that collar left the Were in human form, not animal, which weakened his power. I found nothing about the collar forcing a Pack member to remain in animal form. Nor have I seen or heard any indication that Jake has been dangerous to you since he left your Pack decades ago. Is that why you showed up here? Because you consider Jake a rogue and after all these years you decided you wanted to teach him a lesson? Last I heard, a Pack member can voluntarily leave the Pack, which Jake did, or be beaten and thrown out. It seems all he did was chose the safer course."

"Is that it?" Blair interrupted. "You decided to do the honors now because Jake left without any of you having the chance to beat the shit out of him? You would have thrown him out of the Pack anyway, because he's not wolf. He made his own choice to leave. He made a new life for himself, and he never asked any of you for a thing. I am so glad I'm not a Were."

"You're not helping," Trev muttered under his breath.

Blair turned to the wizard. "Trev, I adore you and I know Stasi loves you, but I'm firing you as my lawyer. Why don't you and Stasi wait outside for me?"

Trev opened his mouth to argue, but Stasi took one look at her friend's determined stance and tugged on her lover's arm.

"Good idea." She pushed and pulled Trev out of the room and closed the door behind them.

Roan studied Blair for several moments. Jennifer remained in the background, still silent but watchful.

"As I said before, it's too bad you're a witch, when you have arrogance worthy of a Were," Roan said with a hint of admiration.

"No reason to be too nasty here." Blair kept her power out in the open, leaving the air heavy with electricity. "I can be bitchy enough once a month without throwing a fur coat into the mix. All I want is the spell. Give it to me and I'll make sure Horace doesn't come for another visit. And let me tell you, if we leave him to his own devices, anything can happen."

Roan took the chair at the head of the table but didn't invite Blair to sit. She chose a seat at the opposite end of the table and leaned back in the high-backed leather chair, her arms resting lightly on the chair arms.

"How did you get the elves to clean up their act?" He deliberately ignored her request.

"I didn't. Agnes did, thanks to her fantastic lasagna and her need to mother, even if it's a bunch of elves. She's in her element when she's in charge of a project and turning those nasty little creatures into clean-cut guys that will enliven the carnival is one of the best things she's done in years."

Roan leaned back and pressed his fingers together steeple fashion as he regarded Blair.

"We never venture into any situation without a great deal of research," he said. "But it seems we didn't do the right kind of research here. We did know that two witches lived up here and owned a great deal of the surrounding land. Still, we had looked at this area for some time and my step-father felt this was close enough to the main Pack's compound, but far enough away that we wouldn't be living in each other's pockets. The fact that the resort was up for a quick sale at a low price was nothing more than a bonus."

"Aren't you the lucky one?" She knew she was tapping big time into her inner bitch and it might not be a good idea since Roan held the spell to release Jake's collar, but she wanted to draw some blood, too.

She also noticed that Jennifer was listening intently to their conversation.

"But after our first encounter I did some additional digging and learned that none of you witches like to follow rules. Obviously, you don't believe in a well-ordered life."

"Too boring," she mimicked his drawl. "The spell?"

"The land?" He cocked an eyebrow. "And don't think about taking this before the Were Council, Blair. We did nothing wrong and we can back up any actions we took."

Blair's brain processed the Were's words and felt her hopes sink like the proverbial stone.

Roan smiled and named a price that was a bare fraction of what the land was actually worth. He was basically holding the spell hostage in return for their selling him the land. Except she still had a few aces up her sleeve.

Oh boy, I'm thinking in clichés!

She stood up while Roan remained seated.

"Thank you, Roan," she said, pleased to see the cautious surprise spring into his eyes. Her smile grew so large her face ached. "You have made this so much easier for me. The good news is, Jake's away from your Pack and I will make sure he's protected against anything you try ever again. He has his own Pack now, and I'm taking the position of Alpha bitch. The bad news for you is you will never get our land. So do yourselves a favor and look for a real estate broker in Siberia." She slapped her palms against the table and walked out.

"Ms. Fitzgerald? Blair?" Jennifer caught up with Blair before she reached the end of the hallway. Blair stopped, curious why the Were was calling to her.

Jennifer looked over her shoulder as she approached Blair. The hallway was empty.

"I didn't know what happened until this morning when I heard the others talking about it. Roan knew Jake would follow him after we left your house," she whispered. "Roan sent me back here. He said he and the rest were going hunting. I had no idea that they did that to Jake."

"Then help me get the spell," Blair insisted. "You must have an idea what they used and how they did it."

Jennifer bit her lower lip. "I—I heard talk, but nothing definitive. And I could be in a lot of trouble if I'm caught." She started to back up as if Blair would overpower her even though her strength was greater than the witch's. Tears glittered in her deep purple eyes. "I'm sorry, I can't."

"Jennifer, please," she pleaded, pulling the words up from her heart. "At least point me in the right direction. Right now I'm willing to steal the spell and never say you helped me. This isn't right. Jake doesn't deserve this kind of punishment. You have no idea how much he's suffering."

Jennifer shook her head and continued to back up. "I just wanted you to know that if there was a way I could have talked them out of hurting him, I would have."

Blair wasn't sure whether to cry or scream. For a second, both sounded good.

"Tell Jake…" Jennifer threw up her hands. "Tell him I'm sorry." She turned and hurried away.

Blair swallowed her frustration and hurried out to the lobby where Trev and Stasi waited.

"Let's go," she said in a clipped voice, walking toward the door without bothering to see if they were following her.

"Magick levels were elevated but not out of control," Trev commented, as he climbed behind the wheel, while Blair huddled in the back seat. "What happened in there?"

Blair ducked her head so she could swipe her hand over her damp eyes without anyone seeing.

"Nothing, other than Roan Thorpe being willing to give up the spell to release Jake's collar—if we sell the land to him." She practically choked on the words.

"I gather your response wasn't what he expected." Stasi turned in the seat and reached out to cover Blair's hand with hers.

"No." She turned her hand and gripped Stasi's. "It was nothing more than extortion and I refused to give in. Jake would have been furious if we had. So I have to find a way to release the collar."

"*We* have to find a way," Stasi corrected her. "We're in this together."

"Why do I feel as if I might need to bail you two out at some time in the near future?" Trev groaned.

"I told you. We covered our tracks very thoroughly when we broke Jake out of the shelter."

"Do not say another word, Stasi! You performed an illegal act," he tersely reminded her. "I'm still an officer of the bar, wizard and mortal. I ought to report the two of you for what you did."

"He gets a bit testy when we break the rules he follows so strictly," Stasi grinned at him and then back at Blair.

For the first time in hours, Blair felt lighter at heart. She wasn't alone in battling Roan to help Jake, and with that knowledge came strength flowing through her veins. "You know what? We're going to win this all the way around. Either Roan Thorpe backs off and settles for what he has, or he can move to Siberia, where I'm sure he'd have all the land he wanted. And we'll get that damn collar off, because I finally got Jake and I absolutely refuse to have a dog for a boyfriend!"

"Is she always like this?" Trev asked Stasi.

She shrugged. "This is actually a good day for her. Sometimes she's worse."

Chapter 14

ONCE SHE WAS BACK IN MOONSTONE LAKE, BLAIR HEADED down to the Sit 'N Eat café, where she found Ginny behind the counter setting plates down in front of hungry customers. The minute she saw Blair, she inclined her head toward the rear of the restaurant while she filled a carafe with coffee.

Blair was barely seated at a table before Ginny joined her, flipping over the coffee cups already set on the table, filling them, and setting down a plate of muffins between them.

"Since I know for a fact that you refuse money for what you do, I can at least feed you," she said, nudging the plate toward Blair, who promptly chose a lemon muffin with lemon cream cheese filling.

"Did you talk to your mother yet?"

"She and my dad left this morning to spend a week at one of the casinos." Ginny breathed a sigh of relief. "She thinks I had a bad allergy attack last night, and I'm wearing so much concealer today that I feel as if I'm wearing a mask."

"You did a great job. I don't see any signs." Blair picked up her bag and pulled out a small, dark-orange silk bag. She pulled open the drawstrings and pulled out a stone disk the same color as the bag. "Leave this under the register. It's nothing major. People will come in and they'll feel hungrier than usual. They'll experience the need to order a side dish or dessert when they normally wouldn't. It will last about six months and after that I can strengthen the charm. It's designed to help the café and not affect you directly."

Ginny shot a questioning look at Blair, who nodded encouragingly. Ginny lightly stroked the disc's surface. "I don't know what to say."

Blair nibbled on her muffin and moaned with delight. "Between you and Mrs. Benedict, Stasi and I should be the size of buildings."

"But you're not, damn you," Ginny teased.

"There are days we worry it will all catch up with us and we'll wake up one morning and find that our beds are broken and we can't fit through the door." She set the muffin down and took a sip of coffee before continuing. "Now, as to Dave."

Ginny stiffened, but nodded and kept her composure.

"Thanks to the key fob I was able to do a location spell last night. I couldn't see much, but I saw enough to lead me to believe he's on an island. And with that I was able to focus a spell on him where he will encounter bad luck at every turn. He'll lose money at local casinos, and he will come under the eye of the authorities, and not in a good way. Who knows, he might even show up in the States again."

Ginny's smile broadened. "This kind of bad luck can turn into a very good thing. I already feel better. I know whatever you laid on him will work wonders, and maybe he'll think twice before he tries to con another woman. The women in this town—and even some men—know what you've done for others, especially what you recently did for Hetty and Jason. Vic is still a jerk, but since that day he's improved his treatment of Jason and his attitude toward Hetty."

"I don't like bullies," Blair said, thinking of Roan and what she'd really like to do to him, if there wouldn't be any repercussions. But she'd rather expend her energy finding a release spell for Jake.

She stayed a little while longer, enjoying the company, pleased to see Ginny smiling and acting more like her usual self. She knew it would take the woman a while to get over her lover's betrayal, but she also knew that Ginny was made of stern stuff and would move forward and eventually meet a man who was worthy of her.

"I'd better head down to Grady's and see how the elves are doing." She said goodbye to Ginny, pulled her leopard print fleece cap down over her ears, and walked swiftly down the sidewalk.

Blair wasn't sure what she'd find, but discovering ten elves swarming over the RV, now painted white, soft gray, and blue to resemble snow and ice, was a major surprise.

Elves 'R Us. Available for parties, fairs, and holiday gatherings. www.elvesrus.net was written across the top in emerald green lettering.

"Hey, toots!" Alberic scampered down a ladder and headed for her. Green paint was splashed across his tiny cheeks. "Whaddya think?"

She stared up at the RV. It looked 100 percent better than the first time she had seen it.

"Is this the same piece of junk that limped into town?"

"Isn't it wonderful?" A paint-smudged Agnes—wait a minute, *Agnes?*—walked around the front of the RV. "I suggested they cut their ties with that odious Mickey

Boggs and go out on their own. Marva even helped them set up a website."

"We promised her no peeing on the trees, no going around naked, no cussing, no getting drunk, and no belching in public." Alberic didn't look pleased with that, but there was something a lot more likable about him that wasn't there before. "And Thaddeas has to stop scratching his balls, which doesn't make him too happy since he's way too fond of scratching his balls."

"Good to know." Blair couldn't stop smiling. "Agnes, I don't know what to say. I mean, I've always known how wonderful you are with organization and getting us to work on your various committees, but this goes way beyond anything you've done in the past. You've caused an incredible transformation in these elves."

"Our website's already got a few hundred hits and some gigs! Our settling in here is the best thing we've done in centuries." Alberic hitched up his sagging jeans. He turned around and frowned. "Hey, you can't make those mountains look like tits! Whadder'ya thinkin'?" He shook his head and returned to the RV where he and a fellow elf got into a heated discussion.

"Settling in here?" Blair wasn't sure she could handle Weres and elves on the same mountain, much less the same town.

"They're very much like children. They need stability." Agnes looked over at the elves indulgently, then fixed Blair with a penetrating look. "What I want to know is, where's Jake Harrison? He's supposed to be helping, and he knows how much I rely on him, but I haven't seen him all day. I was hoping we could finish up with the booths by tomorrow."

"He was called away on family business," Blair lied. "I'm sure he'll be back in the next day or so." She mentally crossed her fingers. "Well, I better get back to my shop. I'm glad to see the elves didn't turn into the fiasco we were afraid of."

"I admit I was very worried when they first showed up considering what all happened that first day, but I'm beginning to see that if you give them some direction, they're perfectly reliable."

Blair looked over Agnes's shoulder and watched one of the elves weave a path between the trees until he faced one and obviously unfastened his pants. Evidently not all of them were keeping their promises, but she wasn't going to point that out to Agnes. She was too proud of her accomplishments and the elves were behaving a lot better than they had at the beginning.

"And they love my lasagna," Agnes confided. "Floyd always feels my lasagna is too spicy, but they prefer it that way."

Blair walked back toward home, deep in thought, mulling over a spell to release Jake from his collar. The first thing she did was run up to the second floor, where Jake met her at the door, tail wagging slowly.

"You look better!" she said with relief, as he leaned his head into her hand. "Feel like coming with me while I check on the shop?"

Jordan, a tall, gangly young man, was just ringing up a purchase when Blair and Jake walked in.

"I sold one of those wooden toy trains you pull along," he told her with his shy smile, brushing his dark brown hair out of his face. "And you got some messages." He nodded toward a few slips of paper.

"Would you be able to work until closing? I'd like a chance to catch up on paperwork."

His face lit up at the idea of making the extra cash. "Sure."

Blair retreated to her office, where Jake curled up in a corner of the room, his bright eyes following her.

Right now, my life totally sucks, he thought. He longed to be able to walk with Blair and hold her hand, steal some kisses, maybe sneak back to his cabin for some private time. Instead, he was lying on the floor at her feet, without much to look forward to besides the beef bone Stasi had promised to bring him for dinner.

Blair sorted through bills and tugged off her boots, wiggling her toes in their thick socks before pulling them off to give Fluff and Puff some air. They immediately began jabbering, but she did her best to ignore them.

Except once she was seated at her small desk, she couldn't concentrate on bills and invoices. She ignored her laptop and rested her chin in her cupped hand, elbow braced on her desk as she studied Jake. He stared back at her sadly.

While he was a gorgeous dog, she really missed seeing flesh and blood Jake. Her anger at Roan grew the longer she thought about the collar around the dog's neck, and she wasn't all that happy with Jennifer for being unwilling to help. She knew it had to do with the Pack mentality. Roan was much higher up in the hierarchy, and Jennifer wouldn't dare mess with the status quo, but Blair didn't really care about anyone's feelings. She wanted Jake back.

"I told that asshole Roan we're our own Pack now, so he better back off," she told Jake. "The bastard wouldn't give me the release spell." Then she yelped as something dug painfully into her ankle. "Hey! Stop that!" She pulled her leg out and glared at Fluff and Puff, whose tiny fangs were buried deep in her skin. "For a tattoo, you guys sure inflict a lot of pain!" Both bunnies started chattering away. She was not in the mood to listen to their rants and raves, but Puff's insistence finally sank in and she listened more carefully. "Cursed." She rolled the word around in her mouth like a sip of fine wine. "Cursed!" She laughed and jumped out of her chair.

"Blair, is everything okay?" Jordan stuck his head through the doorway.

"Everything is fine." She danced around the office then hugged the young man, bringing a dark flush of color to his cheeks. She returned to her desk and retrieved her socks and boots. "I have to go upstairs." Jake stood up, ready to follow her.

"Aren't you going to put your boots and coat back on? It's really cold outside." Jordan trailed after her.

"I'll be fine!" She fairly skipped outside, ran around to the rear of the building, and raced up the stairs with Jake at her heels.

She glanced at the note on the refrigerator door that told her Stasi and Trev had gone down the mountain to do some shopping. She pulled a Diet Coke out of the fridge and a bag of pretzels off the counter.

"A curse. I should have thought of it that way from the very beginning, because that's just what it is. It's not just a spell, it's a curse on you," she told Jake, opening the hidden door to their magick supplies and rummaged through the books there. "If Jazz weren't on that rafting trip, I'd call her and ask for her advice.

Eliminating curses are her specialty, although I'm better known for creating them. I was looking for a way to release you from an enchanted collar, and yes, it's enthralled, but instead of looking for enchanted objects, I'm going to search for cursed items and believe me, there's a big difference. So let's work backwards on this, shall we?"

Jake allowed himself to be cautiously optimistic and stretched out under the table, allowing Blair to use him for a footrest. Bogie hovered around him, half sympathy, half jealousy.

"Curses to trap a being," Blair muttered, leafing through a spell book. "Why can't that work?" she asked, even though she didn't expect a reply. "You're trapped— although, I guess in a sense you're not trapped, not like when Horace was turned into a gargoyle, because you're merely in your other form. Ah, here's one." She munched on pretzels and took a long swallow of her Diet Coke. "Wow, a lot of ingredients here. I hope we have them all. But if we don't, I'll call Stasi's cell and have her do some shopping in town. Some of these I'm not familiar with, so I hope maybe Stasi is, or even Trev." She lightly danced her toes over Jake's thick, soft coat. "This is it! I feel it in my bones." She left the kitchen long enough to get her iTouch and load it in the speakers. Celtic Woman's mellow voices streamed through the room as Blair gathered up the necessary ingredients and made a list of the ones they didn't have.

"I have an idea how we can get the collar off Jake," she told Stasi without preamble when her friend answered her cell. "We've been saying it was enchanted while we really should have considered it cursed. All we had to do was see it as eliminating a curse, not ending an enchantment. I've found a spell that looks as though it will work, but we need some items." She read the list to Stasi, who repeated it back to her.

"We'll get everything you need," she could hear Trev's voice. "Just be ready to work up the spell when we get back."

"No problem." She disconnected and looked down at the spell book and the small glass bottles and jars she already had set out. She crouched down and ruffled Jake's ears. He snorted and tossed his head around, dislodging her touch. "Hey, you wear the fur, you get the doggy treatment," she teased, feeling lighter at heart than she had since this all started. "We'll have you back to your gorgeous self in no time."

Blair's impatience grew with each tick of the clock until she heard the sound of an engine stop by the building and Stasi and Trev's voices.

"We've got everything!" Stasi announced, carrying in canvas tote bags with Trev likewise loaded down behind her. "I can't believe we didn't think of that before."

"Jazz would have, and I really have Fluff and Puff to thank for coming up with the idea." By now Blair was practically dancing on her tiptoes.

"Okay, Blair, take a chill pill, because you're almost flying," Stasi laughed.

"Where's the spell you found?" Trev asked, setting a canvas tote on a chair. He leaned over to read the page, then carefully closed the book and read the title. "You do realize these spells are more appropriate for wizards than witches?"

"And isn't it wonderful we have a wizard in our midst?"

"Could that have been our problem?" Stasi asked, moving over to stand next to him and read the spell. "They used a wizard's power, not a witch's, to bind the power to the collar?"

"And by doing that, they'd think we'd be shit out of luck for breaking the spell," Blair decided. "Except we have a great and powerful wizard. Well, we do!" she defended herself when Trev cast her a wry look.

"Don't lay it on too thick, Blair." He pulled off his leather jacket and rolled up his sleeves. Power started flowing over him, sending his dark blond hair lifting up as if static electricity zapped it, and his blue eyes glowed with an unearthly light.

"Wow," Blair whispered. "I mean, we know you have power, but this is way past cool. I am so very impressed right now."

Stasi laid out the items they purchased in the order needed and stood back.

"First, I want to further examine Jake's collar to make sure we won't be making any mistakes." Trev stepped back and bent down to Jake, who walked forward and lifted his head to reveal the metal collar. Trev's fingertips sparked as he passed his hands over Jake's head and the collar, but keeping them a safe distance from the metallic band. He winced as sparks flew off the collar and hit his palms. Jake whined and backed off, his head ducked down.

"That's what happened to me," Blair said.

"Because it's a wizard's spell that's been layered with an additional spell to deter any witch from breaking it. I'm sure we can easily assume why that was done," he murmured, continuing to examine the collar. "Once it's off I should be able to examine it more thoroughly and maybe even find out who did this."

Trev straightened up. "I'd say the spell you found has a good chance of working."

"It better, because otherwise, I'm going back up to Snow Farms and turning Roan Thorpe and his crew into Chihuahuas that will be neutered before I drop them off at the shelter." Blair's snarl was as dangerous as any wolf's.

"And I'll help," Stasi's grim declaration caused Trev to wince.

"She used to be such a sweet witch, too," he muttered. "Okay you two, stand back and watch the master at work."

Blair and Stasi did just that and watched Trev cover the table with a white silk cloth, set a bowl in the center, then carefully begin to measure each item into the bowl. Wisps of smoke rose up and circled around him before drifting down to hover over Jake. Once he finished, he poured the contents into another bowl and set it down in front of Jake.

"You've got to drink it all down," he told him.

Jake sniffed the bowl and backed off, shaking his head as the acrid fumes assaulted his nose.

"*Drink!*" Trev's no-nonsense voice pushed the dog back to the bowl and even appeared to lower his head.

Jake lapped up the liquid, snorted twice, then tentatively returned to the bowl and drank it—without much relish.

"What binds him will release him. What binds him will free him. What binds him will return him. What binds him was wrong and that wrong will now be made right," Trev intoned.

Blair held her breath, fearing it wouldn't work. That her crazy idea was just that—crazy. It wouldn't be the first time, but it was the first time it had truly mattered. She knew that Trev was powerful; but she worried that he still might not be powerful enough to break the curse on the collar. She felt Stasi's hand slip into hers and grip it tightly, but she could only keep her eyes on Jake.

The mist that had hovered over Jake thickened like morning fog and lowered to blanket him as he lapped up the last of the potion.

Once he finished drinking, he started shaking and fell over onto his side in convulsions, whining and whimpering as the pain gripped his body

"Jake!" Blair started toward him, but Trev grabbed her arm and held her back.

"Don't touch him. You could get caught up in a backlash," he warned her.

She stood there helplessly watching Jake howl and quiver, until his form shimmered and gradually lengthened out, the fur receding and being replaced with skin, hands and feet taking shape instead of paws. His skin was slick was sweat and his hair matted against his scalp. He never looked better to her.

"Jake!" Blair cried and laughed at the same time as he slowly rose to his knees then carefully stood up, still quaking from the spell.

"Wow," Stasi murmured, looking at him in all his naked glory. Trev quickly placed his palm over her eyes, and all her pushing at his hand wouldn't budge him an inch.

Jake was pale and shaking as he turned to Blair. He didn't say a word, but stepped forward and hauled her into his arms, hugging her tightly before he framed her face with his hands and kissed her as if it would be their last kiss on earth.

"Wow for me too," she gasped once he allowed her to catch her breath. "But it was Trev who performed the spell."

"No big. I'm fine with a simple thank you," Trev said with a grin as he held up his hands.

Jake continued to cup her face with his hands and stared at her with a gaze that seemed to warm her all the way down to her soul. "That was for never giving up on me. For telling Roan we are a Pack."

She smiled through her tears. "Trust me, we're a lot more fun, even if we can't grow fur."

"We need to get you some clothes," Trev said.

Jake looked down and grinned. "Yeah, I guess so. We Weres don't have a problem with nudity. Although usually when I return to my human body my clothes come back. I guess the collar took them away."

"I don't have a problem with it," Stasi muttered slyly.

"I do." Trev grabbed her shoulders and turned her around.

"Spoilsport," she grumbled, but she didn't turn back around for another peek.

"I was positive we'd lick this thing, so I picked up some of your clothes in case you needed them," Blair explained to Jake as she brought out jeans and a blue plaid flannel shirt.

Trev bent down and used his handkerchief to pick up the collar, which now lay on the floor striated with charred black marks. He carefully folded the cloth over the collar. "I want to have this checked out to see if there's a chance we can find out who was behind the spell."

"Wizard forensics?" Blair asked.

"Something like that. This shouldn't have been done and charges could be brought against the wizard who crafted this."

Blair reached up to smooth back Jake's hair. "I'll bet you want a shower, too. There's everything you need in the guest bathroom. There's even disposable razors and shaving gel in there." She felt the air in her lungs whoosh out as she looked up at him. "I'll fix you something to eat."

Jake paused long enough to lay his hand on Trev's shoulder. "Thanks."

Trev nodded. "I'm sure you would have done the same."

Jake's footsteps were still shaky as he adjusted to walking on only two feet instead of four and made his way down the hallway.

Blair's legs finally gave out from under her and she sank down into a chair and burst into tears. Stasi wasted no time moving to her side while Trev did what most men did in the face of tears and busied himself with clearing off the table and making sure the stoppers were secure in all the bottles and jars.

"I was so afraid," she confessed. "You and I had looked and looked and it didn't seem anything would work. And now I want to drag out my special spell books and find something truly nasty for the Pack and any consequences be damned."

"We'll think on that one," Stasi soothed her.

"I'd rather do it."

❖ ❖ ❖

While a shower revived Jake, it hadn't eased the fury that had been simmering inside him for the past few days. He wasn't the only one to suffer from the spell. He'd seen firsthand what it did to Blair. How she had worried over him and fussed and fumed, while never losing faith that he'd be free of the collar. And how she had kept sane by plotting some nasty revenge on the Pack. That part he was only too happy to let her do. But he knew that revenge wouldn't solve the problem.

He noticed he still had cuts and bruises, but they appeared to be slowly healing and he felt stiff from walking on all fours for so much longer than unusual. Still, it was good to be dressed and feeling more like himself.

He stared into the fog-shrouded mirror as he towel-dried his hair, then shaved.

He smiled and shook his head in wonderment. "Our Pack."

A moment later his smile dimmed and he knew what he had to do.

He already knew his Suburban was still parked out back and the keys still in their hiding place.

"I've got to run a quick errand," he told Blair after he left the bathroom.

Alarm washed across her face. "What errand?"

"I'll be right back. I promise." He looked into her beautiful blue-green eyes and pulled her against him for a kiss as intense as his earlier one.

"You're going up to the resort, aren't you?" Her fingers dug into his arm, but he carefully peeled them off.

"I'll be fine."

She shook her head. "That's what you said the last time and look what happened. I want to go with you."

He shook his head. "I need to do this on my own."

Trev stepped forward. "I'll drive you up there," he offered. "Don't worry, I'm not going to interfere, but you're still pretty shaky from the past few days." He noticed the darkness flowing over Blair's face. "Jake's right. It has to be done, Blair, and better if you're not there."

"Then I'll drive him."

Jake shook his head. "It's better this way."

While she was ecstatic to have him back, she wasn't going to allow him to go all macho Were on her and think he needed to protect her.

"So the big bad Were and wizard go off to fight the bad guys while the little witches remain home and cook up potions and spin wool?" she snapped. "We can vote now, you know."

"And she's back, in all her hexy glory," Jake grinned, not the least bit awed by her temper.

Jake and Trev drove off with Blair and Stasi watching, the former not happy and the latter amused.

"I don't see what's so funny," Blair grumbled.

"That's because you don't see the red hearts yet." Stasi laughed and ducked the dish towel that came flying her way.

Jake was grateful for the company on the short drive up to the resort. By the time Trev pulled up in front of the rambling hotel, Jake felt in better control of his body and managed to walk up the steps without stumbling.

"I don't need a babysitter," he growled, as Trev walked beside him.

"Never hurts to have a witness." Trev looked around and noticed the small group of Weres lingering in the lobby and the two standing behind the front desk, warily watching him. "Plus, I never like to miss a good show."

"Then get ready for the first act." Jake stalked up to the front desk and slapped the counter with the flat of his hand. "Where's Thorpe?"

The clerk's mouth opened and closed like a gaping fish. "I'm sorry, but Mr. Thorpe is hosting a business meeting. You can always call his assistant for an appointment."

One crafty-looking Were sidled up. "He's in the dining room," he murmured, ignoring the dark look from the clerk.

Jake bared his teeth. "Thanks."

The dining room was almost empty save for a crowded table by the window. Jake didn't miss that Roan sat at the head and, interestingly enough, Vera sat at the other end.

Conversation around the table stilled as Jake approached them. Roan's nostrils flared as he caught the scent of fury in the air, but he remained seated as a deliberate insult to Jake.

"Well, well, look who's here. I'm afraid I have no time to speak with you today—" the words had barely left his lips before Jake pulled him up by his shirt front and punched him square in the face. Roan flew across the room, landing on a table that collapsed under the force.

"Don't even think about it," Trev warned several Weres who started advancing toward Jake. He held out one hand, the palm and digits glowing with a fiery power that would be directed at them if they took one more step.

"Jake! You're acting like an animal!" Vera's face twisted with distaste.

"If you want to talk about animals, look at your other son, *Mother*," Jake sneered before he turned back to Roan, his finger pointing at the Were the way he'd point a gun that he would have loaded with silver bullets. "You committed the unthinkable, Roan. You used your position as Heir to Alpha to bind me in animal form. The best thing I did was leave the Pack, and this was the absolute proof I needed to know I did the right thing. You leave me the hell alone, and you leave Blair and anyone else I care for alone, because the next time I'll do more than just punch you out."

"It won't end that easily, Thorpe," Trev said conversationally. "You made a very major mistake in using a wizard's power to strengthen that curse. You knew Blair wouldn't have a chance of releasing Jake from the collar unless one of us discovered the workings behind it. As a law-abiding wizard, and as a member of the Wizard Bar, I will be filing charges in the Wizards' Council along with sending a report to the Were Council about this transgression. I'm sure that after my report is read, proper action will be taken regarding the offenses against my client."

Roan didn't say a word, but his fury filled the room like boiling acid.

Jake was chuckling by the time Trev drove onto the road leaving the resort.

"We make a pretty good team," he said.

"That we do," Trev agreed. "I've got to say, all that's happened in the past several months sure has changed my outlook on a lot of things. Now there's only one problem."

Jake didn't need to read minds to know what the wizard meant. "Yeah, once we get back to the apartment we're going to have to make nice with two pissed-off witches so we can keep our balls where they belong."

Trev's hands slipped off the steering wheel. "Do you think Blair would do that?"

"Without blinking an eye—and she'd make sure they were dipped in glitter and strung around our necks, too."

"Fine, you go inside first."

Chapter 15

"LOOK AT YOU! YOU MADE IT BACK IN ONE PIECE!" Irma squealed, not thinking as she hugged Jake.

He shivered under the ice-cold sensation and again as Phinneas patted his shoulder, his hand going right through him. Phinneas looked longingly at the four steaming bowls of chili topped with chopped onions and shredded cheese sitting on the table, with bottles of beer set next to two of the bowls.

"So, you were naked when Trev snapped you back?" Horace asked from his perch on the kitchen counter. A smaller bowl sat next to him. "I thought you all did something with your clothes when you shifted. Are the girl Weres naked when they change back? Are there any good-looking ones that like short gargoyles? Or at least don't mind short gargoyles?

"Be quiet and eat," Stasi ordered him.

Blair picked up Jake's hand and studied the reddened knuckles. She arched a delicate eyebrow. "No shifting to heal that before you returned here?"

"I'm holding off on shifting for awhile." He really hoped she wasn't going to withhold food from him now. "I feel like I'm still picking fur out of my teeth."

"Is he seriously hurting?" she asked.

"He was hobbling a bit after he flew across the dining room and landed on a table that broke under him. Smashed nose and black eye, but knowing him, he'll shift fast to heal."

She stood in front of him, processing his words and picturing the scene in her head.

"One punch?"

He nodded.

"I'd rather he would have been slowly eviscerated, but you obviously did some major whup ass, so I'm happy."

"Her love of horror movies comes out at the wildest times." Stasi poured Diet Coke into two glasses. "Let's eat before Blair starts talking about blood and guts."

Jake framed Blair's face with his hands, drinking in her smile and the light in her eyes. "Did you mean it?" he asked in a low voice. "Did you really mean what you said about our being a Pack? You didn't say it just to yank Roan's chain?"

"Of course, I meant it." She spoke as if she couldn't imagine anything else. "And let me tell you, you're part of a very special, very magickal Pack that never derides their family or abandons them. Face it, Jake, you're stuck with me." She stroked his face. "While you make a cute dog, I have to admit I like this face much better."

"And while I'd love to pursue this further, I have to admit I'm starving for real people food."

"Then let's eat." Laughing, she pulled on his hand and led him back to the table. "I haven't had much of an appetite lately, either."

As they ate and talked, Jake looked at the two witches, wizard, gargoyle, two spirits, and an enchanted dog that all managed to crowd around the table like one big magickal family.

My Pack. He felt a tightness in his chest that threatened to overwhelm him at the realization. There had

been loneliness in his soul since he left the Pack and with
Blair's declaration, that sensation had disappeared.

Then he felt silky skin slide over his hand. He looked
down to find Blair's hand covering his in a light touch.

"The elves have totally cleaned up their act and
you're back with us. Talk about a very good day," she
murmured, then raised her voice to tell Stasi and Trev
about her visit to Ginny and what she had discovered
when she checked on the elves, including their plans to
settle in Moonstone Lake.

"See, all we need now is you up here on a full-time
basis," Stasi teased Trev.

"The way things are going, I could use some backup,"
Jake added. "And I don't mean just with Roan, either."

"I know we can't do much except give someone a
nasty cold feeling, but we'll do what we can," Irma
vowed, with Phinneas nodding his agreement.

"You'd think we'd get more respect, wouldn't you?"
Blair said with a long-suffering sigh. "Jazz is going to be
really sorry she missed this." She laughed as Fluff and
Puff added their opinion. "And they're going to enjoy
telling her everything." She suddenly sobered. "They're
not going to give up, are they?"

There was no doubt what *they* she referred to.

"If they can't find a legal way to make your life
miserable, they'll look for an illegal way," Trev said. "I
should be able to slow them down some, since they'll
have to respond to the allegations I'll be filing."

Jake shook his head. "I expect they'll choose the
latter, because Baxter always enjoyed brute force and
intimidation when dealing with his enemies, and over
the years Roan seems to have picked up the same bad

habits. Of course, it's not surprising, considering Vera's made of the same stuff."

"I can throw some extra power into your wards," Trev offered. "You might want some protection around your place, too," he told Jake.

"Wolf traps would work well," Blair muttered into her food. "The big nasty kind that slice off limbs. And we could enchant them to make sure the only ones that would fall into them would be those Weres, so no one around here would be injured by accident."

"Be nice," Stasi chided.

She heaved a deep breath. "My life is so stressful. I thought it was bad enough when we had to contend with no indoor plumbing, washing our clothes in the same creek where we bathed. Rats, fleas." She ignored Jake's wince. "Lice!"

Stasi sighed. "Oh no, she's on that rant again."

Blair also ignored her. "No zippers or buttons. Chamber pots. No central heat or air conditioning!"

Stasi rubbed her thumbs and forefingers together. "World's smallest violins," she murmured.

"Exactly where is this heading?" Jake finally interrupted.

"Nothing, it's just something I had to get out of my system."

"Get her out of here before she moves on to crossing the country in a Conestoga wagon." Stasi started picking up the empty bowls and Trev jumped up to help her.

"Those wagons were torture devices! I thought my back and butt would never recover. I wish we'd waited until they laid all the railroad track from east to west." Blair squealed when Jake pulled her from her chair and directed her toward the door.

"Don't wait up for us," Jake threw over his shoulder, as he pulled a jacket off the coat rack and draped it around Blair.

"You're just doing this to shut me up, aren't you?" She found herself picking up her pace to keep up with Jake's long-legged stride.

"It's time for us to have some privacy." And he knew exactly what he'd be doing with their alone time, too.

She noticed he looked around as they moved down the path that led to the road that ended with his cabin.

"Are you sure you're okay?" She studied him with a keen eye, noticing he seemed much better; but she knew he still wasn't back to 100 percent. "Whatever they tranqued you with was pretty strong."

"I'm fine. Shifting always helps, although the collar seemed to have diminished some of the healing properties," he replied. "Once it was removed, I felt my strength start to come back. And a good meal helped even more."

Blair pulled back long enough so she could shove her arms through her jacket sleeves then quickly caught up with him, sliding her fingers through his. She trusted his enhanced sight to keep them going in the right direction.

"Other than the satisfaction of decking Roan, do you have any recourse for what he did to you?" she asked.

He shook his head. "Trev feels that I do, but Roan will argue he has the right to have me punished for attacking him without an apparent reason."

"So tranquing you, putting an illegal collar on you to force you to remain in canine form, and dumping you in a shelter that intended to destroy you, weren't good enough reasons? When you didn't attack him until after the fact?" She harrumphed. "And I thought we had it bad with the Witches' Council. Eurydice is looking better all the time."

Snow was falling softly when they reached Jake's cabin. He swore under his breath when he realized his keys were in his truck, but Blair easily eliminated that problem.

"It beats carrying around lock picks," she said, zapping the lock and opening the door.

Jake headed for the thermostat and upped the temperature. Warm air soon streamed through the rooms. He fiddled with one of his remote controls and smooth jazz quickly followed.

"Interesting. I figured you more for country western." Blair kicked off her boots and curled up in a corner of the couch.

"I like all sorts of music." He moved across the open space between the couch and the coffee table.

Blair watched him, admiring the fluidity of his body as he paced with the impatience of his Were nature showing in every move he made.

"It wasn't the first time I'd been in an animal shelter," he spoke, but his tone was absent as if he was talking to himself. "I used to tell myself I needed to keep a license on hand, but since I tended to stay away from humans, I didn't think it was all that necessary. Not that it would have mattered this time, since they wanted to make sure I couldn't be found."

"They didn't count on a clever witch breaking into your house and finding something to use for a location spell." She polished her nails against the front of her emerald green sweater. "Or for her to be more than willing to break you out."

"But why?" He turned to face her. "Why after all these years are they stating I'm still bonded to Jen, yet they try to kill me? I no longer have any kind of standing in that Pack, so by all rights they should leave me alone."

"Maybe you're Baxter's secret heir and Roan wants you out of the way," Blair mused. She looked sheepish. "When it's slow in the afternoons I'll sometimes watch the soaps, plus I used to be addicted to gothic novels. Actually, I still am."

Jake moved over to crouch down in front of her. Blair's fingers itched to reach out and stroke the hard muscles of his thighs that were spread before her. After he showered he'd made use of one of the disposable shavers, so his face was slightly pink from the cold air and he smelled of the citrus shaving gel along with the spices from Stasi's chili and just plain Jake.

"Dark, tortured hero, innocent heroine," he murmured. "Well, the former fits."

Blair dropped her gaze, her lashes covering her eyes. "I beg your pardon, milord," she murmured with the appropriate amount of humility. "I only wish to please you."

Jake had brought Blair to his cabin for privacy. Now that they had it, there was so much he wanted to say to her, and he had no idea where to begin.

"You do please me, but not as the kind of maiden that's afraid of the beast within the man." He lowered himself to his knees and pulled her against him. He buried his face in her hair, nuzzling her, imprinting her with his scent while carrying hers away. "You please me with your laughter, your joy of life, and your in-your-face attitude, because you won't allow anyone to intimidate you. At first I felt the best thing for you was to run from you, but you wouldn't let me do that, and I am so grateful you didn't. No one has ever fought for me the way you have." He inhaled the combination of jasmine and vanilla mingling with her own personal scent that guaranteed he could find her even if he was blind.

If you're not careful you'll be bound to her. But then she's your soul mate, isn't she? Why not do the right thing and go the rest of the route? Forget your fears that she'll be hurt. She knows what you are and she's never been frightened.

She tunneled her fingers through his hair. "I'm stubborn that way. So what do you intend to do with me now that you've taken me to your hideaway?"

Jake's face creased in a slow smile. He slowly stood up and gathered her up in his arms. "Let's go find some stars."

"I take it you're not talking Hugh Jackman or Keanu Reeves."

"Something much better." He carried her up the stairs to the loft bedroom and carefully laid her on the bed.

Blair rolled over onto her stomach and watched as he took off his boots and stripped off his jeans and shirt. His skin was dark as if the sun touched it even during the winter, but it was his erection that kept her entranced. She resisted the urge to squirm against the dark gray quilt and instead grabbed a mint green pillow and hugged it against her.

"No pillow." Jake rested a knee on the bed and gently tugged it from her, then stripped off her sweatshirt and jeans but allowed her to keep her bra and panties on.

"Black lace. Very sexy." He pressed his mouth against her shoulder, and then gently nipped the skin, leaving the barest of impressions. "I can see you in black lace, black stilettos, and nothing else."

She tipped her head back, allowing him maximum access. "I'm glad you like it. Although I would think you'd seen it this morning when I got dressed."

"I tried not to peek." His words were muffled against her skin. "But now I want to do more than just savor the sight." He pushed a bra strap down her arm and trailed kisses after it while he worked a hand behind her back and released the catch. "Although more and more I think I'd rather touch than look." He still took his time, dragging her bra across her body and throwing it over his shoulder.

Blair twisted her hips, feeling the heat of his kisses and rough-fingered touch make its way down her body. She returned the favor by burying her face against his shoulder and nipping the skin, then lapping it with her tongue. Jake's moan told her he liked what she was doing.

"It's much nicer this way," she whispered.

"We've got a lot of time to make up for."

"I'm up for it. And it seems you are, too." She wrapped her fingers around his cock feeling the hot, satiny skin throb under her touch. Jake didn't go near her panties that she swore were getting tighter, and wetter, by the second.

"Beautiful." He turned his attention to her breasts, rolling a dusky pink nipple with his tongue until it turned a darker color, moist from his mouth.

"Sexy." She carefully cradled his sac in her palm, feeling the heat come off his skin.

"Mine." He covered her mound with his hand, feeling the dampness through the silk of her panties, her heat, and the musky scent of her arousal. A passion that he knew was meant for him only. He wanted to howl with delight that this witch wanted him as badly as he wanted her, and he wanted to take her with a ferocity he couldn't remember ever feeling. Instead, he forced himself to slow down and make this a night neither of them would ever forget. He slid down the bed and covered the black silk with his mouth.

"Whoa!" Blair arched up against his nibbling kiss.

"This is just the start." This time he slid the silk down and tossed it in the direction of his briefs, then returned to the crisp red curls that fascinated him to no end, along with the pink plump folds that hid what fascinated him even more. He blew gently on the curls then nuzzled the folds, lapping at the moisture that seeped out. He ignored her sighs and whimpers and lapped again, then pressed his mouth against her and hummed.

The vibrations just about sent Blair flying off the bed, or at least levitating, but Jake's hands on her hips kept her firmly in place.

"No fair!" she gasped. "I don't get a chance at you."

"That will come, but not until after you do." He grinned and returned to driving his hexster insane with arousal.

But Jake forgot that Blair had more than her share of tricks up her sleeve, so to speak. She easily twisted in his embrace until she could wrap her hand around his cock and lower her lips onto it. If Jake thought humming against her center was wild, her sending vibrations that thrummed with magick went beyond that. He twisted her hair around his hands as he dug his fingers into her scalp, keeping her head secure as she took him deep into her throat. When she finally lifted her head, she was smiling and she moved up his body to kiss him, their tongues dancing, blending their tastes together, as she sank down onto him.

Jake hissed at the exquisite sensation as her inner muscles gripped him as tightly as a glove and she moved with sensually slow movements that heightened the sexual spell that wove around them. There was no magick involved between the witch and the Were, only the magick between a man and woman who couldn't keep their hands off each other.

Blair felt Jake's body tightening and knew it wouldn't be long now. She increased the rhythm as he lifted the upper half of his body and kept his arms around her, steadying her and kissing her deeply until their bodies seemed to explode around them.

If Jake hadn't been holding her she would have collapsed onto the bed. Instead, he slowly lowered them both back down among the covers and nestled her face against his shoulder. She felt boneless in his embrace and wasn't ready to move any time soon. She was content to lie against his chest and listen to his rapid heartbeat under her ear.

"You can kidnap me and carry me off to your house any time you like," she said finally, feeling the urge to fall asleep, but too happy with the moment to close her eyes and succumb to post-coital exhaustion.

His chuckle rumbled under her face. "I think we embarrassed the guys."

"What?" She lifted her head then turned her head to look down their bodies to see Fluff and Puff hiding their eyes with their ears and uttering whimpering sounds. "Then leave," she told them. "Just get off my

ankle and go downstairs." She sighed at their reply.
"No, I won't return you to Jazz ahead of time. Sheesh,
one of the few times I don't lie and they don't believe
me." She slid off Jake's body and pulled the sheet up;
her overheated body was finally feeling the chilly air.
She looked at the ceiling fashioned of heavy glass. The
clear, star-studded night sky twinkled down on them.
"It must be miserable to heat this place with all the
glass you have."

"Our Were natures prefer the outdoors and this is close
to it," he explained. "I don't get as cold as you would."

"But there's no windows in your workshop," she
pointed out. "Where do you get any ventilation?"

"You didn't look up. There are a lot of skylights that
I can even open if I like."

She thought about the dollhouse and various sketches
she saw there. "Why do you build dollhouses? I mean,
you're a wonderful carpenter and you never seem to lack
for work around here. Come to think of it, why do you
work as a handyman when your dollhouses must give
you more than enough money?" She rolled over onto her
side and propped her head up on her hand.

"It takes a lot of time to build the houses and I have
to pay the people who make the furniture, figurines, and
clothing and any other fabric items in there. A lot goes
into those houses—they're worth the expense. Odd jobs
help even out the cash flow."

"And why you build them?"

Jake lay back against the pillows, one arm crooked
behind his head as he stared upward. "I guess you'd
have to say because of Jen. When I was just a pup, a
lot of the females in the Pack,"—Blair didn't miss that

he didn't say *my Pack*—"were athletic and tomboys, but Jen was always your typical girl. She had a pretty impressive doll collection and loved to put on tea parties. She's a pretty finicky wolf; she didn't even like getting her paws wet. When she was eight, her mom gave her this elaborate dollhouse that resembled a British country house complete with antique-looking furniture and figurines dressed in period clothing. Even then I was fascinated by all the details, the authenticity. I liked to play around with hammer and nails as a kid, so I tried making a dollhouse."

"And?" she softly prompted.

"And my old man said no whelp of his plays with girl toys and he took a sledgehammer to the house. Then he beat me bloody."

Blair stroked his arm from wrist to shoulder then back down again. "Too bad your dad's dead. I'd love to put that collar on him."

He smiled. "I'd like to see you do that."

"Hey, big bad witch here," she teased, nibbling kisses along his lower lip. "I could turn him into a whimpering puppy."

"You did a pretty good job of doing that to me a few minutes ago."

"Yeah, well, you liked what I did, he wouldn't. My da wasn't a mean man, but he wasn't always kind, either. He was a farmer with more rocks than crops, but I can't remember his ever demeaning any of us. No true beatings, but more than a few cuffs at the ears."

"How many siblings?"

She was so quiet he thought she wasn't going to answer.

"Three brothers and two sisters. Another four that didn't live beyond six months of age. My brothers worked in the fields as soon as they could walk and my sisters and I spun yarn and wove wool, which we sold in the village."

"What about your magick?"

"That showed up when I was six; my mother was frightened out of her wits when I lit the fire without using flint. It wasn't long after that that Eurydice visited our cottage and told them what a better life I could have at the Witches' Academy. My da said it was one less mouth to feed and worry about marrying off. So I went with Eurydice that very day and she took me to the Witches' Academy," she said softly. "For the first time in my life I was scrubbed from head to toe, fed a large meal, and wore clothing that wasn't patched. The scholars at the Academy tested me and put me in classes to learn how to control my gift, along with being taught about all forms of magick."

"Story is, you were all expelled."

She nodded. "It was our last year at the Academy and there were thirteen of us. One of us cast a spell on a local nobleman's son, a spell that was pretty nasty, if I do say so myself. Except it wasn't allowed, and since none of us would admit to casting the spell, we were all banished from the Academy. We all agreed the punishment would be dealt out to all of us. To this day, I don't know who cast the spell, and it doesn't matter. The bastard deserved that and much more, so he got off lightly. And we were sent out into the mortal world."

"For one hundred years." He grinned. "I've heard most of the story, but not from anyone who was there at the time.

"For one hundred years—and we could then return to the Academy as long as we behaved, but it seemed our idea of good behavior wasn't the same as theirs. After all, we're still out here seven hundred years later. And I'm glad we are." She traced idle patterns on his chest. "Stasi thinks it's deliberate. That they feel we *should* be out here and additional years are added to our banishment just for show."

"What do you think?" He grasped her hand and held it against his chest.

"That there was a good reason why Stasi was the top student." She snuggled up against him and looked up at the glass ceiling. "A clear night and lots of stars just for us," she murmured. "It's been a good day."

"It has for me." He laughed as Fluff and Puff began to chatter enthusiastically. "Okay, guys, while I can't understand a word you say, I do get your meaning. And thanks. You're awesome."

"Terrific, now their heads will be so swelled my ankle will be lopsided." She tipped her head to one side to look at him. "So tell me, Jake Harrison, are you over this crazy idea that we aren't meant to be together?"

"If I'm not?"

She held one hand up in the air and started tracing figures in the air with her finger. The figures began to move and dance their way down to Jake's lower body.

"Okay!" He almost yelped. "Yes, you win."

"That's better." She kissed him. "The witch is always right."

"I'll make a note of it." He couldn't help smiling, but then, Blair had a way of bringing smiles to his face.

"And while you're at it, make a note of this, my sexy puppy." She wiggled her way on top of him and leaned down for a kiss. Her whisper bathed his lips. "I always get my way."

And she did.

Chapter 16

"So, WE NOW HAVE LIFE BACK TO NORMAL." BLAIR was in the process of whipping up a couple of ham and cheese omelets and had toast browning. She was wearing one of Jake's flannel shirts, which hung to her knees. She wished she had her 1930s hot pink silk robe and matching high-heeled, marabou-trimmed mules, but this morning, nothing bothered her. After she and Jake finally crawled out of bed, her body felt as if she'd been sentenced to a year's worth of high impact aerobics classes. But she knew the internal aches would soon ease—plus they were worth it. Jake was a *very* attentive lover. She felt the smile on her face grow larger.

"You keep that up and we'll be back in bed before you can say 'abracadabra.'" Jake moved up behind her and wrapped his arms around her while he buried his face against her neck. "Um, you smell good."

She felt that liquid feeling again, but ordered Ms. Happy to behave until after breakfast.

"We have to finish setting up everything for the carnival, remember? If it wasn't for Agnes being so involved with the elves, she'd be on the phone with us every five minutes."

"She really did a great job with them." He nibbled on her neck. "Hmmm, you're tasty, too."

Blair closed her eyes and just allowed the sensation to liquefy her bones. "You're very bad."

"Yeah, but you didn't seem to mind last night."

High-pitched chatter interrupted what might have happened next.

"They claim their eyes are bleeding," Blair translated.

"At one point it looked like they were taking notes."

Blair's jaw dropped. She looked down at the bunny slipper tattoo. They tried to look innocent but were far from that emotion. "If you relay one thing to Horace or Felix, I will make your lives a living hell and don't think I can't," she threatened. "Or that Jazz will stop me. She'd probably even help. That bunny jail you were in will be like paradise compared to what I'll come up with." She laughed as tiny bits of paper flew into the air. "Good idea." She used a spatula to ease the omelets onto plates while Jake retrieved the toast and carried plates over to the breakfast nook. Jake opened the café curtains so they had a picture perfect view of morning snow and trees beyond. Blair slid across the curved bench seat and surveyed the food with hunger.

"You know Roan will be there, too," Jake said, his features tightening.

"If he behaves, so will I—and believe me, that's saying a lot." She smiled as he refilled their coffee mugs. "And he better not think about ruining the carnival. This is one of Agnes's favorite activities next to her Christmas plans."

"Don't remind me of that tree we put up in front of the town center," Jake groaned. "I about threw my back out helping with that."

"I'm amazed Agnes didn't think about bringing elves up then. Although she probably already has them scheduled for next December." She forked up her omelet and nibbled away before she tackled the subject she really wanted to ignore. "Do you think Roan will try anything to ruin the carnival?"

Jake worked on his food for a bit before replying. "Honestly? I don't know. He was always Alpha material and between Vera and Baxter he's even more like them. Our old man was bad enough but Baxter made him look like a puppy."

"So what would they do?"

He took his time smothering his toast with razzleberry jam. "Baxter would mow you down… literally. He likes to use muscle. No subtlety at all and it's served him well for many years. Vera's subtler with her attacks. She'd rather find a way to undermine you in such a way you'd be left a shell of your former self." He grinned. "And she's always hated tattoos." His eyes briefly lowered. "She thinks they're low class."

"I figured that when she saw the guys that morning. You know what? She's the one with low self-esteem issues."

Jake almost spewed his coffee across the table. "There's no way we're talking about the same Vera."

"She tries anything else, I'm siccing Eurydice on her. That'll fix her because my money would be on Eurydice. Actually," she warmed to her subject, "that's something I'd really like to see." She glanced at the clock and started eating faster. "We need to get over to the lake and now I'll have to explain why I don't have the dog with me. At this rate, I might have to get a real Border Collie."

Jake shook his head. "Most dogs don't like me. My Were nature bothers them. Same with cats." He quickly finished his food and stood up, taking his plate and Blair's. "I think the only reason Bogie tolerates me is because he's magickal."

"I need to get home and change."

"I'll do the dishes and stop by for you."

"What a keeper! And he does dishes, too." She went upstairs to change into the clothing she'd worn the night before, once downstairs paused long enough to give him a quick kiss, and ran out the back door.

Jake watched her trot down the path and realized just how much his life had turned around.

"The good thing is, I'm in love with a witch. The bad thing is, I'm in love with a witch—because for reasons unknown to me and her I'm putting her in danger. Although knowing her, she'd just dive in and do what she does best and damn the consequences."

"I can't believe we're the first ones here." Blair looked around at the booths that ringed the lake. She smiled at the iridescent snowflakes that had been painted on the sides and front and the darker blue glitter paint that detailed in elegant script what each booth was for. "How cute! These are even nicer than the ones we made last year."

"The kids must have done the extra decorations. They did good work." Jake walked around each booth, making sure they were secure even though he had directed the construction of each small structure.

Blair looked out over the lake. It had been cold enough that a thin layer of ice had formed over the surface. She frowned as a flash of black seemed to streak underneath.

"Did you see that?"

"See what?" Jake took hold of one booth's side wall and shook it, pleased to see it was good and solid.

She frowned as she held her hand shading her eyes and studied the lake, but whatever she saw had now disappeared.

"I guess it was probably a trick of the sunlight." But she couldn't get the feeling out of her head that she actually had seen something in the water that wasn't a fish.

"Are you thinking about all the rumors of a lake monster out there?" he teased.

"You saw the lake monster?" Ashley walked up, hand in hand with Jordan. "Stasi said she'll look after the shops this morning. If it gets too busy she'll holler for help," she told Blair. The ends of her chin-length, light-brown hair under a bright red knit cap swung in her face from the morning breeze and she pushed it back. "Do you like what we did?" she asked them. "The elves came up with the idea of the snowflakes and showed us how to paint them while they wrote the fancy script."

"Are they real elves or just really short people?" Jordan asked with a shy smile.

"Very real. Don't play poker with them. In fact, don't play any type of game that involves money or bartering for anything you own," Blair advised him. "I've never been sure if they're just plain lucky or they cheat."

"Here we are!" Agnes trilled.

They watched the mayor's wife, the elves, and Grady haul sleds loaded down with portable fire pits that had covers on them to prevent sparks from flying out.

"This will be wonderful," she proclaimed, busy directing everyone to their tasks. "Where have you been, Jake?"

"I drove down the mountain for supplies and decided to stay over," he lied.

Agnes stared at him quizzically. "There's something different about you." Then she looked at Blair and smiled. "Yes, well, we missed you." She cast a sly look in Blair's direction. "Of that, I'm sure."

"Definitely." Blair cast Jake a look of her own that warmed him up a hell of a lot more than any heater would. "And now our Jake's back to work his sweet ass off." She began directing Ashley and Jordan to help unload the portable heaters and set them near benches that had been placed near enough the booths to take the chill off, but far enough away for safety reasons.

"I checked the weather report and we'll have clear weather all weekend," Agnes went on, as she studied the checklist in her hand. "Alberic, has everyone tried on their costumes?"

"Check." The head elf said cheerfully. "I think Foster's put on a little weight, so he won't be bending over or those tights will split and you'll see more than you ever want to see."

Agnes moved off while Alberic stayed with Blair. "I heard a rumor that it's you and Stasi who own the lake," he said.

She nodded. "But it's not common knowledge. We prefer it that way." She shot him a look that suggested he remember that and not pass the information on.

"Gotcha. So what's with the Weres? They up here to make trouble? I had a beer with Horace and he said they're from Baxter Thorpe's Pack. Everyone knows they're sons of bitches and Baxter's just plain mean."

"We're not sure what's going on, so if you hear anything I'd appreciate knowing it," she replied.

"Can do."

"If you know Baxter's borderline psycho—"

"Nope, all psycho."

Blair winced. "Okay, 100 percent psycho, why are you guys sticking around?"

Alberic started to scratch his crotch, saw Blair's warning look and stopped in time. "I guess we're still here because of all of you. We know how we were when we first showed up. You could have tossed us out on our asses and it wouldn't have been the first time. Sure, we could have returned to make your lives miserable; it would have only created a hell of a lot of negative vibes. But you showed us we could clean up our act and even make something of ourselves. Aggie is the first human to treat us like productive beings. She makes us believe we can improve our lives."

"Wow, I don't know what to say." And she didn't, because most of the elves she had known were cute, cheerful beings that worked in Santa's workshop and slipped into places to do good deeds. The elves that had rolled into town were the exact opposite, and she had a pretty good idea it was because of Mickey Boggs. She made a mental note to check with Maggie to see if there were any magickal warrants out against him. She couldn't imagine that Mickey could cheat anyone for too long without someone filing a complaint.

"Then don't say a thing. I hate anyone getting schmaltzy." Blair jumped when she felt a pinch on her butt. He winked at her as he walked away. "Can't give up all my bad habits, can I?"

Blair's laughter stilled when she saw more visitors arriving. Newcomers she'd rather see anywhere but here.

"Outer Mongolia would be good," she muttered.

"For what?" Stasi said from behind her.

Blair yelped and spun around. She held her hand against her chest to keep her heart from pounding its way out of her chest. "You startled me! What about the shops?"

"We haven't had a customer in the past hour and a half, so I felt safe in closing them up. Ginny stopped by and had a big grin on her face. She'll be out here in a bit with baskets of food for the workers, so I thought I'd come out and get my share." Stasi snugged her knit gloves against her fingers. She looked beyond Blair at the Weres that stood around talking to Agnes. "She needs to know what they are."

"I was thinking the very same thing." Blair felt an energy sweep across the area around them and if she wasn't mistaken it was caused by Roan and his mother. She smiled as she heard Alberic whistle the first bars from "Peter and the Wolf" and couldn't resist whistling the opening notes for "Who's Afraid of the Big Bad Wolf" back at him. He flashed her a grin and a salute.

As if she heard her name called, Blair swept the area and zeroed in on Jennifer Santiago who stood a short distance away from Roan and the other Weres. She momentarily admired the Were's dark purple parka then tamped down the envy.

"Are you going to do what I think you're going to do?" Stasi easily picked up on her intent.

"You betcha." With steel in her blue-green eyes, Blair headed for Jennifer. When she saw Jake's look and his step forward as if to intercept her, she waved a hand to reassure him. "Jennifer, nice to see you here." She bared her teeth at the Were. "And brave of you to come out."

The female Were backed up a step then moved forward as if refusing to give in to Blair's aggression.

Hm, she might have those oh-so-perfect bloodlines they seem to like for breeding purposes, but no way she can handle being an Alpha.

"Let's chat." A less than subtle push left Jennifer no choice but to head into the trees.

"What do you want?" She tossed her head in defiance. "You have Jake back in human form. You've angered Roan to the point where he's ready to take off anyone's head… literally. Isn't that enough for you?"

"Not really. I want to know what's really going on. Why Roan felt the need to put that cursed collar on Jake that would have guaranteed his death and why you're still considered Jake's fiancée, since he broke the engagement when he left the Pack. This all makes no sense, so why don't you clear it up for me?"

Jennifer's lavender eyes burned with a deep glow. "A bond can't be broken that easily. If Jake was brought back into the Pack, the bond could be broken—the right way."

"So his saying it's off wasn't enough?"

Jennifer shook her head. "There's only one way of breaking it."

Blair mentally sifted through her brain for Were information, but that part eluded her.

"And that is?"

"None of your business." A large hand wrapped around her neck and pulled her backward against a large body.

Blair clawed vainly at the hand cutting off her air supply.

"Roan! Let her go!" Jennifer cried out, grabbing his arm. "You're choking her!"

"She's trouble and deserves all she gets," he snapped, tightening his hold.

By then Blair was seeing spots before her eyes and knew if she didn't do something soon she'd be sleepy-bye, and not in a good way.

"Fire hurts," she croaked, slapping his hand.

Roan howled in pain and released her as the burn covered the back of his hand.

"She can help us," Jennifer pointed out, grabbing his arm before he struck the back of his hand across Blair's face.

"Help you how?" She rubbed her aching throat.

"Break the bond," Jennifer said quickly before Roan could stop her.

Blair backed away. She didn't want to retreat, but it seemed prudent to get back among the crowd where she hoped Roan wouldn't try anything else. She already knew he didn't play well with others and his attack just proved it.

"Jake doesn't want you. Jake doesn't want anything to do with the Pack, so why don't the two of you get hitched, have perfect little furry cubs, and live happily ever after? But think about this, Jennifer. If that happens, then all Roan wants it for is your bloodline, not you. He's like his bitch of a mother and only wants the power that Baxter's giving him. Maybe you Weres look at commitments differently than many of us, but I'd still want a guy to want me for me and not for what I can offer him. Love isn't so bad, you know."

Roan took a step forward with Jennifer still hanging on his arm. "Stay out of our affairs and I'll let you live."

"Move off the mountain and I won't give you parasites!"

Blair took a deep breath and did something that was dangerous to her well-being, but she felt was necessary. She deliberately turned her back on the pair and walked out of the woods.

Stasi saw her first then Jake spied her. Both walked over to her, faces etched with concern, and darkening anger on Jake's as he stared at the rapidly darkening fingerprint-size bruises on her throat.

"I'll challenge him then tear him apart." He started toward Roan but Blair gripped his arm as tightly as she could.

"Take a look at his face," she said under her breath. "That's exactly what he wants you to do and maybe even why he grabbed me.'

Jake followed her direction and stared at Roan who stared back. The Were's eyes were dark and glittering with malice while his lips tipped upward in a cruel smile. Vera walked up and insinuated herself between Roan and Jennifer, linking her arms through theirs.

"One big dysfunctional family," Blair muttered. "They'd be a hit on Dr. Phil."

"Here." Stasi pulled off her scarf and wound it gently around Blair's throat, hiding the bruises.

"How do you feel about being outed, so to speak?" Blair asked Jake.

"No memory wiping if things get out of hand?"

She shook her head. "The residents here are a hardy bunch. Agnes might even look at it as a publicity stunt, but if everyone knows what Roan and the Pack are up to, maybe his plans will be thwarted before he can try anything more."

"He'll also use intimidation tactics that I'm sure he learned well from Baxter."

"And we'll do what we can." Blair mentally geared herself up. "But I want to do it."

"Because it affects our Pack?" Jake asked.

She and Stasi bobbed their heads.

"No one messes with our Pack," they said in unison.

"You're not doing this alone," Jake insisted, taking Blair's hand.

She smiled and turned around to face Roan.

"Agnes," she called out. "Everyone. We have some interesting news for you." She ignored Roan's narrowed gaze and the look of panic on Jennifer's face. The look of calculation on Vera's face made Blair falter for a second, but she knew if she didn't do it now, she'd hold off until it might be too late.

Blair waited until everyone stopped what they were doing.

"It seems Roan has more than a few surprises set up for us," she said. "But since he's too shy to mention them, I guess I'll let the wolf out of the bag. It appears Roan is to be the Alpha of a Were Pack that has plans to expand their territory to most of this mountain."

"Were? Do you mean wolves?" Agnes asked. "I've heard wolves howling some nights, and we all know wolves haven't lived up here for years." She looked at Roan with a combination of fear and curiosity.

"My stepfather is our Pack's Alpha and with our Pack growing so large, we thought we would split and I would rule the new Pack up here. There is nothing to worry about," Roan said in a soothing tone, moving toward Agnes and Floyd, who stood next to her. His Honor looked a bit shaken but to his credit he didn't back away, nor did his wife.

"I admit I don't know a lot about your species, but I do know you need a lot of land and most of it up here is already taken," Floyd contributed.

"And we are ready to pay fair market price for anyone who's willing to sell their land. We'll even help with relocation costs." Roan cast Blair a dark look.

"We've lived here all our lives," Agnes argued.

"There's even more, Agnes," Jake spoke up. "I'm also a Were. I'm Roan's brother."

"More's the pity," Vera was heard to murmur.

"I'd like to see her made into a fur coat." Blair didn't care that the female Were heard her.

"Another wolf?" Agnes exclaimed. This did startle the group.

He smiled and shook his head. "Just that friendly Border Collie you all like to leave treats for."

"Witches and Weres," Agnes's mind was already whirring away.

"Witches who want to live here and Weres who want us out," Blair pointed out. "And something about a bond between Jake and Jennifer that Jake broke years ago."

"It can't be broken that easily," Vera argued coldly, seeming to spout pure poison. "There's only one way the bond can be broken to free the other. In order for Jennifer to become Roan's mate, Jake has to die."

Blair froze at her words.

"Okay, I so did not see that coming."

Chapter 17

"You told me all I had to do was break the bond and I could leave the Pack," Jake shouted at Vera, stalking toward her with his fists clenched. "I broke up with Jennifer and I left—what more do you want?"

"Was I somehow unclear? Baxter wants you dead. Roan wants you dead. That way you can never try to return to the Pack," she replied.

"Hasn't the last seventy years told you I have no desire to return?" He threw up his hands. "I was treated like shit the entire time I lived with you. Why would I want to return to that when I have a life here that I enjoy? A life without any of you," he said it not to inflict pain but to state a cold hard fact. "Jennifer is yours, Roan. There will be no fight, because I'm done with that."

"And he has a new Pack," Blair announced. "A much better one, I might say." She grinned.

"*You will not ruin this!*" Roan's roar was barely a warning before he raced to her side and grasped her by the back of her neck, literally throwing her toward the middle of the lake.

She immediately broke through the thin layer of ice and sank through the frigid water.

I should have learned to swim when I had a chance! swept through Blair's panicky mind as the icy water wrapped around her like a chilly shroud. Her lungs seized up from the cold and her body felt as if it was shutting down. *What if this kills me?* She paddled in the black water, but by then couldn't tell which way led to the surface.

A thunderous sound rushed through her ears as she realized there was no way for her to get oxygen.

I'm sorry, Jake. No idea why the apology, but the words still echoed in her head as she sank toward the bottom.

Just as suddenly, she felt something slide under her limp body. She forced her frozen fingers to grip what felt like a scaly fin and felt herself carried upward, then she was suddenly flung through the air toward the shore.

Instead of landing on the hard ground as she expected, she fell into a pair of warm arms.

"Blair!" Stasi's panic was close to Blair's own state of mind as she pulled off her jacket and wrapped it around her where she lay in Jake's arms.

"I brought a blanket!" Floyd brought up a heavy wool blanket and draped it around Blair as Jake carefully laid her down.

"Sssssssss-omething ssssaved mmmmmeeeee." Blair's teeth chattered so hard she feared they'd fly out of her mouth. She cried out when a burning pain hit her ankle and she looked down to see Fluff and Puff peel themselves off her ankle and fall over on their sides. Fluff coughed up what looked like a gallon of lake water while Puff hacked up water and a tiny fish. "Sssssoooo all I had to do was get ttttossed in ice water for you guys to get off?" she croaked, but she picked them up with her blanketed hands and held them against her so they could also warm up.

"No more of this shit." Jake momentarily pressed his lips against her temple. He straightened up and stalked toward Roan, whose smile was just as feral as Jake's.

Stasi knelt down and rubbed the feeling back into Blair's hands until they turned from an unattractive blue to a healthy-looking pink. Blair whimpered as needles of sensation moved through her body.

"No!" Blair cried at Jake, but it was too late.

As he ran toward Roan, his body shimmered with power and the dog streaked into the air at the same time Roan shifted into the black wolf amid screams and cries from the humans, who ran off to a safe distance.

Blair wanted to cover her eyes, scared to death that Jake would be killed, but afraid not to look. She gripped Stasi's hands, while her friend stayed close to her. Then she shifted her gaze to Vera who looked a little too pleased by the battle. And she knew exactly why.

"Vera." She deliberately raised her voice so everyone would hear her. "No matter what happens today you will not win. I will do everything in my power to make sure of that." She wasn't surprised that Vera didn't reply. The female still felt Roan would succeed, but Blair refused to believe it. Not when Jake had so much to fight for.

The wolf was larger, but the dog was faster, dancing out of the way of the large canines and leaping over the wolf before he could spin around.

"You can't help him," Stasi whispered in Blair's ear when she heard whispered words tripping from Blair's lips. "He wouldn't want it that way."

"I know," she choked. "But that doesn't mean if Roan manages to win because he didn't fight fair that I won't go after him."

"We'll all help."

A vow that was spoken by one, but Blair knew it would be meant by all. Her sister witches would help her in this cause if it came to that.

Blair winced when Jake yelped and leaped back with a tear in his shoulder. But he immediately flew back in and took a chunk out of Roan's haunch that had the wolf snarling and snapping at him.

The battle could have taken hours. It could have taken minutes. For Blair it felt like forever.

Until Jake pounced on Roan, somehow rolling him onto his back and pinning him to the ground. Jake opened his mouth, sharp canines only inches from his throat. Roan stilled, knowing it would only take a second for Jake to rip it out. By all rights, it was his victory. Roan's death was his due.

Blair wobbled to her feet with Stasi's help. All she could do was wait.

For one brief second Blair's eyes connected with Jake's as he looked her way

Instead of killing Roan, he jumped back and shifted to human form.

"Why didn't you kill me?" Roan also shifted back and slowly rose to his feet, unsure what would happen next.

"Because I limit my killing to rabbits and squirrels."

"And if you'd destroyed me, you'd be a target for everyone in the Pack," Roan pointed out.

Jake shook his head. "Didn't even enter my mind. Blair already told you, we have our own Pack and I like it a hell of a lot better. Now you've had your 'fight to the death.' Accept this as the breaking of the bond, mate with Jen, and have all the cubs you want." He spared his mother a brief glance. "Just do us all a favor and find new territory. I'd rather have neighbors I could like." He limped his way back to Blair, who sobbed her relief and wrapped her arms around him.

"I'm building you a dollhouse," he whispered in her ear. "One hex of a dollhouse." He used his thumb to wipe away her tears.

"What does this mean?" Agnes cried out.

"Agnes, go home, have a glass of wine, and I promise I'll be over later to explain it all to you," Blair told her with a weary sigh as she pulled the blanket tighter around her shoulders. "The same with everyone else."

Agnes could be heard sputtering as Floyd hustled her away and the others slowly followed, keeping a wide berth around Roan and his group.

"Wicked fight," Alberic congratulated Jake before he walked off.

Vera's face was ugly and dark with fury as she swiftly moved into Blair's personal space. "You have ruined everything. By the time I'm finished with you, my son will never even want to look at you," she snarled. And Blair wasn't missing that it wasn't the least bit feminine. "It had already been decided that Jake would die, so that the bond would be properly broken and Jennifer would mate with Roan to begin a new dynasty. It's up to the two of them to rule the new Pack. And it's all ruined because of one witch slut and a dog that refused to die." A manicured hand turned to a sharp claw as it lifted ready to tear Blair's face off.

"Don't even try it, Vera." Jake's voice was as steely as his hand flashing to grip her wrist in a hold guaranteed to crush her bones.

"Hey, I'm not the slut here!" Blair wasn't about to back down and started the chant in her head. She briefly thought about turning the Were bitch into a toy poodle. Emphasis on the toy. She even started muttering the spell.

"You will do *nothing!*" The familiar voice rang out clear and strong with so much magick in the tone that the air grew thick with it.

They turned as golden light spilled out over the ground while a portal opened and a tall woman stepped through.

Blair wasn't sure whether to mutter "oh shit," or draw a sigh of relief that there was a chance Eurydice was coming to her rescue before Vera tried to turn her into pet food—although Jake was doing his best to keep the Were from removing her face.

Instead of being garbed in her usual emerald green velvet robes, the head of the Witches' Council wore a wool suit that Blair guessed was Chanel. A gold and emerald pin on the jacket winked brightly and her dark hair was swept up into a French twist. No one would guess she was well over two thousand years old.

Eurydice spared Blair a brief glance before turning to the Were. "This is unacceptable, Vera. You will *not* threaten one of my witches, you will *not* do anything to cause more trouble here, and you especially will *not* stand in the way of Jake's happiness. You maliciously toyed with his safety and you desired his death with no good reason but your own personal vindictiveness. Jake has rescued my witches more than once, and I have given him my protection."

Blair looked around on the ground because she was positive her jaw was lying around somewhere. She was smart enough to keep her mouth shut.

Eurydice stared at the Were. "If you want something to do, work on your Pack before it splinters beyond help, because if you continue on the path you have blazed, that is exactly what will happen. And if it does, you know very well the Were Council will get involved."

Vera's eyes blazed with bloodthirst. "He is *my* son, Eurydice. A bond was struck, a bond he claimed was broken when he left the Pack. But there is only one way to break the bond and that means his blood."

Eurydice's smile wasn't all that pleasant, and Blair was soooo happy it wasn't directed her way. She was content to just stand back and watch the show. She wished she had some popcorn and a Diet Coke, not to mention a camcorder, because she was positive this conversation was going to be good, and no one was going to believe what was happening before her. She was betting heavily on Eurydice.

"You only say that because you wish it to be so, when we also know those terms can be renegotiated when a Pack member leaves of his own accord. And now he is part of a new Pack. An odd one at that." Her gaze sliced toward Blair. "If you try to interfere again, I will have no choice but to bring you and Baxter before the Ruling Council."

Vera's eyes glowed pure yellow momentarily and her wolf soul surfaced but eased back under Eurydice's power. The glance Vera shot toward Blair indicated she didn't feel the witch had won. She turned on her heel and walked away.

Once Vera was gone and Blair had gotten her breath back, she looked at Eurydice.

"Why?"

The elder witch smiled, easily understanding exactly what Blair wanted to know.

"Sadly, Vera hates Jake enough to want to see him dead any way she can, because as long as he lives he is a reminder that he isn't wolf and she sees that as her failure. I wouldn't have allowed her to harm you when you only did what you felt was right. I realize you all think we are hard on you," she said, continuing to smile at Blair's expression. Clearly, that was *exactly* what the younger witch thought. "And we are, but with good reason. You witchlings were the best class we'd had for centuries. Even in 1313, you all had such potential that we knew you would go on to greater things. And in many ways, you have."

"Yes, we have! So why have you been so mean to us for the last seven hundred years?" Blair blurted out then cringed. *Way to go, Blair! Piss off the one who can control some aspects of your existence.*

Instead of pronouncing a few hundred years added to her banishment, Eurydice smiled.

That scared Blair more.

"So you feel we were harsh with you, Eilidh?" Eurydice fingered her emerald ring. "We chose tough love, as they say, because we needed to ensure you thirteen witchlings never tried to abuse your power and that you survived your existence in this world. You all have crossed the line more than once, but I must say none of you have ever crossed so far that you couldn't return to your proper place. The Council has watched over you carefully and noticed that your powers grew over the centuries, but you still continued to do what was right and never exploited what you could do. We have never seen the addition of years as punishment, but as a way to make you think before you leapt the next time." She made a face. "Not that it seemed to work with any of you."

"We do tend to be pretty stubborn," Blair agreed. "But it's hard to believe you haven't allowed any of us to return to the Academy."

Eurydice shook her head. "Witchling, all any of you had to do was ask and you would have been welcomed back with open arms. But you were too content to be out here in the world."

Eurydice looked across the way to where Jake stood uncertainly with Fluff and Puff trying to scramble out of his arms. Not that the bunny slippers would get too close, since the only being that frightened the wits out of them was the head of the Witches' Council. "It's the Weres that feel they shouldn't interact with witches, but then none of you have worried about that. Go to your Were, Eilidh, before he thinks the worst will happen." She snapped her fingers and was gone like that.

Blair looked over at Jake and ran to him, hopping into his arms, wrapping her legs around his waist and her arms around his neck as the slippers chattered away in her face. He laughed and pretended to stagger under her weight.

"She gave us her seal of approval," she told him with a big grin. "My place is closer than yours, plus I'd really like to get into some dry clothes."

"Why, when you won't be wearing them too long and I've got a washer and dryer?" But he managed to carry her all the way back to the building, then dropped her to her feet as Ginny ran up to them.

"I just got the news!" she exclaimed, hugging Blair and sighing over her wet cold clothing, then hugging Jake. "I always knew you were special." She kissed him on the cheek.

"Wow, you've turned 180 degrees," Blair teased.

Ginny almost danced on her tiptoes. "Dave was arrested for conning an island governor's daughter. He's in jail and not getting out any time soon," she announced. "And he hadn't had time to spend all the money, so we'll all receive at least part of what we're owed. I asked that my money be divided among the others."

"That's wonderful!" Blair exclaimed.

"And now you get inside and warm up." Ginny shot Jake a teasing look. "And I know just how you'll do it, too." She practically danced back to her café.

"It's turning into another great day." Blair hitched the blanket up around her.

"Could get even better," Jake said, gesturing toward the street.

The Cadillac Eldorado that pulled up to the sidewalk had once been baby blue; it was now more primer than paint and emitted enough nauseous gray smoke to be a smog hazard all on its own. The driver who stepped out looked just as nasty as his vehicle.

The troll facing them was about five feet tall with a stocky body and ginger blond hair... everywhere. His cross-eyed stare roamed in a haphazard manner.

"Mickey Boggs," Blair said with the same distaste she'd use when describing a dung heap.

"Hey guys. I heard you all had some fun up here. Judging from everyone's smiles it looks like everything turned out just fine," Mickey said, walking up with a cigar jammed in his mouth that smelled so bad Blair almost gagged.

"No thanks to you," she retorted, wondering how he'd look as a bobble-head doll, then decided he'd look just as bad as he did now.

"Good. Good. Well, I just came up to collect the rest of my fee, then I'm outta here." He ran his stubby fingers down the front of his puke-yellow Hawaiian shirt with topless hula girls scattered across the fabric. His wispy ginger-blond beard looked to have half his meal still in it. He looked toward Alberic who stood further down the sidewalk with Agnes standing next to him. "Once you guys are done here, you need to pack up and get the fuck out. I've got a gig set up for you in Omaha."

"They are not going anywhere, and you, sir, do not deserve one penny!" Agnes told him. "In fact, I have suggested that Alberic and his troop sue you for not paying them what is their due."

"Hey, lady, you have nothing to do with this and if you don't pay me, you'll find yourself in court." He took his smelly cigar out of his mouth and used it to stab the air.

Agnes glared back. "We'll just see about that. You have cheated these poor men out of their rightful wages for many years now. That has got to stop."

Blair looked up the street and smiled. "I think that's just about to happen. I swear, the witch's timing is always perfect."

A beat up, dark blue crew cab pickup truck that looked as if it was on its last legs but purred like a panther rolled toward them and stopped. A familiar long-legged blonde in jeans, T-shirt, and denim jacket, with a straw cowboy hat perched on top of her head, climbed out. Magick seemed to seep from Maggie's pores as she greeted them with a broad smile.

"Hello, Mickey, you've been a bad boy, haven't you?" Maggie drawled.

The troll took one look at her and uttered a girly scream, his cigar flying into the air. "No! Not you!"

She tutted under her breath and shook her head. "You've been a very bad boy, Mickey, and I've got a warrant to take you in. I'm sure you're not going to make this difficult for me, are you? If you go quietly, I won't have to hurt you." She pulled out a pair of enchanted handcuffs. Before he could try for a futile escape she snapped them on his wrists and hauled him to the back seat, pushing him inside and closing the door, which snicked with an audible click of the lock.

"You can't let her take me! She'll kill me with Barry Manilow music." He pounded on the closed window as he pleaded with the others. "You know what that does to me."

Maggie reached inside her truck and pulled out a CD. "I've got all his greatest hits. Mickey'll have a chance to hear them all during the drive back to Texas."

"Is she taking him to jail?" a wide-eyed Agnes asked Blair.

"Something even better," she assured her. "So don't worry about him trying to sue you. He'll be out of circulation for some time, so he can't do anything to the elves either." She raised her voice. "Don't forget to play 'Mandy' for him, Mags,"

Mickey's moans and whimpers mingled with Maggie's throaty laughter. "No problem there." She walked around the truck's hood and stood in front of Blair and Jake.

"You two look good together," she said.

Blair grinned first at her fellow witch, then at the Were she loved. "We do, don't we? Maybe you need to find someone, too."

Maggie shook her head. "I doubt there's anyone out there who can kick my ass and make me drool at the same time. Just remember that not only does Blair do revenge very well, she's got friends." She winked at Jake and climbed back into her truck.

Blair turned back to Jake. "What do you say, my sexy puppy? Wanna go somewhere and make out? You did say you have a washer and dryer at your place."

He combed his fingers through her hair. "Sounds like a plan, hexster of my heart."

Agnes watched them head up the road that led to Jake's cabin.

"Don't forget tonight's the meeting to plan the spring frolic! The sooner we begin, the sooner we'll be organized!" she called after them. She frowned as neither acknowledged her words.

Alberic walked up and stood beside her with a cigar jammed in his mouth.

"I don't think you'll see them for a few days. But don't worry, we'll be here to help out."

Between Jake's speed and Blair's magick, they were in his bed in seconds. Clothes flew every which way even as they barely stopped kissing each other.

"My Alpha," Jake intoned, sliding into her with ease.

Blair smiled as she arched against him. "Think you can handle it?"

"Something tells me we'll be an unstoppable team."
He immersed himself in the witch he loved more than
life itself.

She cupped his face with her hands. "Welcome home,
my love."

Afterword

I FOUND THIS RECIPE SOME YEARS AGO AND IT WAS AN instant hit and much requested among friends. I thought it only fitting that Hetty carry it in her candy shop.

—Linda

HETTY'S Marbled Orange Fudge

1 ½ tsp plus 3/4 cup butter—divided

3 cups sugar

3/4 cup whipping cream

1 pkg vanilla or white chips

1 jar marshmallow creme

3 tsp orange extract

orange food coloring

Grease 13x9 pan with 1 1/2 tsp butter. Combine sugar, cream, and remaining butter in a medium saucepan. Cook and stir over low heat until sugar is dissolved. Bring to a boil, cook and stir for 4 min. Remove from heat, stir in chips and marshmallow creme until smooth. Remove 1 cup, set aside. Add orange extract and coloring to remaining mixture. Stir until blended. Pour into pan. Drop reserved marshmallow mix by tablespoonfuls over top. Cut through mixture with a knife to swirl. Cover and refrigerate until set. Cut into squares.

For a change, try chocolate and mint, chocolate and coconut and put coconut in the coconut part, lime extract and vanilla, peppermint, even cinnamon flavoring is great!

Acknowledgments

Many kudos to my agent, Laurie McLean of the Larsen/ Pomada Literary Agency, aka Batgirl, who's always there for me.

I'm so grateful for my editor, Deb Werksman, who loves Jazz and her witch buddies as much as I do. Her associate editor, Susie Benton, who climbs mountains— literally! Danielle Jackson, Casablanca publicist, who does a fantastic job of getting the word out on my witches. And thanks to Lisa Mierzwa who designed my wonderful covers.

My Devoted Niece, AshNay, who may not be my niece by blood but definitely from the heart, and Jordan, who I know will go far.

The Witchy Chicks, Yasmine Galenorn, Terese Daly Ramin, Lisa Croll Di Dio, Madelyn Alt, Candace Havens, Kate Austin, Maura Anderson, and Annette Blair. Your support is much appreciated and I love you all.

And last and certainly not least, the lil sis of my heart, Elaine Charton, who's come so far with her writing and I'm very proud of her!

About the Author

Linda Wisdom was born and raised in Huntington Beach, California. She majored in Journalism in college, then switched to Fashion Merchandising when she was told there was no future for her in fiction writing. She held a variety of positions ranging from retail sales to executive secretary in advertising and office manager for a personnel agency.

Her career began when she sold her first two novels to Silhouette Romance on her wedding anniversary in 1979. Since then she has sold more than seventy novels and two novellas to five different publishers. Her books have appeared on various romance and mass market bestseller lists and have been nominated for a number of Romantic Times awards. She has been a two-time finalist for the Romance Writers of America Rita Award.

She lives with her husband, two dogs, one parrot, and a tortoise in Murrieta, California.

When Linda first moved to Murrieta there were three romance writers living in the town. At this time, there is just Linda. So far, the police have not suspected her of any wrongdoing.

For more from Linda Wisdom, read on for a sneak
peek of:

Coming soon from Sourcebooks Casablanca

The Best Hex Ever

Thea made her way carefully down to the outskirts of the town, the toes of her shoes sending up puffs of dirt, discoloring her expensive Gucci sandals.

The buildings looked ready to fall down if she blew on them, with doors hanging loose and windows grimed with dirt. One building, named Silver Rock Bank, was minus several bars on the windows. She doubted there was anything in there to steal, anyway.

"Hello, girly."

Grateful to hear a voice, Thea spun toward the saloon. A skeleton rocked back and forth just outside the swinging doors, his bony legs shoved into battered brown boots, a faded blue bandana knotted around his neck, and a hat perched on his skull. His jaw made clacking noises as he guffawed at her look of shock. "Welcome to Silver Rock. We've been waitin' for ya."

Just out of Thea's line of sight, a tall figure stood at the iron gates that led to Boot Hill. It was a prime spot for someone wanting to observe the entire town.

Utterly masculine, with an angular face, dark hair the color of fresh brewed coffee under a battered Stetson, and a cigar clamped between his strong jaws, he was the perfect depiction of all of Thea's fictional heroes. The grin on his face was wide and a little too all-knowing.

"Well, look who's come to town."

"What's the matter? Cat got your tongue?" The skeleton chortled, slapping his knees as he rocked back and forth in the chair, which looked as though it might splinter at any moment. Cedric, curled decoratively around Thea's wrist, raised his head long enough to take a good look at the bony creature. "You used to take me to such nice places," he sighed.

"Dayumm! Did that snake just talk?" the skeleton asked. "Wish I had my shotgun. They're right tasty in stew."

Cedric eyed the creature with a slitted stare.

"Name's Julian," he informed Thea. "You Thea James? I guess you must be, since we don't get all that many visitors up this way 'less they're wantin' to visit a ghost town, and that we do have." He chuckled.

"Yes." Speaking to a skeleton that was sentient was nothing new to her, but one that knew her name was definitely startling. "What exactly *is* Silver Rock, other than a town that should have been bulldozed decades ago?"

"We're protected property, missy. We were also one of the best mining towns in this here state," Julian replied with a hint of pride. "I had me a good claim up the mountain." He gestured with a bony arm.

"And now it's just you and me?" She wanted him to tell her this was someone's idea of a sick joke, because the idea of sharing this Hades on earth with a smart-mouthed skeleton was too much to bear.

"Hell, no! We got us a right well-populated town. 'Course, most of 'em don't come out until later, when it's not so hot." Julian looked down the dusty, empty street where even the horse troughs were... well, dusty and empty. "Don't bother me none. I like the heat warming up my old bones." He levered his way off his rocking chair, his bones rattling as he straightened up. "Got you a nice room set up over at Miss Mona's."

"I need a phone." Desperation licked at her senses as she followed the skeleton. She had no idea where he was going or why she should follow him, but it was better than standing alone in the middle of this sad excuse for a street. Thea wasn't used to being outside her comfort zone and this was about as far from her luxurious life-style as she could get.

"You mean those things you talk into? We ain't got 'em." He appeared to eye her disconcertingly with his empty sockets. "But you're a witch, ain't ya? Can't you just pick up a rock and use that to talk to someone?" He cackled and then continued walking through town. "That there's the general store, over there's the dentist. Don't let him pull your teeth unless he gives you the good whiskey. Miss Priscilla has the next shop. She carries ladies' fashions—most of 'em she makes from those pattern books out of New York City. Saloon..." As if the swinging doors weren't enough of a hint.

Panic was rapidly overtaking her. "What is this place?"

"Hades," Cedric murmured.

Julian cackled again. "A damn fine ghost town, I reckon. Population of thirty-two or thereabouts." He walked down the wooden sidewalk, the soles of his boots clomping in an odd rhythm with the rattling sound of his bones as he swung his arms. "Used to be more, but some didn't want to stay around. Don't know why. It's a pretty nice place."

Thea stared in horror at the dilapidated buildings. "Ghosts. And one skeleton."

"Makes me unique, doncha think? So, you're some famous writer? Like Mark Twain or Ned Buntline? 'Course I can't read, but I can usually find someone to read the dime novels to me."

Thea winced. Not at the mention of famous author names, but because of the reminder of her fall from grace, courtesy of poor sales.

"I write uplifting historical romantic fiction," she explained.

"Ah, books for women to swoon over." He bobbed his head, the skull perilously close to falling off his spine. He stopped in front of a fence that had seen better days. "This is where you'll be staying."

Thea's bag slipped through her fingers, dropping to the ground. "It's a boarding house," she said in disbelief.

He chuckled. "Not exactly, but the rooms are nice. You're upstairs, third door on the right. No need to knock. You're expected." He started to amble off, somehow managing to whistle a tune.

"You're just leaving me?" Not that she really wanted his company, but a nonstop talking skeleton was better than nothing. At least until she figured out what was going on and how to get out of here.

"There's no Starbucks," Cedric whispered. "No five-star restaurant. Not even a Jack in the Box."

Thea tried to calm the sick feeling deep in her stomach, but it wasn't about to be ignored. "This *has* to be someone's idea of a nasty joke. I'll go in, take a nap, and wake up in Celestial Gardens, like I was supposed to." She picked up her bag and let herself in through the tiny gate.

"Maybe it's a spell and all you have to do is write us out of here. Or talk to Eurydice." Cedric had left her wrist and moved around to coil on top of her shoulder, his head resting along the top of her ear. A sure sign he was nervous.

"I thought you were afraid of her." Once inside, Thea was surprised to find the interior smelling of roses and lavender instead of must and rot. She peeked into the parlor and noticed the heavy mahogany furniture didn't have even a hint of dust on it. The dark red and gold patterned carpet was clean and showed no sign of the fading you'd expect in fabric that had been there well over one hundred years.

"I am, but if anyone can get us out of here, she can."

Thea had no difficulty finding the room assigned to her. She was curious about the other rooms, but wasn't about to snoop in case any of them were occupied.

The surprise was her room's furnishings. The brass bed had a plump mattress covered with white, lace-edged sheets and many pillows also trimmed in lace. She winced when she saw the china pitcher and wash-basin and wasn't about to look under the bed to see if a chamber pot was there. Instead, Thea dropped onto the bed and fell backwards. Cedric flew through the air and landed on one of the pillows.

"Why does this room seem so familiar?" she whispered

to herself, looking around from her prone position. "I'd never stay in a place this garish and Celestial Gardens was all about serenity. This is all about…"

"There's nothing serene about gaudy red velvet," Cedric commented, staring at the drapes trimmed with gold tassels. "This is a decorator's nightmare."

Thea blinked rapidly to fend off impending tears. "I shouldn't have waited so long to use my reservation. Fiona told me they were sent to this lovely French valley a hundred years ago, and Fredda stayed on a beautiful South Pacific island fifty years ago." She spoke of two friends who no longer took her calls, so she guessed if she was honest with herself they were no longer friends. The same was true of the wizard she'd been dating for the past few months, her attorney, and even her publicist. Damn it! She had taken that woman to Milan for Fashion Week to celebrate her new contract!

She pulled in a deep breath and stretched her arms over her head as if reaching for the other side of the bed. "I refuse to feel sorry for myself."

"Of course you do," Cedric soothed from his spot on the pillow. "There has to be a way you can contact someone to get us out of here. What about that Russian who claimed to be descended from royalty? Or that wizard you met in New York a few months ago? He was very interested in you."

"He was interested in my wardrobe, especially my lingerie. Besides, I should think you'd love it here. Dust, heat, other snakes around." She tried not to think of the latter. A domesticated python bracelet/choker was one thing. A snake in the wild was something else entirely.

"Oh puleeze! I have my standards." His tongue flicked out. "I think someone's coming."

"Oh goody, Julian's back." She closed her eyes. "I want a bath and a nap, and then I'll try to figure a way out of here."

"A bath can be accommodated real easy. Hell, I'll even wash your back for you. And when it comes to a nap, I'll sing you to sleep."

Thea's eyes flew open at the sound of a deep male voice and she just about levitated off the bed. "*You*!" Red sparks flew around the room, sending the china washbasin spinning in the air. A porcelain shepherdess figurine smashed into the wall, shards flying everywhere. All self-pity was forgotten as she jumped to her feet and stalked toward the tall figure filling the doorway. "I might have known you'd have something to do with this." Without a second thought she raised her hands and threw every bit of power she had at him. She wasn't pleased to see it slide right off him like butter off hot corn.

He flashed a white-toothed grin. "Sorry darlin'. Your magick hissy fits don't work on spirits."

"JT, you son of a bitch," she uttered between clenched teeth as she advanced on him.

"Now, Peaches," he said in a low voice that had always been guaranteed to send shivers down her spine.

"Don't call me that!"

He winced at her strident tone. "I can see some things haven't changed over the years. You look good, Peaches." He slipped off his hat and tossed it onto a nearby chair. "Real good.

JT felt a stirring deep down that he hadn't felt in a long time. In fact, he hadn't felt it since the last time he saw Thea. Back then she went by the name Theodora Harris. She had been, and was, a beautiful woman who smelled and tasted like peaches, hence the nickname. Theodora, who looked like an angel but had a naughty side that was pure temptation. He had never forgiven her for just walking away from him without a word.

And now, for some reason, she was back and still looked so desirable it wouldn't take much for him to rip her clothes off and see if the magick that made up Thea was still there. He grinned at the darkness and fury brewing in her eyes. The little witch riled up so easy.

"What are you doing here?" she asked, her voice sharp enough to slice right though him.

"I died in this town."

He watched her features as she processed this information, entranced by the way it took so little for her to shore up her defenses and revert to the cool, collected woman he had known 130 years ago.

He saw her eyes flick to his chest and the five-pointed star pinned to his shirt.

"You're the sheriff here?" He understood her skepticism, since JT had been well known for skirting the law. Many times the marshals had wanted him hanged, and many times the courts exonerated him.

"Marshal," he corrected her. "Someone needed to keep the peace and I got the job."

"Because of the big gun you carry?"

"Why darlin', you remembered." He continued grinning at her because he could tell it irritated her, and Peaches with her feathers ruffled was an even prettier picture. "But then you always were partial to my *big gun*."

Thea had forgotten how very male JT was. Several inches over six feet tall with close-cropped, coffee brown hair, equally dark brown eyes, and a very sinful white-toothed grin that sometimes caused her knees to buckle, and sometimes got her thinking about blasting him. The man looked so lethal and sexy it was downright illegal. He was ultra-male to her female. His Yang to her Yin. His macho bullshit to her feminine wiles.

There wasn't one hint of magick in his gorgeous body, but that hadn't stopped her from falling for the unbearable man, even though her usual rule was to stick to the preternatural communities. She had a ready excuse for breaking her own rule, though: *Just look at him! The man is a walking, talking sex toy! He's been the perfect inspiration for every sexy love scene I've written since then.*

She ordered herself to stay focused. Why was he here? She was beginning to think Hades had played a nasty trick on her.

"If you're a ghost, why are you corporeal?"

JT shrugged. "I don't know."

"Why is there magick surrounding this town? I could feel it the minute I passed that entrance gate."

He shrugged again, leaning against the doorjamb, his arms crossed in front of his chest.

"And why are the ghosts here?"

"It's a ghost town, Peaches."

She ground her molars. "But they usually have a

realm of their own they retreat to except for the days near Samhain. Plus, *I'm* not a ghost."

"No, I've got to say you're still your gorgeous self."

She had a sudden suspicion. "Did you know I was coming? You know why I'm here!"

"Sorry, I don't. All I was told was that you'd be showing up today."

"Who told you I was coming?" Couldn't the man give her *one* logical answer? After so many years she'd forgotten how exasperating he could be. Her fingertips tingled with magick, but what could she do to him? He was already dead.

"A message came over the telegraph wires this morning. First one we've gotten in decades. Said you were to be our guest for a while. I thought it was my birthday all over again." He flashed that grin at her.

"How lucky for you." She walked over to the window and looked outside at the dirt street. All she saw were ramshackle buildings, a skeleton walking down the sidewalk, and wait... faint impressions in the air, as if people were walking along and horses trotting down the street, but they weren't defined enough for her to tell. She almost pressed her nose against the glass. "What on earth?"

She barely got the words out before JT was standing behind her. "It starts to get more active around here later in the day."

"Active as in?" He may have been a ghost, but he still smelled good. That clean male smell he always had. Her fingers started to tingle with the desire to reacquaint themselves with his muscular contours. Start at the shoulders, move down to his chest with the dusting of dark hair, over abs of steel and down to… she shook off the image before she did something unthinkable, such as throw herself into his arms.

"You can see for yourself later." He turned away and headed for the door. "I'm sure it's been a long day for you, so I'll let you get some rest."

"JT." He paused at the doorway. "Why?" she asked simply. So many questions were whirling in her brain, but two definitely headed the list. Why was she here? And… why was *he* here?

Available April 2010

50 Ways to Hex Your Lover

BY LINDA WISDOM

"A magical page-turner... had me bewitched from the start!"

—Yasmine Galenorn,
USA Today bestselling author of *Witchling*

JAZZ CAN'T DECIDE WHETHER TO SCORCH HIM WITH A FIREBALL OR JUMP INTO BED WITH HIM

Jasmine Tremaine is a witch who can't stay out of trouble. Nikolai Gregorivich is a vampire cop on the trail of a serial killer. Their sizzling love affair has been on-again, off-again for about 300 years—mostly off, lately.

But now Nick needs Jazz's help to steer clear of a maniacal killer with supernatural powers, while they try to finally figure out their own hearts.

978-1-4022-1085-3 • $6.99 U.S. / $8.99 CAN

BY LINDA WISDOM

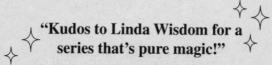

"Kudos to Linda Wisdom for a series that's pure magic!"

—Vicki Lewis Thompson,
New York Times bestselling author of *Wild & Hexy*

JAZZ AND NICK'S DREAM ROMANCE HAS TURNED INTO A NIGHTMARE…

FEISTY WITCH JASMINE TREMAINE AND DROP-DEAD GORGEOUS vampire cop Nikolai Gregorivich have a hot thing going, but it's tough to keep it together when nightmare visions turn their passion into bickering.

With a little help from their friends, Nick and Jazz are in a race against time to uncover whoever it is that's poisoning their dreams, and their relationship…

978-1-4022-1400-4 • $6.99 U.S. / $7.99 CAN

Wicked by Any Other Name

BY LINDA WISDOM

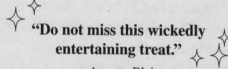

"Do not miss this wickedly entertaining treat."

—Annette Blair,
Sex and the Psychic Witch

STASI ROMANOV USES A LITTLE WITCH MAGIC IN HER LINGERIE shop, running a brisk side business in love charms. A disgruntled customer threatening to sue over a failed spell brings wizard attorney Trevor Barnes to town—and witches and wizards make a volatile combination. The sparks fly, almost everyone's getting singed, and the whole town seems on the verge of a witch hunt.

Can the feisty witch and the gorgeous wizard overcome their objections and settle out of court—and in the bedroom?

978-1-4022-1773-9 • $6.99 U.S. / $7.99 CAN

IN OVER HER HEAD

by Judi Fennell

"Holy mackerel! *In Over Her Head* is a fantastically fun romantic catch!"

—Michelle Rowen, author of *Bitten & Smitten*

○ ○ ○ ○ ○ ○ **HE LIVES UNDER THE SEA** ○ ○ ○ ○ ○ ○

Reel Tritone is the rebellious royal second son of the ruler of a vast undersea kingdom. A Merman, born with legs instead of a tail, he's always been fascinated by humans, especially one young woman he once saw swimming near his family's reef…

○ ○ ○ ○ ○ **SHE'S TERRIFIED OF THE OCEAN** ○ ○ ○ ○ ○

Ever since the day she swam out too far and heard voices in the water, marina owner Erica Peck won't go swimming for anything—until she's forced into the water by a shady ex-boyfriend searching for stolen diamonds, and is nearly eaten by a shark…luckily Reel is nearby to save her, and discovers she's the woman he's been searching for…

978-1-4022-2001-2 • $6.99 U.S. / $7.99 CAN

ROGUE

BY CHERYL BROOKS

Tychar crawled toward me on his hands and knees like a tiger stalking his prey. "I, for one, am glad you came," he purred. "And I promise you, Kyra, you will never want to leave Darconia."

"Cheryl Brooks knows how to keep the heat on and the reader turning pages!"

—Sydney Croft, author of *Seduced by the Storm*

PRAISE FOR THE CAT STAR CHRONICLES:

"Wow. Just… wow. The romantic chemistry is as close to perfect as you'll find." —*BookFetish.org*

"Will make you purr with delight. Cheryl Brooks has a great talent as a storyteller." —*Cheryl's Book Nook*

978-1-4022-1762-3 • $6.99 U.S. / $7.99 CAN

OUTCAST

BY CHERYL BROOKS

Sold into slavery in a harem, Lynx is a favorite because his feline gene gives him remarkable sexual powers. But after ten years, Lynx is exhausted and is thrown out of the harem without a penny. Then he meets Bonnie, who's determined not to let such a beautiful and sensual young man go to waste...

PRAISE FOR THE CAT STAR CHRONICLES:

"Leaves the reader eager for the next story featuring these captivating aliens." —*Romantic Times*

"One of the sweetest love stories... one of the hottest heroes ever conceived and... one of the most exciting and adventurous quests that I have ever had the pleasure of reading." —*Single Titles*

"One of the most sensually imaginative books that I've ever read... A magical story of hope, love and devotion" —*Yankee Romance Reviews*

978-1-4022-1896-5 • $6.99 U.S. / $7.99 CAN

WILD HIGHLAND MAGIC

BY KENDRA LEIGH CASTLE

She's a Scottish Highlands werewolf

Growing up in America, Catrionna MacInnes always tried desperately to control her powers and pretend to be normal…

He's a wizard prince with a devastating secret

The minute Cat lays eyes on Bastian, she knows she's met her destiny. In their first encounter, she unwittingly binds him to her for life, and now they're both targets for the evil enemies out to destroy their very souls.

Praise for Kendra Leigh Castle:

"Fans... little extra som... ekly

978-1-4022-1856-9 • $7.99 U.S. / $8.99 CAN